# YOU ARE MINE

JANEAL FALOR

# OTHER BOOKS BY JANEAL FALOR

Mine to Tarnish (Mine Prequel Novella)

You Are Mine (Mine #1)

Mine to Spell (Mine #2)

Mine to Fear (Mine #3)

Sacrifice of Mine (Mine #4)

Ever Darkening (Darkening Light #1)

Savage Light (Darkening Light #2)

Death's Queen (Death's Queen #1)

Death's Betrayal (Death's Queen #2)

Death's Embrace (Death's Queen #3)

Death's Assassin (Death's Queen #4)

Bound by Birthright (Elven Princess #1)

Bound to Endure (Elven Princess #2)

Bound by Love (Elven Princess #3)

Goddess Ascending

A Genie's Heart

*For Lori*
*Not only an amazing critique partner,*
*but the truest friend.*

# CHAPTER 1

## Serena

M<small>Y</small> <small>BLOOD WILL ENTICE</small> warlocks to ask for my hand in marriage, so of course Father wants it spilled. The sooner the magic within it is measured, the sooner he can sell me off. According to the laws of Chardonia, there's no escaping it. For me that day has come.

From the way Father's bulky frame lounges on the couch in the men's waiting area as he casually smokes his pipe, one would think my testing doesn't matter. I suppose it doesn't, as long as I have enough magic to make him a beneficial connection. The greater the level of magic flowing in my veins, the better the marriage offer will be. And of course, whatever my owner wants, I must deliver. Only, I can't control how much magic is in my blood.

I shift my weight trying not to think about things I can't change, but it's hard to think of anything else as I stand in the cramped women's corner of the testing center. A soft tut sounds from mother. If anyone has reason to be uncomfortable it's her. Eight months pregnant with sweat glistening through her white face paint, though the spring day is just beginning to warm. Too many other women are crowded about waiting with their daugh-

1

ters. Her eyes don't lift to mine, instead staying properly focused on the ground. From the set of her mouth, the lecture about my fidgeting will come when we're home. After I've brought her favorite food to help pacify her a bit.

Keeping my head bowed, I sneak another glance at the men. They're carrying on like men do, with ample space to spread themselves across couches and chairs throughout the plush waiting room, lit by windows that don't stretch to our side of the room. Father is smoking a pipe and motioning for a glass of wine as he laughs at something the warlock next to him has said. He must not have noticed my fidgeting. His ignorance of it will make it easier to appease mother during her lecture. But it's hard to care about possibly getting out of punishment when this morning he demanded I come on the day of my eligibility instead of waiting a year or two like most.

There's movement in the hall across, disrupting my thoughts. All of us girls waiting by our mothers strain forward. They must be as eager as I am to be the next one called. Not to be one step closer to marriage, but to be done with this place. In truth, I am probably the only one eager to be away from here. While the other girls are truly eager to wed and take the only role society allows them, I've had to force enthusiasm. The role of a warlock producer holds no appeal. It's a role mother's failed at—fourteen times— with me being her first mistake. I eye her rounded belly. Maybe this time will be different. Highly unlikely. Not that I'd ever admit it aloud. I'm a mistake enough without being wholly foolish.

Someone steps out of the hall. I lower my gaze to the wooden floor. Today is not a day for getting caught sneaking glances.

"Stephen's daughter."

For once, I wish they'd call me by name. It's not as if Serena is hard to say. I bunch my hands together, but quickly take a step forward, leaving mother and the others behind. Why did I want it to be my turn so desperately only a moment ago? My heart quivers as I near the hall, moving closer to the unknown. Keeping my strides steady, I fight the overwhelming desire to run. My request to Father this morning not to get tested was not only rejected, but my cheek still aches from the punishment delivered for asking. If I publicly defied Father, worse is sure to follow. Not only for me, but for my sisters.

By the time I get to the hall, the man is already striding away. I manage to keep pace with him, feet making barely a sound, head bowed. But each step is harder to take. Each movement taking me closer to the unknown and farther from what little freedom I have.

When he abruptly stops, a squeak of fear almost escapes me as I barely stop myself from running into him. He ushers me inside a tiny room with a grunt. A single wooden chair is the room's only occupant. Otherwise its blank white walls are lit by the strange glow of a single electric blub.

He flips the light off and slams the door, leaving me in darkness. There's no stopping the frightened squeak, but I am strong enough to keep myself from opening the door. Being left in the dark is one thing I hate about being a woman. I never wish I had been born a boy more than when I'm left in the dark. Boys are never left alone in the dark. And certainly not for days. At least this time it shouldn't be that long. They wouldn't want to keep Father waiting.

I reach out until I feel the back of the chair. Once I'm sure of its position, I lower myself onto it. My body refuses to relax, remembering when tiny paws crawled over my feet in the cellar. No matter. Girls aren't allowed to relax anyway. Not unless heavy with what may be a warlock.

The one thing I can do is close my eyes and hum the little tune Bethany sings the younger girls when they're frightened. The humming stays silent, playing only in my head. There would be more punishment if I got caught humming. It's just as well.

Bethany may sound as sweet as a bird, but I'm worse than an old frog.

How long will they keep me here? They could have at least sent mother with me, since she has nowhere else to go. She could stand in one of these corners as well as a corner out there. Did she sit in the same room when she was tested? I wish she would have told me more on the carriage ride here. She only said that I need to have a lot of magic in my blood to be of any worth. My head aches under the tightness of my bun.

The door opens and the electric lights turn on. I squint against the brightness, wanting to look at the light. Our house was only recently wired for electricity and Father rarely wastes it on us. My eyes adjust to the unnatural light so I'm able to see a man, skin like prunes, focused on the papers in his hands. When he looks up from his papers, his eyes tighten. "Get out of my chair."

I jump. Blast! I should have known it wasn't for my use. Why didn't I think of it being there for the tester? I lower my head, hoping he doesn't discipline me for the mistake.

Once seated he says, "Shut the door."

After closing it, I press my back against its hard surface. His focus returns to his papers. No punishment then—at least not immediately.

"Seventeen today," he says. "Need more girls to come in right away on their birthdays."

Does he think I had a choice? Who would come early if they didn't have to? I suppress a groan. Cynthia maybe. She's always been fascinated by boys. And the girls from class. Basically, any girl who's not me.

He delves back into the parchment. His thin nose is long until the end where it bulges out. White hair sticks out from his head as if the remaining strands are trying to escape.

"Very good pedigree," he mumbles. "Father most impressive. Mother's Father is Devon Mullshire. His and his Fathers' powers were excellent. Simply excellent. With that alone I'd say a warlock

4

should court the girl before the month is over. Get over here, girl, and give me your bare hand."

Is this a trick? Some sort of test before the real test? The Woman's Canon says a woman must always wear gloves when a warlock is present. I inch toward him, but leave my hands gloved and curled together. He can't really want me to break that rule, can he?

At my hesitance, he zaps a silver hex at me. The light strikes across my body and I attempt to hide a cringe. I suck in a breath as the feeling of needles poking my skin encompasses me. As the pain subsides, I tug off my glove and hold out my hand, silently cursing him.

The tester's fingers scratch against my hand as he flips it palm up. I clamp my jaw together and force myself not to move. He stares at my palm. Maybe he can see the magic just by looking. Maybe the rumor in class of the tester spilling my blood was to scare us girls.

A spell of black fog dances from his hands, with tendrils darting out of it like clawing fingers. I dig the heels of my shoes into the floor. The fog nears and loses its blur, hardening into a single knife. I pull away, but he yanks me back. The dark blade skims across my palm and stabs my wrist then dissipates, leaving behind pain. I bite my lip to keep silent.

The crimson on my wrist grows and drips. Before it falls to the floor, the warlock emits a faint blue spell to catch it. The light flows up to the cut and draws more liquid from my wound. While the pulling continues at my wrist, I feel a tug snagging deep in my chest. Something inside me protests as the yanking grows. Once there's about a shot glass full, the pulling stops.

A small hiss escapes me, which he thankfully doesn't seem to care about. The spell dances over my skin, closing the wound, and the last trickle of fluid ceases. Dizziness strikes. I wobble and use the still closed door to steady myself. The room sways as the tester waves his hand, and the spell stretches its beam of light and thins my blood out into a flat circle. The sight of my blood like an evil moon before me makes my stomach churn.

The minutes drag by. The dizziness doesn't leave, but lessens. I try to avoid gazing at the crimson circle. The tester's brows furrow as he studies it. My pulse grows faster. I didn't expect it to take this long. I suck in air and gradually release it. Is there something wrong with it? What if there's no magic in it at all? If I were a boy, it would have been checked long ago, but since women don't do spells, there wasn't a reason to check until now. How angry will Father be if there's nothing in it?

I sag lower against the door. The tester fixes a glare at me. I stand straight and proper though it makes the room sway again. His focus returns to my life force. The spelled light pulses twice before compressing my blood. When it's the size of a squashed pea, it merges onto one of his papers.

"Bring your Father." His voice makes me start after such a long silence.

I hurry from the room, grateful to get away. Once in the hall, I give myself a moment to become accustomed to my weakened state. When I think I can handle it, I walk fast down the hall. Or at least as quickly as my faint body will let me.

When I reach the waiting area, mother is still in the corner, but the women surrounding her are different than those who were waiting before. All have varying shapes of tattoos above their collarbones. The center tattoo is bordered by a second in a diverse array of lines, curves, and sometimes another shape. The border indicates they're all married. The daughters must be in testing rooms like the one I just left. Their eyes constantly dart toward the men.

Father lazes, laughing with the men. I position myself where Father can see me, but where I won't be in the way. After a few moments he addresses me.

"Finished then. Let's see how soon some chap will ask for you." He tosses his pipe on a table. "Agatha, come."

The crowd of women parts for my mother, who waddles behind Father. I would rather be headed to class, but wishing won't make it happen. When we're back to the tester, a second chair has appeared across from him. The room seems larger and somehow warmer. I don't know if it's really changed or if it's easier to face with mother here.

Father's frame overflows the new seat, and mother moves to stand behind him. After closing the door, I take my place beside her. The air grows hot with the progressing day and too many bodies in the tight room. I pull at my navy gown, but it goes right back to sticking to my skin.

"Good to see you, Councilman." The tester smiles, making his face appear kind instead of foreboding, though more pruneish than ever. It's almost like he's a different person.

"And you," Father says anxiously. "What are the results?"

The warlock shows Father the parchment with my blood on it. "Take a look for yourself. It's already lost some of its potency, but she's brimming with magic. Good fine stock. Should be able to secure you an exemplary son-in-law within the month."

Father studies the parchment for a moment. "Marvelous. You've done some fine testing."

"Thank you, Councilman Stephen. We've all been impressed with your own work. You're a great benefit to our society. I'll make sure the paperwork gets in right away. I suspect offers will be arriving soon."

"Any good candidates inquiring lately?"

"Matter of fact, the Grand Chancellor's son was recently in. Picked a wench two days ago."

The Grand Chancellor's son? If he hadn't picked a wife previously, would I have made it on his list? I grip my hands together. It's doubtful I could handle hosting the required balls and being watched and gossiped about by all the other councilmen's wives. Having to endure my husband will be hard enough without him being a powerful and influential warlock. More than ever the thought makes me want to be back with my sisters. Father leans forward, eager as the tester continues.

"Lots of other good ones are still looking. Jonathan, Councilman Michael's son was by the other day but hasn't found a wife yet. Neither have Frank or Walter of Norpar."

"Excellent. Would you make sure they are aware of Serena's submission?"

"Of course. I'll pass it on to those of esteem. I keep hoping Chancellor Jacob will come in for a new wife. He needs to get over his dead one. So many admire you council members. He's setting a bad example."

Father rubs his chin. "Can you imagine if she was the Chancellor's wife? That would bring good things for me. Since that won't happen, the most powerful, influential warlock in Chardonia who needs a wife would be fine. Preferably one that can pay a lot."

They both stand. "I'll take care of it. Thank you for bringing her in."

"Just doing my duty. I'm ready for some strapping grandsons."

My insides hurt. I fold my arms across my stomach as they head out, but it doesn't help with the pain. I move to follow.

Mother touches my elbow. The touch startles me to a stop and she lets go. "I remember when I was chosen by your Father. It was a troublesome time, but you can do it. You're strong and your sisters need your example."

I close my eyes and shake my head before opening them again. "I don't think I'm that type of strong."

Mother sighs. "Maybe not, but you still have to go through it, society expects it. You'll have a new owner soon."

She's right. A warlock could ask to buy me at any time. There's nothing I can do about it. I follow mother from the room, bowing my head with the hope that it will keep further attention from me. But it's too late to hope. I will always be owned.

# CHAPTER 2

IT TURNS out the tester was wrong. Very wrong. It isn't even a week before I'm purchased by a warlock. Some man I've never met now owns me. According to Father, this man is wealthy and has had only the best of classes focusing on helping him become a councilman. Someone capable of filling Father's pockets and increasing his popularity. A man whom I'm on my way to meet. Thomas. My new Master. He summoned Father and me to keep him company during the yearly tournament. For a full week I'll be with my owner and soon-to-be husband.

My gut churns. I don't know if my carriage sickness is extra severe today or if my nerves are making it worse. The seat jostles beneath me like it has for most of the day. I bump against Cynthia in the dark carriage. I'm grateful Father let her come since mother isn't permitted to attend the tournament in her state. I just wish Cynthia could keep her excitement over our first tournament to a minimum until we're there. If women were allowed windows in the carriage, at least the scenery would distract me. Instead there's nothing but darkness, bouncing, and sickness. I groan.

"Sorry, I didn't mean to make you feel worse." She stops wiggling, at least for the moment, and I only have to contend with the ruts of the road. She means well, when she thinks about it. "I'm sure we'll be to Thomas's soon, and you can get some fresh air."

"I hope so."

"Can I do anything to help?"

I rest my head against the carriage wall, but lift it when the swaying makes the nausea worse. "Talk to me. Distract me."

"Certainly. I love your two new gowns. They're stunning. The dark green one is my favorite. You'll be smashing. I wish Father would let me get a new gown or two. You're lucky he got some for you."

I think they're all too fancy, but of course she would want them. She has more dresses than she can wear between wash days. I don't know what she would do with more, but Father insisted I needed to look my best for Thomas to show off. "You make your gowns look beautiful, Cynthia. No one will know they aren't new."

"Apart from being out of date. Still, I hope being at the tournament will give me a chance with some warlock. I brought three handkerchiefs to give away."

I groan. "Three? Do you really need more than one?"

"Well, if I can't get in the marriage pool for another year, I might as well spread myself out and practice."

"Practice what? They don't care about anything besides magic and money. We know you have a good pedigree, it's not like you can change the magic in your blood."

She leans back and is quiet a moment before answering. "If I get someone to care enough about me, they may try to find me in the marriage pool. It's not unheard of for men to gain a preference for a woman before her blood is tested, you know. One of them could be better than Father."

I wish this conversation were taking place somewhere easier to think. Somewhere we weren't being churned about. "If anyone can do it, I'm sure you can. But should you?"

"Men aren't all bad. Don't you remember Lewis from our weekly manners lesson? He was always so nice, making sure I was first in line to go home."

If she really thinks that, it's because she didn't see how he looked at her when she was turned away. Or how he pinched the back of my arm while trying to steal a kiss. It left a bruise for two weeks. Though I should have given him what he wanted, I couldn't. Instead, I screamed and received a day-long silence spell. Of all the hexes I've gotten, not being able to talk was minor. And I wasn't forced to kiss his peeling lips.

Dreaming of a nice warlock is a dangerous thing. Yet, I can't take her hope away. Without hope, there's nothing but misery. I know. I close my eyes. "Can we please speak of something else?"

She returns to talking of dresses for a while, then moves on to the sisters we left behind. Little Molly learning to walk. Sally eager to begin classes. Bethany taking care of them all. As she prattles on, it's hard to pay attention, but I let her voice soothe me. No matter how hard I try not to think of them, her earlier words about men being nice come back to me. Despite what she thinks, men are rarely kind unless they're playing some sort of cruel game. To them, women are owned and used, that's all.

Finally, the carriage halts, and Cynthia's chatter ceases. I continue to sway. The bouncing resumes as Cynthia can't contain her excitement, again. I groan and try not to lose my breakfast. Shouldn't have eaten that biscuit.

"Sorry." While she sounds sincere, she continues twitching.

Men's voices drift from outside, but I can't make out what they're saying. As I think of what's to come, the voices I hear and who I'm about to meet, my hands shake. Several more minutes pass before the carriage door opens. I blink against the light. Father pokes his head inside, shielding us from some of it. One glimpse of me and he leans farther away. I must look as ill as I feel.

"Best behavior. Particularly you, Serena." His voice is a gruff whisper. "Remember what's at stake."

For him it's gaining the right son-in-law. Nothing to do with the fact I'm about to meet my new owner. Why does it even matter? It's not like I can be returned like goods at a shop. I'm bought and paid for, no matter what. Unless of course I'm found unvirtuous.

I stare at my gloved hands. I'm trying to keep from being sick, but Father must take it as acceptance because he leaves. Fresh air whirls in. I stay in place, letting my stomach calm. Cynthia tames a few of my locks back with a pin from her pocket.

"You brought hair pins?" I ask.

"Bethany said you would need them."

Taking care of me is such a Bethany-like thing to do, my trembling eases a little. Out of all my thirteen sisters I'll miss her the most. Tears threaten, but I push them away with a glance at Cynthia. We look nothing alike. Her blonde curls are still forced into the tight knot at the back of her head. Green eyes, big and full of life against the pale face paint. Her reddened mouth purses as she fixes another of my stray hairs.

In contrast, my dark hair never stays in place, even though it's straight and not curly like hers. My brown eyes always seem so dull, the few glimpses I've had of them. But the face paint is the same. Of course we have to wear it and follow the Woman's Canon. Mother wouldn't have it any other way.

Cynthia nudges me. If only we were at the house instead of here. Even classes filled with endless dronings about the Woman's Canon and how we must live up to it sound better than meeting the warlock who now owns me. I take one last deep breath and exit the carriage. Despite the circumstances, I try to muster as much grace as I can.

The house is bigger than Father's. Three stories of gray stone, ivy creeping up one side. Bushes cluster around the house reaching the bottom of the windows. Servants line the stairs, at the bottom of which Father is talking to a man who is perhaps five years older than me. Thomas? Taller than me, but about half

Father's weight. Golden eyes. No blemishes on his face, though his nose has been broken at least once.

Mine looked like that after I'd been particularly outspoken. When I lived with it for a week, Father fixed it. Said warlocks would reject me with a nose like that. I wonder why this warlock didn't fix his with magic. It does make him handsome, in a fierce sort of way.

I brush my hands across my dark, wool dress, overly aware of my travel-worn state. Father can't truly fault me for it, but he may nevertheless. Once Cynthia departs the carriage, she slides next me. Together, we walk toward the men.

Motioning at me, Father says, "Thomas, this is your new property."

Thomas bends over my extended hand to kiss it. A tremor of dread starts where his lips touch my glove and travels through me. Not letting go, he straightens. His eyes roam over me. I force my smile to stay, though I'd prefer to glower. No man has ever leered at me in such a way. A chill fans through me. I want an extra wrap. Or three.

"Enchanted. I don't mind getting married, but I believe marriage to this one will make duty a pleasure."

Even through the shield of my glove, his touch makes my insides balk. I yank my hand from his, as politely as I can, and mask my features. Father scowls. Apparently, not polite enough.

"Glad to hear it." Father slaps him on the back. "Wouldn't want it any other way. The other is my second eldest. Turns seventeen in eleven months."

Thomas's gaze leaves me in favor of my sister, for which I am grateful. As he grabs her extended hand and places a kiss on it, the bit of gratitude I felt flees. He shouldn't be touching my sister.

"She's also lovely. I know you mourn not having sons, but if these two are any indication of your other daughters, you have outstanding stock. You'll be rich from the sell of them. If her blood is as potent as her sister's, I hope they pass the multi-wives law before her birthday."

Cynthia giggles prettily. The sound makes me feel as if my carriage sickness is returning in full force.

Father chuckles. "With your lineage and power, I'm sure you'd do the law justice. I'll be pulling for it myself. If it had passed years ago, I might have been able to get a son."

"Then I hope it passes. There may still be time." He winks at me. Though it takes effort, I manage not to glare back. What I can't stop is the chill crawling through me.

His arm drapes around my waist and he pulls me toward massive front doors. He calls over his shoulder to Father. "You must be tired from your travels. I'll have servants attend you, Stephen. Dinner is at seven."

As we ascend the steps, the space between us isn't enough. I suspect it won't be the entire time we're here, but hope it's not always this close. The whole week-long tournament. Ugh. And then the marriage in five months, what will I do? With a slight shortening of my gait, I try to ease from him and rejoin my sister. Thomas clings tighter.

The doors open and he calls out orders to his servants, his voice echoing through the entry. Behind us, Cynthia and Father follow. Several tables decorated with flowers line the walls adding a sharp, floral scent, making me more ill.

"Councilman Stephen, you'll be shown to my best guest room."

"Thank you, Thomas. I'm sure it will be to my liking."

A tarnished servant leads Father up the curving staircase. A second servant, not tarnished, steps forward. We only have the bald, inked-faced tarnished servants at home. The sight of someone serving who looks more like me is jarring. A reminder that anyone can become a servant. Though anyone can also be tarnished should their master deem them unworthy. The thought distracts me from the fact that I'm being left behind. The servant leads Cynthia down a hall to the right, and out of sight. I yearn to follow.

Once she's gone, Thomas puts his nose in my hair and breathes deeply making the ache to be away a physical pain in my chest. "It's unfortunate we can't hold the wedding at the end of the tournament. What a fine thing that would make. Ah, well, make yourself at home, wench. Soon enough, it will be."

He wraps his fingers in my hair, loosening the pins. *Maintaining proper distance is unnecessary with your Master. He sets what's proper.* The words from the Woman's Canon were drilled into me so many times, they echo in my head as if my teacher is actually saying them. *A woman must always submit to her Master's wishes.* At school we learned the only exception is that she remain chaste before marriage. Otherwise the warlock lines might become tainted.

*The law must be obeyed.* I force myself not to let my fist fly like Father has done to me so many times. My arms tremble. "Please stop."

"Ah, ah, ah. You must address me as Master." He presses his lips to my cheek, his hands move from my hair going lower and lower down my back. My muscles tense and my body shakes. Suppressing a whimper, I squirm.

Laughing, he pushes me away. I stumble, but manage to catch myself on a small table. The vase of flowers on it rocks back and forth. I steady it before it can crash to the floor.

"I'm not an Envadi, wench. You'll come to realize my attention is not barbaric, but what you want."

While he ascends the stairs, I hold myself as dignified as I can. At the top, he stares at me. I hold his gaze, unwilling to look away. It doesn't matter he owns me, after what just took place I can't degrade myself any further by lowering my head. A wry grin crosses his features, as if he's won something.

Finally he saunters down the hall. When he's out of sight, I let the air rush from me and rub my cheek, probably smudging my face paint. Though he didn't punish me for the disobedient act, I can't help but feel maybe he did win something.

"This way," says a tarnished I hadn't noticed. She waits next to the hall Cynthia went down.

"Does the place you're taking me have somewhere I can wash?" She nods.

"Good." I stop rubbing my face and anxiously follow her.

The memory of his lips upon my skin distracts me from noticing much on the way in. She leads me to a sitting room I assume will be shared with my sister. It's twice the size of my bedroom. A small sofa and three chairs grace the middle of the room. Paintings of pregnant women hang on the walls. Cynthia enters from an adjoining room, eyes brighter than when we arrived.

"Come see your room. If it's anything like mine, you'll love it."

She rushes me to the door on the opposite side of hers. My temporary room is even larger than the sitting room. A bed and wardrobe occupy one side. On the other is a vanity with a mirror larger than any I've ever seen. At home the few mirrors are the size of a small plate. This one is the size of a large plate and easy to see in. I wonder if Father knows I'm going to a man who doesn't care if women become vain. If I thought it would do any good, I'd tell him. Instead, I'll use the mirror to keep from being punished over wayward strands of hair.

A chair and a table sit in the corner. The Woman's Canon lays on it. No need to bother that area of the room. A doorway leads to my very own water closet. All the space put together is as much room as my sisters have combined. What does a woman need so much space for?

"Isn't it fantastic?" Cynthia asks.

"Different from home, that's certain."

"Would you like me to sleep with you tonight to make it feel more like home?"

I survey the bed trying to imagine what it'd be like not to be kicked by four sisters all night long. A nervous, but excited flutter fills me. "Entirely unnecessary."

She laughs. "I knew you liked it."

"You can come in whenever you'd like, though."

I move to the vanity where an empty bowl, a bowl full of water, and a cloth await. I rinse my mouth first and spit in the empty one. The water is tepid, but I don't hesitate using it to scrub my face. When it starts to feel raw, I realize I scrubbed too hard. Yet it still feels dirty.

"The carriage ride really bothered you this time, didn't it?" Cynthia grabs a brush. "Let me fix your hair before dinner."

I clamp my jaw shut. The dark locks are in disarray, hanging around my now reddened face. Much more damage than a day long excursion will do. I can still feel his hand twisting in them. I scowl at my reflection and hope Cynthia doesn't know why it's such a mess. Her fingers set to the task, just like they would at home. Seeing her work in the mirror is entertaining. Her brows furrow as she tames my hair, her own still impeccable. Somehow, her curly mane always manages to behave better than my straight one.

"You're so lucky," she says. "This will be such a good match for you. Just look at this room. And the house. I don't think you could do better. Well, except for the Grand Chancellor's son, but since he's already engaged, I can't imagine a better catch."

Of course that's what she thinks. The muscles in my shoulders tighten. I roll them trying to ease the tension.

"What's wrong?"

She's always been able to read me too well, but I've never said a word to her before about how I feel. Not one. I want to tell her. Tell someone. My thoughts go against the Woman's Canon, though. I can still feel Thomas's arms around my waist, his gaze raking across me, his fingers in my hair, his lips pressed against my cheek. I've barely spent any time with him, but he already owns me in a way worse than Father ever did. It pushes and tugs against something inside of me until it breaks.

"It's not right." My voice is louder than I intend. I work to make it softer. "It doesn't feel right."

Cynthia stops playing with my hair and looks at me in the mirror. "What do you mean?"

"All of it. Any of it. I'm not ready to be a wife, a mother. To be owned by a husband. Getting away from Father would be, well, you know how Father is, but how do I know Thomas will be better? What I really want is..." What do I really want? I don't know, but not this. Something different. Something that won't require me to constantly submit myself to another's will.

"What is it? What do you want?" Her eyes are so big and innocent.

What I want are things that will lead to more punishment. I can't bring myself to break her along with me. "I don't know, Cynthia. I don't know."

She says nothing, instead finishing my hair. Tears leak out my eyes without permission and trickle down my face. She hands me a handkerchief. Swiftly, I dab the moisture. When all trace of my weakness is gone, I turn to her, forcing a grin.

"I hope that wasn't one of the handkerchiefs you planned on giving away."

"Certainly not." She takes it from me. "It's almost seven."

With my emotions so raw, I want to escape from the men the rest of the night. I think I may know a way, but how will she react to it? "Should we go feast in silence while listening to the men go on about the tournament or should we claim we're too ill from the journey?"

"Let's claim we're too ill." She laughs, easing my fears. "Ever since you were sick on Father's shoes, he no longer thinks it's just an excuse."

"Then I won't be the one to tell him that my stomach is settled."

"I'll find a servant to take a message. Then I'll be back to help you unlace and we can get more comfortable." She scurries from the room.

I scrutinize myself in the mirror. Seeing more of my reflection will take some getting used to. My eyes are a touch puffy, but otherwise normal. The red from scrubbing too hard has faded. I look the same as I did a short time ago, before I turned seventeen and had another owner. Waist-length dark hair, dark eyes, pale face. Inside, I don't feel the same. Even a small amount of time can bring bitter change.

What type of change will tomorrow bring? Mother always talked about tournament deaths, which leaves me unsure. I've seen many injuries, but never seen anyone die. Neither have I met anyone from another country. Though it's doubtful Father will let me actually meet anyone, I'm still curious to see what they're like. Especially the barbaric Envadi. Will Thomas have to duel against any of them?

Cynthia waltzes into the room full of news about treasures she found while searching for a servant. I barely hear, more concerned with what tomorrow will bring. At least while Thomas participates, I will have one less thing to fret over. Except it's those moments when his arms and lips have time to reach me that I dread. I'll hope he does extremely well and has no time to spare for me.

# CHAPTER 3

THOMAS'S BOX offers not only a perfect view of the field where the main events will be held, but also a great place for keeping an eye on other council members and those of power. Especially since we're right next to the Grand Chancellor's box. At least that's what Father has been going on about since we arrived. I can't tell one way or another.

The boxes sit at varying heights and sizes, held up by pillars. There seems to be no pattern, except that none are bigger or taller than the Grand Chancellor's. Our own is several feet off the ground, just a little lower than the tallest. Even so, being this high off the ground has me gripping my chair tight whenever I think on it. I've never been so high before.

The smell of dirt and grass wafts in. Two chairs made of wood waited for Cynthia and me when we arrived an hour ago. It's been making my backside ache ever since. The warlocks have cushioned chairs and small tables nearby to hold their food and drink. On the side by the stairs is a table with a jug of water. Several servants, mostly tarnished, but a few like the one I saw at Thomas's house, stand by it. A canopy hangs over our box, orange like everyone else's from Chardonia. The women in nearby boxes all wear dark colors and an orange band like Cynthia and me. Some gather in their boxes chatting in little groups or stand next to a warlock waiting to be shown off. Most sit alone.

Other canopies and bands come in varying colors, each color representing a different country. Green, yellow, blue, red, purple, white. I don't recognize where they're from. Classes didn't cover the colors of other countries, only our own. And there are so many of them. Never have I seen so many colors in one place.

A few warlocks, mostly those with purple bands, have a gun strapped to their waist. Those with red bands have dark skin and hair, the likes of which I've never seen before. But it's not nearly as surprising as what some of the women from other countries do.

They prance around with no warlock nearby. Not a single man within twenty paces of them! That makes them stand out more than their excessive height, though in truth there aren't more than a dozen. A few of the others, with a white band around their arm, wear shockingly bright colored dresses. A few of the other brazen women walking about wear colors from other countries besides white, but none wear orange. None of these unaccompanied women have marriage or engagement tattoos on their necks. Are they all single or do they not mark themselves as we do? I sigh and slouch in my chair.

"Sit up straight," Father says.

I frown, but resume a more dignified posture and brush the wrinkles from my deep violet gown. Thomas enters the box for the first time since showing it to us. He wears simple black breeches and shirt, with the orange band tied around his right arm, dressed as the other participants from Chardonia. His gaze lingers on me as he walks toward Father. An older gentleman wearing tan robes follows him. White hair brushed back from his forehead in waves contrasts with his dark mustache and short beard. A skinny young man, also in dueling clothes, finishes the group.

"Councilman Stephen, I trust the box is to your liking," Thomas says.

"Very much so, thank you." Father pushes to his feet. "We're grateful to be privileged enough to be next to your box, Grand Chancellor."

The older gentleman nods his head. The Grand Chancellor stands but a few feet from me. My stomach twists. I continue to hold my rigid posture as he speaks. "Pleased to see you here, Stephen. You remember my son, Nathaniel."

"I do. Are you trying to get on the council, Nathaniel?"

The young man, whom Father was so disappointed already chose a bride, looks to the Grand Chancellor who says, "Remember I won't have any political talk during the break."

"Of course not, Your Grace."

Thomas motions toward me. "And this is my future wife." I wonder if it would have been worse if I was Nathaniel's right now instead of his. From the stern expression on the Grand Chancellor's face, probably much, much worse. Thomas continues the introduction, "Councilman Stephen's eldest daughter, Serena, and her sister."

I keep my eyes down and smile fixed like I'm supposed to. Always submissive and pleased with them on the outward, but inwardly wishing they weren't here. Yet, I feel their scrutiny as much as if I looked them in the eye so I'm careful to keep the proper pose. We practiced in class, but having it happen under a real setting, and by the Grand Chancellor, makes it harder not to squirm. Next to me, I can only make out the dark brown of Cynthia's dress.

"Indeed. She's lovely. Heard rumors her blood was good quality."

News of my magic is spreading that much? I should be flattered, instead I feel contaminated somehow. If I'm already bought by another, why does it even matter?

"It's true," Father confirms.

The Grand Chancellor says, "I wish we'd passed the multi-wives law sooner."

"For yourself or your son?" Thomas questions.

The warlocks laugh. I cinch my fingers together.

"What do you think, Nathaniel?" the Grand Chancellor asks.

"Marlene is a good choice for me," a younger voice replies.

"He's quite taken with his intended," the Grand Chancellor says, "but if he hadn't already retained her, whichever of us could persuade you for your daughter would have been the one to claim her."

The men laugh harder. My face burns. Soon they'll be discussing Cynthia like this. The thought shifts the heat from my face to my core. I clench my teeth together and lift my gaze to meet the Grand Chancellor's. The laughter dies off.

"Do you have something to say, my dear?" He returns the stare.

I bite my lip before blurting out, "Perhaps if the law is passed it should include consulting the first wife before taking another one on."

This time the men howl with laughter, except for the Grand Chancellor, who continues to stare at me. I give a forced smile, but my words keep echoing through my head. The laughter lessens. Father frowns.

"It appears you'll have a good source of amusement from your wife, Thomas." The Grand Chancellor finally breaks eye contact. "But as I said, no politics this week. Get enough of that a few months out of the year, eh, Stephen?"

Father's somber expression pulls into a tight smile. "Too true."

I look away. Blast my mouth! Cynthia's hands are twisted together in her lap, mirroring my own. Why couldn't I have claimed I had nothing to say? Or even better, kept my eyes down. I don't know how bad the punishment will be for this, but it won't be a simple fist flying just once at me. My only chance is if Father waits to administer it. The games, if they go well, may soften him some.

"It was good to see you, but I must get to my box." The Grand Chancellor begins to move toward the stairs. "I understand you'll be dueling against Chancellor Jacob soon, Thomas."

"This afternoon, in fact. My first duel of the tournament."

"Surprised he didn't send a marriage contract for your future wife. His old one has been dead four months now. Childbirth. Lost a good warlock babe in that tragedy. Man needs to get himself a new wife. Shame to let such power and lineage go to waste. His choice, though. Best of luck to you against him. He's a powerful one."

Once the Grand Chancellor and his son are gone, Thomas kneels in front of me. When I don't look at him, he yanks my chin until I'm forced to meet his eye. "If you ever embarrass me like that again, I won't hesitate to tarnish you and find myself a more suitable bride."

He flings my chin away from him and strides out of the box. I grip the sides of my chair trying to keep myself from letting my fear show. Tarnished! Stripped of all my humanity, never able to see my sisters again. The world seems to tilt around me.

"Cynthia," Father says, not looking away from me. "Take the servants and get refreshments. Don't return until the curtains are up."

My eyes dart to the tarnished following orders with the other servants. Their dull heads, blank looks, and black lines swirling on their faces make them all appear the same. He could force me to become one of them.

Cynthia bounces to her feet, pulling my fears from those less than shadows. "Yes, Father."

No chance of him calming down first, then. Cynthia hesitates in front of me, her forehead wrinkled and lips pursed. I chance giving her a nod in front of Father, and with a twirl of her skirt she and the servants are gone, the last of their bald heads disappearing from view.

A sky-colored spell tinged with red flashes from Father,

24

leaving me no time to think on the tarnished as the orange curtain lowers. Dread curdles my stomach. His fingers pinch together. The only way I can tell the silencing spell is coming is years of trying to pick out its clear wavering lines. It hits, my throat locking. I grip the seat of my chair and wrap my feet around the legs of it, steeling myself. With my gaze lowered, I pick a smudge on the curtain to concentrate on.

"You will not dishonor me or your intended again." He stalks toward me and yanks me back by my hair bun. "You will do nothing."

A crimson light launches from him, heading straight for my leg. My body jerks with a mute scream as the bone breaks. Tears prick my eyes. I silently beg for the spell to push me into unconsciousness. His hand presses on the wound, the pressure increasing as he speaks.

"He has good lineage, is a powerful warlock, is next in line for the council, and is friends with the Grand Chancellor. He paid good money for you. You will not disgrace him."

The searing agony is so consuming, the world blissfully starts to blacken. My head lolls, and I close my eyes, welcoming the dark embrace.

"Ah ah. You're not getting out of punishment so easy."

The world comes into unreal focus. The pain intensifies. Minutes. Hours. Some time. Too much time.

Finally the pain eases as his grip lessens.

"Will you disrespect me or your intended again?" He shoots the silence spell at me again to reverse its effects.

It takes me a moment to realize what he's saying and even longer to slur a response. "No, Father."

"Good."

His weight lifts from the wound. I crumple against the chair.

"I'll fix you, but know that it's for Thomas."

I try not to let my relief show as he heals my leg, but I surely fail. The pain fades until it's a dull ache. Apparently, he's not healing it all the way. He casts a honey colored spell over me. The light dances in front of my vision. The world takes on an unreal feeling. Colors look off. The sound of the crowd smothered, but somehow sweeter. I want to lie down and listen to them.

"Now, for a little surprise for Thomas. Payment for your rudeness." He holds his hands in the shape of a circle. As he pushes his hands apart black, maroon, and gold burst from them. The colors dance around each other until they form Thomas's family crest, a shield with a hand casting a spell on it. The hand moves and pink light comes from it to create a bouquet of flowers. The flowers fade and the hand casts another spell. It continues casting minor spells, hovering in the air before me.

"Stand," Father commands. I'd rather curl into a ball on the floor, but I'm not about to disobey. Some pain lingers as the crest follows my movement. "Walk to the edge of the box and back."

I do so. Again the crest follows me. Wherever I go there will be no mistaking that I'm Thomas's property. Though it's supposed to be a recompense to Thomas for my behavior, it feels more like a heavy reminder to me. Constricting. The feeling lightened only by the surreal spell encompassing me. When I get close to Father I make sure to keep my head down.

"Get rid of that sullen mood, girl. We don't want Thomas worrying over your gloomy face when he's about to compete. Sit down and pull yourself together."

Finally grateful to obey an order, I do as directed. Instead of leaning back and resting on the chair as I wish, I sit straight and mask my feelings with a pleased expression. Eyes attentive and a small upward turn of my lips. The honey spell he cast makes it easier, not so forced. As soon as I have the expression fully in place, Father raises the curtain.

Some minor duel is going on before us. Lights flash between two warlocks. I lock my eyes on them, but don't really see what they're doing. My leg throbs. I'm cold.

Soon Cynthia arrives, servants laden with food and drink

behind her. She directs them to the table with a jug on it and she prepares a plate for Father. Once he's satisfied, she perches on the chair beside mine. He's more interested in his food and the tournament than us, but we still keep our voices down.

"Father did better than I thought with Thomas's family crest spell. I was afraid you were in for a punishment, but this is magnificent." She stares at Thomas's crest hovering in the air before me as it creates a kitten. It scampers about a moment before dissolving and another spell is cast.

My leg aches. "Yes, Father's a talented warlock."

"Did something happen?" Her hands grip her dark skirt.

With a gesture at the crest, I say, "As you see."

"It's because of what we talked of last night isn't it?" It takes me a moment to remember I told her a little of my marriage fears. "It'll be all right. With this spell, you really look like a grand prize. It's sure to boost Thomas's chances of doing well, which can only aid you. You'll be his good luck charm. No one harms a good luck charm."

Unless it runs out of luck. I can't bring myself to say anything. She's trying so hard.

"You're shivering." She pulls a wrap from my bag and places it around my shoulders, face bunched with concern. "Things really will turn out."

Instead of answering, I nod at the duel. "Can you tell who's winning?"

Her gaze drifts to the field and her expression brightens as a jade light almost hits one of duelers. "It's fascinating, isn't it? Do you ever wish you knew what was going on when someone cast a spell?"

I think of what magic has brought to my life. "No. No, I don't."

We watch for hours. The bright flashes of spells hold no appeal. Neither does the food Cynthia insists I eat. Everything seems drab. The countries' different colors, false. Smells fade to nothing. The people murmuring. The dueling warlocks. Even the flashy, colored spells start to fade. The honey-colored charm Father cast on me must be wearing off. Yet, I've never been under it before, so I can't be sure.

"Chryos brought a good number of supporters this year." Cynthia motions toward the group. "I heard they have around sixty people dueling. But they're supposed to be decent. Some of them wear strange framed windows in front of their eyes though."

I glance to where she points. A large number of participants with black clothes and red bands around their arms watch a duel. "That's more than mother said they had last year. How do you know which ones they are?"

"Some of the servants were chatty while I was getting refreshments. Apparently, Chryos wants to show off their skills."

The normal servants she means. Tarnished aren't allowed to speak freely with us. I peek at the closest one. Though her face is inked with swirls around her eyes and cheeks making emotions hard to gauge, she seems calm. The tarnished catches me watching and stares back. Quickly, I avert my gaze.

Those eyes didn't look calm or emotionless.

The haunted look plagues me as I focus on Cynthia's words, silently begging for distraction. "Lots of people from Arllos are here as well. They're the purple ones."

The purple canopies are straight across the field from us. "What else did you hear?"

"Litilas didn't show, but more Envadi than expected. Look at the bunch of them wearing white bands."

Of course the women without chaperones would be from the most barbaric of countries. I should have realized that before.

"I always knew Envadi were enormous," she continues, "but they need seats bigger than Father's. Only three of them are actually dueling. The Nislia have fewer though. There's only a few of them watching and none of them are dueling. They're the bits of green you see." She sips her drink. "Look, there's Thomas."

He struts out onto the dueling circle closest to us. A man older than him but younger than Father follows. The man angles toward the Grand Chancellor. He appears more aged than I first thought, in a rough way, like his youth was ripped from him. Much of the aging is in his sunken eyes, but also in the grooves on the sides of his mouth. His face is haunting.

"That's Chancellor Jacob. One of the servants pointed him out. It's a shame he never had any children. And to lose the only one he was going to get." She shakes her head.

"It's a shame his wife is dead," I reply. Why am I the only one to ever think of her?

"Must you be morbid?"

Father still appears to be paying us no mind. I lower my voice further just in case. "It's true. Men should be the ones to carry babes since they care about them so much. Then they could die in childbirth and we wouldn't have to fear it."

Cynthia surveys the area around us. "Hold your tongue. You know most woman can be healed. We needn't fear it, but if you keep talking like this you're bound to be punished." She glances at the field. "Look, another duel is starting."

I watch the field only partially paying attention. The men bow to each other and the spells spring forth. Despite my trying not to, I keep thinking on the tarnished and the haunted look in its eyes.

The crowd lets out a gasp, yanking me from my thoughts. Chancellor Jacob is lying on the ground, not moving.

"What happened?" I ask.

Cynthia shakes her head, watching the scene with wide eyes.

The mediator checks on the Chancellor. After a moment he announces, "Dead."

I jump to my feet. Thomas lifts both fists and the people cheer. He pumps his arm, sending yellow sparks in the air. The masses grows louder. My gaze goes to the dead Chancellor. I swallow.

"Thomas is magnificent," Father says. "Did you see that spell? Of course you girls didn't, but it was incomparable."

Certainly incomparable. A man is dead.

"You girls look sick," he continues, "but I tell you it was supreme. Once the shock passes you'll see. My Serena is a lucky girl."

Lucky?

"Should I get the soothing tea?" Cynthia's voice is weak.

"Soothing tea? At a moment like this?" Father says. "It's a time for celebration, not calming, halfwit."

The cheers continue a while longer. My head buzzes as I watch. Finally, the Grand Chancellor stands and raises his arm. Silence. Thomas stands on the ground before the Grand Chancellor's box.

"In accordance with tournament rules, all that Chancellor Jacob had is now yours. Congratulations, Chancellor Thomas."

The horde screams with approval. I collapse in my chair. My stomach churns as if I were stuck in the carriage.

"Just think of all my son-in-law will oversee now," Father says. "No waiting for him to join the council. A Chancellor. A Chancellor!"

My hands shake. Thomas struts around the field casting spells as the merriment focuses on him. He comes toward the box and enters it. Without a word, he kneels before me and the crest. All eyes are on us. I force a pleased smile and the crowd once again goes silent.

An emerald spell is forming on the other side of the crest. After a moment, it weaves itself into the crest, moving and changing it. When it stops, there's a laurel branch entwined with the hand and emeralds bordering the maroon edges. Chancellor Jacob's crest blended with Thomas's. I don't know much, but I do know its lineage rivals that of the Grand Chancellor's.

After a moment of silence, Thomas whispers, "Give me your hand."

The idea of touching this killer repels me, but the memory of Father's earlier hex is still fresh. I reach out my gloved fingers. He takes my hand, stands, and jerks me up beside him. He smashes his lips against mine. The jubilation is louder than ever. I can't think above the ruckus and pressure. I try to pull away from him, but he grasps my head, keeping me close. He tastes salty and rancid.

Finally he pulls away, a gleam in his eye. I force myself not to wipe my mouth. The foul taste of him lingers. He turns to the crowd, raises an arm, and shoots a bigger version of the newly made crest into the air above the field. Father edges closer to us, beaming. Cynthia stands on the other side of Thomas, out of sight and reach. I see nothing exciting about the two men at my side and another's body on the field before me.

Everyone is cheering. The boxes and stands are wild with people. Countries are yelling, though ours is the loudest, with colors waving madly. All except one group. The group that by all accounts should be letting their barbaric nature show the most. The Envadi stand silent.

# CHAPTER 4

"THE WAY you blocked and attacked at the same time," Father's spoon waves about as he speaks, leaving green splatters everywhere, "it was the quickest I've seen anyone move during a tournament."

Never have I seen him so lively. With any luck, the change will mean fewer punishments. The electric lights in the chandelier overhead flicker, casting an odd glow across the far stretching, but mostly unused, table. It makes me nervous. At home, Father makes us eat under candlelight.

Thomas gives a lopsided grin and makes like he's snatching a bug out of the air. "I've always had quick reflexes. Better than those spying Envadi scum. Only someone as powerful as me can have a killing during a tournament. What do you think, Serena?"

My spoon slips into the green pea soup. I've never been required to speak during dinner before. "I agree with Father."

"You must think something beyond that, woman. Don't my spells impress you? My new title make you yearn for when you'll be my wife? I even have a new house. Have you ever been to Chancellor Jacob's manor?"

He stares at me expectantly. Could he actually want an

answer? Why is he speaking to me in such a way? He should know women don't have opinions on things. At least not ones we speak aloud. Of course I don't yearn to be his wife. And I've certainly never had reason to attend a Chancellor's home. Until now. The small amount of food in my stomach protests.

The staring continues. I don't dare pretend to take another bite while he keeps asking questions. "I haven't."

"It's the grandest place I've ever seen. Been in his family for more generations than you can think. But now it's mine. Perhaps if you are good after we wed, I'll let you visit."

"That's a treat indeed," Father says. "Been often enough myself for council meetings. Do you think you'll use it for council meetings when it's your time to host?"

"Chancellor Ryan said I shouldn't bother, but I may anyway," Chancellor Thomas replies and the two go back to conversing without me.

Cynthia taps her spoon on the table to get my attention. With a nod toward my soup, she takes a meaningful sip of her own. I resume pretending to eat. It's difficult to feign hunger while sickened by the day's events.

After finishing an overly sweetened cherry dessert, the men excuse themselves, with a reminder that we're leaving early in the morning to go back to the tournament. I sigh.

"That was the most uncomfortable dinner I've sat through," I say. "How can they eat when they saw a man die? When he killed someone?"

Cynthia holds a finger to her lips and looks around. "Let's go to the sitting room, shall we?"

There are several servants on the edge of our conversation. Mostly tarnished in their strange dark skirts and unmatched, dull blouses, but some of the lower class men wait as well. Servants who are working to pay off debts are trouble. Gossip from them can spread as easily as mother gets with child. "Of course. Might as well take advantage of the space."

We walk to the joined sitting room by our assigned rooms and close the door. A pungent candy-like aroma clings to the air. I spot sachets of dried flowers and leaves clustered on the small table in front of the sofa and chairs. The most offending odor is laurel. The leaves of success. A reminder of my new Master, no doubt. I want to throw them out.

"What has gotten into you?" Cynthia puts her hands on her hips. If she'd been watching mother closer, she'd know they're supposed to be fisted as well. "I know you're unhappy, but you must be more cautious. You can't continue being so out spoken. You've been getting worse ever since your birthday."

The day my future took a path away from her. I clench my teeth. One-by-one I pull my fingers from my glove, then take it completely off. After repeating the action with the other one, I throw them on the back of a chair. The cool air is refreshing against my freed skin.

"He murdered someone. I don't like it. Rather, I hate it. Doesn't it bother you?"

"Of course it does, Serena. I'm not totally unfeeling. But I know when to be cautious. I don't want to see you taken from me. From us."

The words sting with truth, yet they don't change facts. "Thomas already owns me. My engagement ceremony is a little over four weeks away, the wedding four months after that. I'm leaving you. Nothing can stop that."

She plops down in a chair. "But I'll still be able to see you from time to time. Dinner parties, balls, and such. But if you make a wrong turn—"

"Why do you keep thinking I'll do something wrong?"

"Because sometimes you act as if there are no consequences to your words. I'm used to you being this way around Father, but things are different now." She sniffs. "I don't know how I would go on without seeing you again. How are we going to make it at home without you? You always stand up for us and take the brunt of everything. It'll be hard enough in four months. If you become tarnished, it would be terrible. It would be as if you were dead."

Guilt pricks at me. I focus on that and not the fear that's been in me ever since Thomas's threat to tarnish me. I settle on the floor beside her seat. "Hush now. No tears. I don't do as much for you and the others as you think."

"You do. We owe so much for everything you do for us."

"Now you're just being silly."

She sits straighter. "You remember the time you visited Aunt Mary last year?"

"Yes. She has the most lovely peach orchards." The trees were in full bloom and went on farther than I could see. Plus, Uncle wasn't so ready with punishments. I wish he hadn't died so I could go again.

Several moments of silence pass, full of sweet memories of wandering the groves unaccompanied and visiting with Aunt Mary before she speaks. "Father hexed me three times and beat me once while you were away. He beat Bethany twice, and I lost count of how many times he hexed her."

I slouch against the side of her chair, not caring that it digs into my back. Getting away and avoiding Father's punishments came with a price I didn't know I was paying. "Why didn't you say anything?"

"You couldn't change it. When you came home, it was over. And you were happy. You'd never been like that before. Or since. I didn't want to make you lose that joy faster than you had to."

"Then why tell me now?"

"Perhaps I shouldn't have, but I don't want you going to a place that prevents you from ever returning home. If you're not careful, you will."

As if she would know. One week of me being gone didn't seem to change her behavior any. "Silly frills and finding a mate are all you ever care about. You have no idea what it's like to worry."

"I worry more than I let on. But do you know what I do,

Serena? I hide those thoughts and feelings, and move on with my life."

The impact of her words jerk through me. If that's really the case, have her big smiles and infatuations with boys been hiding her worry all this time? She's much better at it than I am. My guilt builds, yet I can't help but wonder why she hides it. If she stood up more often, would Father see us as more than property to be sold? Ridiculous thought. Of course he wouldn't.

"I'll try harder." I rise and head for my temporary quarters. "See you in the morning."

Cynthia follows. "I'm sorry, I didn't mean to upset you."

"Don't be. Thank you for telling me, it's given me something to think on." Even if I don't want to think about it. The weight I've always carried for my sisters seems heavier.

"I really am sorry. I just don't want you to go."

I force the corners of my mouth to lift. "All will be well. Goodnight."

"Night, Serena."

I cross into my room, shutting the door behind me. After a moment, her footsteps recede. I slump against the wall and slide to the floor. My sisters. I've worked seventeen years to protect them. Apparently, I haven't been doing enough. Yet, the little I was able to do, I'll no longer be able to provide. Marriage will stop me from being with them more than she thinks. I'll never be more than I am now. Only less. Less able to help them in any way. My ability to choose will fade. I'll take on the role of a breeder.

Or worse. I'll become like that haunted tarnished. Bald. Inked. Barren. Emotionless. Not worth the shadow I cast.

* * *

THE WEEK MOVES in an odd sort of time. Like at the house when I have to wait for Father to leave for a meeting or stand at attention while awaiting punishment. Moments with Thomas are always the slowest. Agonizingly so. When he's not dueling, he's dragging me from one box to another exclaiming over his new title and riches. Sometimes people find us, which is only an improvement because Cynthia is there.

On occasion while Thomas is dueling, Father leaves to do whatever it is he does. Warlock matters, I suppose. Whatever it is, he's usually with other old, paunchy men. During those moments Cynthia and I discuss things with less restraint, though eyes are still on us and we can't become too heedless. Several times I have found I'm being watched by various Chardonians. Other times I just feel it. The Grand Chancellor is especially unnerving. Why he finds me worth such observations, I'm unsure. But his son or another warlock usually regains his attention before it becomes too excessive.

There are eight more deaths. None of the deceased were as prestigious as Chancellor Jacob. Not even anyone who was on the Chardonian council. Most were from different countries. One benefit of having Thomas drag me around was only witnessing one of them. It was just as horrific as Chancellor Jacob's death, but easier to turn away from. Or rather, run away from to visit the privy. At least that was the excuse I used.

Cynthia stays. She watches the duels with eager eyes. No doubt, trying to ascertain who her escape will be once she's tested. I can't agree with her line of thinking, but at least she has a plan to get away from it. Even if it's doomed to fail.

Upon my return from the privy, she explains that the winner was awarded the dead man's things as has been done with the others. Whether they are Chardonian or not, warlocks who enter agree to the terms and thus forfeit their possessions if killed. Not that a dead man cares. But one of the losers is already married, and as such, the new widow is set to become tarnished. That fact gives me more pause than any of the others she loads me with.

Tomorrow is the last day of the tournament. I'm aching for my own bed, though it's shared with my sisters. The bed here is too big and cold. Since we're staying at the tournament tents while Father and Thomas enjoy the feast, tonight's bed will be a cot next to Cynthia's. Then once the tournament is over tomorrow, we'll be back at Thomas's. Despite my words when I first saw our quarters, I haven't enjoyed having my own space. Even the cot sounds better.

"What are you thinking?" Cynthia asks. "You've gone quiet."

"Going home. I miss being there instead of being stuck with Father here at the tournament. A whole week of freedom, wasted."

"I suppose, but you should still be discreet with your words." She returns to watching the final duel of the day. I try not to think of where our last conversation that began this way went. Cynthia adds, "And think of all we'd be missing."

There's nothing to miss.

Bright yellow flashes and a winner is called out. The events for the day are finally over. With evening coming, darkness is falling. Warlocks send yellow sparks across the field, lighting torches all around. I lean back in my chair, grateful we're staying here for the night. Maybe I'll be lucky enough that Thomas will have less interest in me with so many others about. Then I'd really enjoy the evening.

"Do we have to wait for Father to go to the feast?" Cynthia asks.

"We'll give him a little while. If he doesn't show, it's probably all right for us to take a servant."

In the box next to ours, the Grand Chancellor stands. I point him out to Cynthia. The crowd goes silent. A breeze picks up, carrying a scent of bad cabbage with it.

"What an impressive tournament we've had the privilege of observing. As the last rounds are fought tomorrow, I wish the finalists good luck."

While he's speaking, a tarnished is led to a newly placed stone slab in front of the Grand Chancellor's box. It's the size of my bed at Thomas's, except with bumps and dips giving it a more ragged appearance. They reach it and stop. Dressed simpler than usual in nothing but a tunic, it's clear the tarnished is a woman. Her face is void of emotion.

"Before we celebrate the final night of the tournament, we have one last honor to perform."

Father appears at my side and whispers, "This is what happens to some of those who are tarnished."

My gaze darts to her. The threat was clear. That could be me, standing alone, marked as something less than human. My limbs grow heavy watching her stand without wavering. What are they going to do to her? This was never covered in any class or gossip. Tournaments are a place we let our owners show us off, not watch a tarnished.

The Grand Chancellor leaves his box and strides forward. He motions to the stone past the lit torches. Still without any hint of expression, the tarnished lays on it. In the dim light, she looks like she could be any girl I know.

"Sacrifice." His voice booms through the field.

The cool night air sharpens. Realizing what the stone is, I clench my hands together. An altar. His words make sense. My mouth goes dry. I'm about to witness my first human sacrifice.

It was talked about. More rumors flowed about it than I want to admit. Boys bragging they had seen it done at tournaments. Girls wishing they had. I never wanted to hear it. Never wanted to pay attention. Never wanted it to be true.

I thought I could avoid it. Thought that maybe, somehow, it was a story meant to frighten us and nothing more. Right now, I wish it was a story. I wish my avoidance of it could continue. I wish there was some way for me to be anywhere but here.

Silver light seeps from the Grand Chancellor's fingers and slithers toward her. It sharpens as it grows closer to her neck. I tilt my head away from the scene and squeeze my eyes shut. The silence pulses through me. I breathe slowly, waiting for a scream.

And wait.

And wait.

I slide one of my eyelids up a touch, then open them both wide. The Grand Chancellor is glowing. Faintly, but even with the torches lighting the night, it stands out. Sometime while my eyes had been closed, his skin became luminescent. Next to him, the girl on the table lies dark, unmoving.

# CHAPTER 5

THE GRAND CHANCELLOR claps his hands. Sparks fly from them, darting through the night sky. "Let the feast begin!"

The memory of his voice continues to boom against me as the spectators break into a cheer. Father whoops. My insides hurt. A gnawing, uncomfortable feeling. I force it to stay inside.

"You girls make sure you're in the women's tent before curfew," he says and steps out of the box.

No chaperone in public for the first time. Must be a perk of tournament excitement, not that I'll enjoy it. Keeping my gaze away from the altar, I try to gather a sense of normalcy, but struggle. There's nothing normal about any of this.

Cynthia's pale.

"Can I get you something?" I hope she doesn't ask for the calming tea. Mother's forced it on me so much I've grown to abhor it.

She shakes her head.

Grateful she's strong enough to not want the tea, but not knowing how else to help, I stay by her side and try not to think of the sacrifice. I can't help it though. The few images I saw keep playing through my mind, vivid and life-like. The tarnished. The altar. Her lying there, almost seeming human one moment then gone. Just gone.

People drift from their boxes, onto the field, and to the side where I can't see. The area will have entertainment and tables laden with food and drink. It no longer holds any appeal for me. In the growing dark of our box, no one seems to notice us. The jubilation of the crowd carries, faded by the distance, and the smell of rotten cabbage strengthens.

After a while Cynthia says, "I'm not hungry as I thought I would be, but you can go to the feast if you want. I think I'm going to lie down early."

I sigh with relief. "I'll go with you."

"You don't have to."

"I want to."

She stands and we make our way out of the box onto the grass. Just a few steps out, someone grabs my hand and wrenches me away from Cynthia. My chest tightens. I strain against the cloth covered muscles. The odor of sweat clogs my nose. Thomas. I stop struggling. A few people stop walking to watch us.

The Woman's Canon says his closeness is acceptable. Not only acceptable, but that I must submit to his wishes. It makes my stomach churn as if I was riding in a carriage. Despite his arms wrapped around me, holding me flush against him, the words are law. Shoving him away must only take place in my imagination.

"Where have you been?" Pungent wine is heavy on his slurred words as he dips closer.

Forget the law. I try to ease away from him, but he grips tighter.

"We've been in your box like we were supposed to be. We just decided to go to the women's tent for the night." From the scowl on his face, I know that was the wrong thing to say. "I want to be rested before your duels tomorrow."

"None of that. Your sister can go, but everyone will be expecting to see you with me."

"I can come if you'd like, Serena," Cynthia offers.

Her color hasn't returned yet. If she feels as ill as I do, I can't ask for her presence. I fake a smile. "It's fine. I'll see you before curfew."

"If you're sure?"

"She said she's fine," Thomas says. "Get on with you."

I give what I hope is a reassuring smile as he drags me off. Before I can see if Cynthia moves to follow us or heads toward the tent, we round the corner of the box stands. I hope she makes it to the tent without me, that no one stops her. Or that she doesn't get distracted and not make it back in time. How badly would they punish her for that?

The rotten stench grows, mingling with roasted meats. The noise increases. People talking, laughing, singing. A few vomiting. Spell lights flash all around, haphazardly landing on food, the ground, and people. Everywhere. Nothing is immune to a burst of color. A turquoise one lands on my shoulder. I jerk back, but it's already disappeared. Thomas laughs and threads through the crush. I hope the spell didn't do anything.

After dragging me to the table, he lets go. I inch to the side and behind him. Close enough he can find me, but not so easily seen and remembered. Without bothering with a plate, he grabs whatever food is closest and shoves it in his mouth like an animal.

A woman with lots of jangling jewelry, an orange band, and no ownership tattoo, shimmies close to him. She must still be under her Father's rule. She whispers in his ear. He angles toward her and laughs, some of the chewed meat spitting from his mouth. If the sacrifice and vomiting hadn't already sent my hunger fleeing, he would. He grabs a cup of ale from a passing tarnished's tray, sloshing half of it on the table. With one swig, the cup is drained.

Up and down the table, men and a few women are doing the same with varying degrees of crudeness. Wilted-looking cabbage on plates every foot or so must be the cause of the smell permeating the air since the tournament ended. Even the foul-smelling vegetable is jammed in their mouths.

It's as if no one was murdered. And I suppose there wasn't. A tarnished isn't anyone. Who would miss them? Why do I even care? I don't know. It goes against everything I've been taught, but it's bothering me. I want to push it away, but it lingers.

Without staring, I try to watch the tarnished. They move through the crowd with uncanny ease. Replacing empty plates with full ones. Cleaning spills. Standing in the darkness, waiting and watching for a moment when they are needed. They are the shadows I've always been taught they are. But don't I sometimes do the same with Father and my family? Stand back where I can't be seen, waiting and watching. I brush the thought away. This night really is muddling me.

Father comes by. Once he finds us, he pulls me from the fringes, through the growing mass, back to Thomas's side. A few people examine me, but don't bother long, shifting their attention to my owner. Father stays close. He speaks of Thomas and me, of our engagement ceremony in four weeks, of his position on the council, of his relation to the new Chancellor, to anyone who will listen and some who won't. His voice grows louder as more warlocks gather. I ignore what I can.

The Grand Chancellor walks by the crush surrounding us. He stops to talk to a wiry man, but his eyes never leave the swell of people Thomas has gathered. Does he regret awarding Thomas everything now that he has seen what has come of it? Not that he had a choice. Laws are always followed unless changed and you can't change law in the middle of a tournament. Too many women present.

A ringing sounds. I strain to hear more. A bell chimes ten more times, barely heard over the din. I allow myself one deep breath and tap Thomas on the shoulder. Nothing. I tap harder.

"It's almost curfew."

He drapes his arm on my shoulders. "Eleven thirty already?"

"Soon enough."

His eyes narrow and take on a lusty glow. "I'd best see you back then."

I edge away. "You don't have to leave the party. I can see myself."

"Nonsense. The party will be waiting for me when I return. Won't you?" Affirmative shouts clamor all around. "Not a problem." He turns to his supporters. "I'll return shortly, after ensuring my future bride doesn't break curfew."

Cheers and laughter follow us as we nudge our way out of the throng. A few other women trudge in the direction of the tents. Why do they have to extend women's curfew on tournament nights? Balls I can understand, but this? I hope he never wants to take me to another tournament. Though, as a Chancellor's wife there is little hope of that.

He trips into a warlock at the edge of the crowd.

"Oops." Thomas laughs. "Had a bit too much to drink tonight." A gray apology spell, the kind I only ever see given to men, floats to the man he knocked into. I don't think the light means anything other than an apology, but maybe the spell does more than I know.

The man grins. "Win the tournament tomorrow and we'll call it even."

"I will." Thomas says, earning him a cheer.

I sigh as he pulls me from the crowd. We walk, rather I walk and he stumbles, as we move away from the buzz. The noise weakens, and for a few minutes, there is silence save for his greetings to those we pass. All seem to know him and call after him.

Eventually, we make it to the tented area. Most of the participants and spectators have been housed here all week. Father, and mother, always stayed in the tents before. Another reason for Father to adore having Thomas and his close house in the family.

The first tents are all around my height and gray. Men and women laugh and chatter as they dash in and out of sight. These shelters eventually give way to ones towering over them. The new tents are almost as large as my family home. Though I saw them when we were shown around earlier this morning, I still can't fathom why they are here. Who would bother with such bulky things? They would be a lot of work to put up, take down, and carry from place to place. As we move through the unreasonable-sized shelters, the noise of others fades.

The only people left in sight is a couple, embracing. This close, their height astounds me, but there's something more shocking. Their touch. A Master can touch his possessions, so I shouldn't be so surprised. Yet, this is different. It has a hesitance to it. His arms drape around her. Words pass between them too quiet for me to hear. The woman brushes her fingertip across the man's chin before dancing into a tent with a giggle.

"Stupid Envadi." Thomas sways closer to me and trips over nothing, pulling on me. "Can't even party properly. Shouldn't even be here. They'll only spy on us more, try and steal our spells and our women. I'll show them tomorrow when I beat the last warlock they have in the tournament. I'll massacre him."

I lean away from him as he chortles. Suddenly, he switches directions and hauls me between two of the tents. With his staggering, I didn't think he had much strength left, but the resistance I give might as well be nonexistent.

"What are you doing? This isn't the way." I tug harder, but he clutches me to him.

He moves closer, encircling me with the stench of alcohol and body odor. I want to scour everywhere he touches and breathes. With all the strength I can manage, I shove him. He falters back, taking me with him. For a moment we totter toward the ground, but I lean backward saving us from falling. He snarls.

"None of that, wench. My possessions don't get away from me. Besides, we'll be married soon enough, I just want a little taste."

My pulse quickens. "No."

The leer morphs into a snarl. "Don't you dare tell me no."

Grabbing a fistful of hair, he yanks my head back. I scream. His hand clamps down on my mouth. Panic bubbles in me. I fight it and let anger boil from deep within. I didn't mean to steady him, as well. If only he would get his hands off me.

Punishments have never included such close contact. Tears build in my eyes. I can't let him compromise me. Even if I have to break other laws to do it. I just want him off. I get ready to knee him in the one place I know will weaken his hold. The one place a woman is never to harm.

A hand grabs my shoulder. I'm caught. Will they tarnish me if I didn't commit the offense? Time slows. A fist swings toward me. Before I can pull back, it slams into Thomas's face. He flies backward into the tent wall. It sags against his weight until he crumples to the ground.

I stare down at him. What just happened? Did someone accidentally hit Thomas instead of me? I look at the hand that steadies me, and move my gaze up. He's taller than any man I've ever met. About a foot taller than me. An Envadi.

"Why're you standing around?" He spits and kicks Thomas in the stomach.

I blink. He meant to hit Thomas? And kick him? What did Thomas do to him to cause such anger? If he's willing to do that to another warlock, what are the Envadi willing to do to me? I grasp my trembling hands together. Going to the tent should be my goal, but I can't move. Thomas is still motionless on the ground.

"He'll live. Get a move on."

He shifts far enough to the side that I can skirt past him. If he wants to keep his anger directed at Thomas, I won't stop him. My feet can finally move. I need no more encouragement. Not looking at Thomas again, I dart past and break into a run. The large tents give way to orange tents my height. My breaths are short, painful gasps.

More people mill about, mostly women, but a few warlocks stand guard around the edges of the tents. While steadying my breathing, I slow to a fast walk until I'm safely inside my tent. A slew of women look up as I stumble in. The cots fill the tent barely leaving room to walk.

As soon as she spies me, Cynthia weaves her way to me. "What happened?"

"I—I..."

"You're shaking. Follow me." She guides me to my cot and helps me sit. The tent is almost full. Most of the women must be in already. And they're all watching me.

I give a shy smile and say loudly, "Too much partying for me, I think."

The women return to their own business, a low hum of words. A few snippets of Thomas's name. My hands shake.

Cynthia settles next to me and leans closer. "What really happened"

I pick a twig off my dress. "Thomas insisted on walking me."

When I stay silent Cynthia says, "Did something happen with him?"

A cold wave washes over me. I rub my arms. "Almost. It almost did." My voice catches. "But Cynthia, someone came." The women around us are still paying us no mind. Just to be safe, I lower my voice further. "Before he could do anything, Thomas was knocked out by an Envadi."

She gasps. The women closest to us look at her. She gives a false laugh. "There were mimes? I shouldn't have come back early."

After the women turn away from us, I whisper, "What's a mime?"

She shrugs. "Don't know. I've been listening to the others. Did anyone else witness it?"

"No one. Only Thomas and he were there."

"Chancellor Thomas. You've got to remember that." She shakes her head. "Is he angry?"

"I don't know. He wasn't conscious when I left." I swallow

when I realize what that could mean for me when he wakes. "The Envadi said he'd be fine. Thomas had a lot to drink though."

She lifts her eyebrows at me. "And you left him?"

"I had to return before curfew. Besides, he was making me uncomfortable."

She bites her lower lip. "Turn around. I'll help you out of your dress."

I twist until my back faces her. As she unfastens my dress, I think of Thomas and the Envadi. Their barbaric ways are widely known. The one that attacked Thomas had continued to kick him after he was down and unconscious. Yet, I don't know what would have become of me if the Envadi had not come along. Which of the two is really worse? I can't decide, but my mind keeps remembering Thomas laying on the ground, the Envadi looming over him.

# CHAPTER 6

As Cynthia and I leave the tented area, Father strides toward us. I keep my expression serene despite the quivering inside me.

"Why weren't you here sooner? Chancellor Thomas's duel is about to start." He squeezes both our upper arms and directs us to the box. I hold back a wince at his grip. "He was furious he didn't see you this morning, Serena."

Fear pricks my heart. I took as long as I could getting ready, even applying extra face paint to delay this moment. We enter the box. "Did he say what he wanted?"

"What do you think he wanted?" Father lets go and I scurry to my chair.

To tarnish me for my crimes, for not letting him be my Master. For leaving him unattended while unconscious with an Envadi. My sins are many.

"You're his bride," Father says. "Everyone was asking after him this morning and he wanted you at his side. Once he came to himself that is. Woke in the Envadi section of camp not remembering how he got there. Drank a bit too much last night if you ask me. Took some extra spells to fix that."

I relax into my chair. He doesn't remember what happened.

Cynthia and I exchange a glance. The wrinkles in her forehead smooth.

Though I shouldn't speak, I can't help but try to take the conversation somewhere safer. "Is he the first duel of the day?"

"Yes. He's paired against that Envadi. Massive brute that. Must be what's gotten him this far. No other Envadi have made it to the last day. Should be easy enough for Chancellor Thomas to best him. With any luck, he'll take the day. Not that he needs the prize money now." Father chuckles. It stops when he looks at me. "Why am I wasting this talk on you halfwits?"

He storms out of the box. I don't watch to see if he's going to Thomas or somewhere else. What happens to Thomas gives me no concern. Win or lose, I'm still his. Unless he does remember something from last night that he didn't want to discuss with Father, only me. I shift in my chair. Even if he does want to talk to me about it, I'm going home tomorrow. I won't have to use this facade much longer. By the time we are living under the same roof, as a Chancellor he should have other things to occupy him. Still, I'll have to come back and return to masking my feelings toward him.

Except he could require me to stay. The contract is sealed. As his possession, he could force me if he so wished. I rub my forehead. No sense worrying about that. No one has required that of their possession before they've become wed.

"You look ill." Cynthia moves closer to me. "It appears you have nothing to worry about. Chancellor Thomas is going to duel and win from the sound of things. He'll be in a good mood then."

"I suppose."

"He will." She relaxes in her chair. "Do you want any breakfast?"

"No. But get yourself something."

"It's probably not a good idea. There's likely to be more deaths today. More of them happen today than any other day."

"You've been talking to the servants again?"

"A woman in our tent last night." She shrugs. "We likely won't have to witness most of it if we don't want, but there's still a chance. Would you like me to get you the soothing tea to ease your nerves?"

"No. Mother's not here and Father won't care if I'm myself while he's in the Grand Chancellor's box."

"Mother said I should take it today and get you to, as well." She pauses as if thinking to herself. "I think I'll abstain. I'm not curious what it's like."

"It's strange to feel calm about everything whether you wish to or not."

"I can imagine. You're always so weird after drinking it."

"Happy to hear it."

"I didn't mean anything by it." Cynthia jostles her necklaces between her fingers. "You just seem so different. I don't want to be anything other than myself."

"As you should." The brewed concoction makes me feel distant from myself and leaves me with a headache. Though usually when I take it, the headache is the least of my problems. I've gotten adept enough after hexes and beatings that mother rarely makes me take it anymore. The threat of more deaths must have Cynthia nervous, though she tries to cover it with chatter.

"Two Arllos and three Chryos made it to the finals. Can you believe it?"

"I don't really know. Is that unusual?"

"Apparently. And with the Envadi that Chancellor Thomas is up against, it's quite the foreign showing. Hope they don't beat us. It'd be rather embarrassing."

The duelers gather on the field, but I don't spy Thomas or the Envadi he's pitted against yet. Not that I'd recognize his face, but it would be easy to tell him apart by his size.

"Chancellor Thomas will be a fine match for you. I know it's hard now, but it'll get better," she continues. "Everyone likes him so much. He's definitely the favorite of the day."

"For some," I murmur.

The first duel is announced. Thomas struts onto the field waving and casting all sorts of colored spells that don't appear to be doing anything other than flashing about. Without knowing more it's hard to tell for sure.

He pivots in our direction. His hand reaches toward me as if he could touch me across the many yards between us. I tense as the memory of him pressed against me invades my thoughts. I don't want to think on it. But Father did say he was furious. What punishment does he have in store for me?

A burst of maroon, gold, black, and green fly from his hands and sail straight for me. I start, but the spell comes to a stop before hitting me. The crest that followed me around the first day forms. The crowd cheers. I let the tension ease from me.

Sometime during the display, the Envadi has made his way to the circle. Thomas resembles a gawky teen next to the stoic giant. The Envadi simply stands, wearing the black dueling outfit with a white band on his arm, doing nothing to give away his feelings. They're far enough away that details are difficult to pick out. If they were physically fighting, Thomas would never best him. But magic comes from blood, not size.

The judge motions for them to enter the circle and the audience grows quiet. They face each other, Thomas grinning and the Envadi expressionless. At least from what I can see from here. Why do men always wish to fight? At least here it's with each other instead of picking on us.

The judge signals for them to start. There's no slow building of spells. They both blast at the signal. Thomas's lights are bright and zinging. Sometimes sparkling or jumping to the air. The Envadi's are nothing like them. A few bright-colored spells fly from him, but mostly dark, serpentine ones. Those stay focused around his opponent's spells instead of darting about like Thomas's magic does.

I tilt forward. The crowd has never been so riveted by a duel and their interest pulls at me. For the first time, I want to know what those flashes of light and color are doing. A yellow one opens a gash in the Envadi's arm. He thrusts a charcoal light back. It bursts into a cloud of darkness around Thomas. During the distraction, the Envadi focuses a teal spell at the wound. It knits closed. The crowd boos. A moment later, Thomas flings a burst of white light in the sky, clearing the cloud cover.

Thomas throws his head back in a laugh. An amber spell shoots from him, hitting with a pop. The Envadi staggers. Before he rights himself, he casts his own spell. Unlike those before, it doesn't smash into Thomas's or explode. It surges straight for his adversary. The silvery light slams into Thomas's chest. His mirthful face freezes. The life drains from him. His expression crumples. A strange, croaking sound escapes his mouth. He collapses to the ground.

The crowd jumps to their feet with a gasp. I stare at Thomas's form, looking so much like it did last night. The judge races for his body. It only takes a moment to reach him. As he looks Thomas over, I come to my feet and move to the front wall of the box. I lean against it, my body swaying.

All is silent as another warlock rushes to the judge's aid. Together, they work on Thomas. Both cast numerous spells. But as far as I can tell, Thomas doesn't move. Not a flinch, not a sound. Their spells slow until they completely stop. The judge stands and looks, not at the Grand Chancellor like I'm expecting, but right at me. His eyes wide.

"Dead."

The masses let out a cry. Some fall to their seats. Dead? How can he be dead? He's supposed to lord over me, not die. Can I really be free of him? My chest lightens.

Someone tugs on my arm. Cynthia. She forces me to drink the brew I avoided earlier. Then another. With shaking hands, she drinks one herself and helps me to my chair. Everything goes abnormally silent. The soothing concoction already sweeping through me. I grow distant from myself. The scene before me further away than ever.

The Envadi bends to the ground, his fingers swirling in the dirt. His lips move with words, but they don't carry, even in the silence. Once they stop, he brushes the dirt off and stares straight at me. Even from my distant state, goosebumps raise on my arms.

"Citizens." The Grand Chancellor's voice draws my gaze. He stands, face void of expression. "We will all mourn the loss of Chancellor Thomas. He was a rising star, fated to leave his potential unfulfilled." He pauses. "As our tournament rules dictate, Envadi Zade now becomes Master of all Chancellor Thomas had." He holds his hand out to the Envadi. "Chancellor Zade."

The Envadi's eyes are still watching me. He nods his head.

Suddenly, Father is yelling from the Grand Chancellor's box. "You will not have her!"

The words take a moment to find me through the muffle my world has become. As the significance of his words take hold, the field becomes splotched with black. I blink a few times. The whole world darkens.

# CHAPTER 7

"SHE'S COMING AROUND." Cynthia's voice floats somewhere above, but close. My tongue is thick and heavy and tastes coppery. Something wet brushes my forehead.

"Good. I want her presentable," Father says. "Make sure to fix her face paint. Give her something nicer to wear. Maybe I can still convince them she shouldn't be given away."

The sound of footsteps crunching through dirt is followed by silence. The cool cloth dampens my forehead again. It leaves. I open my eyes and blink against the light. Canvas hangs above me. I don't remember being in a tent. Last I remember, Father was yelling and—Oh!

"Hush, now," Cynthia says. "I'm here."

She holds a cup to my lips. "Come on, drink up." I shake my head. "Don't worry it's just water."

I gulp the cool liquid. After finishing, I lay back. "What happened?"

"What do you remember?"

Squeezing my eyes shut, I say, "Father yelling that the Envadi can't have me."

I look at her. She nods and sets the glass and cloth on the

nightstand. "That went on for a while, until they realized you'd fainted. Father's request was denied and you were brought here."

"How long has it been?"

"Longer than I thought you'd be out. After about five minutes you seemed to be coming around. Father got to you though and I believe he spelled you to stay unconscious. It's been seven hours."

"Seven hours?" I clutch tighter to the blanket on me. "The tournament?"

"Over. The Grand Chancellor's son, Nathaniel won."

"What about..."

She looks at the tent entrance. "The Envadi has been waiting outside this whole time, even forfeiting his place in the tournament. I think Father finally realized waiting longer wouldn't do any good."

A chill sweeps across me. I pull the blanket higher. "I'm his then?"

Cynthia places a hand on my arm. The touch is foreign, but soothing. "It appears that since your marriage contract was signed and sealed by both Father and Chancellor Thomas, that yes, you are the Envadi's." She pulls her hand away and clears her throat. "How are you feeling? Are you ready to sit so I can fix your face paint?"

"I'd rather stay here."

"I know."

I groan. After putting it off another moment, I roll onto my side and sit up. My body is loose and limber. After everything that's happened it should feel worse. "I feel better than I have for a while. Aside from being engaged to an Envadi."

"Father must have healed you as he woke you."

I put my hand to my leg. It's not tender anymore from my punishment earlier in the week. Why would he choose to do that now? Cynthia hands me a mirror and starts applying the paint. My skin is perfectly smooth and clear, not even a blemish. I haven't been free of those since I was twelve. I didn't know magic could get rid of them.

"Is he angry?"

She applies pink powder to my cheeks. "Not at anything we can change."

"It's going to be difficult when we get home."

"Unless something perks him up soon. Stop talking so I can paint your lips." When I close my mouth, she smoothes the cold cream across them. After she's finished, she points to a gown on the foot of my cot. "Father wants you to wear this. Let me help you with it."

My dark emerald one is wrinkled, but still presentable. "What's wrong with the one I'm wearing?"

She shrugs. "I think he's hoping to remind everyone what a good catch you are. Maybe then they won't be so willing to give you to the Envadi."

That explains the healing then. Will it work? I stand and face away from her. While she loosens the laces, I contemplate my fate. I didn't think it could get worse than marriage to Thomas, but clearly I was mistaken. The dress slips from my shoulders and I step into the mud colored one. It's not my favorite, but it matches my eyes. Cynthia tightens the laces. I hold a breath in so I'll have more space when she's finished.

An Envadi. How could this happen? The memory of the one helping me after the feast comes to mind. He did come when I needed aid. I don't know any warlock that would assist a girl in such a state. It's more likely that he was looking for someone to thrash rather than aiding me. He was rather rough with Thomas.

"Are you finished?" I ask.

After a final tug around the neck of my dress, she says, "Done. Do you want me to come with you?"

Yes. "No. I'll manage." While pulling my gloves on, I face her. "I'll be back soon."

She sniffs and nods. "He's giant. Don't let it scare you."

"I won't." I flee the tent before I tear up.

Outside Father waits, fat lips crinkled into a scowl. Next to him is a law officer, thin with a bushy mustache, tapping his foot. Behind them people are gathered, watching the scene. The majority are warlocks wearing Chardonian orange band on their arms. A few others with purple and green bands, along with a few women are here as well. None wear the white Envadi band. I scan them until someone rises from sitting on the ground. The Envadi. A different one from last night, but he still looms above everyone else. I don't know how I missed him, even on the ground.

He's tall. A couple feet taller than me. Perhaps not that much, but I could walk under his arm if he were to stretch it out and I'm taller than most Chardonian women. On the field he looked big, but standing next to me he's sky breaking.

I gawk at him. He might crush me if I look away. His green eyes, pupils rimmed with gold, stare back at me. He's young, but strong. What if one murder wasn't enough for today?

Father snatches me to his side and scolds me under his breath, but I still can't take my eyes from the giant. If he really is my new owner, I have more to fear of him than Father. An Envadi, my owner, I clutch my stomach.

"Are you ready to get this over with?" The Envadi's voice is deep. Deep enough to send quivers through me. Or maybe I'm just scared.

"Of course I am, that's why I'm standing here," Father says.

The Envadi's piercing gaze moves toward Father. I'm grateful it's not directed at me, I'm still shaking even without it. "I asked your daughter. She's my property now. Not yours."

Father's hands clench. His arm lifts in what I know is the start of a spell.

"I am," I say to distract him.

Father falters and the spell never happens, but he stays in a defensive posture.

The Envadi nods. He swishes his hand in a circle. A salmon-colored spell flies around us and forms a dome separating the four of us from the crowd and the tent. It's quiet. The only sound is breathing and the rustle of my dress as I shift positions.

"Now we can't be overheard," he says. "Since I am to inherit immediately, I insist Serena move into one of my properties today."

My legs weaken. There's nothing for me to hold onto. I will them to stay strong.

"That's absurd," Father says. "The engagement ceremony has yet to take place, let alone the wedding. You can't take her from me."

The law officer coughs. "Excuse me Councilman Stephen, but I'm afraid he can. The law states that once the contract has been signed, the woman is his property and he can do with her as he pleases as long as she remains chaste before the marriage."

Father's eyes widen. "But no one takes a bride before the wedding."

"I do." The Envadi sounds relaxed, but his body is taut. Why does he want to take me with him? Is he going to take my virtue and purposely get me tarnished? The world tilts around me. A foul taste invades my mouth. I'm going to be sick.

The law officer addresses the Envadi. "You do understand, Chancellor Zade, that if you dishonor her, she will no longer be yours, but will be tarnished and you will forfeit all claims."

The Envadi's jaw flexes several times before he says, "I'm aware."

"Then what purpose does it serve?" Father says.

"It seems you keep forgetting she's my property, which means it's my concern. However, I know the importance of family. Any family is welcome to stay for a visit."

"That's the only claim you'll give me over her? A visit?" Father says.

The Envadi folds his arms. "You heard me."

"You can't do that." Father shakes with fury.

I cringe away from him.

"Technically he can," the officer says. "You know he has full rights to your daughter now."

"Is there any way to get out of it?" Father asks.

"There are two ways for the betrothal contract to be broken. A man can simply withdraw, but in such case the woman is automatically assumed unfit and will become tarnished. Or a woman found to no longer be chaste. In which case she will also become a tarnished. If it's before transfer of ownership, a sum is paid by the girl's Father for a false claim. If it's after transfer of ownership, she'll be tarnished with no recompense."

"I already know that, fool. I meant is there anything else."

"There isn't."

"Look at her. Just look at her. She can't go to him. Do you know how much magic is in her blood?" Father splutters, his face growing redder by the moment.

I inch farther away from him. I'm getting the chance to leave him before my marriage. As he starts yelling curses, I realize I don't have to return to his house. I can't believe it. I can't.

The Envadi strides over to me. If killing Thomas is any indication, he's a powerful warlock. The lightness within me sinks into a massive horde of fear, heavy and repressive. This stranger is going to be worse than Father. More powerful and bigger. He'll be able to inflict even more damage. Trying to hold back a whimper, I bite the inside of my cheek.

Father spots the Envadi next to me and howls. With a flick of his wrist, he emits a scarlet spell. The light flies toward the Envadi. Before it can reach him, the Envadi casts his own spell of silver in front of him. The scarlet smashes into the silver, both dissolving on impact.

The Envadi says, "Please remove this dangerous, unstable man."

"Sorry about that, Chancellor. Didn't expect it out of our good Councilman." The law officer bends to whisper in Father's ear. As he listens, his eyes tighten into narrow slits. The officer pulls back.

"Forgive my violence," Father says. "It wasn't intended for you. Today has been a shock."

"Indeed." The Envadi's mouth is a tight line.

Without another word, Father and the law officer depart, the salmon dome closing after them. The spectators' lips move, directed at Father. He looks back at me, an expression on his face I don't recognize. Longing? Regret? But it can't be either of those. After it morphs to a scowl, he and the law officer stride off.

The Envadi's focus is fully on me. I grip my hands together and demand my gaze reach up to meet his no matter that my body doesn't want to cooperate. Now that I'm getting used to his height and seeing more of him, I realize he's younger than I previously thought. Perhaps three or four years older than me. Young and strong.

"Would you prefer to stay at Thomas's home or Chancellor Jacob's manor?"

My gaze wavers. The question wasn't what I expected. I expected to be taken, well, I don't know where, but wherever the Envadi wanted. The strain of the day must have addled him. I won't be the one to remind him it's not my choice. If I never have to be in Thomas's house again, I'll be happier. "The manor."

"Very well. Your things will be sent after you."

He waves his hand and the salmon light pops into nothing. Even without the spell, it's oddly silent as the crowd watches us. Without another word, he strides through the cluster of people.

# CHAPTER 8

"I'm glad Father let you come," I say to Cynthia. My carriage sickness abounds, but I do my best to ignore it. She's overly pale and in need of more comfort than me. "Nothing will happen to you, I'm sure of it. You're still Father's property, that will mean something. He wouldn't have sent you if it didn't. The Envadi won't hurt you."

In the faint light coming through the cracks of the carriage door, Cynthia shakes her head. "I doubt it."

She's probably right, though I don't dare correct her. "I'll keep you safe."

"You can't protect me like you did at home."

What can I say to that? There's no reason to think it'll be the same and every reason to think it'll be much worse. I won't be able to protect her or me. "I'll keep you hidden in my closet. He won't find you there."

She gives a mirthless laugh before sobering. "You might as well know I've been sent to spy on you and the Envadi."

"Oh." It makes sense why Father would send her, though why the Envadi offered in the first place is unfathomable. "Did Father spell you?"

"Not that I know of. He sent a note with the directions I was to come and report everything to him with letters, so I think it unlikely."

"Well then, you're free to tell him whatever you like. I have nothing more to hide than I did for seventeen years, and I could care less what you tell him about the Envadi."

She snorts.

Attempting to keep myself from being sick, I breathe evenly. "If mother heard that you would be given a Woman's Canon lecture."

"And you're not going to take her place?"

"Only if you don't."

"Splendid." The carriage dips and bounces back up. "Rough road. How are you faring?"

My stomach churns. I'm hot and sweaty and uncomfortable. "Rather well, considering. Would you keep talking though?"

"Of course."

Cynthia talks and talks of all sorts of things. Stories from when were children. Of the sisters we left behind. Of mother and the unborn babe. She stops only to help when the ride makes me ill. If she had accompanied me on more trips, I wouldn't have despised the carriage quite as much.

The journey is long. Longer than it takes to get to Thomas's from Father's house. Part way through I realize I have no idea what to expect. We could be headed toward a run down cottage. Though since Father and Thomas seemed pleased with the new property, it can't be too awful. But something about it has me nervous.

As time passes, Cynthia's chatter becomes more stilted, and my retching into a pot more frequent. From the aching tiredness of my body, I can only assume night deepens. I'm beginning to think I've made a mistake in choosing Chancellor Jacob's house. No wonder the Envadi let me choose, he wanted to see what type of torture I prefer. Chancellor Jacob must have stayed in the tents instead of traveling everyday like Thomas. Father often stays overnight when there is to be a council meeting and Chancellor Jacob must have done the same. I can't imagine doing this route regularly.

When the carriage finally stops, I've long since lost any sense of dignity. I groan. I can't help it. Cynthia reaches over and squeezes my hand. The stench from my troubles is so foul, I want to rush from the carriage. Of course I haven't the energy for it nor am I so reckless as to open the door on my own. That rule was hexed into me long ago.

I haul myself into a sitting position and try to reacquaint myself with the stillness of the world. Cynthia moves, but I can't tell what she's doing. Probably trying to clean. When the footman finally opens the door, I'm a bit less peaked, though more than ready to be done with the carriage for a lifetime.

The light of dawn pours in. Not how I wanted to greet morning. Cynthia waits for me to exit the carriage, though I imagine she's almost as eager as I am to leave it. Maybe even more so. The crisp air hits me as I step onto the cobblestone, rushing life back in me. I take several deep breaths of earthy fragrance. Beside me, Cynthia gasps.

"What?" I look at her then at where she's staring.

I gasp as well.

It can't be the proper place. We must have made a wrong turn. But the footman is speaking to a servant at the base of the mansion. The servant nods to whatever he's saying and faces us. Still, once I catch my breath I call out, "Is this Chancellor Jacob's?"

"It is," the servant replies. More servants, both tarnished and lower class, make their way outside. More than I've seen gathered in one place before. Are they all for this place?

I look back at the manor. They must be. If there were any fewer, cleaning would never be done. Four stories of stone stacked upon one another and more windows than I could ever hope for. There's a turret at each corner of the manor, rising two stories above the rest of the house. I count the stories again. At least four.

I've never been above the first floor of Father's house. Is it safe? Council meetings were always held on the second floor, so it must be. Yet I can't imagine how a person doesn't fall through. How are the upper floors able to stay up and not come crashing down?

"How much of this land do you think belongs with the manor?" Cynthia asks.

For the first time I glance around. Lush grass all around and a forest off in the distance. To one side of the house there looks to be the edge of a lake, though I'd have to circle around the house to know for sure. In front of the manor are hedges and flowers. Blues, purples, pinks, yellows, oranges.

"I've never imagined anything so grand," I say.

The Envadi dismounts, looming over us. I didn't realize he rode here as well. My astonishment at the house dampens. I thought he decided to stay, well, wherever it was he was staying, but clearly he didn't. At least with a house this vast, I'll be able to secret myself within, even if I'm restricted to the first floor.

"Your things from Thomas's will be by sometime later this morning," he says. "The rest of your things will be gathered from your house and sent over. You both can have whatever room you like."

I can do nothing but stare at him as he heads to the servants. Several listen to him. A tarnished, with a chiseled face, replies. One of the other servants, a lower class girl only a few years older than me, steps out of line and comes to us.

"When you're ready, I'll give you a tour and you can pick out lodgings most to your liking."

Cynthia's eyes are as wide and confused as mine feel. Once I'm finally able to speak, I say, "Are you sure we're to choose our own rooms?"

"Yes, if you wish." She studies us for a moment. "I can pick instead, if you like."

Cynthia and I exchange a look. She's smiling. I've never before seen such a smile from her. All remaining tiredness and sickness flee.

"The tour would be perfect."

"Very well. If you'll come with me please."

As we follow her into the house, we pass the Envadi. I clench my shaking hands and risk a peek back. His gaze meets mine, though he's still speaking to a servant. I trip and hurry to right myself, this time sure to watch where I'm going. Though I don't look again, I feel his gaze still on me. What is he planning to do to me?

* * *

BY THE TIME I plop down on the window bench in the turret, I don't think I will ever stand, and certainly never walk, again. It's the last room of the tour. We haven't seen the grounds yet, but I could not care less. Cynthia slumps beside me.

"I didn't think this day could get any more exhausting," she says. "Two days now, I guess."

"Can I do anything to help?" the servant asks.

I look around the room for the first time. The walls are curved all around as they were in the other turrets, except for a little flat portion hiding a water closet. Next to which is a privacy screen and I assume there is a bathing basin behind it like others we've seen. This room is a full circle, the only access is a door at the top of stairs, leading back where we came from. I can't possibly climb them right now. It's a wonder I even made it up here. Though the floors seem to be holding our weight just fine, which eases some of my worries.

There's plenty more furniture than I need, chairs and sofas and tables, but I only have eyes for the bed. Not as massive as the one at Thomas's, but big enough for me. My choice is the only choice

I'm really allowed given my current state. Did the Envadi plan it this way?

"I think this will be my room. If it's acceptable."

She nods. "I'll let you know if there's a problem."

"Perhaps I'll take the one at the bottom of the stairs," Cynthia says. "That way we'll be close."

"Would you rather have this room? You can if you would like."

"Oh, no. If it wasn't for you we wouldn't be here anyway. Besides, you'll enjoy all these windows more than I will."

Things like this remind me how wonderful she can be. "That's true."

"Can I bring some breakfast?" the servant asks. "Or would you prefer I draw a bath?"

I'm sticky from traveling, but also have an empty stomach. I don't remember the last time I ate. "Breakfast, I think."

"Yes, food would be most welcome," Cynthia says.

The servant nods. "I'll get two trays and your things sent up." She leaves.

I try to pay more attention to my new room. My very own. Not just for a week, but for good. Or at least until I marry. I don't suppose he'll let me stay here. Mother's room was always close to Father's. I shiver and chase the thought away, replacing it with ones of furniture.

The bed has its headboard curving along the wall. Night tables on each side are also curving. By the window where we're seated are a small table and three chairs. There's also a vanity curving like the others. A small mirror rests on it. More like the one at home than at Thomas's, but easy to see into. Above it is another window. A third window lies between the stairs and the bed.

"It's rather large," I say. "Less cramped than our house full of girls."

"Yes," Cynthia replies, but with a wistful note. "Certainly quieter."

She always did spend more time with our sisters than I did. I suppose I spent too much time trying to hide from Father or taking their places for punishments. I still miss them. Perhaps not the same way that brings longing to Cynthia's eyes.

A short while later the servant returns with two trays. She stands off to the side as we settle at the table. Biscuits and chocolate. I devour them, not even taking the time to dunk the thin, sweet wafer in my thick drink. Once my appetite settles, I slow and eat some fruit as well.

I peek at the servant often throughout the meal. As it comes to a close, I work up enough courage to ask, "Do you know in what room Chancellor Zade is staying?"

"I believe he's chosen the back turret on the west side of the house."

Can I really be that fortunate? All the way on the other side of the house?

"You should easily be able to hide from him if that's the case," Cynthia whispers.

The servant's face remains impassive.

I respond, "At least until the wedding."

# CHAPTER 9

THE FREEDOM I gain from being in a new house is odd. All chores are done by the servants. No sisters to keep an eye on and shield from Father. Only Cynthia, but even my relationship with her is changing. There's no need for me to cover for her. It's brought such a relief, more than I thought would happen.

We spend several days staying mostly in one of our rooms. Because of it, I find it easier and easier to wear less face paint, something I've always wanted. Though I do put on a bit more when we attend dinner with the Envadi. Those affairs are more quiet than at home. The Envadi never speaks as Father would. Not to yell or punish, yet no babbling on about other warlocks either.

But this morning, something changed. When a servant was clearing my room, which is strange enough to get used to, she said we didn't have to stay here all the time. We're free to explore the house and the grounds at will.

I don't know if she has the authority to give permission, but I can't help but want it to be true. The rooms, despite their size, have grown confining in the last few days. Cynthia doesn't seem to mind the confinement and chooses to stay in her room, but I'm not wasting an opportunity to get out.

"Are you sure you won't join me?"

She doesn't look up from her embroidery. "I can't believe you're going. The Envadi is probably setting some sort of trap."

"I'm tired of these rooms. We didn't have a lot of space at Father's, but at least we could go outside and to class. Never thought I would miss class." I shake my head. I don't really miss learning how I'm never going to be up to the standards a woman should, but this monotony is overbearing. "If something bad happens, it won't be any different than before."

"Before you avoided trouble instead of racing headlong into it."

Except for the times I said too much or took on my sisters punishments, which was all the time. "I'll be cautious."

"I'll be here when you need a shoulder to cry on."

"I don't cry."

"Just the same, I'll be here."

I pick at my gloves hoping she's wrong and exit the room. The house is lovely. Lovelier than I remember, though I suppose being well rested, fed, and not having the shock of my intended being killed and replaced by a barbarian before looking it over, helps.

Rugs cover the length of the halls, cushioning my steps. Pictures, mostly nature scenes, cover the walls. A few women with their large, rounded bellies, and several with warlocks are scattered among them. Tables sit every few feet with vases of fresh flowers, filling the air with their subtle and sweet fragrance. Though I enjoy their scent, keeping so many fresh flowers with a house of only three occupants and their servants is a lot of extra work.

I randomly pick doors to open and peek in, though I avoid the area by the Envadi's turret. There are so many rooms, all with such varying styles and colors. Nothing sticks out. I wander through halls and stairways until I open a door to reveal something different.

This one is as big as one floor of Father's house, smelling of old paper. Shelves cover the walls, floor to ceiling, books filling them. I never knew so many books existed. Father has some, but those wouldn't fill one bookshelf here. What other words could they contain? If they're all like the Woman's Canon, I've no use for them. Still, the idea they might have more tugs at me until it pulls me further into the room. I'm not supposed to touch them. What if someone caught me just being in here with them? I focus on other things, while the books linger in my mind.

Curtains hang from the ceiling to the floor in several places. When I pull one open, there's a window taller than me looking over the front of the manor. The others open to reveal more of the front and lake side of the manor. The lake is bigger than I thought it would be, swelling across the land. On the side closest to the manor is a little dock with a boat bobbing beside it.

After letting the curtain fall back into place, I try to continue ignoring the call of the surrounding books. I focus on all the chairs, sofas, and tables. The council meeting was off limits, but I imagine something like this would suit their needs. Lots of places for warlocks to sit and do whatever it is they do. Memories of being confined to my room on those days are hot, sticky, and unpleasant. I push them away.

Several minutes pass and nobody has wandered in. The books are still calling. What if they aren't all like the Woman's Canon? They can't all be, can they? I move closer to them. Most are thinner than the only book I'm allowed, a few are fatter.

No one is around, what harm could it do to look?

I peruse the bookshelves, searching for something worth the risk. Something that will show a world outside the Woman's Canon. My search stops on one titled *The Light of Day*. I rest my hand upon it. Supple and bumpy. Still, no one comes.

With a tug, I remove it from the shelf. It's tiny in my hands compared to what I'm used to. Easier to hide. I run a finger on the edge of its spine. It's softer than the Woman's Canon.

With a silent hope I'm not bringing trouble on myself, I open it. The smell of old paper grows stronger. I flip a few pages, then hear footsteps thumping down the hall. Hugging the book to me, I lunge to a nearby couch and hunker behind it.

The hinges of the door squeak as it opens. A slight pause, then the footsteps enter the room. I quiet my breathing. Oh, how Cynthia was right! I'll be punished for this. The extra space the house provides can't hide me if another comes in the same room as me. I shouldn't have given in to my desires on the word of a servant. Warlocks have the final say, always.

My legs burn from keeping huddled. It's been too long since I've used my muscles for such a purpose. It's silent for several minutes. The pang in my legs increases to a stab. If I continue like this, I'll give myself away. I peek my head up. The Envadi!

I duck my head down and hold my breath. He's staring at a nearby bookshelf. Just staring. My lungs start to burn from lack of oxygen. I resume breathing, but it's too loud. I hold it again.

My muscles throb. Gradually, I lower myself to the ground. My dress rustles. I bite my lower lip. The footsteps move closer. He's at the bookshelf just a few steps from me. Of all the shelves in this room, why did he have to pick that one? If he turns his head he'll see me. I close my eyes.

My hands tighten around the book. The book. I shouldn't even have this. How much worse will my punishment be if I'm caught with it? Can I shove it under the couch? Maybe, but it might make noise and catch his attention. Blast.

After a few moments, the footsteps return, but this time leading away from me. I let out a breath as quietly as I can. The door squeaks open and closes. Did he leave?

I wait another few moments in silence. I hear nothing. Did he really leave then? I peek around the room again. Empty. I sigh and rub my sore legs with my free hand. Once they feel a bit better, I grab the back of the couch and hoist myself up. My hands are shaking.

Wasting no time, I head for the door until I realize the book is in my grasp. Do I take it with or put it away? It almost got me caught. Almost brought punishment. But it didn't and I want to know what it says. The brief glimpse I got seemed different than the Woman's Canon. More than ever, I want something new. Can I compound the rule I've already broken by taking it with me?

Cynthia says I'm reckless. Reckless I'll be. Book in hand, I move to the door. I twist the handle and ease it open a crack. No one appears to be in the hall. I ease it open further and stick my head out so I can see deeper into the passage. Still no one.

I slip from the room and close the door until the latch gives a faint click. I head for my own room. In my panic, it takes me a moment to orient myself as to where I am and where I need to go. Remembering the lay of the land outside the book room window, I head toward the direction my room should lie in. Things soon look familiar.

I finish climbing to my room. Once there, I do another thing I have never before attempted. I lock my door. Just to be safe, I curl up in my bed so I can hide the book under my pillow if need be and claim I was resting.

I open the book again and let its scent fill me. The words quickly consume me. It's nothing like the Woman's Canon. Almost being caught was worth it. As long as it doesn't bring trouble and punishments my way, I think I'm going to like it.

# CHAPTER 10

BESIDES THE TERRIFYING BOOK INCIDENT, the only time I've seen the Envadi is at dinner. I've never tried to contact him in any way, nor has he tried to contact me. Until now.

I stare at the note he sent, not sure if the contact brings good or bad news. Mother's coming to dinner. Tonight.

The servant girl finishes tugging my hair into a knot and reaches for a paint pot.

I steel my resolve. "Not tonight. That will be all."

"But you have to," Cynthia says from the window seat.

"Not tonight." I turn to the servant. "You're dismissed."

"Thank you." The servant departs.

"I'll never get used to having someone else do so much for me," I say.

"Oh good." Cynthia walks over to me. "When you said that, I thought you meant you were going to dinner without your face paint. It's odd having them do everything all the time."

"It is odd, but I didn't mean that I intend to do my own face paint. I'll go to dinner without."

Her eyes widen. "You mustn't. The Woman's Canon—"

"It doesn't demand that we wear face paint, only that we look our best." Besides, the book I stole has a girl in it that only mentions face paint once and how she never wears it. If I had known it was a choice sooner, I would have done the same.

"Mother always said we must wear face paint when we turned twelve."

I give her my full attention. "You said you weren't going to take mother's place."

"I'm just worried for you."

I stand and hand her the note. "Don't worry. Mother will be here to scold me herself."

"She's coming? Then you really must put some on."

Purposely ignoring her, I stride to the door. "I believe it's time to go. Mother will be here soon, if she isn't already."

As we walk to the dining room, my face feels naked. I never realized how much I draw on the face paint to mask feelings. I fight to keep my nerves from showing and quicken my pace. I've been away from mother almost two weeks, I'm not sure if I'm excited to see her, or dreading it.

"Mother isn't going to like this," Cynthia says, a step behind me.

"I'm not residing with her anymore."

"What if Chancellor Zade doesn't like it either?"

I shrug and try to put the thought from my mind.

"You really should put it on. Think of what he could do. Has it really been so long that you've forgotten all of Father's punishments?"

My steps falter for a moment before I continue. "I've been punished enough times, I don't think one more will make a difference."

Cynthia grabs my arm pulling me to a stop. "But he's much bigger than Father and more powerful. What if you're seriously injured? I know you don't want to think of it, but he could do worse things. Don't you remember the incident with Thomas?"

Gently, I push her hand from me though her words strike unease. "Don't fret so much."

She bites her lip. "Are you sure?"

"Of course I am. Now we must hurry or we'll be late, which is worse than absent face paint."

Keeping the fear away is a struggle as Cynthia's words haunt me. I doubt myself. Why did I feel this was necessary? Trying to be like a girl from something I shouldn't be reading anyway. What possessed me to think it was a good idea? I don't want this marriage, but the alternative makes me ill. Soon enough, we are in the sitting room right outside the dining hall. The forest green sofas and chairs are empty.

"Perhaps I should..."

"Should what?" The Envadi's voice comes from behind me.

I can't imagine how someone so huge gets around without being seen or heard. He must use magic. Following a moment's hesitation, I turn my bare face directly to him. Cynthia moves closer to me. The Envadi says nothing, merely raises an eyebrow.

No immediate punishment. The tightening in my chest loosens. "I should check if my mother has arrived."

"Indeed I have." Mother enters from the same door the Envadi used, her burgundy dress tight against the swell of her belly.

The Envadi says, "Should we go in to dinner?"

We watch, waiting for him to take the lead. He catches my eye a moment, then goes to the door and opens it. "After you."

We stare at him another moment. Mother takes a tentative step. Before she gets any farther, she looks at me for the first time and gasps.

"What is it?" the Envadi asks. "Have you fallen ill?"

Mother stares at me another second with wide eyes. They narrow and I ready myself for a lecture. "I felt faint for a moment. I'm well now."

"Are you certain? You can rest a minute."

"No need to fuss, I'm well."

"Let's see what cook has made then. I'm sure we're in for another treat."

Mother scowls at me and pads into the dining room. Cynthia and I follow. The walls, tables, and chairs are all made from a dark wood. Though the table is long enough to sit twenty, there are only four places set.

Cynthia and I stand by our customary chairs. Mother stands behind a chair across from us. As the Envadi does every meal, instead of taking his seat as he ought, he motions for the servants to help us all sit at the same time. It takes mother a moment to follow suit, but once she's settled we fall into our silent meal.

When the dessert course is set before us, an assortment of fruit and vanilla cream, I go straight for the strawberries. Before I can take a bite, the Envadi breaks the silence.

"Fruit from the garden. Apparently the main gardener owed Chancellor Jacob's family some money and they settled by using his magic talent on the grounds. They say he has a knack for getting things to ripen whenever he desires. These peaches are tasty." The barbarian wishes to discuss fruit? With us women? He turns to mother and says, "Don't you think so, Agatha?"

Mother drops her fork. "Why, yes."

"Which is your favorite?"

Tentatively, she says, "The peaches. As you said, they are good."

He nods. "And you Cynthia, which one would be your favorite?"

"The peaches, Chancellor."

He takes another bite while we stare at him through lowered lashes. "What do you think, Serena?"

I hate peaches, but I'm not supposed to contradict him. With Father I always knew where my boundaries were. Now, I'm not so sure. Time to find out. "I like the strawberries best."

Mother and Cynthia gape at me. The Envadi smiles. "A dissenter? Granted, the strawberries are good, but not as good as the peaches. They've ripened to perfection."

"Then you must eat mine. I can't abide them." After taking my cup off its saucer, I place the strawberries on the plate. I pick up the dessert dish and set it next to him. Let him punish me, then I'll know what to expect.

Mother's face is drawn in horror, but the Envadi laughs. "And I won't let good peaches go to waste, but there are apples, too."

"I'm finished with everything there."

"I'll make sure nothing is wasted then." He scoops the remaining fruit onto his plate.

I'm not going to be punished? Why? Not that I wanted it, I only wanted to know what it took to get it and how bad it would be. I fork a strawberry while pondering it.

He takes several more bites. "Agatha, Councilman Stephen's note mentioned you were going to be returning later in the week to assist Serena in preparing for the engagement ceremony. What day, or days would you like to come? Is there anything you need that I can help with?"

Mother's gaze darts between me and the Envadi. Finally, she picks up her fork and responds. "Any day is fine. My schedule is clear."

"You're welcome on all of the days then. In fact, you can stay with us while you make your plans."

Mother stares at her plate. "I don't believe Councilman Stephen would care for me to be away from him that long."

In truth, I'm surprised he let her come without him, even with a male servant to chaperone. Though the Woman's Canon says a warlock always knows where his wife is and what she's doing. Perhaps he thought the servant was sufficient.

"Of course you must please your husband. I just don't want you worn out with the traveling."

The remainder of the meal is silent. Though not much of a meal. My strawberries have hardly any taste with such strange goings-on. Mother pushes food around her plate, but Cynthia and the Envadi finish their fruit. When he pushes his chair back and stands, we jump to our feet.

"Would you like to enjoy some time in the sitting room with us, Agatha?" He says it as if we do it every night, but we never have before.

"No, thank you. I believe I must be off."

"So soon?"

Mother nods.

"Then I'll let the girls see you out. Feel free to take my offer for dinner when you come again. A guest room can be readied easily enough if the Councilman allows."

I tense as the Envadi gives a nod and strides from the room. Mother moves to the door. When I don't immediately follow, she snaps. Cynthia and I hurry after her.

"Not you Cynthia. You can go to your room and do whatever it is you do in this big place while I'm at home slaving over twelve girls and preparing for another babe."

Cynthia opens her mouth to speak, but closes it again with the shake of her head. She scurries from the room. I make a note to be extra kind to her tomorrow and follow mother out into the hall. Our footsteps are quieted by a brown rug. Once we're no longer within hearing of the servants, she turns to me with a hiss.

"Where's your face paint?"

I swallow. "I was in a hurry, so I thought that—"

"You don't think. If Father knew..." She frowns and rubs her lower back before pulling a compact version of the Woman's Canon out of her pocket and turns right to the page she wants. "A woman must always look her best." She snaps the book closed. "You won't go without it again. Ever."

The command makes me grit my teeth. "Yes, mother."

She watches me closely and sighs. "Have you given any thought to the ceremony?"

More than I wish. "Some."

"Good. We don't have nearly as much to do as we will when it's time for the wedding. Mostly, we need a dress. I'll bring one with me when I come tomorrow and see if it fits."

"I'll be ready." Like I have a choice.

"See that you're wearing face paint when I arrive. I'd hate to see you punished for breaking the Woman's Canon this close to your wedding." She straightens. "I'll see myself out."

I watch as she waddles down the corridor, wondering what tomorrow will bring.

* * *

"Quit fidgeting," mother says around a mouth full of pins.

"Ouch!" A pin stings my leg.

"I told you. Now hold still so I can finish."

I try to hold still. Really, I do, but I can't help it. The dress is awful though I have yet to see how it looks on me.

Mother moves to my stomach and starts pinning the material. "We'll have to take it in, but I think it will work. I can't believe you're grown enough to wear it. Seems like only yesterday I was wearing it to my own engagement ceremony. Finished. What do you think?" Mother's face glows at me, but from her chair nearby, Cynthia is passive, save for a tightening around her mouth.

I turn toward the mirror, my painted face reflected back, trying to guard my reaction. It's more like a slip than a dress. Flimsy black material clings to me, held up only by two thin straps. Right now it reaches a touch below my knees, but mother has plans to hem it three inches.

I detest it. "This is what you wore?"

Mother nods. "I know it's different from our customary dress, but men like to show off their new things."

"I'm practically naked."

"Serena! Language." She puts the rest of her sewing kit away. "Your dress is acceptable for an engagement. Chancellor Zade informed me it didn't have to be as traditional. The gowns now days are not nearly as modest as this one. We can get one of those if you like."

They can be worse than this? "He said it didn't have to be as traditional?"

"Yes. I don't think he cares too much, and I thought you would prefer this, but obviously not. We can get something more showy. There's plenty of time to run to the closest town."

Cynthia meets my gaze in the mirror, slowly shaking her head like she knows what I'm thinking. I ignore it and grab the opportunity to wear something else.

"I'd like a gown that covers more."

"Really darling, this dress covers as much as you can for an engagement ceremony. Perhaps too much." She eyes the dress, then pulls the pins out. "We don't want you getting punished over this."

I hold my hand out. "No. I want something that doesn't leave me feeling like a red tarnished."

Cynthia gasps.

Mother's face whitens, her lips tighten. "We will see."

She turns to a nearby servant. "Please inform the Master that his bride is refusing my choice in engagement gown instead desiring for something that's highly unsuitable."

The servant nods and scurries from the room. Mother sits in the corner and picks up a blanket she's embroidering for the baby. Sky blue, of course. Cynthia's worried eyes watch me.

"What are you doing?" she whispers.

"Would you wear this in public?" My heart beats faster. She'll have to wear something like it when she gets engaged. I wonder how long it will take the servant to return a message. Or what if the Envadi returns with him to see what all the fuss is about. I hurry to my clothes. "Help me change into a real dress, Cynthia."

She sighs and stands to help. "We've always known the engagement ceremony attire is more revealing than generally permitted."

"And that makes this acceptable?" I motion to the garment

now laying on the floor. "I think not. I'm not keen on marrying anyway, I refuse to wear something I'm so uncomfortable in."

Cynthia picks up the discarded dress, throws it over a chair, and helps me into a forest green one.

"Too much freedom," mother says from across the room. "If your Father were here, he'd skip a beating and go straight to a hex. If that Envadi has half your Father's wits, he'll do the same."

I bite my lip as Cynthia finishes tying my dress. Mother's right, but I don't want her to be. Being here has made me too lax. Rarely seeing the Envadi and no negative consequences when I disagreed with his choice of fruit, made me unwary of how severe punishments can be. I wanted to know how far I could push him, but by barely crossing the line, not bounding over it. Is he coming to hex me now? Or will he wait until I've chosen the wrong gown and hex me then?

The servant enters the room. Mother puts down her work. "Well?"

Instead of addressing mother, the servant walks to me and hands me a pouch. "He said to tell you the carriage has been sent for. You can go to town and pick what you like. The money should be enough to cover what you need."

The bag is heavy. I can't move. I can't breathe.

"He did what?" Mother's eyes grow with disbelief.

"Sent for the carriage."

"He didn't want to do anything?"

"He did ask if she'll return in time for dinner."

Does this mean not only can I go to town, but I can skip another stiff dinner? "Inform him that I won't be back, but mother would be happy to attend."

"She's not going with you?" the servant asks.

"No. Cynthia, would you like to join me?"

Cynthia looks at mother. "I'd better not. Perhaps you shouldn't either. If you insist on going, at least take a chaperone."

That's right. I don't have a chaperone. The Chancellor didn't offer or provide one. What will happen if I go without?

"Don't you do this," mother warns. "He's laying a trap for you and you're falling right into it. He will beat and hex you before tarnishing you."

I ignore her.

"Enjoy your dinner, Cynthia."

"Serena, please don't," mother says.

Still pretending she's not speaking, I head out the door. For the first time in my life, I will do something wholly by myself.

# CHAPTER 11

THE SEAMSTRESS KEEPS STARING at the door after I enter. I glance at it. Nothing special there. The rest of the shop is customary. An area for chaperones, cushioned chairs, and tables laden with things to eat. To my right is a harder area for women to wait. Both are empty. Material and clothes are in the back.

The seamstress huffs, getting my attention. She's an angular woman with no engagement or wedding mark. Probably a lower class trying to help her family make ends meet until she can fulfill her purpose by marrying and producing babies. A warlock sits behind the counter next to her, reading a book. I can't tell if he's the owner of the shop, or just supervising. Either way, I wish he wasn't here.

"When's your Father coming?" the seamstress asks.

"It's just me." Her eyes grow over raised eyebrows. Using Father's example, I try to sound authoritative. "I need a dress for an engagement ceremony."

"Ahem. Yes." She looks at the door again then grabs a few sheets of loose paper. She thumbs through the pages a moment before stopping. "Here they are. Basic patterns we can alter to suit you. Your figure isn't perfect for an engagement dress, but not bad."

Cynthia wouldn't have gotten that criticism. "It's what I have."

She continues as if I didn't say anything. "We can come up with something suitable for your Father to approve when he has time."

I let the barb and the comment about Father go. What could I say anyway? I inch forward so I can see the pages she's referring to. Instantly I avert my eyes. Mother was serious when she said her dress was old fashioned and modest. These gowns make mother's choice positively chaste.

"I was thinking something a little well—well more."

The shopkeeper nods. "It's not what you're used to, but they're perfectly respectable for an engagement ceremony."

"I understand, but would still like something different for my own dress."

The shopkeeper's face tightens with a false smile. "Why don't you come back later with your Father and mother? They are so helpful."

I slap on an emotionless mask and take a breath. "My parents nor any other person will attend me. I want a dress that will cover me properly." The warlock finally looks at me, but I keep my focus on the seamstress. "And in a color too, I should think."

"Color?" she says. "Engagement dresses never have color. Black and black only. For humility, worthiness, and submission to your intended. Black gives in to all. A bride must do the same."

"Are you saying you won't make what I'm asking for?"

"Course I won't. Are you addled?"

"Excuse me, I find I won't be needing your services today." I leave as she continues to yell at me to bring my Father. I take a deep breath. Getting clothing was never like that before, but I always had the one thing she wanted. Father. Maybe coming without a chaperone wasn't a good idea. Especially when I'm asking for something so different. Never know until I try. I head for the next shop.

Three stores later I have similar degrees of failure, but a variance on rudeness. One store flatly refused to speak with me without a chaperone, and the last store said I might as well go to a tarnished store, except tarnished never marry so it wouldn't carry such a thing. In spite of the no marriage thing, I thought it sounded like a good idea. They make dresses, it can't be much different to make an engagement one. Can it?

I give the driver instructions to find a tarnished seamstress. He lifts a brow, but doesn't say a word as I climb in the carriage. At least some men seem to care about their job and not harassing women. Luckily it isn't a far enough drive to make my stomach feel ill. Yet, as I stand in front of the shop, I feel ill anyway. A tarnished clothing shop. What was I thinking? I might as well give in and let myself become a tarnished. Mother's dress will be fine. She was right. I sigh and head toward the carriage.

A bell rings and a woman's voice calls out, "Excuse me."

I pivot toward the voice. A woman with the black swirls of a tarnished on her narrow face occupies the entrance to the shop. Her dress is a two piece in differing colors of dark gold and black, wild as I expect a tarnished not serving in a prominent house to be. I step back.

"Excuse me," she says again, "I noticed you've been standing there staring at my shop for a while. I wondered if there is something I might help you with."

Not only is she speaking to me, but she has a nice, soothing voice.

"I don't know. I need a dress, but I suppose I'm in the wrong place."

"A dress? I can help. Come in." When I hesitate, she opens the door wider. "Please, come in."

The driver pays me no mind at all. It's a better reception than before. I enter the shop. There are no men anywhere in sight. Not a warlock, not another tarnished. No one else at all, except her. As strange as it is to be without a chaperone, it's even stranger for there to be no men at all.

It's a simple room with a few dresses displayed in the tarnished style on one side. No hard-seated waiting area for women. I am wondering if I'm supposed to stand when she directs me to the other side where a sofa with a low table in front of it and several chairs wait. Not just comfort for warlocks at this shop, I suppose. That makes me more at ease already. Once I'm settled, she sits across from me.

"I know it can be hard coming here for the first time, but I'll help you as best I can. When are you to be inked?"

"What? You think I'm—" My hand moves to my face. "No, no. I'm not to be tarnished." I brush my hands along my skirt. Do I look like I'm about to be tarnished?

Her smile vanishes beneath a hardened face. "What are you doing here then?"

"I'm in need of a dress."

Her eyes tighten. "There are plenty of seamstresses on Harrington."

"I know. I've been to many of them already, but none of them would help."

She shakes her head. "I don't—"

"Sorry, I know I shouldn't have come." I stand. This was the stupidest idea I've ever had. Not only have I made a bad impression on so many people, I'm getting myself compared to a tarnished. Probably will be punished for it, as well. My frustration bubbles up. While moving toward the door, I say, "I was hoping I could find an engagement dress that wouldn't make me feel as if I'm in my underthings. It was silly. I'm beyond ridiculous today."

I shove the door open.

"Wait!" The tarnished's voice startles me enough that I follow the command despite my intentions to leave. "Please come back.

Forgive me for being rude. I've just never had a customer like you before. I'm Katherine."

Tarnished have names? That's strange. Still, I hover at the entrance.

Her lips hint at a smile. "We can find you something."

I raise my brows. "Something more than a slip of a dress?"

The inked skin bunches and becomes fuller on her checks as her smile widens. "A modest dress then. Any other thoughts of what you would like?"

"C-color?"

She claps her hands. "A modest, colored engagement dress. That's an unusual request. When's the ceremony?"

Is she really going to do this for me? Hope flickers within me. "Six days."

Her face falls for a moment, and then returns to beaming. "Not long, but I'll figure something out. Please, sit back down. What's your name?"

"Serena." I resume my position on the couch, back straight. "You'll really do this? I can pay you." I give her the pouch of coins.

"Oh, posh. I can't turn you away now. This will be more than I need, but I'm not sure how much this type of material will cost. May I give you the change later?"

Is this acceptable? I've no idea. Until a few hours ago, I'd never even touched money. "That should be fine."

She tucks the pouch under the counter and grabs a book and material swatches before sitting back down. "To be honest, I've always thought those engagement dresses and bridal gowns were rather absurd. I've never needed one myself though, obviously, and neither do my usual customers so I've never done much with the thought."

This feels unreal. She opens the book. I wonder why we need the Woman's Canon until I see several basic dress designs. The tarnished use books in at least one more way than I'm supposed to.

"While you look at these, can you tell me about yourself?"

So I do. It takes me a few minutes to warm to her, but soon I'm telling her everything. We spend the next hour conversing. Instead of being something less than a shadow like I was always told, it's like finding another sister, except she's not afraid of Father and doesn't criticize my unconventional choice. And she likes chocolate, though she has only tried it once.

After a while, she sketches while we talk, making changes here and there, her smile growing with each line. How did someone like one of my sisters, get mixed up with others that are just shadows of people?

"What do you think?" She shows me the sketch.

My breath catches in my throat. The back of my eyes burn, but I blink away the tears before they can manifest. "Perfect. Will you be able to make it in time?"

"I'll make it. Do you know what color you want?"

Talking to her about what has happened made me realize, I don't want just any color. I don't want to just stand out. I want to feel it. "The color that started it all."

# CHAPTER 12

IT's dark when I open the carriage door. Though the ride wasn't far enough to make me too ill, the clean air helps soothe my jumbled stomach. The excitement of the day stays with me as I imagine wearing my engagement dress. It will be the best I've ever worn.

Mother's carriage is gone. A knot of tension in my stomach eases. I hope she won't be displeased with my choice. Or the Envadi. Her words come back to me about him trapping me. He did let me go rather easily and gave me money. It's probably to catch me making worse choices than just asking. My excitement drains.

I should send Katherine a note telling her not to make the dress. But she's doing me a favor, already working hard to get it ready in time. And it's what I want. What should I do? I don't know. I trudge inside and down the passage. An electric light is on in the book room, glowing through the slit in the doorway. I stop and peer inside.

My hand covers my mouth to keep from making a sound. The Envadi is conversing with another giant. It must be someone else from his country. There are never many Envadi in Chardonia.

91

What's he doing here? Even after leaning closer, I can't hear what they are saying. A spell perhaps? Except there's no telling salmon-colored light like he used before. Just the faint glow lightening the area directly around them.

"I can't," Chancellor Zade says, his voice finally growing loud enough for me to hear. Not a spell then, just caution.

"You must at least keep up appearances. What would your Father say?"

"You know he doesn't want me here, let alone encouraging me."

"As a parent, that may be so, but as a—"

"Wait." The Chancellor stalks to the door. "Who's there?"

My heart pounds and my mouth goes dry. I've pushed enough boundaries today without making it worse. I nudge the door open. Both men watch me. I lower my head wondering what hex he'll use. Or is he going to come close enough to strike me? I move deeper into the hall.

"Glad you're back," the Chancellor says. "I wanted to make sure you returned safely before going to bed."

Not what I was expecting to hear. I peek at him through my lashes. Returned safely or that I'm truly making stupid choices? More likely the latter. It has to be the latter.

His companion clears his throat.

The Chancellor says, "Oh, yes, I'm an idiot." Did he really just call himself that? "This is my manservant, Chadwick."

Does the introduction mean Chadwick will be administering punishment for eavesdropping? Father never foisted the job onto someone else, but I've heard of others doing so.

"A pleasure to meet you, madam."

The unusual greeting puzzles me. It doesn't seem like he's going to punish me, though he could if he tried. He's not as tall as Chancellor Zade, but taller than Father. There's a boyishness to his face at odds with the gun at his waist. I'm not sure if it makes him less of a threat or more of one. Chardonian warlocks never carry one.

"Come in, come in," Chancellor Zade says. "No need to hover in the hall."

At the reminder of my spying, I flinch, but edge in as he wishes.

"Did you find something to suit your taste?" His face gives away nothing.

I swallow. Mother was right. It's going to be a trap. "I did, Master."

"Good." He moves closer to my side, towering over me. I try not to shrink away from him. "No need to call me Master. Zade is fine."

"Yes, Chancellor Zade."

Chadwick chuckles and the Chancellor joins in. What's so funny?

"Just Zade."

"But the Woman's Canon says we must address you properly." Not that I want to follow it, but it's expected.

His lips press into a tight line. His eyes narrow. I avert my gaze to the floor.

"This is not your Father's house. Here I'm Zade, nothing more."

Chadwick coughs.

Zade grunts. "Do you need anything else for the ceremony?"

"No, Chancellor." Realizing I slipped the wrong name out, I cringe. It's not like I can call him by just his name, even if he says I can.

"Let me know if that changes. See you tomorrow."

I stay in my spot for a moment before I realize I can take that as permission to leave. Not wanting to make my sins greater, I dart out and head for my room. Why hasn't he punished me yet?

* * *

"DID YOU FIND A DRESS YESTERDAY?" Cynthia asks.

"A woman is making one for me."

"Is it what you want?"

"Yes."

She pats the seat next to her on the sofa. "Tell me about it before mother gets here."

Do I tell her that a tarnished is the one making it? She's here as a spy after all. Spy or not, she's my sister. "I'm not sure it will be done in time. I should've thought of it sooner. There's more material to it at least."

"That's good. I hope I can find the same when it's my turn. That thing mother had you try on was terrible."

She doesn't need to know how much worse most of the options are. At least, I hope she never does. I sit next to her. "I'll help you."

"Help her with what?" Mother waddles in the room.

Cynthia gives me a grin before turning toward my mother. "Picking a frock for tomorrow."

Mother hmpfs. "If there's nothing better for you girls to do, then I suggest you come home and help out."

Cynthia's face pales.

"It's my fault, mother," I say. "I was looking for a distraction. We're to polish the silver as soon as you leave."

Cynthia gives me a nudge of her elbow at the lie.

Mother glides into a chair, as well as any woman with a babe can glide. "You know better than to teach your sister to focus on such fanciful things. I suppose polishing is fine though. Maybe I best not stay for dinner."

I keep a smile from my face. "Only if you think the Chancellor wouldn't mind. We were supposed to be working on it right now, but with you coming we haven't the time."

Cynthia presses a gloved hand to her face.

"I guess we should hurry then," mother says. "Come here, Serena."

Mother sags, kneads her belly, and closes her eyes. Perhaps I shouldn't have made up the polishing chore. Making the journey so often in her condition must be miserable. It's hard to stop myself when the words come to mind.

I lean over to Cynthia and whisper, "Don't give us away."

"Father would've beaten you if he found out such a tale," she whispers back.

Her words won't affect me. I won't allow it. I stand and go to mother. At the swish of my dress, she opens her eyes.

"I brought the gown with the alternations."

"I've found a replacement."

The lines in her forehead multiply, cracking her face paint. "Indeed. Well then, Cynthia, you won't be needed today. I suppose you can get started on the silver. And there's a servant in the hall, tell her to enter in ten minutes. Make sure you don't say anything else. She could gossip."

"Yes, mother." Cynthia gives me a look of longing before leaving.

"Sit down, Serena."

I pull a chair closer and slide into it.

"I know you find me silly sometimes." I open my mouth to speak, but she stops me. "Don't deny it. I suppose I am rather silly at times." She sucks in air and holds her belly.

"Are you all right?"

Her voice is strained. "It's nothing." After several seconds her face relaxes. "When my Father told me it was time to enter the marriage pool, I was nineteen and enjoying life. So I refused."

This is not my mother. My mother has never refused any order from a warlock. It's not possible she's ever acted like this, except she has no reason to lie. My hand covers my mouth.

"I went in my room and shoved the bed against the door so no one could come in. It didn't last long. My Father spelled through it easily enough. He dragged me to the testing center. After I was tested, he chained me to a wall in the basement until the engagement ceremony, rarely fed. He spelled me to have nightmares about my worst fears. The only time I saw anyone was when mother brought food and begged me to repent. She wasn't even allowed to take the chamber pot."

Of all the punishment I've lived through, none have been that horrid. "I didn't know."

"Of course you didn't. I went to the engagement ceremony, returned to my Father's house repentant, got married several months later, and have spent a life time trying to make up for that stupid choice." She moves closer. "I don't want to see you go through something like that."

I don't want to either.

She slouches in her chair. "Father asked me to give you some gifts.

"Gifts?" My mind is still on mother's reveal. It takes a moment for her words to make sense. "But those are only for warlocks."

"A woman occasionally receives them." A woman with black eyes and a shabby olive-green dress enters the room carrying a small parcel. "Phyllis, I was just telling Serena about you."

She stops next to mother.

"Does she have the gift?"

"She's your gift, silly child. Father sent her. He thought being in such a grand house, you'd need a personal one. Though she will be Father's until you wed, then she will be your husband's, she's to wait on you. Chancellor Zade already approved her."

I stare at Phyllis, who stares back. No tarnished marks or marriage tattoos. Must be a lower class. Her hair is as dark as her eyes. The dress hangs on her frame.

Mother winces, her face crumpled with pain.

"Are you well?"

She lets out a slow breath. "Fine. Just a little false labor."

I crouch directly next to her. "Are you sure it's false?"

"I've had more than enough babes to know. Stop crowding me."

And I've delivered enough to know. After taking a step back, I say, "I can send for the doctor to make sure."

"You're the child, not me. Do you want your gift or not?"

The memory of the last babe coming before she thought it was time is hard to forget. The hex Father delivered for my not calling for the doctor sooner clings to me. I grip my hands together and inch back, watching for any other sign I'll be delivering another babe and punished for it.

"It's only—" I shake my head. Saying something won't do any good. "What's the other gift, mother?"

She motions to Phyllis who hands her the parcel. As she speaks, she unwraps the bundle. "This is for the engagement ceremony and after when he brands you. It will make it easier to bear."

I stare at the bottle of herbs unable to move. "Branding?"

"You know all engaged and married woman are marked, Serena. Don't go senseless on me now." She folds the cloth over the bottle and hands it to the servant. "Phyllis will prepare it for you, so you needn't worry about that. She can get more if you should need it. I strongly recommend doing so for your wedding ceremony. That's all Phyllis."

As Phyllis leaves, I move toward my chair wondering what is in that bottle.

"Not yet," mother says. "Come here."

I step closer to her. When she motions to the floor, I kneel next to her.

"The Chancellor doesn't know I'm giving this to you." In light of her earlier revelation, I'm surprised she would do anything without permission. "Father thinks you need it. But you must not say anything to anyone else."

That explains it.

She continues, "Not all men care for a woman to have it. They sometimes prefer us to be more feeling than the herb allows."

"Is it like the soothing tea?"

"No, this is much, much stronger. It has some negative side effects as well, but if you don't have it, you'll ruin the ceremony."

My stomach knots and I grip her armrest. "What happens at the ceremony?"

"The spell from my own engagement prevents me from telling you or I would. They prefer to keep it a surprise." She grabs my hands with both of hers. "No matter. I'll be there for you Serena. As much as the events of the day allow, I'll be there for you."

Tears sting my eyes. I blink them away before they can spill out.

"I'll be next to you at the feast afterward. You look to me if you encounter any problems."

She changes the topic to the state of the house without Cynthia and me around, but the ceremony clogs my mind. A spell is what blocks woman from speaking of it? That explains why I haven't heard anything about it before, from her or in class. And branding? I rub my neck just above my collarbone where I know the mark will go. What will the Envadi choose to leave permanently on my skin?

"Serena?" mother says.

"Yes?"

"You should eat something dear, you're looking peaked." She scoots to the edge of her chair and heaves herself out of it. "I should leave anyway if you are to get the silver polished."

"You don't have to."

"Nonsense. I'll see you at the ceremony."

She surveys me a final time and is out the door. Now my guilt for scaring her off earlier intensifies. I'm not ready for her to go.

# CHAPTER 13

PHYLLIS SHOVES another pin in my hair. It scrapes my scalp. I bite my lower lip to keep from crying out. Father's gift doesn't have a light touch. I miss Cynthia's deft hands. Even my own would be better than this. She moves to pin another wayward strand and I hold my breath. A knock at my bedroom door stops her.

"Come in," I call.

"According to the Woman's Canon," Phyllis says, "you shouldn't holler. Next time, I'll attend to it."

I ignore her and face who I suspect is Cynthia, looking for some relief to her boredom. When Katherine's inked face comes into view, arms laden with a large package, I spring to my feet.

"You're dismissed, Phyllis."

"But I'm not fin—"

"Katherine can help me if I need it."

"Your Father won't be happy to hear about this." Phyllis whips away from me and heads from the room, bumping into Katherine on her way out.

Father may not be happy to hear, but he's not my Master. As long as he doesn't tell the Envadi, I should be fine. I hope.

"Have I interrupted?" Katherine asks.

"No. Sorry about Phyllis. My very first present. Can't say I'm glad to have received it."

Her footsteps slow. "That woman was a present to you?"

I sink into one of the chairs around the table. "Honestly, I think the word present is used to make her sound better. She's worse than mother and continually referencing Father. I'm sure she's telling him all my misdeeds. A great many, I fear. I'd much rather go back to having things between just me and Cynthia."

"Maybe this will cheer you." She sets the package on my lap.

It crinkles as I run my hand across it. "Have you really finished it?"

"With little time to spare. And some extra coins you should keep for an emergency."

"Women can't keep money."

"I do and I'm a woman. Besides, you never know when you'll need a little extra."

The bag is heavy in my hands, though lighter than when I first gave it to her. Can I really keep it? "I don't know."

"Just keep it and enjoy your new dress."

"I wouldn't even know what to do with it. Giving it to you was the most I've ever done with money."

"It's easy to figure out." She reaches over and opens the bag and pulls out a handful of coins. She quickly explains the gold ones are worth more than the silver, and the brown ones are the least valuable. "It's strange using them at first, but you'll get used to it."

I put the pouch on the table, for now, and concentrate on the package containing my dress. "This will be better than the other choices. I'll be more comfortable in it, at least. Mother talked to me earlier and, well, it didn't help with my nerves. Do you know anything about the engagement ceremony?"

The smile on her face transforms into an expression I can't read. "Very little."

"Sit down if you'd like, Katherine. Make yourself comfortable."

Her eyebrows raise, but she settles into a chair next to me. "I understand it's difficult to endure."

I pull the package closer to me, causing more crackles. "Do you know why?"

"No. The only thing I know is that you can't make a sound during the ceremony unless they ask you to or they'll cane you."

"How do you know this?"

"Some of the tarnished who have been servants to a newly engaged woman have noticed things. The women seem jumpier, more distracted, bruises. I wish I knew more."

I rub my forehead. Katherine stands, walks over to me, and wraps her arms around me. The touch makes me stiffen.

"It's fine to be scared, Serena. You can make it through this. I know you can."

It's strange to have another person touch me, but I collapse against her, the contact more comforting than I expected. A tear escapes. Blinking, I try to prevent any more from coming. After a minute, she eases away. "You can make it through this."

I nod, but don't know if I can.

"Good. I wish I could be there to help you get ready, but I'm afraid my presence would make things worse. Let me help with what I can today."

"Thank you, for bringing this and working so hard on it."

"Don't thank me, yet. You haven't opened it."

I tug at the strings trying to keep my fingers from shaking. Once the strings are loose, I pull the wrapping back. My fingers brush against the satin as I hold the dress. The feel of it is different from any other dress I've owned.

"It's perfect."

"I'm happy you like it." She spends the next ten minutes showing me how to get in and out of it by myself. After I've practiced a few times, she helps me into my original gown and wraps up my new one. "Try to get dressed as close to the ceremony as you can. The fewer people that see you in the dress beforehand, the more likely you'll be able to wear it."

"There are going to be problems?"

"You're breaking rules wearing this, so yes, there'll be problems. Can you manage them?"

"It's what I want, so I'll figure it out." At least I hope I can.

She hands me a parcel. "Some ribbons for your hair if you decide you want them. I'd best be off."

I hold the parcel close to me. "Why have you done so much for me?"

"You paid me."

"No, it's more than just me paying for your services. You care. I didn't even know tarnished could care. Why do you?"

Her lips form a thin line. "People like me are more than you've been taught."

"Oh." Guilt heats my face.

Does this mean she's not the only kind tarnished? Not the only one who's more than a shadow? Is that true, or does she just want it to be? It's hard to think all those years of them being only in the background, and being told they aren't even real people, were wrong. But I've trusted her this far.

"I feel like I owe you something more. What else can I give you?"

"Nothing. You just be as strong as you can for the ceremony. I'll visit afterward when I can."

"This means so much to me."

She gives me another embrace. "I'm grateful to help."

# CHAPTER 14

I TUG AT MY ROBE, wishing I could put my dress on. Though if I could, it would mean it was time to go and I don't want that either. I'm not ready to go, just ready for it to be over. The tiny dressing room in the hall where the engagement ceremony takes place, feels smaller with Phyllis hovering. Its bland walls are adorned with an oval mirror and table with face paint pots and a jewelry box. I'm in the only chair, leaving Phyllis to hover over me.

She sets a tea cup before me. "Drink up."

I eye the earthy smelling tea. "I'm not sure I—"

"Drink it. Your Father said if you didn't, I'm to get him. Is that what you want?"

For a lower class servant, she's not as docile as I'd expect. I grab the cup.

"Good. As soon as you're finished I'll do your face paint."

"I'll do it myself."

She grunts and moves behind me. Her fingers rake through my hair. She reaches for a black ribbon.

"Wait, use the red one."

Her mouth purses. She picks it up as if it were a bug. "Why's it red?"

I breathe deeply, trying to pull in strength. "I just wanted a bit of color."

The corner of her lips pull to one side and she ties the ribbon around my hair. "Now, let me help you dress."

"I would prefer to wait. I don't want to crease it."

"Jewelry?"

"After I dress. I don't want it to snag the cloth." She takes a step toward the door. What if she goes for Father? "Perhaps if you helped me with a small piece, it won't harm the dress."

Her face relaxes a little. She drapes me with jewels. A ring on every finger and a few on my toes, a reminder of the fewest warlocks I'm to have, though it didn't work well for mother. Seven necklaces, reminders of my fiancée's claim. They feel like chains, weighing me down. An arm band, five bracelets and five anklets on each limb feel the same. But no earrings. Nothing to block me from hearing the requests of my future husband.

"There now. That's the last jewelry you'll ever wear. When your owner takes it off tonight, you'll never don another. Would you like me to help you into the dress your mother sent?"

I hide a grimace at the slight thing. "No, thank you. It's the only time I can dress myself." Which is true, but not in the way she thinks. She doesn't move. "Alone, if I may."

"You haven't sipped your tea."

The cup is cold in my hands. I put it to my lips and sip. The liquid is tepid and tastes of leaves and dirt.

"All of it."

I glare at her and she glares back. The threat of Father is too heavy for me to ignore. Trying not to think about it, I down the tea as fast as I can.

She nods. "You have fifteen minutes. If you need help, I'll be right outside the door."

Without another word, she leaves. As soon as the door latches,

I shed the jewelry. With every piece, a load is taken from me, not just physically, but deep inside, lightening my very being. Once they're all back in their box, I apply the face paint. Not a lot, just some color on my eyes, cheeks, and lips. Finally, I grab my package. I pause for a moment. It would be easier if my sisters were here. Perhaps Katherine as well.

My fingers quiver as I unwrap it and put it on. The laces gathered on the front slow me a moment, but then I have it tied. The dress is silken against my skin.

I'm a little dizzy as I look in the mirror. The dress is a blood red, draping past my feet. The material is tight on my arms, but not restrictive, and comes down to my wrists where the back half bells out to the floor. The neckline is square and modest, but leaving my collarbone free. My lightly painted face smiles back.

There's not long before someone will come to get me. I'd prefer to go out there where there's less likely to be a scene. I hope. At least I'll be one step closer to where I need to be wearing this dress and one step farther from being forced into the slip.

Before I go, I stop at the jewelry box and make one concession. A silver necklace with a single square ruby. Mother's favorite. Whenever we take the jewelry box out, she threads it through her fingers and admires it before putting it back. As I put it on, my head feels a little fuzzy. The world tilts before righting itself. When the dizziness stops, I let the jewel rest against my chest. After several deep breaths to try and clear my head, I open my door and stride into an antechamber.

Father is talking to Phyllis and doesn't notice me. The world starts to pull away. Or maybe I'm pulling away from the world. Things seem far away. Off. A door closes somewhere.

Phyllis spots me and yelps.

Father follows her gaze to me and halts whatever he had been saying. "What is that?" He gapes at me several moments, his face growing redder by the second. "You will change into the dress your mother provided immediately."

I don't want to, but my far off body turns toward my room. A hand closes around my arm, stopping me.

"Don't change." The Envadi lords over me.

"Do you see what your future bride is wearing?" Father says. "She's dressed like a harlot."

How can he think that? My dress is infinitely more modest than the traditional one. Yet the words bite. I've never been called such a name. I want to hide, but my body doesn't respond.

The Envadi's face is hard, his voice just above a whisper. "I gave her permission to wear it."

"Are you mad? You must call off this ceremony immediately. You obviously can't control the wench. I'll take her in hand until she's subdued enough for the ceremony."

"And how long do you think that will take?"

"Certainly no less than a year."

The Envadi scoffs. "The ceremony will happen today and she will continue to reside at the manor."

"You can't mean that." Father's voice is lower now, but more dangerous. "You'd have her dressed as a red tarnished?"

No one says a word. I feel as if tears should be forming, but nothing comes. It's hard to be grateful I'm not fighting the weakness when I can't seem to do anything. Finally, the Envadi speaks.

"The ceremony will take place now or you will face the penalty of a broken contract."

Why is he sticking up for me?

Father pounds toward me, hand raised.

"Any punishment will be doled out by me in private," the Envadi says.

My stomach cramps. This is why he's sticking up for me. Mother was right. It's a trap. He'll see how far I'm willing to take my mistakes so he can punish me more. I'm only saved from losing my breakfast by the detachment that's plagued me.

Father growls and, instead of hitting me, yanks me to him. "Come. You're about to be sacrificed."

What?

My feet move without my telling them to as my heart pounds. What did he mean by sacrificed? Phyllis opens a door and Father moves through it, dragging me along.

The chattering in the room silences. All faces stare at me, but I don't know what their expressions are like. One thing has captured my attention. A sacrificial altar. Just like at the tournament, but resting on a floor of stone instead of grass.

Who are they going to kill at my engagement ceremony? Whose life will be on my hands? It was hard enough so far away at the tournament, but now I'm a few feet from it. I'd run if I could.

Father lets go and I sway. He waves his hand. A blue thread of light travels to me and bursts under my feet. I'm flung in the air. I try to scream, but my body doesn't respond as I soar upward. Air rushes past. The ceiling grows closer. The crowd more distant. Just before I hit the ceiling, the ascent stops.

If it wasn't for the tea, I would be screaming in terror, disregarding Katherine's warning from when she dropped off the dress. The crowd watches me from fifty feet below as my dress flaps in the breeze. The extra length is even more appreciated now.

The watching crowd unnerves me as I float there. I gaze upward. The arched ceiling is ten feet above me. I focus on it and try to ignore the feeling of air brushing the skin of my feet.

Abruptly, I'm yanked downward. The ceiling grows farther and farther away from me. My hair streams above me. Those gathered come back into view. I'm going to smash against the rock floor. The fear while falling is worse than soaring upward. My heart pounds.

My body won't move in any way to help protect me from the fall. The Envadi's face flashes by. I stop. It takes a moment to realize I didn't crash. A faint spell flows from Chancellor Zade, cushioning me to the ground.

His face is taut, void of expression except his eyes. They burn with barely controlled rage. I try to bow my head so I can't see how furious I've made him, but my head won't move.

From the side of me, Father grabs my wrist and thrusts it toward the Chancellor. "She's yours."

Chancellor Zade grabs my wrist and with his free hand, unties my hair ribbon. The strip of red floats to the floor as my dark locks fall to my waist. He scoops me into his arms.

The ceremony is over. He's going to carry me to the carriage and I'll be able to go to the house. Find Cynthia. Figure out how to get rid of this fog clouding my attempts to do anything.

When he places me on the cool stone, I know being finished was too hopeful a thought. My body shivers. It comes to me.

There's no tarnished coming today.

I am the sacrifice.

"Don't move. Don't speak," the Envadi whispers.

His words mean nothing to me. I want to run screaming away from the altar I lay on. But I can't. I can't do anything on my own. Just his exact words. Don't move. Not even a twitch. Despair engulfs me.

The Envadi moves my arms above my head and shackles them. His hand encircles my ankles and places them in shackles on the other side of the altar. As if I could move anyway. If I could, I would fight with everything I have.

He can't kill me though. If wives were killed before marriage, none of us would be here. The thought should comfort me, except he's clearly going to do something. But what? I watch his every move.

He stands at my side facing the crowd. His hands hover over me as if he's about to cast a spell. Nothing. The longer I stare at those hands, the more I need this tea to wear off so I can move. I have to get out of here.

"Happiness." His voice booms through the room.

Sunny light burst through his hands. As soon as it hits me, I'm laughing, so full of joy to be laying on this altar for him.

"Sadness."

A deep blue is cast on me this time. I sob, tears stream down my face, wetting my hair and the stone beneath me.

"Hunger."

The straw-colored light hits me and my stomach spasms. I'm hungrier then when I had to go a week without food. A moan escapes me.

"Satiated."

The spell fills me and the pain stops.

"Health.

My body brims with strength. If I could rise, I would break through the shackles.

"Sickness."

Olive green slams into me. Aches and chills. I dry heave.

"Pain."

A scream bursts from me. My back arches off the table.

"Contentment."

I fall back to the table, but it feels as if I'm on a feather bed. I sigh.

The feeling leaves. I'm sweating. I want to cry. Or rage. Or scream again. But I can do nothing. My body doesn't respond to anything I try.

"All thoughts and feelings will be mine."

He reaches to his waist. A clang reverberates through the room. He holds a dagger above. I am going to die. For a moment, I panic, then peace fills me. There will be no more punishments, only darkness. I hope my sisters can survive without me. Please let them survive.

"Blood of thine." He thrusts the knife toward me, slicing my neck. The wound doesn't hurt. I won't be afraid as I wait for it to lunge at me again. I won't.

He raises the dagger. It angles toward his own arm and makes a small cut. Why did he cut himself? I can't figure it out, but relief that I'm still alive fills me.

He sets the blade on my breast bone and holds his hand out. A midnight blue spell slinks to my neck and coaxes my blood into the air. It reminds me of getting tested. The light forms a sphere above me, tugging and jerking deep inside. It hurts, the pain growing and gnawing in me. I want to cry out. A stream slips from the orb and flows to the Envadi's cut.

"Becomes mine."

The tugging stops. The orb shrinks as the last of my blood he must have wanted flows into him. I'm woozy seeing my life's blood go to him. The metallic smell makes it worse. But I can't do anything about it. The nick on my neck stings.

He grabs the dagger and sheathes it. With the aid of a spell, he floats up until he's standing on the altar next to my waist. A mass of colors and sparks fly from him, dashing around the room. The crowd murmurs. Blues, greens, silvers, yellows, all invade my sight. One slips to my neck and the sting eases.

Sparks pop faster among the colors. The colors sparkle, glitter, and dance. All at once, they're gone. The Envadi stretches out his hands, then yanks them higher. I spring upward until the chains are tight. My pulse is erratic as I hover in the air, still on my back. My waist brushes against the Envadi, my arms and legs aching against the chains.

He blasts a dark spell over me. "You are mine."

# CHAPTER 15

I KNEEL in front of the altar. The stone chills my legs. Something is bound around my neck. The Envadi holds a leash. I choke back a cry. Or maybe a shriek. But the tea still has me under its power.

I've been collared like an animal. The Envadi glares at me. His lips tighten and he looks away. He's more barbaric than I thought.

The gathered crowd shuffles. I realize all women in attendance are being leashed like me. The Envadi yanks on the leash and strides down the aisle. I scramble after him still detached from myself. If I could control my body, I would fight against him. Or at least I think I would. Maybe I wouldn't. The fight is in me, I'm just so tired.

As we pass the crowd, they fall in behind us. Women with their heads down and men leading them along. We move through the room and into a long passage. The stones are cold beneath my feet. As we walk, the world comes closer again, more in focus. Still not normal, though. I can't quite reach myself.

The smell of buttery rolls and roast venison wafts to me and grows stronger. We walk into a banquet hall. A feast awaits.

I'm led to the middle of the main table, a long rectangle, with a throne-like chair where the Envadi takes a seat. When he says and does nothing further, I hover behind him, grateful I'm more in control of my actions, but still not fully connected. Like some part of me is forgotten. The Envadi hasn't forgotten me though. His grip tightens around the handle of my leash.

Father sits on the left. The woman on his leash is not my mother, but a tarnished scantily clad in red. I stare at her hoping for some clue why a red tarnished has taken mother's place, but she doesn't glance my way. The Grand Chancellor takes the chair on the right. The woman on his leash isn't tarnished, but has a stark black star on her neck, elaborate swirls around it. His wife? She kneels on the ground before him. The others sit and some kneel or lay on the floor. Only one other woman stands behind a man's chair. Once everyone is seated, the Grand Chancellor gestures at the Envadi.

He jerks the chain. I fly toward the table. "Get me food, wench."

I stare at him, willing my gaze to make him disappear. Instead, his jaw clenches. His thumb rubs my leash. Not wanting to make him throw me around more, I face the table.

There are so many choices, I don't know what to grab. What will he do if I pick the wrong thing? My hand shakes as I lift a fork to a whole boar, with onions and carrots surrounding it. Its sides are carved into slices. I dish several onto the plate. A pheasant is nearby so I add that, as well.

The dish is nearly full from the meat I've put on it. More than I thought. Not much of a meal. I grab a hunk of bread and spoon on some peaches. The food trembles as I carry it back. A peach slice falls to the floor. I freeze, staring at the offending piece.

The plate is yanked from my hands. "A drink, woman."

No complaints or punishments for the dropped food. I release the air from my lungs. The drinks have to be on the table. Certainly there's enough food, it can't matter if a little is on the floor. I grab a goblet and inspect the jugs. Wine, ale, or water. Two of the three choices are acceptable to a man, yet I still have to deal with the Envadi tonight, so I grab the unacceptable choice. With a goblet of water, I return to him. It can't be what he wants but if he'll accept it without backlash, it'll be worth the risk.

He takes it from me and drains it. The men cheer. He casts a powder-blue spell. The cup glides through the air to me. It's warm against my palms.

The other women in the room move to the serving table. I refill the goblet, grateful water appears to be an acceptable choice and return it. The Envadi looks me in the eye, a blaze still burning in him. He points at the floor. Despite his power, I don't want to lower myself to him anymore. But my body is so tired. It's hard to keep it up. I sit, curling my legs under me. It's what is expected of me.

The men talk and laugh. Women walk back and forth between the food and the men, but the Envadi never asks for anything more. Rather than demanding things, he ignores me. He laughs and talks with Father and the Grand Chancellor. Though I know he's a barbarian, he sounds just like the other warlocks.

Other men come by with their leashed women. They send their women for drinks and food for him. Some of the women ignore me. Others gaze at me with sympathy. A few glare at me. One walks up to me, but instead of stopping, kicks my legs before falling to make it look like she tripped over me. I ignore them all.

Vaguely, I'm aware that I should be hungry. I ate so little for breakfast, and my body is exhausted. But none of the food appeals to me. If anything, I feel nauseous. My dress clings to my skin. Sweat beads on my forehead. I lean against the throne. It's cool against my side and face. My eyelids give a heavy blink and close.

Without warning, I'm wrenched to my feet. The Envadi wraps his arm around me, half carrying, half hauling me along. I try to clear my mind as we move past whooping men. The women keep their eyes to the ground, some frowning, some smiling, and some expressionless.

I stumble as he stops to open a door. Frigid air blasts, bringing me fully conscious. My gown does little to protect me from the coming storm. A carriage waits at the end of a pebbled walkway. A footman opens the door. I half jump, am half pushed inside. As I collapse on the seat, the door closes. I pant in the dark.

The carriage moves. My stomach twists. I fumble for the pot kept beneath the seat. There's nothing in my stomach to loose, but my body tries anyway. Over and over again. The ride is infinitely longer than this morning. Rain patters on the roof. The horse's hooves clop on the road. The carriage dips and bounces. I heave again.

When the carriage finally stops, I stay slumped against the seat. The cold darkness bears down on me. The door opens. I flinch at the torch light carried by the footman, but don't move from my seat. After a moment, the footman peers in. With a groan, I sit up. I rub the back of my hand across my mouth. The fresh, rain-scented air eases my stomach. I drag myself from the carriage, quickly becoming soaked by the downpour. Thankfully, the Envadi is nowhere in sight. But Phyllis is.

"Come. I've prepared your room."

Not wanting to think what that means, I let her guide me into the house, and through halls and upstairs, dripping on everything. In front of Cynthia's door, I pause. Phyllis snaps at me. With a groan, I climb the stairs after her to my room and head straight for the bed, not worried about drying off.

"Not yet. I'm under orders to prepare you for the Chancellor."

I shiver. The branding. I almost forgot about it. I want to forget about it and have everyone else do the same. The bed sits there. I want to collapse on it. How much longer will this day be? I wipe a tear before she can see it. My little table has bowls, ink, and a needle on it. I avert my gaze from the tools to the vanity. It has a tea set on it. I sit in front of it. She grabs a brush and works on my tresses.

"You'd better drink your tea."

I pick up the cup and smell it. The earthy smell from the morning invades. I slam it down, some sloshing out.

She stops brushing to top off the cup. "Your Father said I'm to inform you that you may be out of his house, but your sisters are not."

I grasp the table. There's no way to direct the attention onto me if I'm here. I swig the drink. She refills it and hands it to me. She frowns with concern, and for a moment I think she's going to apologize, but it deepens into a scowl.

"Drink up."

I close my eyes and down the second cup. When she fills it a third time I say, "No more. One was fine for the ceremony. Two is more than enough."

"I suppose it will do." With a shrug, she resumes brushing my tresses.

I avoid looking at her in the mirror. I want to throw the teapot across the room. And maybe cry, but not while she's here. Oh how I wish there were no warlocks controlling my life.

"Do you need help with anything else?"

"You've helped more than enough."

"Very well. I'll leave the tea in case you change your mind. Ring if you need me." Before departing, she points to the cord by my bed that lets the servants know I need something.

Once she's gone I grab the pot and hurl it against the wall. It shatters to the floor in pieces. I fling the cup after it. I slump in my chair, with my elbows on the table and my head in my hands. Tears sting my eyes. I breathe deeply and close my eyes until they leave. The earthy smell fills the room. I should have thrown the pot out the window.

My head grows dizzy. My body harder to control. It's easier to recognize now that I've already been through it. The detachment is almost a relief, but I still wish I could have avoided drinking the tea. While I still have control, I walk to my window seat and curl up on it, tucking my dress around me. The pouring rain soothes me.

Sometime later, a knock echoes in my room. I try to yell 'go away', but nothing comes out. The knock sounds again and the door opens. The Envadi is in my room. The dagger responsible for cutting into me rests in his sheathe. I blink at him. As soon as our eyes meet, he lowers his gaze.

"You can't talk about the ceremony. The spell cast at the end will turn you mute forever if you even try. You must not." He moves closer. "Do you understand?"

"Yes." My mouth responds without my telling it to. I try to ask him to explain, but nothing comes out.

"I would like to—No, finish the tattoo first, then we'll talk."

He proceeds toward me. I try and try to tell my body to stand. To back away. To do something. At least take whatever is coming standing up. It refuses to move.

My pulse increases. He stops and kneels until his face is even with mine. Faintly, there is the sound of metal sliding against metal. He hovers there.

"Your brand. Would you tilt your head back?"

I try to force it not to move, but my efforts don't make a difference. It tilts back. The ceiling is rather a bad distraction. A blank canvas of cream paint. My neck grows sore after several minutes, but I can't do or say anything. He moves away and returns. I wish I could at least look at him. What's he doing? Why's it taking so long?

"This isn't working. I can't..." He grunts and stands. "Come here."

Against my will, I crush myself against him, resting my head against his chest and wrapping my arms around him. I feel his heart beat increase through his shirt. I shriek at myself to get away from him. I beg and plead. But I remain plastered against him.

He pats my shoulder and takes a step back. I move with him.

He backs up again and I follow. He maneuvers us to the table and chairs. His hands grasp my waist. I want to beat my fists against him. Mother's warning was right. I shouldn't have worn the dress. He's going to take my virtue because of it, and I'll be forced to become a tarnished. The memory of Thomas groping at me surfaces. I struggle to move myself from his grasp, but my body still won't respond.

He grips my waist tighter and sets me on the chair. My insides shake with relief that he doesn't seem interested in me. Once he sits in his own chair, I stop trying to move. Without being under my own control, this may be the best I can hope for. He twists a ring on his right hand.

"Are you all right?"

Not even close, but my body refuses to say that. "I'm well, Master."

"Are you sure?" He cocks his head to the side. "You seem a little... different than usual."

"I'm sure."

He leans forward, elbows on his knees, and frowns. My mouth mimics his frown. "I know this situation hasn't been ideal, but I'd like it if we could get to know one another better before I have to..." He glances at the equipment on the table. "I know about your parents and Cynthia. What about the rest of your family?"

I don't want to say a word about my sisters. "There's me then Cynthia, then Bethany, Preshea, Julia, Grace, Ada, Emma, Sally, Beatrice, Phoebe, Ruthie, Stella, and little Molly."

"Wow. That's a lot to remember."

"Don't worry, you won't have to remember." Egh. They're more worth remembering than he is. Stupid tea.

"Uh—" He sits back in his chair. "That's a big family and all girls. I only have one sister." Only one? Must be because they had him first. "Do you miss your sisters?"

"Yes." My voice cracks.

He moves to kneels by me. "Hey, it's all right. You can be sad about it. Even if you need to cry about it, it's fine."

Tears gush from me like a spring river.

Zade holds a handkerchief out to me. "I didn't mean you had to cry if you don't want to."

My tears stop. Thankfully.

"What is wrong with you?"

So, so much. "What is wrong with me?"

He casts an aqua spell. It traces over me. "You're not spelled. Are you sure you're all right?"

"I'm fine."

"No. You should be doing more," he waves his hand about, "normal things."

"What do you want me to do?" My voice doesn't sound like my own. Too breathy.

He clears his throat and looks around the room. "I just wanted to—" His gaze stops on the broken teapot. He stands, his forehead wrinkling. "What happened?"

"I broke it." My body giggles. Blast it.

He strides to the tea pot and picks it up. He holds a broken piece to his nose and sniffs. His eyes tighten. With a wave of his hand, he casts a muddy spell over it. After a moment, the spell stops. He stiffens. With his hand clamped around the piece, he strides toward me. He thrusts the broken piece toward me.

"Did you drink this?"

"Two whole cups."

His nose flares. "You're trying to get rid of my ownership of you so they'll have grounds to make me lose the Chancellor's position. Who put you up to this?" He throws the already broken piece at the wall. "Who was it?"

My eyes tear. At least he's getting to the information I want him to know. "Phyllis."

"The servant your Father sent?" He paces the room, clenching and unclenching his hand. "I should have sent her away the day she got here. I just didn't think you'd go along with their plans. I should have never agreed to marry you. Stupid wench."

He stops in front of me, leans down, and puts a hand on each of the arm rests. Punishment is coming. Some good will come of my detachment. I'll finally know what his punishments are like.

"Why did you go along with this?" His voice is menacing.

I cringe. For a moment I'm grateful my body is finally responding to what I want it to do, but then it speaks without my telling it to. "So my sisters wouldn't get hurt."

His face relaxes and he stands. I jump up and put my head against his chest again. Tears stream down my face. Stop crying. Stop it right now! He's going to punish me, don't let him see what it's doing to me. But of course I continue crying. The Envadi doesn't move.

"I didn't mean to get upset." His voice is calmer now, like that I'd use with one of my youngest sisters. "It's all right. Why were your sisters threatened?"

I sniff. "When I wouldn't drink the tea, Phyllis said Father had ordered that if I didn't, they would be punished."

One of his hands rubs my back. I snuggle closer to him instead of running like I want. He jumps from me and moves to the other side of the room.

"I don't have the antidote. Sit. Don't touch me or come any closer to me."

My body freezes. This isn't as good as being in control but less troublesome than before.

He flicks his dagger on the table next to the branding items and paces before coming back to me. "Give me your hand."

I hold out my hand. He pricks my finger and sheathes the blade. He holds my finger over the bowl. There's already some clear liquid in it, but I can't tell if it's just water or something else. The fluid turns pink and darkens as my blood flows into it. Once the liquid is a shade lighter than blood, he heals my finger.

"Sit back and don't touch me."

I sit back in my chair and watch every move he makes. He grabs the dish of ink and dumps it in. Using a small spoon, he stirs the mixture. After a minute, he says, "Look at the ceiling while resting your head on the back of the chair."

I don't want to take my eyes from him, but I can't help but comply.

"This will hurt."

A moment later, he puts a hand on my shoulder and something pinches my neck, just above my collarbone. And pricks again and again and again. My branding. I try to wonder what it will be like instead of thinking of the pain. How will it be seeing it every time I look in the mirror? I start to enjoy the distance the tea forced on me and fall more deeply into it. I close my eyes. At some point the pricks stop and the pain eases. I'm being lifted to some place warm and comfortable. Everything fades.

# CHAPTER 16

LIGHT STREAMS INTO THE ROOM. I roll away from it. A breakfast tray sits on my bedside table. I groan and pull a pillow over my head. Then I realize I'm still wearing my dress and necklace. I bounce up, flinging the pillow from me. My hand goes to my neck where I was cut at the ceremony, then to where the pricks hurt me last night. My skin feels as smooth as always. My head was so distant last night, perhaps none of it was real.

Grateful I don't have to pull the cord that rings for Phyllis, I grab the tray and set it on my lap. A note waits with my name on it. I ignore it in favor of strawberries and some pastries. Once my stomach isn't so ravenous, I grab the note.

*TELL PHYLLIS THAT COUNCILMAN STEPHEN won't be rid of me so easily.*
*~Zade*

I LURCH TO MY FEET, and the tray falls to the floor with a crash. I step on a strawberry, squashing it beneath my foot, as I hurry to the mirror. Just above my right collarbone is a hollow circle, like a ring, about cherry-sized. A thin line curving around the top, thickening as it bends toward the bottom. I brush my fingers over it. My brand.

"Doesn't look like a new mark. Skin's not red enough."

I jump and almost scream, but stop the sound from escaping. Phyllis stands behind me.

"Don't startle me like that."

"I knocked but you didn't answer, and it's almost lunch time so I figured you should be awake. It's plain for an engagement brand." She sounds more curious than disdainful like I'm expecting.

I look back in the mirror. Definitely not as elaborate as some, but he could be saving that for the wedding.

Phyllis clucks her tongue. "My, you made a mess this morning."

Suddenly, I'm aware of the wet, mushed strawberry beneath my foot. As I peel it off, I notice it left pink marks across the rug leading to the dropped tray. I hope Phyllis isn't too upset over the mess. It'll be a pain to clean. I move to help her, but stop when I remember the tea.

"The note might as well be for you. Take it with you when you're done cleaning."

I grab clean clothing, and leave without another word, slamming the door. Cynthia should have been awake hours ago. In fact, I can't believe I slept so late. I pound on her door with my free hand. A moment later, it opens.

Cynthia takes one look at me and opens the door wider. Once I'm in, she closes the door and leans against it. "How was it?"

I throw my clothes on a table and slump into a chair. "I can't talk about it."

She eyes my brand, but doesn't mention it. "Is there anything I can do?"

"Unless you can get rid of Phyllis, no."

"Phyllis?" She moves to the chair across from me. "What does she have to do with it?"

"If she ever offers you tea, turn it down. If anyone offers you tea that smells like dirt, throw it at them."

"Are you well, Serena?"

"No. It was awful. It made me not myself. I was far away and couldn't control my actions. Whatever I was told to do, I did." I put my hands to my face. "Just promise me you'll never drink anything that smells like dirt or that someone says will help when it's your time for this."

"If it makes you feel better, I promise not to."

It doesn't matter what she promises. If someone threatens her, she won't have a choice.

My dress is wrinkled from being slept in. Part of me doesn't want to take it off, the other part wants it gone. Mostly, I hope there's no punishment for wearing it. I rise and begin unlacing my dress. "Would you help me change?"

Cynthia stares at me a moment before saying, "You can unlace your dress? I didn't know we could have ones like that. Where did you get it?"

"It's from my engagement ceremony."

She throws my change of clothes back down and comes closer, inspecting it. "That's your engagement dress?"

"It is."

"But it's not black, and it's an actual dress."

"Rather lovely isn't it? Crinkled and in need of a good washing now." I glance down at it. "Perhaps I should just burn it."

"What? No, don't do that. If you really want to be rid of it, I'll take it for you."

I resume unlacing. "Why do you want it?"

"Why don't you?"

Because I can still feel it flapping in the air while I'm plummeting to the ground. Because the cold stone of the altar seeped into it. Because my blood might as well be one with it.

Neither of us say anything as she helps me into some clean clothes. A bath would feel nice, but I'll wait to draw one for myself when Phyllis isn't around. I ball up my red dress and throw it toward the door. Cynthia goes after it.

"Just leave it. If you want it so bad, I'll clean it for you."

Ignoring me, she picks it up, folds it, and places it on a side table. Her fingers continue to pick at it. "You don't have to tell me if you don't want to, but yesterday, was the Envadi barbaric as it's said they are?"

I adjust my sleeves. "I wish I could tell you everything. Nothing was as I thought it would be, not even the Chancellor."

I take off the necklace, never to wear another. The Woman's Canon says that a woman who is engaged or married must never wear jewelery as if we'll somehow use jewels to gain freedom. If that was the case, I would have used them to fight against Father long ago. I sigh and slip it into Cynthia's jewelry box. "Would you like me to do your face paint?"

She hesitates by the door, looking over my clean face. "Yes, but I'd prefer it on the light side."

Once I'm working on her paint, things feel more natural. Though I've enjoyed having more freedom from it being caked on, the motions are familiar. Comforting. A few minutes after I've finished, a knock sounds.

"Come in," Cynthia calls.

A tarnished enters. "The Chancellor would like to see Serena in his study."

I swallow and put the brush down. "Tell him I'll be right there."

She nods and leaves, closing the door behind her.

My legs wobble as I stand. This is ridiculous. I handled the ceremony, I can handle the punishment for my dress. Why doesn't my body get the message?

Cynthia puts a hand on me. "If he sends you away, will you come and say goodbye first?"

Her hand looks so small on my arm. Fragile. "If I can."

I leave, not daring to look back for fear of losing control of my emotions. The house is void of servants. Not a sound can be heard, save for my light tread. When I arrive at the study, I pause at the door and raise a hand. My arm shakes. I let it fall to my side. How much worse can he be than Father? All this time without punishment has left me too weak. I wanted to find out how barbaric he is. I can do this.

Without further wavering, I knock.

"Come in."

With a steadying breath, I turn the doorknob.

Chancellor Zade is working at the desk. "I'm just finishing some business. Shut the door behind you."

I enter, closing the door behind me. This study is different in every way from Father's. There are two windows instead of one, ending waist high instead of going to the floor. The Envadi's desk is between them. Couches and chairs litter the room. Not a bookshelf in sight, though with a whole book room I doubt he needs more here. I wonder how much of this was Chancellor Jacob's and how much he brought.

I clasp my hands together and use good posture. Nothing of my behavior will give him reason to make the punishment worse. Does he prefer hexes or beatings? I bite my lower lip. How will it compare to Father's punishments?

After pushing his things aside, he rises. "Thank you for waiting. I'm not used to having such duties." He draws nearer, his muscles evident even beneath his coat. Despite telling myself I wouldn't show fear, I can't help but retreat to the wall. "We'll be seeing more of each other. Might as well get used to it. Would you like some tea?"

A tea set and cakes wait on a table I didn't notice before. Perhaps poison is his mode of punishment. Or he wants to force that awful concoction from last night on me. I shake my head. Not if I can help it.

He shrugs, grabs a cake, and shoves the whole thing in his

mouth. It's harder to be scared of him as he brushes crumbs from his face and clothes. After shoving another in his mouth and eating it, he says, "I skipped lunch."

So, he doesn't like to do his dirty work on an empty stomach. The cake tray is loaded. I hope he wants them all. Maybe then he'll be in a better mood. Or too full to be severe.

Two more cakes are demolished. "You're not a chatty thing are you?"

Is that good or bad? Am I supposed to respond? I settle for shaking my head again.

"Guessed that when you girls never say anything at dinner. I thought a change of setting would help. Come in, sit down."

I ease to a maroon chair and perch on it. It's harder than I was expecting. Maybe all those years of not being able to sit in Father's study isn't such a loss. He lounges across from me. A crumb remains on the corner of his lips. I concentrate on it.

"Did you get my note this morning?"

I tense. "Yes, Chancellor Zade."

"Did you do as it said?" He studies me, gaze unyielding.

"I gave it to Phyllis."

"Would you be willing to let me cast a truth spell on you, and ask you about the incident further?"

No. Please, no. He's a hexer for sure. "Do I have to, Master?"

When he doesn't respond right away, I realize my answer was too brash and brace for punishment. His eyes tighten as he studies my face. Finally, he lounges back. He waves his hand. I flinch and he puts it down.

"There's really no need for one," he says. "You were telling the truth last night and if your Father gets the message, it's enough."

Tension eases from me a bit. No punishment then. At least not now.

"Shady business. I'll take care of things though." He grabs another cake from the tray. "Dinner should be good tonight. Cook's really working hard."

The room is silent for a few moments. What is he leading to? I bunch my hand into a fist.

"I guess dinner doesn't interest you either." With a sigh, he stands and gets something from his desk. "Women here are weird creatures."

"No odder than yourself." I clamp my jaws shut. Why did I say that?

The Envadi's brows rise. He stalks toward me and raises his arm. I flinch. Here it comes. He lowers his arm. What is he doing?

"I just wanted to give you this." He raises his hand again, and I realize he's holding a note. It was foolish to recoil. I take it from him. "Councilman Stephen sent it after I asked where your mother was yesterday."

The note is small in my hand. I open it.


ENVADI ZADE,

*Agatha gave birth to a girl two days ago and was unable to attend.*
*Councilman Stephen*


I READ IT TWICE. That's why mother wasn't there. I slouch in my chair. A girl. Another one. The news should be familiar by now, but it still hurts. How is mother doing without me there? Without Cynthia? Is one of my sisters being beaten in my place?

Chancellor Zade kneels next to me so our eyes are level. My heart clenches as I realize the coming threat. "Congratulations on another sister."

The sting of my sorrow sharpens. Of course I shouldn't have gotten my hopes up that he wouldn't punish me. It's only fitting I'm punished. He's just a different type of punisher than Father. False good wishes over another sister, burning the already painful news. I glare at the note and will the tears rising in my eyes to go away. His hand raises. I duck.

With a grunt, he pulls himself up and goes back to his desk. "That's all." I hold the note out, but he brushes me away. "I don't need it. You can keep it. Show Cynthia."

I clutch the note to me as I escape the room. Not only does he want to torture me, but Cynthia as well. The pain grating in my chest intensifies. This subtle form of punishment is worse than being hit or hexed. Much worse.

\* \* \*

THE SOUP COURSE IS SERVED. I watch Cynthia. Her eyes are puffy. She must have cried for some time after I told her the news. Potato soup. I concentrate on not spilling. The Envadi's gaze is on me, but I avoid looking at him. Too much pain there. I didn't think my new Master would be so cruel as to rub in the fact we have another sister.

The courses continue as such. Me peeking at Cynthia. Chancellor Zade peeking at me. Silent. Just like a woman is supposed to be. Except in those moments I can't stop myself from mouthing off.

Finally, dessert is served. A creamy peach treat, though cook has added some strawberries to my plate. At least some good has come of my mouthiness. Someone knows I like strawberries and is going out of their way to give them to me. Bless her kindness, but I don't have an appetite. I dip my fork in, but before I can eat, the Envadi speaks.

"I have a council meeting here tomorrow. You ladies enjoy dinner without me. Best do it in your rooms though. In fact, stay in your rooms all day. Dinner will be brought to you."

Since we aren't allowed on the second floor at Father's, I've never seen the council room. The Chancellor hasn't given us that restriction. I wonder what room he'll use for the meeting.

Eating dinner in our rooms, that will easily be accomplished. Cynthia grins at me and, though I don't feel any joy, I return it. We haven't had a dinner to ourselves since Chancellor Zade's last council meeting. They're always my favorite nights.

"Would you like me to request anything special from cook?"

I stare at him, but Cynthia says, "Can we have duck?"

How can she answer him so casually?

"No problem. I shot a few this morning, I'm sure cook would be willing to prepare them. How would you like it?"

"It doesn't matter, I love duck. She prepared it once before when you were at a meeting and it was simply delicious."

"I'll speak with her. What about you, Serena?"

My name on his lips sounds different. "I haven't had enough variety to know."

"Then we'll have to change that. Did you like the duck, too?"

"It was unusual, but gratifying."

"I had to bribe her into trying it," Cynthia says. "You should have seen the look she gave when they brought it out still looking bird-like. I feared she would forget her manners and leave me to dine by myself."

I glare at her. Why is she telling him this? "I wouldn't leave you to such a fate."

"You did the time Father ordered the whole boar brought to the table."

And was hexed for it later. Chancellor Zade's laughter booms through the room.

My cheeks heat. "I was seven. Things are different at that age. I feared he would spring to life and eat me."

I attempt to mask my embarrassment as his laughter grows and Cynthia joins him. They're absurd. At least I had the excuse of being young, they have nothing. I spear a strawberry.

"I didn't know that was the reason for your running away," Cynthia says. "How awful. Should we tell cook to be sure and cut the duck before it's brought out?"

Ridiculous. "A duck isn't large enough to eat a grown woman."

Chancellor Zade nods. "It's true. Ducks don't eat women. If we ever have boar though, I'll be sure they carve it before bringing it out."

Cynthia giggles.

I jolt to my feet. I won't sit through this if I don't have to. "If you will excuse me, I'm exhausted."

I escape the room wondering if a hex will shortly follow like Father would have cast, freezing me in place to keep me from running. When nothing happens, I give a sigh of relief and hurry to my room. When did Cynthia decide to consort with the Envadi? Didn't his punishment affect her as much as me?

# CHAPTER 17

PHYLLIS POURS TEA for Katherine and me. Though I have obeyed the Envadi's request not to leave my room, Katherine managed to sneak in the servant's entrance. I'm grateful she did, her presence is a welcome relief on a day like this one. Though I hope the fact that Phyllis knows she's here doesn't cause problems.

When Phyllis finishes setting up the tea tray, she hovers close by.

"We have no further need of your services, Phyllis," I say.

She eyes Katherine. "I don't mind staying."

"That will be all. You're excused."

Katherine raises an eyebrow at me. After tisking us, Phyllis exits the room. Katherine opens her mouth to speak. Shaking my head, I raise one finger at her. I wait a moment, then move to the stairway. No one is hovering nearby. I close the door, just in case.

"There. No prying ears." I place a few biscuits on a plate and pour some tea and hand it to Katherine. "Father's gift is a trifle overzealous."

"Still having problems with her?" Her voice is strained.

"Under Father's orders, she forced me to drink a tea that made me obey other's commands. Twice."

With a peek at my empty cup, she says, "That explains you not having any tea."

"I've sworn it off. My expectation of it is rather dismal."

She sets her own cup aside and nibbles on a biscuit. "What did it taste like?"

"Dirt. Or what I would expect dirt to taste like."

"Califrasum root. Nasty stuff. It's supposed to be banned, but Councilman Stephen would have access to it, no doubt."

"Califrasum? I've never heard of it before."

"The council keeps it quiet." She sets her half empty plate down. "Does this mean your engagement ceremony didn't go well?"

"No." My own treats look rather unappealing. "Your dress was perfect though. It was hard enough, but having to go through it in the traditional dress would have been ghastly. Your design really helped me feel more comfortable."

"Any trouble over it?"

I shrug. "Nothing unmanageable. I'm still here."

"I'm grateful you liked it and the Envadi didn't punish you for it."

"I am wondering," I begin to ask, but then pause. Am I really brave enough to do it?

"What is it?"

"I'd like a new dress. But the only money I have is what is left over from before." Technically the Chancellor's, not mine, but he hasn't asked for it.

"What type of dress were you thinking of?"

Somewhere a clock chimes. I fuss with my sleeve. This is more rule breaking, and asking her to break it, as well. "An everyday dress but more like what you made for the ceremony. Something I could get in and out of myself and not have to rely on Phyllis."

She grins. "I'll do it, and you don't need to pay me for it."

"I must give you something for it."

"I'm not taking the little money you have for such a request.

What about something like what I'm wearing, though altered for society."

I take in her clothes. A burgundy blouse tucked into a deep violet skirt. They have minimal adornment, just a few buttons down the front.

"I do like the simpler design. Less fanciful is more to my taste. Mother would never hear of it, but the Chancellor shouldn't care." Unless his punishment with my newest sister is an indication of how things are going to be. But I think I'm willing to risk it.

"I wasn't referring to the embellishments."

"What then? The two-piece?" A laugh escapes me. When her face stays earnest, I stop. "You can't mean it."

"You don't have to."

I spring from my chair and pace in front of the fireplace. "A two piece? Do you know what that would mean?"

She moves in front of me. After grabbing both of my hands in hers, she looks me in the eye. "I know. We would start out subtly. Make them the same color. And fancy them up. You may like simple, but this is too simple for the company you'll be keeping.

"I'd tailor them to look closer to a one piece and put false buttons on the back so it would still look like you needed help. If you're never comfortable, we wouldn't do anything further. But if you like it and no one rejects it, we could maybe try for something else."

Tarnished clothes. She wants me running around dressed as a tarnished. If I haven't doomed myself to be banned yet, this certainly would get me there. Society would shun me. Yet, I did want something better suited to my difficulties with Phyllis. Dressing such seems like going too far. It is going too far. But her gaze is so earnest. Would I like wearing a two piece?

"Why do you want me to dress like that?" I ask.

Her eyes squeeze shut. "Don't you ever tire of wearing what others demand of you?" She opens them and I can't help but think how right she is. I'm so tired of it. "Plus, you're a Chancellor's bride. If you happen to mention where your new, fashionable gowns come from, it could mean more business for me."

I laugh, draining some of the tension. "So, even if you don't accept payment, it's still about the money."

"Money does help. I can't survive on my own without it." Heading back to her chair, she says, "What do you think?"

"I don't know. It's like what I wanted, but a lot more. I've never done anything like this."

"The engagement dress I made was a much bigger step than this."

"That doesn't count. The other options were worse than wearing my underthings."

"And you liked not having to do that, right?"

I sink into my chair. "That's true."

"And how could more freedom with your clothes be bad? Freedom not just for one day, but any day you want it."

"I suppose it wouldn't be all bad." My gloves suddenly feel oppressive. One by one I pull at the fingers and discard them on the arm of the chair. "What I'd really like freedom from is my life." Did I really blurt that out? Surprisingly I find myself meaning it, but still. To say it out loud? Is freedom even an option?

Katherine goes still. "Would you escape if someone helped you?"

"There's no escape when your fiance is a warlock." Of course it isn't an option. A bitter laugh escapes me. "I suppose in contrast, a little wardrobe change isn't so dreadful."

"Good. I have the perfect outfit. I'll adjust it and have it sent. May I stop by next week?"

"Of course. Perhaps Cynthia can join us. I'd like for the two of you to meet."

"And I'd like to meet your sister." She stands.

"Would you mind coming on a council day? The Chancellor would be gone then, though I don't know when it will be."

"I'll figure it out and come when he'll be away."

"Hopefully, I'll see you soon then."

* * *

TWO DAYS LATER, I stare at the package Katherine sent. I should ring for Phyllis to help me dress, but instead pick up the package. It feels heavier than it really is, as if the weight of my trying to gain more freedom in clothing is weighing it down. Not having to bother with Phyllis will be better than any consequences this new outfit could bring.

Chancellor Zade sent a note with breakfast saying he has a gift for me, and wanted to see me in the study. The last, and only, gifts I received were horrid. Despite possibly causing more problems, the dress helps me feel more confident. Will he like it? Hate it? Punish me over it? Or just ignore it? Pushing away my misgivings, I focus on the package.

The strings come undone easily. Beneath the wrappings are a charcoal colored blouse and skirt. I hold them up. Buttons line the front and back, though on closer inspection, only the ones on the front are workable. It's embroidered with a darker shade of thread. Tasteful, but not overdone. Other than being two pieces, it's too elaborate to be a tarnished ensemble.

I like it, but I don't know if I can wear it. The thought of getting dressed myself encourages me to try. I step into the skirt and put the blouse on, button it, and place the belt over it like the instructions suggest. It's easier than I expect. Almost like helping my sisters, but on myself.

The mirror beckons me. I hesitate a moment, then stride to it. The outfit looks good. Really good. I can't believe how much I like it. The blouse is elbow length and has matching gloves. A thick black belt is over the top of the skirt and blouse making it appear that I'm wearing a one piece with the top puffed out. The belt seems masculine, but holds a certain appeal. The material is soft as I brush it with my fingers. The front buttons are appealing rather than confining. They're the size of a strawberry, and spaced apart with fabric covering them instead of tiny ones clustered together. But is it acceptable?

I adjust the belt, though it was perfectly fine, and head for the study. I pause just outside it. When will I learn to take problems on at full force? Not today. I can't bring myself to touch the knob.

"You can go in." I jump at Chancellor Zade's voice. "It's all right."

I put a hand to my chest. "I thought you were in there."

"No, I was taking care of a few things."

He brushes against me to open the door. "Go on in and pick a seat."

I walk past him, aware of our close proximity. The maroon chair was unlucky for me last time, so I pick the sofa. No word about the dress. Maybe he didn't notice, or even better, is ignoring it.

Chancellor Zade opts to sit next to me. Why is he getting so close? The memory of Thomas attacking me surfaces. I inch away from him, ready to defend myself if needed.

"Serena, my family learned that I'm getting married and wants to meet you." The thought of having to meet another warlock isn't as bad as being attacked, but not something I'm eager to do. "They can't come now, so they sent a gift instead."

I won't have to meet them then. Realizing this, I want to relax, but the threat of a gift still hangs over me.

"They are sending a lady's maid. She should be here next week."

Another living gift? His family wants to spy on me, as well. I force my expression to remain pleasant. How am I to handle two spies? Three if you count Cynthia.

A thought hits me. "Wait, what's a lady's maid?"

"She'll basically do what Phyllis has been doing. It's what we call them in Envado."

"What will happen to Phyllis?"

"I'll send her to the kitchens with a note of apology to your Father. We can't refuse a gift from my family, it would be rude, and you've been able to use Phyllis for a little while at least. Unless you'd like to keep her?"

Keep her? I'm ready to load her in a carriage. "No, that will be fine."

Chancellor Zade shifts toward me. Closer than he's been since my branding. "I think it's important to tell you, that while Waverly's condition of being here is a gift, she agreed to it and will be paid for her services."

"She's not working off a debt then?"

"No debt."

"That's different. It's—" How do I feel about this? I suppose it's rather like paying Katherine for making a dress. What if I could work to pay her? Have my own money? Silently, I laugh. An engaged woman never works. Only singles and tarnished. And a woman like me isn't supposed to have money. "It's good."

Chancellor Zade relaxes against the sofa. "I was hoping you'd think so. She won't pose the same problems as Phyllis."

That isn't certain. "A warlock could still make her do or say what he wanted."

"She's an Envadi. Things are different for her than they are for you."

"But if a warlock casts a spell upon her, she wouldn't have a choice."

He takes my hand. It's big and strong. It's harder to think with him touching me, even through a glove. I don't know if I want him to let me go or take hold of my other hand, as well. "Don't worry about it. Like I said, she's different. She can take care of herself."

No woman can do that. The Chancellor wraps his other hand around ours. "You can trust her. With anything."

"Except things I want to keep from you." After the words leave my mouth, I flinch. I want to go back in time and clamp my lips shut. Stop those words from escaping. But it's too late.

He raises an eyebrow. "You have secrets you want to keep from me?"

I swallow.

He gives my hand a squeeze. "I have secrets, too. We all do. I give you my word she's trustworthy and that I have not and will not force her to reveal anything to me you haven't given her permission to do so."

I hold his gaze. My throat tightens.

"I know you won't be comfortable with it, but you can trust her," Chancellor Zade says. He looks at the clock. "Phyllis will be coming by soon." He squirms. "There's one favor I, uh, wanted to ask of you."

I cock my head toward him, curious about his change in behavior and wondering what he could possibly ask of me.

"It seems that most engaged men are more, uh, amorous with their future wives. I haven't wanted to—I don't want—" He glances away before looking me straight in the eye. "Phyllis reports to your Father. I wondered if we might show her something favorable to report."

"What type of something?"

"I'd like to be kissing you when she comes in."

This is wrong. He's sort of doing what I first suspected, but not even close to how I suspected it. "Why are you asking? Warlocks always take what they want."

A light pink fills his cheeks. Is he—? He's blushing. It's strange for him to have the bit of color. I didn't know men could do that.

"Envadi aren't as aggressive with their kisses."

I realize my hand is still in his. It's warm. Too warm. I withdraw. "I see." I fold my arms then unfold them and place them in my lap. "Why did you want to leave this impression again?"

He pulls at the cuff of his sleeve. "It seems word has gotten around that instead of harming your virtue like everyone thought,

I've been too cold and distant. They're saying you should be taken away from me and given to another."

"And this is a problem?"

"They only way they can legally do it, is if I'm dead."

"Oh." Why does he not force his kisses upon me then? I still don't understand. But I'm sure I don't want to go back to Father's house. "I suppose it would be fine."

Instead of relaxing like I expect, he looks more nervous, scratching the back of his neck. He scoots closer to me and puts an arm on the sofa behind me. I become rigid.

"Before I came here, I was engaged to a girl back home."

The shock of the statement shoves the tension from me. "When did she die?"

He gives an unhappy chuckle. "She's perfectly alive and healthy."

"But you can't possibly be my intended then."

"Laws are different there. Engagements aren't as binding. We don't have a ceremony until the wedding and no contract is ever sealed. Just an agreement made, which I broke at our engagement ceremony."

Another should have belonged to him, not me. I should be back at Father's house or owned by someone else. An odd pang trembles through me.

He clears his throat. "I'm telling you so you know why I don't act like the typical groom."

I nod, though I really don't know why it matters. At least to me. It's easy to see why he cares how others may view it, but why does it matter if I know?

"May I kiss you now?"

No. Kisses leave me feeling sick. "I suppose it would be for the best."

He leans closer. I want to pull away. Thomas's kisses were callous. Painful even. The thought of more of that makes me feel queasy. But giving my permission somehow makes it harder to pull away.

His hand reaches up and brushes my face. Flecks of gold are mixed with the green of his eyes. Suddenly, he scoops me into his arms and plops me on his lap. I yelp.

"Sorry, I guess I should have warned you first."

After straightening my skirt with quivering fingers, I hold myself stiff. His nose nuzzles against the side of my neck. Warm lips brush my jaw and sweep along my cheek until they reach the corner of my mouth. My breath comes in shallow gasps. He smells lightly of citrus.

I don't move. His fingers tangle in my hair. His lips hover over mine. A nervous flutter grows in my chest. The creak of the door opening spurs him into action.

His lips touch mine. Flowing and sunny. They grow firmer. It feels so much better than I thought it could. His fingers run through my hair, the tendrils falling out of their confinement. Heat grows between us. He pulls me closer to him. Not only do I manage to refrain from fighting him, but I want to draw even closer.

"Ahem." Phyllis.

He leans away, though still only inches from me. "Why are you interrupting?"

My face feels flushed. I try to slow my breathing.

"Sorry, Chancellor. I was told I was needed in here."

He turns on her, face tight. "You are, but not now. Didn't you get my message?"

"What message?"

"My family also gifted Serena a servant. She'll need to be shown your duties when she gets here."

"My duties, Master? Not hers?"

A grumble sounds from him, vibrating his chest. "No. You'll be working in the kitchen. We're grateful for you services so far, but with this new servant, you're needed elsewhere."

"I see."

"Then leave. I'm busy right now."

My face grows hotter. He presses his lips back on mine. It's much different than when Thomas kissed me. Softer. Slower. Comfortable. Nicer than I thought kissing could be. I don't even mind it. In fact, I think I like it.

Suddenly, he pulls away and sets me back on the couch. Why did he stop? I realize Phyllis is no longer in the room. When did she leave? My face heats. I put a hand to my tingling lips. The fabric of my glove may be soft against them, but feels coarse after his touch.

He clears his throat. "Thank you for your help with that."

"Certainly." Just doing my duty as your possession. Though it felt like more. More what, I can't be sure of.

His lips press together. It's silent a moment before he shakes his head and says, "There's one other thing I wanted to discuss. It's customary for council members to hold a ball the day before they get married."

The council? Why do they even care? "It is?"

"Looks like it. Council members are usually married before they're on the council, so it's not done often, but I've been told we'll need to hold one. Would you be willing to arrange this? I can give input where needed and Waverly's good at that sort of thing. You could ask for help from anyone else you want."

Exactly the sort of thing I hoped never happened. Not like I can refuse. Or maybe I can, he is asking, and he let me pick my dress and go shopping on my own. It could be possible to say no.

I smooth the gown of my charcoal skirt. Perhaps Katherine could make a ball gown for me. I could wear it and tell those who are interested in it who made it. It could aid her, if they like it. But in doing so, I'd create another dress she wouldn't get paid for.

"Will you plan it?" His voice pulls me from my musing.

"Yes, Chancellor Zade."

He brushes the seat of the sofa. "One thing. As part of this type of ball, there's a sacrifice. That will be mine to take care of. If anyone wants to know about it, send them to me. Okay?"

A chill runs through me. I nod.

"Good. Everyone on the council should be invited and those of rank. You probably know better than me." He waves his hand. I duck, but no spell comes. "Maybe not. I'll get you a list."

It sounds daunting. "I'm not very well versed in things like that. Cynthia's good at it. Bethany's better."

"The third oldest?"

"Yes. She loves things like that. She wanted to go to the tournament, but wasn't allowed." I didn't need to say quite so much, but he doesn't look upset.

"I'll ask your Father if she can help."

My load feels lighter already. "That would be fantastic. I'd love it if she could stay with us." Avoid whatever punishments she's been taking in my absence. Hopefully very little.

"I can't guarantee anything, but I'll try."

"Thank you, Chancellor Zade."

"We'll consider it repayment of the favor you just did for me." The vague reference to the kiss makes my face heat again. There's no reason for me to act this way about my duty. He stands. "And you can call me Zade."

That's absurd. Why does he keep bringing it up? "I believe it would be improper."

"Improper? We're getting married."

I rise. "Mother always calls Father Master, Councilman Stephen, or Father."

He shakes his head and rubs his shoulder. "I have to be Chancellor Zade everywhere else. I'd like one place I don't have to be. Please just call me Zade."

A barbarian does own me. "If you insist."

"I do." He moves behind his desk. "Let me know if you need anything else."

"Of course."

"Nice dress, by the way."

I trip over the rug. "Thank you."

He likes the outfit. Called it a dress, but that's probably a good thing. He didn't notice that it was too different. Katherine is wonderful.

As I head back to my room, there's a lot to think on. Much more happened in that room than I expected. A new servant. No matter what he says, I doubt I can trust her. A ball to plan. I don't know how I'll ever manage. Hopefully, Chancellor Zade is able to convince Father to let Bethany come.

And the Chancellor. His attention was much different than I thought it ever could be. Though I continue thinking about all that happened and all that I need to do, the memory of his kiss lingers.

# CHAPTER 18

I WAIT in the entryway for my new servant. It makes me feel like
mother. She often stood waiting for guests or Father like this,
though always people of note, not servant girls. Cynthia lingers
beside me playing with her beaded necklace.

Chancellor Zade didn't stay with us, instead rushing out to
greet her. Treatment of servants in Envado must be more
different than I presumed.

"I can't believe you're getting an Envadi servant," Cynthia says.
"It will make you the talk of the town. Everyone will be jealous.
No one's ever had a servant from Envado before."

"One that's paid? Doubtful they'll be envious."

"Paid?"

"Apparently, it's how things are done there. Chancellor Zade's
manservant must be as well."

"That's different."

I almost mention how I like the idea, but hold back. I don't
want my own sister to think I'm going mad.

The front door opens and the Chancellor strides in, a huge
smile on his face. Behind him is a woman. She's almost as tall as

my intended, but not quite. Certainly taller than my sisters and me. She's wearing a serviceable gown. Dark blue, appropriate length, not too fancy, but neat and clean.

She's close to my age, though older or younger than me, I'm not quite sure. Her face is smooth, cheeks still a little babyish, but she carries herself as if she were, well, as if she were a man. Long striding steps, full of confidence and power. Intimidating. She's very pretty though. Her long blonde hair complements her tanned skin.

"May I present, Miss Waverly." Chancellor Zade gives my new servant a genuine smile.

She looks down at me with piercing brown eyes and grins. "A pleasure to meet you."

This is so different from customary servant behavior, I can do nothing but stare.

"Are you really from Envado?" Cynthia asks.

"I am."

"Do they host balls there?"

What's she getting at?

Waverly tilts her head to the side, brow crinkled. "Of course we do."

"Then you can help us plan." Cynthia turns to me. "Isn't this perfect Serena? She can help make the ball really stand out. Now if only Father allows Bethany to come, it will be the best Chardonia has ever seen."

"You're planning a ball?" Waverly asks.

"I—" The Chancellor clears his throat. "This is something I just learned about. I hoped you'd be willing to help with it."

"I'd love to help." Waverly faces me. "Balls are my favorite sort of thing."

"Let's get you to your room." Chancellor Zade turns to a waiting servant, Phyllis. "Show Miss Waverly to the servant quarters. Once she's ready, show her around and explain her duties."

"Yes, Master," Phyllis says.

He scowls until Waverly says, "Wonderful. I'll see you soon." She curtsies at the Chancellor. "Master." She turns to me and gives another curtsy. "Mistress."

A smile flickers across his face. Phyllis leads her from the room. What sort of servant have I been gifted this time?

\* \* \*

CYNTHIA'S really taken to talking during dinner. I don't believe she's taken a bite of dessert. Rather unfortunate. It's yummy, a sort of flaky shortbread with seared and chilled bananas.

Her excitement about the festivities is a relief, if a bit much to listen to. Inviting adequate dance partners for her will have to be one of my priorities.

I polish off my dessert and wait for Cynthia and Chancellor Zade to finish. And wait.

"We must make good use of the gardens. It might be cool for the fall, but the trees will be lovely colors. If only more flowers would be in bloom."

"We could spell them to bloom for the night," the Chancellor suggests.

"You can do that? That's wonderful. Don't you think, Serena?"

"Yes, it will be. If you'll forgive me, I must excuse myself." Jumping at the chance, I stand.

"I've got to leave, too," Chancellor Zade says, already on his feet.

His dessert is untouched. Come to think of it, he didn't eat much at dinner. And why is he leaving at the same time as me?

"Goodnight, Cynthia," he says.

"Goodnight," she says. "I have more ideas we can discuss in the morning."

Zade leads me through the halls. The farther we go, the more my nerves jitter inside me. It seems to take longer than usual.

What could he want? Is he going to punish me for something? When we stop at the foot of the stairs leading to my room, he pulls both of my hands into his. I'm sure he can feel me shaking, but whether it's from worrying or the contact, I don't know.

He says, "If you have any issues with Waverly, will you tell me?"

Why's he so concerned? Is it for me or her? It must be for her. He's never been this way with me before. "If you wish."

"Thank you. Please be nice to her. It's difficult being in a new country with unfamiliar people."

"Is that how it is for you?"

His lips turn up in an almost smile. "It was. Sometimes it still is. A lot of times, I guess. Notably when I attend council meetings. I'm growing more comfortable with it, though it hasn't been long. I'm sure Waverly will adjust quickly."

The way he says her name, it's different. Protective. Fellow countrymen have to stick together. Still, it's weird for him to care so much about a servant girl, even if they're from the same country. Maybe there's something else. Not just the way he says her name, but how he acted around her. Almost like caring. There has to be more to it. Maybe she's running away from the law and he's trying to help her escape. We're housing a fugitive!

"Is she supposed to be tarnished?"

He drops my hands. "What?"

"I don't mean to be rude, it's just, if you're going to break the law, the punishment will come down on me, as well. I've a right to know." Really, I don't, but I want to know, and he's been more forthcoming than any other warlock.

He folds his arms. "What if I am breaking the law?"

I am being too forward. But, he didn't indicate a punishment with the question. And if it's to help someone like Katherine, I understand, maybe even agree with it. If he's not really breaking the law though, saying I support it could wind up with me being punished. Or turned into a tarnished myself. There's not an easy way to answer.

He stares at me, his face growing harder as time passes.

"I'm sure a Chancellor does what's right," I say.

"She's not on a tarnished list. We don't have tarnished in Envado."

It's my turn to stare at him. Once I'm recovered enough to speak, I say, "What do you do with non-magics or those who break rules then?"

"They're punished according to what fits their crime. Sometimes imprisonment, sometimes they have to fix something or help with the community. It depends."

"What about Waverly then?"

"What about her?"

"Why's she a servant?"

"She chose to become a servant."

"Oh." She chose it? How does a girl choose something? I have fifteen reasons for wanting to know. And counting. A few more months and mother will probably announce another pregnancy. "How can she do that?"

He huffs. "She just decided she wanted to do it and did." He shifts away from me. "Council meeting tomorrow, so I won't see you until the day after."

Tension moves between us with intangible waves. The line must have been crossed somewhere. He's acting so odd, but I can't say I regret asking. Despite his behavior, I know more than before, and without getting punished for it. "Goodnight then."

"Night." He heads down the hall away from me.

I head up the stairs. I said too much. When will I learn to hold my tongue? Punishment would have been dealt at home. At least a knock on the head. But Chancellor Zade didn't do that. He didn't do anything. My steps slow until I come to a halt. He never does anything.

The only spells he's ever cast on me were part of the engagement ceremony. And he's never lifted a fist at me. Perhaps he's trying to lull me into state of ease so the punishment feels harsher when finally dealt. But those kisses. If that is how he's going to treat me, will society have a problem with it? They always accept that men punish us. And how would it be for me? I resume my ascent, but continue wondering about his actions, and what will happen because of them.

# CHAPTER 19

ONCE I'M in my nightgown, I sit at the vanity and work on taking my hair down. It's rather pleasant doing this myself. I keep thinking of how Chancellor Zade noticed my dress and said it was nice. I hope Katherine comes tomorrow while he's gone. I'm excited to see if she's willing to design a dress for the ball. Maybe even another dress or two for the week. That's a lot to ask without pay though. I wish there was a way for me to earn some coins like Waverly's doing.

When my hair is down, I grab a brush and work through the locks. After a few strokes, there's a knock on my door. Cynthia must have an idea that she can't wait to share. "Come in."

Waverly bounces in the room. "Evening." She sets a tea tray on the vanity before me.

I stop brushing my hair mid-stroke. This was supposed to stop with Phyllis. Perhaps it's some other tea. There's no reason to tamper with me when I'm just going to bed. Even if it's not the Califrasum, I've no use for any type of tea.

"What's wrong?" Waverly asks.

I stare at the tea tray. "Nothing."

"Clearly something." She grabs the tea pot and lifts it to a cup. "We can talk about it over—"

"No." I slam the brush on the vanity. I won't be forced into drinking it again. She stops. Is this going to bring problems like it did with Phyllis? Please tell me it won't. "I mean, no thank you. I wouldn't care for any tea this evening."

Her forehead wrinkles. She looks from me to the tea tray and then laughs. "Oh, don't fret. Zade told me about the Califrasum fiasco." His name rolls easily from her. "I wouldn't drink tea either if something like that happened to me. This is just warm milk."

He told her about that? She pours a cup and then grabs another that I hadn't noticed. "I thought we could get to know each other so I can better serve you, and warm milk is always soothing before bed. Or any time really."

I've never heard of a stranger servant. Though perhaps since Phyllis was the only one I've had, I don't have enough to compare with. "I haven't ever tried warm milk."

"Try it for a couple nights. It may seem strange at first, but soon you'll be asking for it. I promise to have your chocolate in the morning."

I take the proffered cup. It doesn't sound like anything a person should drink, only calves. Her eyes are so big and her smile so encouraging, I find myself taking a sip anyway. My face scrunches. It's not right.

She laughs. "Try it a few more times. If you don't grow to like it by next week, I'll quit pestering you." She pulls a chair beside me and pours her own cup of milk. "Now then, what sort of things do you expect of me? Is there a particular way you like things done?"

I set my cup down. "No. I don't think so."

"There's got to be something."

"What type of things are you expected to do?"

She studies me. "Is this a test or don't you really know?"

I shift in my seat. "We had servants at the house, one for mother, but mostly they did things for Father. My sisters and I helped with chores and taking care of each other. I can't imagine needing a servant. The only one I've ever had is Phyllis, whose job you are replacing."

"It's hard for me to understand that. Families in Envado aren't big like yours. Usually they have one child, maybe two."

"The only big families are those who produce a lot of boys. Once they have a girl though, they stop. And families like mine who can't produce a boy."

"I see." Her brows draw together. "Sisters would have been nice, I think. But as for being your servant, I can help with dressing and cleaning. Drawing baths, doing your hair and face paint, bringing you treats, delivering notes. I'll help with the ball of course."

"It sounds like too much. I'm fine with doing things myself. Except for planning the ball. That I could use help with."

She finishes her milk and sets down the cup. "I'll help with that, but Zade said I was going to get paid extra for it, so I'll need some other duties. Let's start with this one." After grabbing my brush, she stands behind me. Part of me wants to be grateful for her assistance, but the other part is resentful that she's taking it from me. "Your hair is so long. It must be hard to take care of."

I shrug. "We aren't allowed to cut our hair, only trim it. With so many sisters, we take care of each other's hair. But being here, I've been doing it on my own. Until Phyllis came that is. Sometimes Cynthia and I still assist one another."

"Well, I'm a bit rusty at doing hair, but I'll soon remember and can help make up for your other sisters not being here."

The brush moves over my hair as if one of my sisters was using it. Once she's done, she turns down the covers.

"If you need anything, feel free to ring for me."

"I will." Except I won't. It seems odd to have someone at my beck and call.

She gives a half smile, as if she knows what I'm thinking. "Goodnight."

"Night."

Once she's left the room, I climb into bed. Yes. The strangest woman I've ever met. I blow out the candle and pull the blankets over me. Strange. I think I like her.

* * *

A NOISE STARTLES ME AWAKE. Moonlight shines through my window. What woke me? I stretch out on my back. Usually it's one of my younger sisters that wakes me, scared or in need of a drink. That chore often goes to Cynthia or Bethany, but sometimes it falls to me. Won't happen here though. Unless Cynthia comes, which she hasn't in the two and a half months we've been here.

The door is closed. It's hard to tell in the dark, but I don't see her coming toward the bed. Maybe something in my dream that woke me.

I curl up on my side, facing my window seat. I wonder how Cynthia's getting along. Many times I've awakened in the night at Father's, she was up. If I can't get back to sleep, maybe I'll go visit.

My eyes give a heavy blink. My limbs relax. Tomorrow then. I'll see her tomorrow. My eyes close. Then I jolt awake. Did that shadow just move?

Sleep flees from me. My body tenses. The shadow isn't moving anymore, but I can't think of any object in my room that would cast it. It's a lumpy, round shape, sort of like a person crouching. Someone's in my room.

Do I feign sleep or call for help? Who would even be in here? Has the Envadi come for me? I swallow, trying to force the fear down. The action does no good. If it is him, no one may come for help, but I won't sit by and do nothing.

There's nothing close by I can use to defend myself. The best I can do is ring for help and try for the door. Where to go after that? I don't know if anywhere is safe. I hope someone comes when I ring.

With several deep breaths, I bolt from the bed, yanking on the cord as I pass. The rope burns my hands as it slides through. I dart for the door, not daring to check behind me. It's still too far away when hands grab my waist and I'm knocked to the floor. My head bangs against the wood. Blood fills my mouth. I thrust my head back, slamming into my attacker. He grunts.

Hands scramble across me. I claw at them.

"Wenchit!" A tenor. Not the Chancellor. Who's attacking me?

The pressure lifts off me. I scramble on my hands and knees toward the door. Before I get more than a few feet, I'm flipped over onto my back. Meaty fingers wrap around my wrists and hold them above my head. He smells of damp earth and body odor, sort of like Thomas.

"Get off me!" I buck and kick, trying to get free.

A slap stings my face. "Where's the Envadi?" What? Why do they want him? "Where is he?"

The door opens.

"Help!" I yell and struggle to get my hands free.

A crack. The pressure is gone from me. I flip back to my hands and knees and crawl away.

"Light a lamp!" A female voice. Waverly?

Whack! A green spell zaps toward her. She twists away and it crashes on the wall behind her.

I rush to my night stand and light the lamp.

A man in black has his hands wrapped around Waverly's throat. She reaches up, trying to pry his fingers off her. No luck.

If I do nothing, she's going to suffocate. I jump onto his back, hitting him with everything I've got. Immediately, he releases her and casts a maroon spell at me. I drop to the ground before it hits.

A teal and pink spell hurtles toward the attacker. Where'd that come from? Does the attacker have help? I look around for more intruders.

Chancellor Zade stands just inside my room. "What are you doing here?"

Without hesitating, the attacker flashes an orange spell out the window and bolts after it. The Chancellor darts after him, but stops at the window. He throws several spells from the window and then shoots one through my door.

"Are you both well?"

I'm trembling, but don't think I'm injured. "I'm well. Waverly?"

She coughs. I fill a glass of water and bring it to her. Dark bruises are already forming on her neck. She croaks out, "I'm all right. Or will be."

He crosses to her, puts a hand on her throat, and emits a faint blue light with streaks of red. When he takes his hand away, the marks are gone.

"Thank you." Her voice back to normal.

His mouth thins. He comes to me. "Do you want me to heal you, too?"

I put a hand to my cheek. "It's nothing."

"Are you sure?"

Very. I don't want magic cast on me ever again if I can help it. "Yes."

"What happened?" Chancellor Zade asks.

Next to his presence I feel as helpless as I did a moment ago while being attacked. I shiver and Waverly wraps a blanket around me.

"I woke to a noise and rang for help. Waverly came before anything really happened. He asked where you were."

His face hardens. "Speak of this to no one. I'll put extra guards and wards around the house. Let me know if you have any more problems, but you shouldn't."

With that he leaves the room. What's going on? Does he expect there to be more problems?

Wavely's pale. "Did you need anything else?"

"No, I'll be fine."

She nods. "Ring if that changes."

She helps me into bed, tucking the blankets tight around me. After she leaves, I stare at the window. Why is someone trying to attack the Chancellor? Is it because he's not acting eager to marry me? The kiss was supposed to fix that. I toss and turn, fear chasing away any hint of sleep.

# CHAPTER 20

A KNOCK SOUNDS at my door, and Waverly enters, carrying a tray. I leave the window seat to sit at the table.

"Are you all right this morning?" She sets the tray down and pours some chocolate.

There's no sign left of the struggle last night on either of us or the room. Inside myself though, the same couldn't be said. I'm exhausted from jumping at every noise I heard last night. "Shaken."

"Me, too. If truth be told. I didn't sleep very well after that."

"Me neither. Do you know any more about why it happened?"

"Only what Zade has told me." She looks at the tray. "Have some chocolate, maybe that'll help."

I take a biscuit and a cup. "Thank you."

"No problem. Warm milk soothed me, but I figured this would work better for you." She fixes a crease in my already made bed. "A note was sent for you. Someone named Katherine will be by to see you this morning."

"Good, I was hoping to see her soon."

After I've eaten and dressed, Cynthia enters wearing a dark teal gown with matching metal bracelets and necklace, and helps herself to the last biscuit. Part of me wants to tell her what happened last night. But I don't want to scare her and Chancellor Zade said not to tell anyone.

"I've heard your famous seamstress is going to join us. Is it true?" Cynthia's eyes are bright.

"It is."

"Oh, goody! Do you know when she's going to arrive?"

"She should be here about now," Waverly says. "Would you like me to send her in if she is?"

"Please do," I say.

Waverly leaves and a few minutes later returns with Katherine who's laden with packages. While setting them on the bed, she says, "You're not wearing the dress. Didn't you like it?"

"Come sit," I say, some of my stress from the previous evening grows lighter at seeing her. "Have some chocolate."

"Chocolate?" She hurries to get a cup. "Thank you, but is this your way of not talking about the dress? It's fine if you hate it."

"No, I just remembered you like chocolate. The dress I love. I wore it yesterday. I was just telling my new servant, Waverly, about it." I gesture to Waverly. "The Chancellor's family sent her to me from Envado. I'm already learning new things from her. She's wonderful." And she risked her life for mine last night. I motion to my sister. "This is Cynthia, the eldest of my sisters."

"Good to meet you both." Katherine gives them both wide grins.

"I've been anxious to meet you since seeing Serena's engagement gown," Cynthia says. "It was superb."

A small smile graces Katherine's mouth. "Thank you." She turns to me "You liked your new dress then. Good. Did you wear it for the Chancellor?"

For some reason, my cheeks grow warm. "I did."

She tilts her head closer to me. "And what did he say?"

Waverly and Cynthia also give me their full attention. My cheeks grow warmer. "He said it was nice."

158

They smile.

"Good for him," Waverly says, but her expression is more subdued than usual. Why is she somber? Did she not want my dress to get approved? Does she think it gives me too much freedom? It better not become an issue she convinces Zade about. I like it too much to have her pushing me back into traditional dresses.

"Wonderful," Katherine replies. "It means the things I brought won't go to waste."

"What did you bring?" I eye the packages on the bed.

"Work's been a bit slow lately. I had to do something to keep me and my workers busy." Her face glows, but I can't help but feel guilty. Doesn't she need something she can get paid for?

"Please tell me they aren't all dresses for me."

Her cheeks grow rosier. "They are. There should be enough that you won't have problems finding something to wear."

"All the time your workers spent and the materials, I simply can't accept this. You should try to sell them in your shop."

Katherine frowns and moves to the bed. She opens a package on top. "No tarnished would wear such a thing, and you are my only other customer."

In the package is a black gown. She holds it up. Another two piece. Embroidered with silver thread, almost too light of a shade to be acceptable, but such a small amount, it will pass. She's right, it's decorated more than anything a tarnished would wear.

"Katherine, it's—" I don't know what to say.

"It's lovely." Cynthia moves to brush the gown with her fingers. "It matches your hair."

"That's what I was hoping," Katherine says.

I press my lips together and reach for one. "May I?"

Katherine says, "Please do."

I take the string off it. Another lovely two piece awaits. We all start opening packages. The joy within me grows with each new reveal. Dresses with laces in the front and two pieces with buttons. Matching gloves and ribbons. It's too much, but it's perfect.

I tell Katherine, "These are beautiful."

"Let's try them on and see if they need any adjustments."

So I try things on and stand while things are pinned. Then another dress. And another. Most need few, if any, adjustments. Katherine got them just right. Waverly and Cynthia ohh and ahh over the choices. I feel like doing the same.

"Well, I'm starved," Cynthia says when I've tried all the dresses and I'm back in one that fits. "Why don't I bring us a tray for lunch? Then I'll help with some of the sewing if you'd like, Katherine."

"You can sew?" she responds.

"She's the best seamstress in our household," I say.

"I can get the food so you can stay and work." Waverly stands.

Cynthia beats her to the door. "I'll grab it. It'd be nice to stretch my legs."

"Let me help at least. It's part of my job and I don't mind"

"That'd be great. We'll see you ladies soon," Cynthia says.

After they've left, Katherine says, "They seem nice."

"Cynthia's sweet. I don't know much about Waverly, yet. Did you know that in Envado, servants are paid?"

Katherine keeps her gaze on the skirt she's hemming. "I'd heard. How do you feel about that?"

I lower my voice. "It's a little strange, but a good idea. As much wealth as the Chancellor has, I don't envision it being a problem, but if we ever get close to going into debt, it would be nice to work it off before becoming indentured."

"Could you handle a life of work?"

"I think so. I wasn't pampered at home. I did as much as the servants both here and back at Father's. Maybe a little more work. I suppose I wouldn't really know until I tried. If I become tarnished, I will find out."

Katherine looks up from her work. "Do you think it's a possibility?"

"It's always a possibility now that I'm engaged. I'll spend the rest of my life worrying it may become my fate." My gaze roams over her inked face. "Not that I mean to imply your life is undesirable."

"It's not for everyone, or even most, but sometimes it's for the best."

What can she mean by that? She goes back to stitching, but keeps darting her gaze to me. "Do you ever think about escaping?"

"I've thought of it more than I should," I whisper. Since coming here and discovering things are different than I was always taught.

She finishes the hem and sets the skirt to the side. Grabbing a hold of my hand she says, "Serena, I can help. If you ever want to escape, or need to, I'll do whatever I can to help."

I glance at the door. If anyone should overhear us talking like this, what would be our fate? I don't want to find out, but I also want to know what she means. "How would you do such a thing?"

"We'd make something work." She gives my hand a squeeze. "Will you come to me, if you need to?"

I think of what I've been through. Do I want to leave? Truly leave? What would my sisters do without me? "How would I ever promote your dresses if I weren't here?"

She sits back and smiles. "It'd be harder. But the offer stands." She grabs another skirt and threads a needle.

"Do you mind if I ask a personal question?" I say.

"You can ask. I may not answer."

"Fair enough." I shift in my chair, wishing my stitches were good enough to help. If I could maybe it would keep us away from this conversation. Or at least give the appearance I was doing something useful instead of delving into questions a woman shouldn't ask.

"How did you get to be a tarnished?"

"Ouch!" A dot of blood forms where she pricked her finger.

"Are you all right?" I move to help her, but she stops me with a wave.

"Happens all the time." She grabs a discarded piece of fabric to dab it with. "I became a tarnished like everyone else. Why do you ask?"

"Father and mother threatened that if I didn't behave, my future husband might force me to become one. I wondered what it was like."

"Most male tarnished become so at their three-year-old test. Without magic, they're never given a chance to know anything else." A bitter edge taints her voice.

"You don't agree?"

"Who am I to say what the council laws should be? I'm not a man and certainly not a warlock."

"But if you were, would you agree?"

"If you were, would you?"

I watch her hands deftly weave the needle in and out of the cloth. Should non-magic men be tarnished from childhood? Should they experience a life more like what I grew up with instead? Living a life of hard labor whether with a warlock or trying to make things work on their own like Katherine? They still have choices, but not as many as the warlocks do.

"Are many tarnished children beaten?"

For the first time since the subject began, she looks at me. "What?"

"I know your men can't hex anyone, but do the caretakers beat them?"

Her lips tighten. "Tarnished children have already been through testing and taken out of their homes. That's hard on any three-year-old. We know better than to beat them."

"No one ever does?"

"Sometimes it happens, but it's the exception. Personally, I'd never raise a hand to a child and neither would any other tarnished I associate with, man or not."

Perhaps the compulsion comes with those who use magic. "I think that—"

My door opens. I exchange a look with Katherine. Did they hear us? The conversation is over. For now, at least. Cynthia and Waverly enter with trays of food. I rise to help, hoping my actions will help them think everything is as it should be.

"This looks delicious," I say. "I don't know which I'll eat first."

"You should have seen Phyllis's face when we came to grab a tray," Cynthia says. "I don't think she's very happy with you."

No hint that she overheard something she shouldn't. I shrug. "I wasn't happy with her either."

Once the plates are dished and my hunger abated somewhat, I say to Katherine, "These clothes will be more useful than you know. Apparently when a council member gets married, they hold a ball. It will give me the perfect chance to show everyone your dresses."

Katherine eyes widen. "When's it taking place?"

"You'll get paid from all those warlocks who attend and don't want their possessions out done." Cynthia laughs. "It's the day before the wedding. I can't wait."

"A ball before the wedding?" Katherine says.

I wish the wedding didn't have to be associated with it. Every time it's brought up, my insides mush together. The ball though, it's coming together better than I hoped. "I'm trying to get help planning everything. Cynthia has many ideas. Hopefully, my other sister Bethany, will be able to help. She's always had a knack for helping mother plan, though she hasn't attended any as of yet. And instead of just helping put everything together, maybe Waverly can give us an Envadi flare."

"I don't know how things differ, but I'd be willing to tell you what things are like in Envado," Waverly says.

"We've already discussed how I can't pay," I say, hoping I'm not being too forward. That she really does want people to see me wearing her things, "but maybe you could make my ball gown? I might be able to get you some new orders from it."

"Sounds good, if we can convince the other guests to buy something. And for your dress, it'd be a thrill to do. I'll get started on ideas right away." Katherine stands. "I must go anyway. I'll take these dresses and get them to you as soon as they're finished."

"You're already doing so much. Thank you, and don't rush. I'll manage with what I have," I say.

"Then I'll only work on outfits I want to. Let me know how the ball plans go."

"I will."

Waverly gathers the dresses that still need alterations and packages them. The rest go in my closet. Tomorrow, I'll be able to dress myself and I owe it all to Katherine's generosity. But the conversation about the tarnished makes me wonder if there is more to her than just the generosity she has shown.

Cynthia's moving toward the door to help Katherine, when it bursts open. Chancellor Zade looms before us, his gaze stopping on Katherine.

My hand goes to my throat. Is he going to chastise me for having a tarnished over? Will he punish her for being here? It's my fault, not hers.

"I heard you had a guest," he says.

I lick my lips. How much do I tell him? Is it worse if she's here for no reason or if he knows what she's been helping with. No reason would be worse. "Y-yes. My seamstress."

He does the most astonishing thing. He walks to her with his hand outstretched. "Good to meet you, I'm Zade."

With more confidence then I'd have, she places her hand in his and tilts her head down. "I'm aware of who you are Chancellor. If you'll excuse me, I was just leaving."

"I didn't mean to scare you off."

"We finished what was needed."

Will he ask what we did? If he sees the dresses, will he make me give them back? Punish her for them? I grip the side of my chair.

"I'll see you out then." He takes a few packages from her and looks at me a moment before they depart.

The packages were within his possession. Will he open them while escorting her out? My grip tightens as I worry about what he'll do if he discovers just what kind of dresses a tarnished has been making for me.

# CHAPTER 21

A COOL BREEZE sends a shiver through me. Or maybe fear is making me feel colder. I pull my shawl tighter around me. Though there are guards posted and protection spells, I can't help but check around for an intruder. If I wasn't so sick of being inside, I wouldn't bother venturing out. But staying indoors has been hard.

Stopping in front of the biggest water feature in the garden, I scan the area for signs of trouble. When none appear, I let myself relax a bit. There's been no further sign of problems. Maybe Chancellor Zade took care of them.

The pond is decorated with fish and lily pads. Flowers are blooming all around, just like the rest of the garden. With a bit of work, in two months it will be a beautiful sight and hopefully fall won't be too cool for our guests to enjoy.

I debate if I'm brave enough to go further into the garden when I hear the clomp of footsteps. I whirl toward the direction the sound comes from. Am I about to be attacked again? There's no way to ring for a servant out here. If I scream, will a guard be close enough to hear? Or will the attacker cast a spell to keep anyone from hearing my cries for help?

The sound moves closer. What should I do? Before I decide, Chancellor Zade strides around the hedge. Most of the tension drains away. Not an intruder, just the Chancellor. He's most improperly attired without his coat. Though I find myself not wanting to, I avert my gaze anyway. He doesn't look angry. Maybe he's not upset about the dresses. Or perhaps he didn't even open them.

"Enjoying the garden this morning?" His casual question eases my worries over Katherine and the dresses.

"Yes, it'll be a fine addition to our party." My eyes drift back to him and I hurry to look away. "Aren't you cold?"

He laughs. "I'm hot. That's why I'm not wearing my jacket. I live in the mountains back home and it's always much colder than this."

"Oh." I wonder what that would be like.

"I can run back to my room and get my jacket, if it'd make you more comfortable. I was working in my study. Didn't think to see you this morning, but something came for you."

I think about his offer. I'm not sure more comfortable is the right description. It would be easier to look at him without feeling... different. "What came for me?"

"Well, it came for me, but it's really for you." He holds out a letter, his face impassive. "It's from your Father."

From the lack of emotion on his face, I can't tell if it will hold good or bad news. My hand quivers as I take the note. "Have you read it yet?"

"It was addressed to me, so yes I did."

"Is it about Bethany?"

"Yes."

It takes me a couple of tries before I'm able to open it.


*ENVADI ZADE,*

*I received your request for Bethany's aid in addition to Cynthia's for planning your upcoming ball. It is a very hard request to comply with since the two older girls are already with you. But upon consideration, I realized you can't possibly manage without more help.*

*I must inform you that at times Bethany can be willful. You have my permission to punish her. She should need it often as Serena does. Expect her this afternoon.*

*If you have any further need, let me know and I will assist in any way that I can.*

*Councilman Stephen*


BEFORE ROLLING THE PAPER UP, I brush my fingers across the words. I hand it back and sit on a nearby bench.

"I thought you would be more excited to hear," Chancellor Zade says. "Are you unhappy?"

When I stay silent, he sits next to me. I glance at the letter he still holds.

"It's not that. I'm pleased she's coming." But hearing about liberal punishments is too much. Chancellor Zade hasn't done much to me yet, but he could. Father obviously thinks he should. Now the Chancellor holds that power over my sister, as well.

"Are you upset over my power to punish her?"

I clench my fingers together and say nothing.

"If it is, I can assure you she'll come to no harm, just as I haven't punished you."

I should stay silent. Bethany would be shaking her head at me right now if she was here. "Yet, you have punished me once. I'm sure you have plans for more."

"You must be confusing me with someone else. I've never lifted hand nor hex to you."

"You didn't have to. Punishment was delivered all the same."

He squeezes the bridge of his nose. "Sorry if I've offended you in some way. If you don't mind me asking, how did I do it?"

"How can you forget something so cruel?"

He jumps from the bench. His words harsh. "Forgive me if I remember doing nothing cruel. Please feel free to remind me."

"Your phony congratulations over my new baby sister. Taunting me with the note of her birth and insisting I share it with Cynthia. I would have preferred the customary beating for another sister instead of your false words."

He spins to face me, dropping his hands to the side. After a moment, he says, "You thought that was cruel?"

"Of course." But even as I say the words, I can't help but doubt them. He looks so shocked, his face drawn, brows raised, he's earnest.

He kneels on the ground before me so we're about eye level and takes my hands. "Serena, I beg for your forgiveness. I had no idea of you being hurt by my comments. In Envado, a birth is always treasured and my mother taught me to treat those surrounded by a birth with respect."

I stare at him, unable to comprehend his words. Could it really be? Did he truly not mean to hurt me? Does he really not mean to ever punish me or my sisters? His eyes search mine. I can't help but want to believe him. A small flame of hope lights within me.

"How do I know your words are true and not meant to set me up so the punishment is worse when delivered?"

He hangs his head. His words are barely audible. "What have they done to you?"

After a moment, he lifts his head and gives my hands a squeeze. "I doubt anything I say or do will make a difference on how you feel, but I'll give you what I can. You have my word that I will not intentionally harm you or your sisters. If I do, tell me and I'll fix it."

His hands are so firm, but giving, wrapped around mine. I don't know if I should believe him. I nod to let him think he's getting his way. At the very least it will give me time to think on it.

With a sigh, he withdraws his hands and retakes his seat next to me. "Is that why the note bothered you?"

"Yes and no."

"Tell me what else bothered you."

I hesitate then say, "The note was just a reminder of where I used to be and where my sisters still are. Without me there, I don't know what's happening to them."

"Do you want to talk about it?"

"No." I slump back. He sits without saying a word. "Is it like this in Envado?"

"I hope that my actions have been a good example of what things are like there. Here though, everything isn't just different. It's wrong."

"Wrong how?"

He looks as if he's going to say something, but shakes his head. After a moment, he says, "It doesn't matter. I have a council meeting I should prepare for, and you probably have some arrangements to make for your sister's arrival."

"I suppose I have."

But neither of us move. Cynthia readied a room across from hers, in hopes that Bethany would come. There's not much else to do until she gets here. I wonder what Chancellor Zade must do in preparation for a council meeting. I watch him from beneath lowered lashes. He slouches against the bench, eyes unfocused. Whatever he does must require a lot of thought. What is he thinking about?

I watch him for a minute before building enough courage to ask, "Is it hard getting ready for a council meeting?

His eyes come into focus. "You really want to know?"

I lick my lips. He said he wouldn't punish me. Gave his word. Did he mean it? I steel myself in case he didn't. "I do."

"Why?"

Why? It's something I've never thought of before, but all my life Father has attended council meetings. Warlocks discuss them all the time, even ones not on the council, though in general terms. Only tiny bits of clues slip out as to what goes on. I want to know more about those little hints. Know why I'm forced to marry when Father says I must. Know why my sisters and I must be punished.

I straighten my skirt. "It seems to me there's a lot more going on than I always thought, and it'd be nice to know. Perhaps attend a council meeting." I slap a hand over my mouth. After backing as far away from him as I can, I watch for signs of delivering pain. I've never been so outspoken before.

"Are those your thoughts or did your Father put you up to this?"

Not moving my hand from my mouth, I shake my head.

His voice grows quieter. "No to which one, Serena? You have to tell me."

I put my hand on my skirt and clench it. I don't dare take my eyes from him. "Not my Father."

"I need to be sure. Would you be willing to let me cast a truth spell on you?"

I bite my lower lip. He's asking and not just doing, that has to be better, right? Still, I don't want a spell cast on me.

"I won't do it without your permission, so if you want continue this discussion we can after you answer a few questions under the spell. Any time you want to stop, we will, nothing further. You don't want to do it, fine, but I can't tell you more until I know for sure."

If I don't continue it now, I'll never do it. How much do I trust him? Not at all. Or perhaps some. He's more trustworthy than Father. And I do want to know more about the council. The tarnished. The multi-wives law. The sacrifices. Why are those necessary? The fate of me and my sisters. Is having the chance to know a little more about them worth allowing a spell?

"If I let you cast the spell on me, will you answer my questions?"

"I'll answer what I can. There are some things I can't say. Like the engagement ceremony."

I nod. That I understand. "Cast it. Before I change my mind."

"Let's do it then." He lifts his hands and I can't hide a flinch. "It won't hurt."

A white light shines from his hands and encompasses me. I feel only the air around me though, nothing more.

"Have you ever had a truth spell cast on you before?"

"No. Father never did." He mistakenly assumed I'd never dare lie to him.

"Tell a lie then, any lie, so you know what it will be like."

Lie on purpose, what does one say to that? I go with something easy. "I've only brothers."

The light surrounding me pulses and becomes dark.

"To get it back you need only tell a truth. Remember, if at any time you'd like to stop, just let me know and we will."

"All right."

The light goes back to white. Chancellor Zade moves closer to me on the bench. "Are you asking questions about the council on behalf of your Father?"

"No."

"Why are you asking about it?"

"I'm curious about what's happening. I want to know more." The light remains white.

"Are you in any way trying to get me off of the council?"

"No."

"Are you associated with anyone trying to end my life?"

I tilt my head to the side. Though I know of the intruder searching for him, I wasn't expecting the question. "I'm not."

He nods like he anticipated my answer, but a few of the lines ease from his face. "What do you know of my family?"

"Your family? Why is that relevant?"

"You can answer the question and we'll talk about the council, or we can be done."

I didn't know his family was such a taboo subject. "I know very little about your family and just what you've told me. You respect your mother."

He gives a small smile. "What are your intentions toward me?"

My intentions toward him? "I have none."

The light turns ashy. He lifts his brows. I look at the fountain. Why doesn't the spell like that answer? Why don't I? "I don't know what my intentions are." The light pales a bit, though still off. "You're different than other warlocks, but I don't know if I can trust it. If you're true to your word, I wish you nothing ill."

The light flashes back to white. "And if I don't stay true to my word?" He holds up a hand. "Never mind, don't answer that. I'll stay true to my word. I didn't cast this spell to invade your privacy."

He waves his hand and the spell lifts from me. "Your Father wants me out of the council and I have to protect myself against that. Thank you for being willing. What do you want to know?"

It almost seems silly now, wondering about the council. But one thing did make me wonder. "Why did you ask me if I was associated with those trying to end your life?"

"There have been more death threats against me than the attempt you know about. A few, not enough to get concerned over, but I want to make sure before I tell you too much."

"A few?" As in more than one? My mouth goes dry.

"Nothing to get concerned over."

It sounds like something worrisome. "Do you know where the threats are coming from?"

He shakes his head. "A few guesses, but no evidence of anything. In fact, I would feel better if you learned to use a gun."

"A gun? Me? I'm not sure I'm supposed to touch one." No one in Chardonia uses one, man or woman.

"I checked the laws, there's nothing that says you can't. The idea might sound foreign, but it'd help me out if you had some sort of protection if they come to the house again. It's warded, but sometimes that's not enough."

This is something he seriously thinks I should do. Remembering how scared I was when I heard him coming, thinking he was an intruder and not knowing what to do, helps me understand where he's coming from. But one of those guns in my hands? "I don't know."

"You can think it over, but it'd be best." His expression eases. "Didn't you want to know something about the council and not things about me?"

After talk of guns, my brain feels muddled. "I don't know what to ask. It was silly of me."

"Not silly. You were willing to put yourself through a spell of honesty. If you ever think of anything, please come ask me."

"You asked me what I know of your family, is there something I should know about them?"

"I guess if we're to be married, you should know something. They're nice. Different from your parents. A lot different. Mom never lets Dad tell her what to do. In fact it usually goes the other way around."

I'm stunned. "Your mother punishes your Father?"

"No, never that. Mom's just the bossy one."

"Oh." The concept is still foreign to me. How can she be bossy without getting punished for it?

"Do you have any other questions?"

The only one I can remember right now is the major slip I let out about going to a council meeting. I'm not bringing that up again. "If I think of anything, I'll let you know."

"Good." He pushes some rocks around with the toe of his boot. "If there's anything else you'd like to ask me or do with me, I could fix that, too."

For some reason, the statement makes my face hot. There's nothing for us to do together until we marry and that's not a part of my life I want to contemplate. "Like what?"

He gestures at nothing. "Anything."

"What did you do with your other fiancée?"

An unhappy chuckle snorts from him. "She's not like you." I try not to bristle as he gets a faraway look in his eyes. "We danced at balls, had dinner together with our families, had tea together with our mothers. Talked. That sort of thing."

So the dancing thing is one of them, and he has met my family and talked to them. "We haven't danced at a ball, but how's the rest any different?"

"She's just—"

"Serena," Cynthia calls out, interrupting our conversation before I can learn how his fiancée is better than me. I'm not sure if I want to know more about her anyway. Zade seems more attached to her than I thought and it makes my insides give an odd twist.

# CHAPTER 22

FEELING RESENTFUL, I watch Cynthia round a hedge, her chocolate-colored dress trailing behind her, a matching set of jewelry with it. "There you are. Father's carriage is coming down the lane."

The resentment is replaced by excitement. "He sent word Bethany's to join us."

"He's letting her come? Why aren't we out there yet?"

She races back to the house. I follow her as fast as my legs will let me without running. Chancellor Zade strides ahead and opens the door for us. Once inside, we follow him through the halls to the entryway where he once again holds the door open for us.

I rush outside, then remember myself and take the last few steps at a more sedate pace. Cynthia dashes all the way to the carriage. I suppose I should just be grateful she came and found me before running out.

At the bottom of the steps, I wait. The Chancellor must have decided to wait inside or went to do some work because he doesn't follow. A footman opens the carriage doors. Bethany emerges looking as if she's grown since I last saw her. Her dark-blonde hair is pulled back away from her face showing off her sparkling green eyes and innocent face. She smiles as Cynthia launches into a narrative of our dealings. At one point Bethany nods, but Cynthia doesn't stop long enough for her to do any more.

Finally, Bethany gestures to the house and the girls walk toward me. Every bit of lightness is instantly gone. My heart sinks to the pit of my stomach. I want to cry, but hold it in and let myself seethe. Bethany is limping.

Any accident would have been healed already. Father punished her and thought the crime warranted natural healing. But she's never been rebellious or as outspoken as me. I can't imagine her doing anything to cause such punishment. Maybe it's meant as a reminder to me. Breakfast sours in my stomach. I can't get away from him even here. I'll always be owned and I or someone I love will suffer because of it.

I think back to the letter he sent. It implied that the Chancellor has been punishing me, so maybe I really have nothing to do with why she's been hurt. Besides, Father's never hurt one of us to teach another. Though he did threaten to if I wouldn't drink the tea, but I'm sure it's only because he knew it would work. I don't know if he thinks it would be an effective punishment for me or not.

Bethany manages a smile when she reaches me, but her eyes are tight with pain. She's hurting worse than she'd like us to know. Cynthia falls silent.

"Hello, Serena."

"Bethany." I try to pour all of my love for her in that one word. "Welcome to the Chancellor's house."

Her gaze travels over the manor behind me. "It's huge. I wonder how many times Father's would fit inside it?"

"About seven and a half," Cynthia says. We both look at her. "What? I know I shouldn't have, but I was curious as well."

Bethany giggles, but it doesn't last long. I'm hurt, angry, sad for her too much to bother with more than half a smile. She still has to get up the stairs to the house then there's all the stairs to her chamber. Even with the servants' help, she'll hurt too much. It won't do.

Bethany says, "I'm excited to see the room we'll share. If the outside is like this, I can't imagine how big it is inside."

"There's absolutely no sharing involved," Cynthia says. "Serena wouldn't let me, even when I tried."

"How do you manage to sleep without an elbow in your ribs?"

"It's easier to overcome than you might think," I say. "Cynthia, would you mind taking Bethany to the parlor? A little refreshment would be good before setting her loose on the place."

Bethany glances at me as if she knows I'm trying to help ease her pain, but doesn't say a word.

"Certainly," Cynthia says. "Cook makes the most wonderful treats."

We start up the stairs. While I hover around Bethany in case she needs me, Cynthia prattles on.

"And Serena will have to show you the new wardrobe she's acquired. It's the most wonderful thing I've ever seen. Just look at the dress she's wearing now. Those laces in the front, see them? Those are the ones that tie so she doesn't have to have help getting in and out of it. Isn't that wonderful? Her seamstress, Katherine, is fantastic. I can't wait to see what she comes up with for Serena's ball gown." She stops long enough to open the door. "I'm glad you're here to help. We've so many things to do."

Something is weird with Cynthia as well. She's always chatty, but not to the point of excluding other's from the conversation completely. Doesn't she think anything about Bethany's pain?

"I'm glad, as well," I say, forcing myself to be heard over Cynthia's next sentence. "In fact, I'd be rather lost without you." We reach the top of the stairs and enter the house. The Chancellor is nowhere in sight. Blast him.

"I'm glad to be here," Bethany says, her voice betraying her pain.

"Good." I don't want to leave, but can't help if I stay. "Now I'm afraid I must attend to something for just a moment, then I'll be back and we'll get you settled properly."

Bethany nods, her face pale.

Cynthia gives me a look, part curiosity and part upset. She says. "Don't worry, I'll see to her."

"Thank you." And I'm off. I'm being a bad hostess, but I can't worry over it. I stop the first servant I see. "Do you know where Master Zade went?"

"To his room. Just a few minutes ago."

I hurry passed him to Chancellor Zade's section of the house. Once I reach his door, I pound on it. A moment passes. I knock again. I'll give every bit of freedom I've tried to gain if it means he'll help her. He opens the door, takes one look at my face, and opens it wider. "Come in. Have a seat. I thought you would be longer with your sister. Is everything all right?"

Not bothering to move from the doorway, I fall to my knees. My dress pulls downward but instead of adjusting it, I clasp his hands. Touching him feels wrong, but I'm desperate. Plus, the anchor may help my shaking. He's so high above me. It would probably work better if I lowered my head, but I'm afraid he won't hear me. He's so tall.

"What are you doing? Get off the floor."

"Chancellor Zade."

"Just Zade, and please, please get off the floor."

I don't move from my kneeling position but give in to his other demand "Zade, I know you have no reason to, but I beg of you to please help my sister. She hasn't said anything, but I know Father's punished her. She's limping. She's trying to hide it, but she's in pain. So much pain."

And it's all my fault.

My eyes fill with tears, but I blink them away before they can make him angry at my weakness.

He kneels in front of me, our hands still clasped. "Serena, you don't have to beg. You only have to ask. I don't know if I can fix it, but I will try. Where is she?"

Relief fills me so violently, I collapse on the floor. "The parlor."

He helps me stand and keeps an arm around me, steadying me, as we head to the parlor. It's not life threatening, but it feels urgent. My sister is hurting and I wasn't there to keep it from happening.

When we get to the tea room, Zade opens the door and ushers me inside. Cynthia's next to Bethany biting her lower lip. Bethany rests in a chair with her head relaxed against it, her eyes closed. I cross to her side and Zade follows. As we near, she opens her eyes and gives a polite smile. Though the pain isn't as obvious as before, her face is still masked. Sitting must help.

"It's nice to finally meet you, Bethany. Your sisters have talked a lot about you."

"And you as well, Chancellor."

"Your sisters care a great deal for you. In fact, Serena mentioned she noticed you had a slight limp. Could I take a look? I'll need to take your ungloved hand, if you'll allow. It's easier to detect and heal injuries that way. Nothing more."

"I'm feeling better since I sat down. You needn't worry yourself over me."

I give her shoulder a squeeze. "Would you please let him? It would make me feel better and I'll be right here."

Her head hangs. For a moment the room is silent. Finally, she lifts it. "Father did say Chancellor Zade was over me while here."

"That's right. We can't have it any other way." I keep my hand on her shoulder as Zade ambles over. After removing her glove, she holds her hand out to him. Slowly, he takes it in his own and concentrates on the floor.

Time passes. More than I expected. Cynthia's face is scrunched with worry.

Beneath my hand, Bethany relaxes. Deep blue sparks dance across her. It looks more like a hex than a healing spell. I want to scream, but the lines are easing from her face. It's the only time I've ever asked for one of my sister's to be spelled instead of taking the hex for them. Yet, whatever he's doing must be helping, not hurting. I force myself not to move.

After a few minutes, the sparks disappear and Zade releases her hand. She stirs and opens her eyes.

"You're going to be pretty tired," he says. "Rest here a while and then let Cynthia show you to your room. I'll have cook send something to eat. We'll have dinner together when you're feeling better."

"Thank you," Bethany says and closes her eyes again.

Zade glances at Cynthia. "If you need help, let one of the servants know."

"I will."

After watching me a moment, he leaves the room. Bethany's breathing deepens. Cynthia and I move to the side.

"I think she fell asleep," I say.

Cynthia nods. "He's a good-hearted man."

Watching Bethany sleep, I can't help but feel the same. There has to be something to his statement that he wouldn't hurt us. Not only has he stayed true to it before he even made the promise, but he's gone farther by healing her. Something sparks within me.

# CHAPTER 23

I HEAD FOR MY ROOM, but decide to search Zade out instead. Bethany was right to thank him and I should do the same. Is he back in his room or did he go to the study or gardens? The study is a place I'd prefer to avoid. Since he was in his room when I sought him out before, I head that way. A few hallways later, I find him staring at a portrait on the wall.

I move next to him. The portrait is of a woman, a rare one because she isn't pregnant, sitting next to a table of flowers, smiling. Her expression is so genuine, I can't help but wonder who she is.

"Chancellor Jacob's wife before she got sick," he says.

"She's lovely."

"Indeed. There's something I need to tell you." He shifts, but continues staring at the picture. As I wait to hear, my trepidation increases. "Your sister's injury was a magical one. A potent, magical one. It's contained now."

I twirl a stray lock of hair, then brush it back. "Would you please tell me about it, Zade?"

He turns to me, his brows lifted. "Are you sure you want to hear about it?"

No. "Yes."

For a moment, his gaze pierces mine, like he knows I don't want to hear this, but I need to. "Very well. From the injury described, I was expecting to find a sprain or pulled muscle, something like that. There was nothing. Physically, your sister's fine. She hasn't had an injury in six months."

She hasn't been beaten since I lived at Father's. The news should comfort me, but it doesn't.

"After I kept searching, I noticed an unusual type of magic all the way through her, with a high concentration around her leg." He pauses to gauge my reaction. Despite my feelings, I keep my features schooled. "I studied the negative energy there and realized the magic surrounding all of her was a type of pain spell. She's been in constant, severe pain since the spell was cast."

My stomach churns. I lean against the wall, wishing there was a place to sit down. "How long has she been suffering?"

"Don't know for sure, but it's been some time. There has been a little variance on the amount of pain."

The sick feeling completely engulfs me. "I wish I'd never left the house."

The hall is silent. I can't believe I said that out loud, no matter how true it is. Father's wrath was directed at me more often than not. And when it wasn't, I could usually get it there. It's not surprising he picked someone new with me gone. What else did I expect to happen?

Zade moves closer to me and puts a hand on my shoulder. "This isn't your fault."

I clamp my jaw. He's wrong. All wrong. A few tears escape me. I clench my fist and hold my breath, but they keep coming. Soon, I'm crying in earnest.

He sweeps me into his arms and strides through the hall. What's he doing? I'm embarrassed, but the tears won't stop. I bury my head in my hands. With a twitch of his arm beneath my knees, a spell opens a door. He sits and pulls me close to him, rubbing my back.

My heart aches with tears. His actions only spur them on harder. Embarrassment fills me. Why can't I control myself? I've always been able to keep my tears under control. After a few painful minutes, they slow.

"I suspect you've needed to do that for far too long." He tilts my face toward his. With a kerchief, he dabs at my tears. Something warm flickers in me. Being here, in his arms, it feels good. Much better than I would have thought. The warmth grows until heat burns my cheeks. I climb from his lap, as dignified as I can.

I clear my throat and sit on the couch opposite of him. The heat recedes, but not as quickly as I'd like. That can never happen again. Though I'm sure he won't forget my weakness, I act as though it never came. "Thank you for helping Bethany."

"It was nothing. I wish it wasn't needed in the first place."

"I'm grateful she's here now. We'll get her settled and hopefully things will be better." I can't allow myself to think of what may be happening to my other sisters. It's out of my control.

I inch to the edge of the sofa, but he says, "Wait a moment, please. There's something else I wanted to talk to you about."

"What is it?"

His hand clenches. "While I was healing her, I found out that she's been spelled to spy on us, though she's not aware of it. Everything she learns will be recorded through a spell that allows the caster to see and hear anytime he desires it."

"Father." I jump to my feet and pace the room. "I can't get away from him and now my sisters are caught between us more than ever." Strange how everyone always speaks of the Envadi spying on us, but it's only other Chardonians who actually seem to do it. "Cynthia was talking about the ball and our rooms and our lack of chores. He'll know you've healed her."

"Yes."

"I don't think he would care much except I'm the one that

begged you to. If he finds out it'll be seen as a weakness." For a warlock, it is a weakness. But it feels like strength. I take a step closer to him. "Why did you do it?"

"A better question is, how could anyone not do it?"

His face doesn't hint of a smile or laugh hiding behind his sorrow. He's serious. It was the right thing to do in his mind. I slouch against the sofa. How can he be like this? It should be a test of how long I'll continue being willful. As soon as I believe he really means his kindness, he'll transform it into punishment, but he hasn't yet. He moves to levels of compassion I've never seen. I've never had someone test me this long before. Can he really be so kind to a woman?

"Do you think your Father will demand her return?"

I shake my head. "I don't know."

"We'll hope it doesn't come to that. Do you have any idea why he's so intent on spying on us?"

"No idea. Why are you even asking me?"

"You've grown up here. You'd know things like that better than me."

"Us women aren't told things like that. What do you think?"

His fist raps against the arm rest a few times. "Venturing a guess, just a guess, I'd say it's two fold. If he can discredit the barbaric Envadi that has snuck onto the council, it would gain him much favor. At council meetings, he makes his dislike for me very apparent."

"That sounds like him. He never says much about his job, but I know he was hoping to be one of the next Chancellors." It's strange to discuss warlock issues, but somehow natural at the same time. I want to learn more. "What's the second part of the guess?"

"You. The law is a little different if I'm an unsuitable owner. If he can find and prove that I've broken the law before we marry and you become pregnant, you'd be returned to his ownership.

He'd have the chance to arrange another marriage that would benefit him."

There's another way out of the law besides me becoming tarnished? Looking at Zade now, I'm not sure if that would be to my determent or aid. I'm still uncertain about him, but more hopeful than I've ever been. I know I never want to be owned by Father again. "I didn't know I was so valuable to him."

"Very much so. If I were to die or be discredited enough to be kicked off the council and exiled from the country, he would get some of my money and possessions. Unless he's also rendered incapable, then it would go to the next closest relative."

Everyone else is dead. But it doesn't matter, Father isn't going anywhere.

He says, "Can you see why Councilman Stephen would be eager for something to happen to me? Not only would he have some of my money and possessions, but he'd be able to obtain even more power and money with another son-in-law.

"He's renewed the application for your entrance into the marriage pool, just in case something should happen to me. Many of those previously seeking your hand who haven't found a wife are aware and have been encouraged to keep an eye on me."

The thought of being in the marriage pool again, having to put up with someone like Thomas instead of Zade sickens me, but with under-lying flames of anger. No wonder his life is being threatened. "Do you know our laws well enough not to break them?"

"I do."

"No Chardonian would have healed Bethany. You aren't from here and you act like it."

"Trust me, I'm very aware. But you might be surprised by some of your countrymen," he says. "I know the laws. I can keep up well enough in public. I'll just have to be more careful at home than I was already." After a moment's hesitation, he says, "Especially with you."

Not me. I knew it sounded too good. I don't want to do this. Anything else but this. But he just healed Bethany. I have to. "Are you... did you want to leave a bruise now or later?"

Zade springs from the chair, his face contorted with anger. "I'm not going to hurt you. I won't go back on my word."

"But the laws."

"The laws say nothing about beating and hexing women. Nothing."

Shock jolts through me. "It doesn't?"

"No."

My whole life, I thought Father had to punish women. We are such an unwieldy gender, he needed to at least take one of us in hand. "How can it not say that? I thought—He always—" I try to gather my thoughts. "What does it say?"

"It says a lot, but little on women. Estate things like I mentioned. It says once married she must bear children, or her husband may tarnish her. The only other things are about your engagement and wedding ceremony which you already know or I can't reveal."

"Nothing about punishments?"

"Not one, single, thing." He paces the length of the room and mumbles, "This is exactly why I—" He shakes his head.

After a few minutes of watching him pace the floor and trying to wrap my mind around the new concept, I ask, "What did you mean then about being careful with me?"

The pacing stops. His cheeks pink. "I meant something more along the lines of getting caught kissing again."

"That's a law? Father never behaved as such."

"Yes, but your Father isn't about to be married and already has children."

My own cheeks heat. "So, it's like the same reason you wanted to kiss me in front of Phyllis."

"Yes. The law that has to do with you bearing children. It's expected that I'm to be anxious for it." He clears his throat.

"I suppose I understand what they mean." I grip the arm rests feeling a little anxious myself, though exactly why I can't say. "Are you sure it's necessary?"

A mirthless laugh escapes him. "You offer to let me hurt you, but don't want to kiss me?"

The memory of his lips pressed against mine surfaces. The comfort there. And something else. Do I want to kiss him? The room grows hot. Not really wanting to talk about it, but sort of hoping we will, really hoping we will, I shrug.

He snorts. "Forget I mentioned it."

Air rushes past as he storms from the room, not bothering to close the door behind him. I stare after him long after he's gone, my lips tingling.

# CHAPTER 24

I HURRY to finish my breakfast so I don't have to be around Zade longer than necessary. Still, the meal drags on. The silence has grown uncomfortable between us. Prickly. Perhaps it only bothers me. He eats as if nothing's wrong, even taking his time over a cup of warm milk. Like there aren't people trying to kill him. It's unbearable. At least when Father grew silent at meals I knew what to expect.

I don't finish my chocolate before excusing myself. Once out of the dining hall, I stroll through the manor, then the gardens. The morning sun's warmth soothes my skin. I head for the fountain in the middle of the garden. It's becoming my favorite. Halfway there, Cynthia and Bethany come into view.

Bethany looks as good as I remember. Better actually. Relaxed, but there's more change than that. The last of her baby fat has thinned from her cheeks. Her dark green dress fitted until her waist where it fans out. She looks like a woman.

"How are you feeling this morning?" I ask. "Any lingering pain?"

"I'm fine. Thank you for getting Chancellor Zade."

Fine except for the spy spell lingering on you. I wish I could tell her about it. Instead I have to minimize what she knows. What she could pass on to Father.

"I only told him you had a limp. He insisted on fixing it himself, though I'm sure your gratitude would be appreciated." Usually lying isn't so bad. I've done it often enough to Father. Never once have I felt guilty for telling one, until now. This is so different and much worse. It feels like it's eating at me from the inside. I can't think like this. Lying to Bethany is like lying to Father, for now at least. The reminder doesn't help.

No one speaks. It really hits me that my sisters are only allowed to be here to spy on me. I can't trust them with anything, and as soon as Father has no further need for spying on us, they'll go home. If his plans turn out like he wants, I'll be going home with them. My stomach churns at the thought.

"This is another of Serena's new gowns." Cynthia finally breaks the silence. "Isn't it lovely?"

"It is," Bethany says. "I wish I could have one like it."

"Best of all it's a two piece." I grin. Father should hear this. It will make him furious, but it's not unlawful. Or maybe it was too impulsive. Will he find a way to punish her from a distance? Or what if he punishes my other sisters? There's nothing I can do to protect them.

"I didn't realize before, but I see it now. How clever." Bethany grins. "I'm going to enjoy your new wardrobe. I wish we were the same size so I could pilfer a dress or two."

I laugh. "And I'll be glad we aren't."

"You should meet Katherine," Cynthia says. "Didn't Waverly need to talk to her anyway? We could go to town and stop by for a visit."

Will letting Bethany meet Katherine put the seamstress in danger as well? If Bethany is to help with the ball, she'll have to meet her sooner or later. I'd like to see Katherine anyway.

"But we don't have a chaperone," Bethany says.

Cynthia starts to protest, but I stop her. "She's probably right. I like going out on my own, but Chancellor Zade scolded me the other day for it. I'll see if he is interested in going to town today."

Cynthia scrunches her nose. "You're so strange sometimes. Go ask then. We'll want to spend all day there if we can. Especially to make the carriage ride for you worthwhile. We'll meet you back at the house."

I head back for the Chancellor. After trying so hard this morning to avoid him, here I am rushing back. I go straight for the dining room, hoping he's still there. When I enter he's still at the table, spells hovering before him. More spells of different colors flash through the window every so often, joining the others. I wait at the other side of the room where he can see me, wondering what the spells are for.

Several minutes later he says, "Why are you standing there?"

"Because I need to speak with you?"

"Then come and talk."

I don't dare get any closer. "What are those spells doing?"

He looks at the lights, then at me. With a wave of his hand, a black one zooms out the window. Though there are still several in front of him, no new ones appear. "They're bringing news from home and around Chardonia."

"How can you get news from light?"

"Come here, I'll show you."

I hesitate a moment, but not long. I'm too curious. Once I'm next to him, he waves his hand and a green light moves to the front. I gasp. From this angle, the light is made of words.

"I've never seen anything like it."

"I don't suppose you would. Seems like Chardonians like to keep most magic from women."

Could it be true? It makes sense. Most spells I've seen have been hexes. Father occasionally did something different like chill his wine, but that happened rarely.

"I know you didn't come here to talk about this. What did you need?"

"You've been scolding me," I blurt out, still thinking of how I know mostly hexes. What else can they do with magic?

"No, I've been reading the paper. If you're referring to last night, forget I mentioned anything. About the kiss any way. I'm serious about everything else that was said."

My face warms at mention of a kiss. "Not about that. I told the girls you've been scolding me for going out on my own."

"Why?"

I lower my voice. "Because we're being spied on and it just isn't done. I love doing it, but it gives an impression you don't want to make. Sure it's not against one of the laws you listed, but it's still expected. This is a good way for you to show your dominance. Take control of your possessions." When he says nothing, I continue, "Unless you don't want to take us to town. We could stay home. That would show your dominance as well."

He rubs the bridge of his nose. "What are you doing in town?"

"Taking the girls to see my seamstress."

His voice deepens. "We've got to get ready for the ball, woman. Call for the carriage."

I gape at him. He waves a hand at me and I stumble from the room feeling confused. Why did he suddenly become so harsh? After a few moments, I realize he was teasing. It's something I've done with my sisters, but never a warlock. Not sure how to feel about that, I find the girls and call for the carriage.

Once everyone is ready, we begin loading into the carriage, except Zade who rides alongside on horseback. Waverly pouts over not being able to ride with him. He insists it isn't proper in Chardonia. When Cynthia and Bethany aren't watching, he winks at her. I spin away from them, a twisting in my gut.

The ride is filled with talk of the ball, Cynthia and Bethany quickly drawing Waverly out of her pout. I stare at the solid doors, wishing I could watch the scenery go by. If I learned to ride a horse like Waverly, I could be out there as well. If it got rid of dealing with carriage sickness, it would be worth it. Wait— What am I thinking? Horses are huge and have big eyes. Not to mention, Zade's right, it isn't proper.

When the carriage stops, the footman opens the door, and everyone else piles out. I wait, giving myself a minute to let my stomach settle.

Zade leans in. "Are you coming?"

A breeze blows in from outside, cooling me. "Yes, I just need a moment."

"She gets carriage sickness," Bethany calls out.

"You do?" Zade asks.

"Yes."

"That's easy enough to fix. I have a spell that would help if you'd like."

Should I allow him to cast a spell on me? I've never wanted a spell cast on me before, but it would be nice not to be ill. The truth spell wasn't so bad. "Does it hurt?"

"Not at all."

Maybe spells other than hexes aren't so bad. The light spell he showed me that brings news wasn't. I take a deep breath. This will help me feel better. I can let him do it. "Then yes, would you please?"

"Of course." A blue light glides from his hand and surrounds me before penetrating my skin. My stomach instantly settles.

"How's that?"

"Much better, thank you."

"Glad I could help."

He holds out a hand. An unfamiliar tingle races through me as my gloved hand touches his. As soon as I'm on the ground, I let go of his hand, though part of me doesn't want to, but the feeling continues. After I straighten my skirt, he pulls the door of the shop open. I'm more aware than ever of his close presence when I pass him.

Katherine looks up, with puffy eyes, from speaking with

another tarnished. "Welcome. I'm so glad you came. This is my assistant, Mavis. Please, come in."

Everyone moves to stand next to me, Zade entering the shop and closing the door once we're all in. I wait for Zade to say something, but he only stares at me. It makes his role appear less domineering, but hopefully a minor detail.

"Morning, Katherine," I say. "You've met everyone except my sister Bethany."

"Nice to meet you and welcome to everyone. Please pick a seat. Mavis will you help them get settled?"

Mavis, who has a narrow, happy face, steps forward. "Of course."

"Thank you." Katherine turns to me. "Would you help me gather some refreshments?"

I wonder at her asking me and not Mavis, but I've done more than enough in a kitchen to know my way around. Really, it's been too long since I've helped. Plus, the distance from Zade might help clear my awareness of him. "Of course."

I follow her past the main seating area down a small hall to a tiny kitchen. She pumps water into a jug and directs me to cut the stems off some strawberries.

In a lowered voice she says, "Chancellor Zade visited a few days ago."

"Zade?" I pause cutting. Once the shock has worn off, I resume, fear making me smash the berries more than slice them. "Was he angry about the dresses?"

"Not at all."

While I'm grateful he didn't punish her, why else would he visit? She pulls out a tray and fills it with glasses. When the tray is full, she turns her attention on me. "I thought you should know he finished paying for the entire wardrobe I gave you and commissioned ball gowns for you, your sisters, and Waverly."

"He did?" I'm too stunned to put the strawberries in the jug.

Katherine takes them from me and does it. Dresses? Not only mine, but Cynthia and Bethany's? And Waverly, a servant?

"Actually, he overpaid. Insisted on it."

She grabs a plate of biscuits and places it on the tray. It's all ready to go, but we stand there. Hearing this is not helping to distract my thoughts from him as I'd prefer. I don't know what to think of him.

"Why did he pay you?"

"I don't know, but I wanted you be aware of what he did," she says. "He's different. Next time you need something, ask him for the money. I doubt he'd want to know what it's for."

Would he really be so careless about his money with me? "He's supposed to let me know when I need something."

"But men don't always know, do they?"

They rarely do. "But that's not how it works."

"It will if you ask."

I look at her swollen eyes. "Are you all right?"

She rearranges the glasses. "I'm fine."

"No, really Katherine, how are you? You don't seem yourself."

"I'm not," she whispers. "But no one can do anything about it."

"What happened? At least let me try."

"It would only lead to more trouble."

Despite my protests, she picks up the tray and leaves the room. What could possibly be the problem? She's done so much for me, I hate to see anything bad happen to her. It's easier to focus on her situation than on Zade as I grab the jug and follow after.

Everyone is settled on the chairs and sofa. Katherine has left the tray on the table and is handing everyone a glass. After pouring everyone some strawberry lemon water, I set the jug on the table next to the tray and pass around the biscuits. Once everyone is served, I grab my own and take the only free space left, next to Zade.

"Waverly," I say, "the idea of having an exotic theme is a good one. Can you tell us more about balls in Envado?"

"Well, I've never been to a Chardonian one to compare it to, but next to weddings and babies, they are the most celebrated events. Magicians come from all over to cast for them."

"Spells at a ball?" At the one I attended, there weren't any.

"What sort of spells?" Cynthia asks.

"The gowns for one," Waverly says. "It's one of the few times women wear formal dresses, the type that takes two or three people to get you into. All of them are spelled in some way. They change colors, styles, they sparkle. They vary as much as the people in attendance."

"A spelled dress?" Katherine says. "I've never thought of that."

I say, "You haven't? Seeing the dresses you've created so far and hearing your ideas, I was sure every idea for a dress had crossed your mind."

"Would you be able to spell a ball gown or two for me, Chancellor?" Katherine asks.

"Changing colors is simple if you have examples. Sparkles or flashes easy as well. But, I've never been great at switching styles. It'd help if there were two dresses I could spell to become one alternating piece."

Wearing more new dress styles? How will people react to this? Will we get in even more trouble for it? I don't know if having spelled dresses is a problem or not. Despite what that may arise, I'm curious to see what they'd be like. Maybe even wear one. And wearing one that Zade helped to spell for me? The thought brings the tingling feeling back.

"It sounds as if you've had a lot of experience with this before," Cynthia says.

"A few times. I've a sister I help on occasion."

"And your sister told me you—" Waverly starts, but Zade interrupts.

"She was always grateful for my help. Always."

She giggles. "That's not what I heard."

"Servant gossip is highly unreliable." He scowls.

"Actually," Katherine says, "servants are one of the best sources of information."

"Hah!" Waverly says.

"Envadi servants aren't like the ones from here." Bethany's quiet voice sounds for the first time.

We all look at Waverly who blushes. "Sorry."

Everyone bursts out laughing, except Waverly, but she quickly joins. The topic drifts back to the ball. The girls soon have lost me with the details. So many things to plan, but I can't manage to keep track of them.

"Serena?"

I glance at Katherine. "I'm sorry, what was that?"

"I said I've finished altering a gown if you'd like to take it home. You're welcome to try it on."

"You work fast. I'm sure it will fit fine."

"Try it on," Bethany says. "I'd love to see what another one is like."

"Why don't you?" Zade asks. I stare at him and he grins. "I'd like to see it as well."

That's as good as an order, yet I know I'm blushing because of it. Asserting himself is coming a little too naturally. But that must mean he does want to see me in it. "I suppose I could."

"Please make yourselves comfortable, Chancellor, girls. Let Mavis know if you need anything," Katherine says. "Waverly and I'll have Serena back soon."

She leads Waverly and me to the changing room. Katherine hands me a gown.

"You can change in there," she points to a curtained off section of the room,

The dressing area has a small chair and a place to hang my current dress. I change, still amazed at how quickly I can manage, and by myself. I step out.

Waverly claps her hands. "Wonderful."

"Yes, the fit is better. I added holes in all your right pockets so you could get your gun."

"My gun? I don't have one." I put my hand in my right pocket, and sure enough there's a hole big enough to pull out a gun.

"Chancellor Zade's orders." He must have been more serious than I thought about making me learn. I lock my jaw as Katherine continues. "There's a mirror you can use." She points to a full length mirror to the side, standing on a black frame. Anxious to see, I step to it.

"It does look good." The maroon material hugs me, but gives with my movements until my waist where it flares and flows to the floor. "I should show my sisters."

"And the Chancellor," Katherine says.

What will Zade think of me? I don't move from in front of the mirror.

Katherine says, "I know you don't want to marry, but you can't change it now." She comes closer to me and adjusts my sleeve, whispering, "Unless there's something you want me to help you with?"

She did offer to help me escape. But the offer seems even less appealing than it did before, if it would actually work. "No."

A mischievous grin transforms her face. "What if you tried to make him fall in love with you?"

The memory of his lips on mine, makes my hands shake. The warmth there. "What do you mean?"

"You're dressed nice. We could do your hair a little fancier and give you some face paint. If you did that more often and then spent some time with him, try to find something you have in common."

I play with the hem of my sleeve.

"Maybe love is too strong of a word. But you could at least be friends."

Friends. With a warlock?

"Do you really not want to marry him?"

Whatever I say, Waverly could tell him. Yet, he said I could trust her. Even if she does tell, it won't change anything. She's been oddly silent during the whole exchange. I watch her from the corner of my eye. She's paying very close attention.

"No. I don't want to be married at all. Whether to him or someone else. It's not what I would choose for myself or my sisters. Not that women really have a choice. The thing is…"

"Go on," Katherine says. They both look so concerned, like they really want to know.

I stare at the dress in the mirror. It laces across the front, allowing me to dress myself. Giving freedom, unless someone catches me breaking rules. Deep inside, my feelings burst. "You're right, Katherine, I don't want to be married, but things are different than I expected. He's never hurt me, at least not intentionally. Zade's rather kind. He's given me a lot of space and freedom."

And how I feel around him. I don't want to think what that means. I pick up my skirt. "And apparently helped pay for clothes that I didn't need, but wanted. The freedom is wonderful, but it feels sort of false. He still owns me. Nothing will change that. How can I be friends with someone who owns me?"

I force a laugh. "Listen to me complain when I don't even have to work. I'm sorry. If I could change things for the two of you, I would."

"Oh posh," Katherine says. "I'm as free as I can be and you've already helped me more than you think."

"And I wanted to be here," Waverly says. "The laws aren't what I'd like. My mother almost fainted when I told her, but it was my choice."

Does that mean the laws are different in Envado?

"See," Katherine says. "You're only telling us what we asked for. Now, we can't do anything about him owning you, but we can make him glad he does, which should make things better for you. The closer you get to him, the less you'll be a possession."

"We shouldn't make her if she doesn't want to," Waverly says.

Katherine catches my gaze in the mirror. "What do you say, Serena?"

I lick my lips. "I suppose it wouldn't hurt."

A grin spreads across her face. "Waverly, will you redo her hair? I've seen some of the things Envadi do with hair. Don't let her get away with this severe bun thing anymore. I'll grab some face paint."

# CHAPTER 25

FIFTEEN MINUTES LATER, my hair is braided and twisted around the back of my head, with a few wisps left by my face. Not a style seen in Chardonia. My face paint is subtle, but makes my eyes look bigger, my mouth a little redder, and my cheeks as if I'm blushing. It looks good.

"Why don't you go out so you can see his face when she comes out?" Waverly suggests.

"Yes, all right," Katherine says. "You can do this, Serena. Don't forget to smile."

After she hurries out the door, Waverly says, "You really don't have to do this if you don't want to."

Part of me really wants to and part of me is shying away. I shrug. "You've already transformed me. If I don't want to do more than that, I won't."

Her lips tighten. "Be careful." She opens the door and I follow her through the hall. When we reach the receiving room, she holds up a hand for me to wait and enters.

"May I present Serena, Master Zade."

Does she know she broke protocol by announcing my name first? No corrections are forthcoming. At least not in front of everyone. I try to calm my nerves, but my hands start shaking. I paste a smile on my face like Katherine said to and step into the room. My sisters look at me, but I watch Zade. His expression changes to something I don't recognize. After a few moments, he scowls. As soon as he does, I want to scowl back, but decide to pretend like it doesn't bother me. Dressing up feels good, I don't have to let him ruin it.

Zade's hand bunches into a fist on his lap. "Have you drank that tea again?"

"What? No." Where is this coming from?

"Then someone slipped it to you."

"Zade," Waverly says, "I've been with her and no one gave her anything. She didn't eat or drink while we were back there."

His eyes never leave mine. "Is this true?"

"It is."

"Then why is your face paint different, and your hair? Why are you smiling?"

The smile falls from my face. I made the wrong choice. I knew there was something awry with smiling. And the hair and face paint. Why did I let them talk me into it? Waverly hides her face behind her hands and Katherine chuckles. Them finding humor in the situation makes my muscles tense.

"Forgive me," I say. "I was pleased with the new dress."

"Oh." His face pinks a bit and he sits back on the sofa. "Oh." He stares at nothing and shakes his head. "You're never like this. The smile, never. And when you do, it's so rare and quick." I rarely smile? "I thought... I'm a complete idiot."

"No need to worry about that, Master Zade," Waverly says.

For a moment his scowl deepens before lightening. "It's a nice dress. Your hair is good, too."

"Waverly styled it differently."

He grins at her. "I like it."

I'm still trying to get over him calling himself an idiot again to think what their banter means, but a tiny knot forms in my stomach. Maybe he likes Waverly's styling, but not me trying it.

"Please, sit," he says. "There's no need for everyone to stay on their feet."

As Waverly and Katherine find their seats, I take my place back on the couch. I'm still overly aware of his presence next to me, but now it's charged with my failings.

"The dress really is nice, Miss Katherine," Zade says. "It's good of you and Waverly to put a smile on her face. Sorry I was so surprised at it."

"Thank you. It was a pleasure making it for her and Waverly has a hidden talent for doing hair."

Waverly shrugs. "It's how we do hair at home, just what I was asked to do."

"Well, it's good." Zade leans toward her a moment, then seems to catch himself and leans back. The knot in my stomach multiplies. "Tell us, Miss Katherine, where do you get ideas for your dresses? I'm not overly familiar with women's fashions, but I can tell these are different from usual Chardonian dresses."

"Please do tell," Cynthia says. "I love what you've done."

While she talks, I grab a biscuit and nibble on it

"There's not much to tell, I'm afraid. Most of my ideas come from mixing what the tarnished have with what the wives wear. More practical, yet still beautiful. A few things from other countries. Where ever I can find inspiration."

"No one's done it yet, though," Cynthia says.

"A few have tried. Not exactly like my designs, but similar. None have succeeded."

"I for one hope you do," Zade says. "You've done well. We'll have to see what we can do to get Serena to show the dresses off."

"I was thinking of wearing them while delivering some of the invites," I say.

"Splendid idea," he responds.

Katherine's face lights up. "That'd be kind. Thank you."

"Do you have any other designs we haven't seen yet?" Cynthia asks.

"Mostly variations on things you have seen, but there's one other thing."

"What is it?"

"I'm not sure I should say." She eyes Zade.

"Go ahead. I won't get after you for having ideas."

She shifts in her chair. "I've made a few pairs of female britches."

My sisters and I all gasp. Waverly laughs. "We wear those all the time."

Even if they do it in Envado, it certainly isn't done here. All of Katherine's ideas have turned out to be good, but this one I don't think I'll ever like. Besides, society would never allow it.

"I had heard Envadi woman wear them," she says. "That's why I made some."

Zade says, "Perhaps you can talk these three into trying some."

"I'll see what I can do." Katherine laughs.

"I think the gardens will look lovely for the ball," I say, desperately trying to change to subject. I can't imagine wearing breeches. Having those things clinging to my legs all day, I don't think I could stand it. And such little material? Hardly fitting for a woman.

Talk of the ball resumes. Which girls we went to class with that we should invite. Who of them will probably come. What will they likely wear. The talking continues so long, the girls soon have me lost with all the details again. I yawn.

Zade stands, causing the conversation to halt. "You ladies carry on, I'm going to run some errands while in town."

As soon as he finishes, they continue, but I say, "Yes, Master," and look him right in the eye, silently pleading for him to take me with.

"I told you—" his expression lightens, before becoming stern, "woman, that you weren't leaving my side today. Stop being lazy and let's go."

The conversation halts.

"Yes, Chancellor Zade." I put on a sorrowful face for the girls. "Do you mind continuing without me?"

"No," Cynthia says. "We'll take care of things."

"I don't know what I would do without you," I say.

"Not have a good ball," she says.

"Very true."

The girls laugh and I join them. I grab my cloak and exit the shop with Zade.

"Thank you," I say to Zade. "I don't mind a few details, but that was too much. I don't know why they enjoy it so much."

"So, they'll basically plan it for you?"

"Shameful, isn't it?"

He walks away from the carriage.

The day is clear with a light breeze, but I shouldn't just walk around town. It wouldn't be seemly. At least, Father always said it wouldn't. "Where are you off to?"

"Nowhere. I don't really have any errands. You're not the only one that couldn't sit any longer."

"Should we take the carriage?"

"Why? It's such a nice day."

"Should I really be going around town this much? Besides, this is the tarnished side of town."

"So? You found Katherine here."

That I did, but how does that make this acceptable? Before I can argue further, he sets off. I pull my cloak tighter around me, making sure it covers the engagement mark on my neck. It feels more conspicuous in the tarnished section of town. Though without being bald and having an inked face, it matters little. It makes me less jittery though.

We walk in silence for a while. Soon, I grow more comfortable and take in my surroundings. Despite always hearing about tarnished being less than nothing, it's a nice area of town. Nicer than some areas inhabited by warlocks, and not at all like the rumors. The shops are tidy. We peek in a few windows. I'm surprised to see they don't look any different than the regular shops, except for the people running them, of course.

When we move to the housing district, the yards are trim and well-kept. The houses are smaller than Father's, but have more wild flowers growing next to them. The walkways are neat and clean. We come to a park, not a person in sight.

"Would you like to wander through?" Zade asks.

"It looks lovely."

As I follow him into the park, the space between us lessens. I have the strangest urge to touch him. His arm maybe, or perhaps his hand. A part of me really wants to, but it seems like the wrong thing to do. I let a bit of distance grow between us and try to focus on the scenery. There's green everywhere with lots of winding paths. A small river runs through part of it with a bridge over it. A man appears in the distance. I think nothing of him until Zade slows.

"What is it?"

He shakes his head, but there's something. Everything about his movements becomes stiffer. My nerves heighten in response. A small part of me wishes I had a gun to pull out of my pocket. But it wouldn't help anyway, probably would only get us in more trouble. No matter what Zade thinks, women don't carry guns. A moment later the man is upon us.

"Chancellor Zade, didn't think to see you here. This is—" His gaze roams over me. "Your intended? What are you bringing her here for?"

It's then I realize that this is a warlock. No tattoos and a full head of hair. Do they wander down here often? His words to Zade make me think not, yet he is here. Better than him being the person threatening Zade's life, yet my muscles grow even more taut. What if he sees the dress I'm wearing?

"Just showing her where she'll end up if she misbehaves. Really none of your business though, Councilman Barkley."

Another councilman. Worse and worse. My chest tightens. I step back and lower my head, watching them interact through my lashes.

The man casts a gray apology spell. "So magnanimous of you to share such a grand idea. I'll have to bring my woman here next time she misbehaves. We have children so I can't really do it, but she doesn't need to know that."

Memories of Father punishing mother surfaces. A part of me wants to force this man's ideas back on himself. The other part wants to find his wife and comfort her. Maybe even hide her from him. But none of those things can happen. I'd be dead or tarnished and Zade along with me.

"If you think it will help," Zade says.

"Course it will. The only thing that scares them more than us is the thought of becoming tarnished. Isn't that why you brought her here?"

"Women behave differently to punishments is all."

"No, no, you've finally stumbled on a good idea. You haven't owned a woman long enough to know, but they need a firm hand. Remember that advice with your new toy."

I'm not a toy. Anger burns deep in my chest, but I do nothing. There's nothing I can do.

"Course Envadi scare them plenty. Must work well for you, huh?" the Councilman asks.

"As you say."

"Your woman does seem upset." His eyes roam over me and I'm extra grateful for the cloak hiding my dress. I try to pull my expression into a neutral one. When did I get so bad at hiding my feelings?

Zade steps in front of me. "She's not yours to worry over."

"Right you are." The man chuckles. "About the proposed tarnished law, you're going to support it."

"I haven't researched it enough to know, yet."

"Best get to it then. Being nineteen doesn't excuse you from not doing your work." He's only nineteen? I didn't know he was so young. The man continues, "The Grand Chancellor was working on the council at eighteen. You've no excuse. We expect better."

"That we can agree on."

It's silent. The type of silence there used to be before Father punished me. I shift so I can see the Councilman. His eyes are narrowed at Zade as if searching for a deeper meaning. "Good. Best be on my way. Got a lunch appointment waiting for me, if you take my meaning. Before you leave, you should take her by the Red District, too. That will put the fear in her."

My cheeks flame as he passes by, his gaze lingering. Zade moves in front of me again. The man laughs as he passes out of sight. I can't decide whether I'm more angry about his behavior or my inability do anything about it.

Quietly, Zade says, "Sorry."

Despite the warmth of my cloak and the mild day, I shiver. "It's not you."

"But I want to—" He huffs and puts his hands on his hips. "Things shouldn't be like this, for you, for women, for the tarnished."

"What should they be like?"

He finally looks at me. "Different."

What does he know that he's not saying? Maybe he doesn't know anything. Maybe he's just wishing aloud. I've wished it enough myself. Yet, there has to be more. I want there to be a reason behind the thought. How can things be different?

# CHAPTER 26

A COUPLE WEEKS LATER, I debate whether or not to include Waverly in on an idea I have. She would be the perfect person to consult, but something about how close she and Zade are stops me.

"Anything else?" she asks.

"No, thank you." I'll ask Cynthia to assist. Bethany may help mother with the parties, but Cynthia helps mother with the furniture. And I won't have to spend extra time around Waverly wondering what's between her and Zade.

I head for Cynthia's room and knock on her door.

"Morning," she says. "Come in. One of the servants wanted to fix my hair, but she couldn't get it the way Waverly has been doing yours. I was going to attempt it myself, but if I can't figure it out either, I was going to give Waverly a ring. What do you think?"

"Let me help." I settle myself behind her.

While I do her hair, I worry over asking her. Maybe I shouldn't. Women don't make decisions like this. We always wait for the men to tell us to do them. But I really want to do something to help Zade. Forget what others think I should be doing, I

will do this. "When we're done here, would you help me with
something."

"With what?

"The Chancellor isn't comfortable in any of the furniture we
have. We should get him items that are bigger."

"That's easy enough to fix. Did he have anything specific in
mind?"

"Not really. At least one bigger chair." It seems silly not to
correct her, but it's strange for me to do this without being asked.
And he would be more comfortable in things his size. Besides it's
a way I can return the favor for everything he's done. "And I
haven't seen his bed chamber, but perhaps a bigger bed. A better
chair in the dining room, as well. Things for his study?"

She nods. "Perhaps we should look around the house and see if
anything would work. It'd be faster than waiting to order it."

"I didn't think of that. It's a splendid idea."

"It may help give us a better idea of what he needs if we see
what he has currently. Is he in today?"

"No, there's a council meeting."

"I wonder what they talk about so much." A faraway look
enters her eyes.

"Me, too." Like, what that tarnished law Councilman Barkley
in the park was talking about. What is it all about? Will it affect
Katherine?

"In any case, it will give us a chance to look around without
bothering him. Father always hated it when mother and I tried to
figure out what furniture he needed while he was getting work
done."

Sounds like Father. But I don't want to think of him. "Let's go
then."

We cross along the length of the house. It feels strange not
taking any stairs to get where we are going. I twist my hands
together. Maybe this wasn't such a good idea. I stare at his door.
"Are you sure we should check now?"

She nods vigorously. "You remember the time Father hexed you mute for a week?"

"After I claimed you'd done it because I said you had to." The memory is at the back of my mind with all the others I keep pushed back. "I never knew what you were doing for that one."

"I was going through his study taking inventory of what he'd broken and needed replaced. While working I made the mistake of singing and he came in and caught me at it."

"That explains the muteness. I never did get the chance to ask. By the time I got my voice back, mother had another baby."

She plays with her fingernails. "Thanks for always doing that for me. I never told you, but it meant a lot to me."

"Oh, Cynthia." Remembering how it made me feel when Katherine wrapped her arms around me and I hugged her back, I can't help but try likewise with my sister. At first, she's tense under my embrace, but soon she relaxes into tears. I pat her back. "It's all right, Cynthia."

"It's not," she says between sobs. "You were punished so many times for me."

"And I'd do it many more."

"I don't deserve you for a sister."

"You're planning my ball, I'll call that good enough."

"It's not enough, but I'm trying my best." She sniffs a few times before pulling away. "We should investigate his room before I end up crying all day and night and he comes home to us blocking his room."

I grin at her. "I don't think he'd hex us mute because of it."

She grins back.

A cool breeze rushes past as I open the door and enter. "That was odd."

"What was?"

"Didn't you feel that cold air?"

"No."

"Huh. Must have been a breeze or something." The room is the same shape and size as the one I use. The only difference is a desk shoved in by the window and a razor, soap, and towel scattered across the vanity. And it smells faintly of citrus, just like he does. "Look at this. His furniture is the same as mine."

She runs her hand across the back of a chair. "We'll need a few chairs to replace these. He has a desk in here which I wasn't suspecting. Perhaps we should get two for him. One for the study and one for in here. Two beds as well, I should think. You'll need the extra space when you're wed."

My cheeks heat. I want to be anywhere but here. "I suppose." I scramble for the door. "We should go through the house for some furniture."

We exit, making sure to leave everything as we found it. Starting from Chancellor Zade's side of the house, we work our way through the rooms. The top floor holds nothing useful for Zade, but plenty of space for guests during the ball. If I find any guests I'd rather be near, I'll put them here. Father will be on the ground floor.

On the next floor, we stop when we find a grand suite. An entry with a few chairs and a sofa leads to two private chambers off to the sides, each with their own receiving rooms, wash rooms, water closets, bath-rooms, and bedrooms connected by a door. I've never seen a personal bath-room before.

The rooms are richly dressed with colors, fabrics, and paint-ings. When we come to a chamber containing dresses, face paint, and a canopy bed, a thin layer of dust covers everything.

"This must have been Chancellor Jacob's wife's." Though it's bigger than I expected the woman's side to be. I remember the picture I saw of her. "Do you know what her name was?"

"I don't." She runs her fingers across a book shelf, three rows deep of books, and there are still more on the floor. "Maybe Chancellor Jacob kept some of his books in her room? It's rather strange though."

"No stranger than Chancellor Zade."

"That's true." She bounces on her toes and moves to the vanity. "She has lots of face paint. More than even mother. I didn't know any woman could beat her with that."

"She didn't have much on in the painting I saw of her downstairs."

The Woman's Canon lies on the bed stand. Next to it is an unlabeled book and a strange looking pen. No ink pot around. Why would a woman have a pen in her room? We can't use them. But what would it be like if I could?

I bite my lip and stare at the pen a moment before picking it up. It's light between my fingers. Its metal feels cool even through my gloves. I glance at the unmarked book. My pulse increases. I've not ventured into the book room again, but I've read the book I stole until I've memorized it. I'd really like another.

With my free hand, I grab the new book. Is it some sort of extension to the Woman's Canon? I've never heard of one. But what else would she be permitted to keep in her room? She did have a pen here as well so perhaps it's something different. I want it to be something different. With a peek to make sure Cynthia isn't watching, I flip the cover open.

To my dearest Julia,

*I give you this gift with the hopes it will help heal your heartache. No matter what they say, you are the perfect woman for me.*

*Faithfully Yours,*

*Jacob*

NOT RELATED to the Woman's Canon. My fingers shake as I trace the words and read it again. It stirs something within me. Something deep and abiding. I turn the page. Inside it's lined and filled with a flowing script. Did she write this herself? I know how to read, but I've never written anything. I sit on the bed as I read of her heartache over not having children and her love for her husband.

"What's that?"

I snap the book closed and throw it on the table. How could I be so careless? "The usual."

"I thought you hated reading the Woman's Canon." Cynthia heads for the door. I sigh, grateful she didn't realize it was something different. "There's nothing here that will work."

It takes me a moment to remember what she's speaking of. I don't feel like searching the house, instead I want to read more of Julia's words. When Cynthia's out of view, I grab the book and hide it in my blouse, thankful I'm wearing a loose one today.

I glance down. A little squarish around my stomach, but hopefully she won't notice. I think of a way to get this hidden in my room and follow her out.

"Maybe we should go order things," I say. "Even if we find something large enough, he really could use more than one or two items."

"I'm sure if we keep looking, we'll find something here though."

"What if we ordered the things and looked when we returned? That way, the furniture would be on its way sooner, but if there's something, he'd be able to use it in the meantime."

"Can we take the carriage into town today?"

"You're asking if we can go without a chaperone?"

She bites her lower lip. "Only if Bethany doesn't want to come. She said she had some things she wanted to talk over with Waverly today, so I suspect it won't be a problem."

The fact she doesn't want to take Bethany is a relief. I can't forget she's a spy. I should be better around Cynthia, but she knows I've been out on my own. With all the time she's spent with Zade, I doubt she really believes he's suddenly trying to be harder on me anyway. "I suppose it'd be fine, as long as we don't go anywhere besides the wood worker."

"Let's go then. We can't have the Master of the house uncomfortable."

"You really want to go out without a warlock to chaperone?"

"Well, Zade isn't here and it needs done. Nothing's happened to you yet."

"Your first unchaperoned outing. I'll hold this memory forever."

I laugh. She goes on ahead to call for a carriage while I hide Julia's journal in my room to peruse later. Hopefully, Waverly won't find it while she's cleaning.

# CHAPTER 27

SEVERAL DAYS LATER, Zade corners me on my way out from sneaking a snack in the kitchen. Thankfully Phyllis wasn't there, but she may have been a better choice than him. His face is stern, not a hint of lightness in his eyes. Did he find out we were in his room? Is he angry we went to town and ordered things without him?

"Today, you're going to use a gun."

Not problems with the furniture then. I'm not sure this is any better though. "I don't know if that's a good idea."

"You will learn to use a revolver."

The air is sucked from me. He's never forced me to do anything. I hate the change so much, I'm willing to risk contradicting him. "I don't care what the law says, women don't touch them."

"Most don't live with a man who has a price on his head."

He has a good point, but is such a drastic action needed? He leans against the wall next to me. Our arms brush. A tingle rushes through me.

"How seriously are they trying to harm you?"

"The intruder in your room was the first attempt. I finally

caught up with him. Seems someone mixed up our rooms. He's taken care of now."

Taken care of? I shiver. "First attempt? Don't evade me this time, how many more have there been?"

"Enough that you need to protect yourself."

Still evading, but it sounds bad. I clench my jaw. I don't want anything to happen to him. I want to do this, or... maybe I do, but it's still hard to ask. "Will more kissing help?"

He pinks and shrugs.

My chest stings at the rejection. "Is there anything I can do?"

"Learn to shoot."

I bite my lip. "What about Cynthia and Bethany?"

"I'd like to teach them, but with your Father still their owner, I have to be careful. They've got extra wards on them."

"Can't you do that for me?"

"I'm doing what I can, but I can't do everything. You shouldn't worry about them. You're around me more than they are. Plus, you're the one engaged to me, not them."

"I don't think it's a good idea."

"You need some means of protecting yourself, though I pray you never have to use it. Please do this for me."

I don't want to touch a gun, let alone use it. But people rarely use the word please, and never a warlock. Plus, there was the moment when we met Councilman Barkley that I wished I had a gun. "When do we start?"

He slouches against the wall a moment, before coming to his feet. "Right now. Follow me."

We leave the house, but instead of going to the gardens, we go to the side, trailing along until we come to a field. My muscles tense more the closer we get. One side has stacks of hay set up. He leads me across from the hay about two hundred paces away.

"This is your revolver. When we're not using it, keep it strapped to your leg where you can reach it through the pocket Katherine made for you." He pulls out a black gun and lets it rest in the palm of his hand. The sun glows on it, making its deadliness shine.

I swallow.

"Never, ever point this at something you're not willing to destroy."

"This really isn't a good idea."

He grabs my hand and presses the gun into it, wrapping his own hand around it. "You can do this."

The metal is cold against my skin. He takes his hand off mine and points to the long end of the gun. "This is the barrel. This is the hammer." He flips a lever back. "Pull it half way to open the loading gate." He pushes it back up. "You try it."

My fingers quiver as I pull it back. "Now what?"

He spins the middle part of it. "This is the chamber that holds the bullets. How many are there?"

I reach up to spin it myself and count. "Six."

"Right. Always keep track of how many you've shot." He reaches into his pocket and pulls out some small brass items. "These are bullets. You slip them in the chamber with the point side down." After showing me once, he holds them out. "Give it a try."

I don't want to touch those things. With shaking fingers, I pick one up and point it toward the chamber. Instead of going in, it falls to the ground. "Sorry."

"Don't worry about it." He fishes it out of the grass and smiles at me. "See, no harm done."

Some of my nervousness dissipates. I grab another bullet and try again. It slips in without a problem. After I get the other four loaded, he says. "If you're not going to use it right away, put the hammer up. If you're going to shoot it, pull it all the way back."

He demonstrates then has me try. The gun is heavy. I pull the hammer back.

"Good." His hand runs along my arm straightening it and sending tingles through my body. "Now aim at one of those haystacks and pull the trigger. When you get good enough, I'll put up a bull's eye for you."

"Are you sure I should be doing this?"

"There's no one else around. You won't hurt anyone, we're just practicing."

I bite my lip, lift the gun, and shoot. My arms jerk back and the noise hurts my ears. I yelp. The odor of smoke fills my nose, but it's unlike anything I've ever smelled before.

Zade laughs. "Try again. This time, look at your target. I'll spell your gun so it's easier to see where it goes."

I scowl. The stacks seem so far away. He casts a tan spell that hovers over the barrel of the gun. I look at the middle of the hay stack and try to shoot.

"It's not working."

"You have to pull the hammer back."

"Of course." I feel foolish.

After pulling the hammer back, I look at the hay stack again and pull the trigger. The sound is just as loud, but doesn't startle me as much. Zade's spell flies from the gun, and flows through the air following the bullet, lowering until it hits the ground. It's only half way to the hay stack.

"Better."

"That was better?" I groan.

"Don't worry about it, progress is good," he says. "How many bullets do you have left?"

"Um... four?"

"Good. Always keep it in your mind so you can remember without stopping to think. Now, try again."

I grip the gun tighter in my hands, aim, pull the hammer back, and fire. This time the spell show's it going farther, but to the right.

"I can't aim this thing."

"Sure you can, it's just nerves. Let me help you."

He steps behind me, and wraps his arms around me until his

hands are over mine. My skin warms. He smells of the earth and citrus. His breath tickles my ear.

"The gun isn't the enemy here. You've no reason to fear it if you treat it properly. Is it comfortable in your hands?"

Right now, none of me is comfortable, primarily where he's touching my back and arms. Compared to that, the gun is like a brush in my hand. I know better what to do with the gun than with him. "It's fine."

"Are you sure? You're shaking."

My breathing quickens. "There's not much I can do about it."

"True. Go ahead and aim again."

I point the gun at the hay stack. He lifts my arms a little higher. "Take a breath and hold it."

When I do, his scent mixed with the smell of the gun-smoke fills me.

"Pull the hammer back and fire."

It's easier to pull the hammer back. I shoot. The spell shows that the bullet plummets just short of the hay stack.

Zade moves away from me, leaving me cold even though the day's warm. "Good job. You're getting better."

We practice for a while, though he doesn't put his arms around me again. I wish he would, but it's easier to concentrate without them. I've managed to hit the stack a few times when he says we're done for the day.

He hands me a box of bullets. "Keep these somewhere safe."

I nod.

"You can practice whenever you want. At least once a day. I'll help you when I can. Waverly can give you some tips, too. She's great with a gun."

Of course she is. "I'll keep that in mind."

"I'm going to stay out and practice. See you at dinner."

"Until then."

I head back for the house, the gun and box of bullets clunky in my hands. Before I turn the corner, I glance back at him. He casts a spell that looks like a bird and shoots at it. The bird wavers and falls apart. He must have hit it. Why does he bother shooting when he can just cast a spell?

I'm not sure, but I can still feel his arms around me. Comforting. Guiding. The metallic smell of my hands stays with me all day, reminding me of him and the threats lingering over him.

# CHAPTER 28

THE NEXT WEEK, I'm sitting in the garden reading Julia's journal. It's much easier than shooting like I've been practicing. It's fascinating to learn about her life. She's unlike any woman I've ever known before. The pain she writes about is as real as I've felt or seen my sisters and mother go through. But instead of her husband being the cause, she speaks of how he helps her through it. Then she moves on with her life. She sounds more like a man.

The bench creaks beside me. Zade. My heart quivers. I've been caught. I close the book as quietly as I can, hoping he doesn't notice it's not the Woman's Canon. I give him a small smile. What will happen if he catches me?

"Good book?" He asks.

I cling to it. "Fine."

"Did you find it in the library?"

The unfamiliar word breaks through part of my fear. "What's a library?"

"The room with all the books." His eyebrows bounce a couple times, lips tugging upward. "The room I found you hiding in shortly after coming here."

My hand flies to my mouth. "You saw me?"

He chuckles. "Yes, but you didn't look like you wanted me to, so I didn't say anything."

I reach my other hand to cover my whole face. "I can't believe you saw me. I thought I got away with it."

"Got away with what?"

Being from another country, he might not know the rules, so maybe I shouldn't tell him. Except he did say he knew the laws well enough to keep from getting in trouble. Trouble that would lead to his death. He has to know about it. Besides, maybe this is a good way to figure out how he'll react if he figures out what I have. "Being caught with a book besides the Woman's Canon."

"Woman's Canon should be burned."

I take my hands off my face. His eyes are wide, face pale. He looks... Is he worried about having said that out loud? Does he really feel that way?

He scans the garden. No one is around, yet he casts the salmon-colored spell around us, keeping our words safe. "Please keep it a secret. I shouldn't have even told you. But since it slipped out, I'm hoping I can trust you with it."

It's been long enough that I feel I know him. Know when he's telling the truth and when he's keeping things to himself. This feels like truth. If the council found out, the threats on his life would quickly multiply. Why would he want to burn the book that tells women how to act? I know why I do, but why would he?

"I suppose I could keep it secret."

"Thank you." He points at the book in my hand. "Is that one I'll need to burn or something else?"

With what he revealed, maybe I can reveal a bit of truth, as well. "It's different. It's writings by the woman who used to live here."

"Julia?"

"How did you know her name?"

"I made it a point to know."

None of this seems to upset him. In fact, he seems interested.

Could he really be fine with me reading? "Then perhaps you will know if her journal entries are based on fact or fanciful ideas."

"Since I haven't read it myself, I don't really know. From what I've gathered, she wasn't the fanciful sort. I could read it through if you'd like and give you my opinion."

Though I've already read the whole thing, and am just picking out bits and pieces, I'm not sure I want to give it away. I grip the book tighter. "May I have it back when you're finished?"

"Of course."

I bite my lower lip and hand him the book.

He takes it and runs his fingers over the cover. "It means something to you?"

Something, but what I'm not sure. Not more than the novel I pilfered from the library, but different. I want Zade to be kind and caring like Jacob, but without us dying. Perhaps Zade is? "I'm not sure as of yet."

"Maybe we can talk about it after I've had a chance to look through it." As he settles further onto the bench, I contemplate what that may mean for me. For him. For us. Us.

His next words startle me out of my daydream. "I was wondering if you'd like to deliver invitations with me."

"I suppose."

"I can take them if you wish, or we could have them delivered. I just thought you'd want to."

"I do." I smooth a wrinkle from my skirt. "It's just that I've never done anything like this before. Mother always said I was too much trouble to go."

He rests a hand on mine, stilling my nervous action. "You're good with people, I'm sure you'll do fine."

He's warm through my glove. Sustaining. "How much time do you think we need to get them delivered?"

"It depends on how many we decide to hand deliver. We should at least visit all the council members, a few other prominent warlock households. After that, how about we see if you feel like doing more?"

It depends on how I feel? "That would be fine." More than fine. "We should get them out in the next two weeks though. Bethany will get after my manners if we don't."

He chuckles. "I've a council meeting the day after tomorrow, but none next week."

The garden is silent. With the spell and us not talking, it's an eerie sort of sound. It gets me thinking about the tarnished park. Zade said I could ask anything. Finally, I work up the courage to say, "The other day at the park, Councilman Barkley said something."

He rubs his forehead. "He said a lot of things."

"The tarnished law he spoke of." When he stays silent, I go farther. "What did he mean by that?"

His face darkens. "Some of the unmarried women have started rebelling."

"Women like my sisters?" What do they have to do with the tarnished? And why are they rebelling? How are they rebelling?

"Not them. Those you call tarnished. The women are seen as the problem, but I believe the men are rebelling just as much."

"What are they doing?"

He faces me. "Some have been escaping to Envado and other countries. Enough have left that it's caused a strain on the working force. The council and upper class don't like losing their workers."

"But there are so many of them. Plus, they're always threatening to make more. And the lower class owes debts that they repay with work. Isn't it enough? Is it really a problem if people want to leave?"

He shrugs. "If it was just that, I don't know, maybe the council would leave them alone. I doubt it, but maybe. What's seen as the real problem is that some of them have started harassing council members and a few powerful warlocks."

The death threats jump to mind. "Are you in any danger?"

"I'm safe enough."

It doesn't sound like he really is. The weight of the gun on my leg is comforting, though I'd do little good with it should the need arise. I want him safe. "But what of the problem we had and the others you've mentioned?"

"Not related."

How can he know? At least this isn't a threat, as well. "And what of the new law? What are they proposing?"

"They are trying to implement more restrictions, and make current laws more severely punished."

Katherine flashes through my mind. How will this affect her? "What type restrictions?"

"You're very inquisitive today."

I blush. "Sorry. I didn't mean it." Except I did, and I want to know. I just don't want to push the one person who's giving me answers too far.

"Don't be sorry, it's a refreshing change."

He wants me to ask? I lick my lips and say, "Would you tell me more about the restrictions then?"

"Of course." He clasps his fists together and I lean forward to better catch the details. "All those considered unfit will have their ink spelled to change colors on a monthly basis. They'll have to check in monthly which will include being tracked all the time."

"How would they be tracked?"

"A certain spell can be used to find those who participate. Mostly, they'll use it to restrict their movements. If a person with their spelled ink goes out of an allowed area, severe pain will befall them. If they don't hurry back, they'll die."

"Die?" My heart is cold.

His nose flares. "In some cases."

"Will they be speaking of this at the next meeting?"

"They always talk about it."

This is too much for me to hold still. I stand and cross to a table. Its surface is hard beneath the weight of my hands. They want things worse for Katherine. And what about Katherine's workers? And the other tarnished?

The council wants to make life harder for them. One small step out of line and they could die. Gone forever. Not even something less than a shadow deserves this. And Katherine is worth more than a shadow. She's worth more than any warlock.

Whirling around, I ask, "Will you take me to a meeting with you?"

He jumps to his feet. "You want me to take you to a meeting?"

Though he's a several feet from me, he still towers above me. I cower back. "It was just a thought."

"Sorry." He sits back down and rubs the back of his neck. "You want to go to a council meeting?"

"I, um—is there a law against it?" I wish I had access to the laws and not just the Woman's Canon.

For a moment he's quiet. "There's usually only the council and servants, but no. I don't think there's a law against it."

I step forward. In my mind, I keep the image of Katherine taking one step outside of safety and dying. Nothing that bad will happen to me just from asking. But so much could happen to her. I can be strong enough.

"Maybe you could take me. Make it a show of dominance for the council."

"No."

The sharp reply silences me. If I persist, he may break his promise and a fist or hex will fly my way. Except, this is Zade. Not my Father or another warlock. He's only ever encouraged me. I have to believe he's different and if he's not, I want to know.

"Why not?"

He looks me straight in the eye. "I don't want you there."

The reply stings. "Because women are supposed to be silent child bearers."

His head lowers to his hands. "That's not it. There are things you don't understand."

"Right." He still thinks of me as only a woman, even if he doesn't punish me like he should. I'm sick of being just a woman.

He shakes his head before raising it. "Not like that. Just–just let me think about it, all right?"

The answer is so stunning, it takes a moment to reply. "Yes, of course." I back away from him. If he wants to think, I'll give him space to do so. "I'll leave you to it."

Before I depart, he says, "Don't forget, you're delivering invites with me."

"I won't."

I hasten from the salmon spell, feeling nothing as I step though it. Zade sits within its confines, lost in thought. I want to do this. For Katherine. For the other tarnished. If I can't free myself from a warlock's control, I can at least try to help others. But even that depends on what my owner allows.

# CHAPTER 29

DELIVERING invites drags on longer than I expected. It starts at the Grand Chancellor's house. His son, Nathaniel, greets us and accepts the invitation. We don't stay long before moving on to Chancellor Ryan's house.

He's nothing like Zade. Arrogant to the point of thinking we delivered his invitation before anyone else's, even the Grand Chancellor's. I guess being only one of two Chancellors could make a person think they're above everyone, but he pushes the limits. At least none of the other councilmen we visit are as arrogant. We call on several more before heading home. After another long carriage ride this morning, we're ready to deliver more.

I stare at the next door, belonging to a house not far from my Father's where we just came from. No one came to greet us. We had to leave the invitation with the footman. I haven't even seen my littlest sister yet. Does she look more like mother or Father? What will her fate be?

After that disappointment, I was hoping we could be done, but I suppose we do need to deliver as many as we can. I brush one of Katherine's best dresses free of wrinkles and try to prepare myself for another forced conversation. At least they haven't lasted very long. Yet.

"You're doing fine," Zade says.

Though his confidence in me is heartening, I shake my head. Before I can respond, the door opens.

Like before, Zade steps forward and says the line Bethany quietly suggested. "We've brought an invitation for the household."

"Please, come in." The thin footman moves aside and motions us inside.

The hall is elegant. Stone tiles line the floor. White walls reach far above even Zade's head, with windows at the top. We enter and the footman closes the door behind us. The morning sun warming us from the many windows, it's a pleasant temperature. Much better than the fall air.

"Please wait and I'll see who's available."

Once he's gone, I whisper, "It feels good in here."

"It's spelled to feel the perfect temperature," Zade says.

"They can do that?"

He nods. "The same spell is on our house, too."

That explains a lot. "This is nice."

"Yes. Councilman Daniel is level headed. Hopefully his wife is the same."

The footman returns. "Follow me."

He leads us to a nearby sitting room. There are more windows, lighting the golden colors of the room. Matching golden sofas and chairs are clustered together throughout. A woman waits in the middle, by the closest set. "Welcome to our home."

This is the first time we've been greeted by a woman. It's usually been a warlock, sometimes a wife in the background. She's much shorter than me and a pudge of a woman. The tattoo above her collarbone is a triangle with v's cut out of each corner, ringed by interlacing triangles. Simple, but unique. Her brown eyes are full of life.

Zade recovers much faster than I do. "Thank you."

"You'll have to forgive Councilman Daniel, he's unavailable to greet you himself."

This explains her sole presence. Yet, why let his wife greet us by herself instead of a servant?

"Don't worry about it," Zade says.

"I don't believe we've been properly introduced. I'm Annabelle, Councilman Daniel's."

"Pleasure to meet you. I'm Chancellor Zade and this is my intended, Serena." I give a curtsy enjoying this introduction better than the one Thomas always gave at the tournament. "I've enjoyed working with Councilman Daniel. He's a good man."

"Yes, he is. Won't you please sit?" She indicates a couch with a table in front of it filled with refreshments.

I perch on the couch. Once I'm arranged, Zade says, "You have some nice hunting grounds. I wonder if you'd let me explore them."

Annabelle's smile widens. "Please, feel free. Would you like someone to show you around or do you prefer solitary exploration?"

"Solitary exploration suits me." He kisses my gloved hand. Heat floods my checks. It must have been to help spread word that he's interested in me as a wife. Though it's only to save his life, it doesn't stop the warmth sweeping through me. "Enjoy your visit." With a bow at Annabelle, he leaves the room.

I stare after him feeling lost. He's taken charge of everything until this point. I squeeze my hands together, wishing they were free of their gloves.

"Just us girls then." Annabelle settles in a chair across from me.

I pull the invitation out of my handbag and give it to her. Before I have too much time to think on it, I say, "We're hosting a ball and would like the privilege of having the company of your husband and you."

"Hand delivering the invitations, what a nice touch." Her eyes brighten as she scans it. "And it's been spelled. However did your future husband come up with the idea?"

After grabbing a cup and saucer off the tables, I take a sip of lemon water, trying to think of what I can say and what I should avoid. "He's Envadi, you know. He has new ideas about a great many things."

"I've heard." She grabs her own cup. "If you don't mind my asking, what did he think of your engagement dress?"

The cup slips on my saucer. I hurry to correct it before it spills. Either she was there or word must be traveling about my taboo incident. She's curt. Two can play at that game.

"He approved. Did you know that in Envado, they don't have engagement ceremonies and when they marry, the bride wears a white dress sort of like a ball gown, trimmed with their favorite color of ribbons and flowers?"

Her brows shoot up. "I hadn't heard. I would've enjoyed a wedding dress like that."

My breath goes out of me. She's perfect to introduce to Katherine. Afraid it will give away my shaking hands, I set my cup down. "If you're interested, I know someone who creates magnificent dresses. She's making my ball gown. In fact, she made this as well."

"That dress. Really?" She sets her own cup down. "It's beautiful, but does seem a little different."

I take a deep breath. I want to help Katherine, but I don't want to endanger either of us or Zade. Whatever trouble I get in will reflect poorly on him and make things worse. "The buttons in the back are only decoration. These laces in the front are the true way of tightening and loosening the gown. I often dress and undress myself."

"Often? You have other dresses like this?" Her face is void of emotion.

Suddenly, I feel as if I've said too much. Given too much away.

I haven't mentioned Katherine's name yet. Perhaps she can escape punishment. But I've put myself and Zade in danger.

A moment passes. Though I try hard not to, I end up fidgeting with my gloves. How can I reply to ease her fears about me?

"I'm afraid I've been too frank," she says. "I didn't mean to scare you. It's just, your engagement dress was a welcome change. To know you've also managed to change your everyday dresses is unbelievable. I'd love to know who your seamstress is and utilize her."

Relief rushes through me. "Your husband wouldn't mind?"

"No more than yours." She grins.

But will she mind the seamstress? "What are your feelings on the tarnished?"

She mumbles, "We, uh, don't have any tarnished servants."

"You don't? How do you manage without them?" I've never heard of such a thing before. Even Zade has tarnished servants.

A high-pitched laugh bounces through the room. "Oh, we get by."

"Your husband must be owed a lot."

She grabs a pastry. "Before getting on the council, he was a banker. Met a lot of people who were trying their best to stay out of debt but struggling. He now hires some of them and pays them to help keep them out of debt."

This is going better than expected. "Our owners are more alike than we first thought. Mine also pays his workers, though he also employs the tarnished at the same price instead of giving them just food and shelter."

The pastry falls to her lap. "He pays the tarnished?"

"He does."

She picks up the fallen pastry and sets in on a plate. Then she brushes the crumbs from her skirt. "I've never heard of such a thing. It may be something I should mention to Daniel." Her voice trails off.

"Have you spoken to many tarnished?"

233

"Not a one."

I can do this. "My seamstress is a tarnished."

"Your seamstress? How did that come about?"

"None of the regulars would make what I desired for my engagement gown."

Her eyes widen. "But she did?"

"Yes. I've discovered the tarnished are very capable." More than capable.

"Perhaps I'll get one. The ease of dressing myself would have advantages."

I don't mention the breeches. That's too far for me. Or the gun slit in my pocket. I've no idea how she would react to it and I've pushed everyone's safety enough for one day.

She scoots closer to the edge of her chair. "Who's this seamstress?"

I give Katherine's information, all the while silently hoping good things come of it and not ill. After that, our conversation drifts into the more mundane. Despite the shift in topics, she's still not afraid to say what she means.

A while later, Zade returns. Having him back in the room fills me with relief, though he's breathing hard and his clothes look a little ragged. My shoulders roll down as the tension seeps from them. I feel as if I succeeded with Annabelle. At least I hope I've helped Katherine without making anything worse for Zade.

"Your grounds are great. If Daniel ever needs a hunting partner, be sure to let me know."

"Only if you'll bring Serena to keep me company."

He grins at me. "A woman does need a break from her intended once in a while."

She laughs. "I'll be sure to give him word."

We're shown out and Zade escorts me to the carriage.

"You two seemed to get along."

"Better than expected. She has Katherine's information, though only time will tell if she makes use of it."

"Good to hear. I had high hopes for them. Let's end the day on that note." He scans the area around us.

I look around, but see nothing. "What are you looking for?"

"Someone followed us here." His jaw tightens.

After a second look, I still see nothing. "Trouble?"

"Nothing new."

But from the set of his jaw, I can tell it's serious. He hurries me into the carriage and gives directions to the driver to head home. My gut twists. I think someone just tried to kill him. Again.

# CHAPTER 30

THE LAST CHAIR is set in place. I survey Zade's room. A few servants are putting the remaining pieces of the desk together. The woodworker did a good job adjusting things to the proper size. Or at least it looks that way. It will be hard to know until he uses it. As long as everything is big enough, it's perfect, and the project somewhat helped to distract me from the fact that someone is trying to kill him.

All his chairs have been replaced with larger ones, except for one, which is left for a guest. The bed matches my new one perfectly, except mine has a canopy with a soft indigo cloth draped across it, an idea I borrowed from Julia's room. The size of the bed is too much, but something about the folds of cloth around me is comforting. Cynthia and I couldn't see Zade wanting the canopy, so his is plain.

The new desk will be left by the old one when it's assembled. There are so many papers, we didn't want to move any of them. The woodworker said if it works, it would be easy enough to make a second for his study. I rest in an over-sized chair, Cynthia across from me in the regular sized one.

"You did a good job. Thank you," I say.

"Do you think Chancellor Zade will like it?"

I shrug. Maybe? It's hard to know, but I do. I hope he does, as well. If it helps him feel more comfortable, it will have been worth the work. I want him to be comfortable. And safe, but I can't do anything about the latter. "We'll see."

"If he doesn't like it, he can donate his bed to me and we'll get another canopy. Yours is fantastic."

"It's big enough, I could probably go back to sharing it with you and our sisters and not even notice."

She giggles. "It is most likely. Perhaps we should go to dinner."

"What we should have done was think ahead and had it brought to us. I'm exhausted."

Me, too, but hopefully it is worth it. "If the Chancellor doesn't like the furniture, we'll tell them to put it in another room up here so the servants don't have to keep moving everything."

"We could ask them to bring dinner up, I suppose."

"After all that, I'm not really hungry."

BAM!

I twist toward the noise. In the open door way, Zade's a tower of rage. I freeze in place. Cynthia cowers in her chair.

"Get out!" he yells.

I can't move. The remaining servants scamper away. He pounds into the room. Black spells fly from him darting around. One zips close to me. I jolt back in my chair. After it whizzes past, I spring from my chair and hover in front of Cynthia.

"What are you doing in here?" He thunders closer, dark spells stained with red blasting around him.

I flinch. He stops, smashing his palms across his face. The spells finish rushing around the room, rebounding to him. Some of the tension seeps out of him, his shoulders slumping. My own pose doesn't relax. I realize I'm shaking.

"Sorry for losing my temper." His face tightens and he closes his eyes for a moment. After several deep breaths he opens them again and his face eases. "The council meeting didn't go as planned and I've been worried about—" He sighs. "Never mind. It doesn't matter. I still shouldn't have lost my temper."

He collapses onto the chair I vacated, face drawn except his lower lip which is pushed up. With a more subdued voice, he says, "What's going on?"

Still uncertain, I stand at attention making sure I'm blocking Cynthia from view as well as I can without looking at her. "It's my fault. I thought you could use some furniture that fit you better."

His gaze roves around before glancing at the chair he occupies. "I didn't realize…" With another glance at me, he hunches in the chair and his voice softens further. "I'm not going to hurt either of you."

I stare at him, knowing there's going to be more.

"Sometimes I lose my temper and yell more than I should, but I'll never purposely hurt you. I won't break that promise."

It's true, he hasn't yet, but those spells were dark and flying fast. I struggle to normalize my breathing. Cynthia nudges my leg. I glance back at her.

She mouths, "I'm fine."

The expression on her face is sincere. I purse my lips. After considering a moment, I move to the rug next to her, curling my legs beneath me.

"Don't sit on the floor." He stands, moving toward the desk. "Let me get you a chair."

"I prefer the floor."

He grumbles back into his seat. With another survey of the room, he says, "This is great. The desk looks like it'll fit my needs. This chair is the best I've sat in since I got here. I can't believe you both did this for me. I'm such a fool."

"You didn't tell Serena to do it?" Cynthia asks.

I cringe. For a moment, he's thoughtful. "I guess I did. It just turned out so great."

My face heats. "Glad it meets your expectations."

It's clear he doesn't know what to think as he cocks an eyebrow at me.

"We're delighted," Cynthia says. "We've been waiting for it and worried you wouldn't like it after all the work we've been through."

"It's really great." He sets his elbow on the arm of the chair and rests his chin on his palm. "While you were getting it ready, did you happen to come in here?"

Trouble. "Yes. Sorry, I wanted it to be a surprise when it arrived."

"Of course. When did you come in?"

"A couple weeks ago," Cynthia answers. "You should have seen the shopkeeper's face when we went without you. But as soon as he realized the order was for you, he promised he'd have his servants working full time on it."

"I expect he'll be sending you a rather large bill soon," I say. Will it bring more trouble, or does he really like it?

"I'll watch for it." He chuckles. "Next time you want to surprise me, don't use my room. Or tell Waverly. I knew someone had come here and was worried."

The comment about Waverly bothers me, but I focus on his last thought. Did he think we were one of those trying to take his life?

"How did you know we were here?" Cynthia asks.

"A spell that always wards my room. Usually, it tells me who's been here. But it didn't this time. I thought it must have been a powerful warlock, but now I'm wondering if it's the strength of magic concentrated in you two interfering. Naivety can be powerful. And Serena's blood is strong with magic. Its made my own powers increase ever since..."

"Ever since what?" Cynthia asks.

But I know he won't say. He can't say anything about the ceremony when my blood, teeming with magic, joined his. Did that mean something more than just tradition? I shyly peer at him. It's not like I can ask with the spell preventing me from talking about it.

"Not important." After gazing back at me a moment, he shakes his head. "I wonder if you're as strong as your sister, Cynthia."

Behind me, she wiggles. "You can check if you'd like. But I must warn you, blood isn't my favorite thing."

The fact that she asks should surprise me more than it does, but I must be too used to her talking of marriage. This is a way to know what her offers will be like. It breaks a rule though, to ask Zade to do it. She's spending too much time around me. Becoming more and more outspoken and careless of the rules. I doubt it was a side effect of spying Father wanted. "She usually faints at the sight of it."

Something whacks me on the shoulder. I twist and wink at her.

She blushes. "It's true."

"Blood isn't necessary. It's a little more accurate, but not much," Zade says. "I'd only need to hold your hand. It's not a problem for me, but are you sure you want to?"

"I'm sure."

He crosses over to us and sits next to me, but facing her. His body heat brushes my arm. A faint scent of citrus drifts from him. I move around so I can watch.

Cynthia holds her hand out to him and he envelopes it with his own. He stares into her eyes. It's uncomfortable to watch. I brush a speck off my dress. This is silly. She's bound to be like me. We shouldn't have him check. It could get us in trouble if someone finds out.

"Amazing," he whispers. They let go of each other, but he stays next to me.

Cynthia looks like a Chancellor's wife situated above us. Straight back. Head lowered. Hands clasped on her lap. Her silver earrings and necklace wouldn't be allowed, but otherwise, she's perfect. Except it's not her. I'm the one who will fail at it.

"Well?" She says.

"I almost don't believe it," he says, "but it's true. You possess even more magic than your sister. I've rarely, if ever come across such strong magic. Just think what you could do with that kind of power."

"Father will be anxious to marry me off."

"No," I shout. Their gazes flash toward me. I swallow and lower my voice. "She doesn't need to worry about a husband, yet. There are a few months left."

When she doesn't contradict me right away, I wonder if she's too angry to speak.

"Surely not," Zade says, his voice going cold. "I forgot myself. If you ladies will excuse me, I've had a long day."

I bound to my feet. "Yes, of course. Will you be joining us for dinner?"

"No, I'm afraid not. I asked cook to send a tray."

Cynthia stands. "Thank you for checking."

He nods, but says nothing.

With no sign of hesitation, she wraps her arm around me. The gesture is new, but feels as if it's meant for sisters. She must not be cross with me. "We'll see you later."

I follow her example and we're out the door. When we're part way to our room, I work up the courage to ask, "Are you well?"

"I'm fine."

"Indeed?"

She sighs. "It wasn't a shock, but something I hoped for. Now that I know for sure, well, I guess I'm glad." It takes her a moment to continue while we walk through the passage. "It's just, seeing your relationship with Zade, I don't know if anyone who asks for my hand will be able to compare with that."

Our feet shuffle through the hall. I let her words absorb into me. She's right. No one can compete with how Chancellor Zade treats me, but does he see me as more than just a possession? I want him to, but I'm afraid to hope.

# CHAPTER 31

A KNOCK STARTLES ME AWAKE. It's still dark. I groan. It sounds again. Not one of the servants or my sisters, they would just come in. Who would want to bother me? There's no one else. I haul myself out of bed. After throwing on my robe, I rub my eyes. The knock comes a third time before I answer it.

Zade stands before me, dark circles under his eyes. "Better get dressed if you're coming to the council meeting with me."

I slam my door closed. Did he really just say that? I open it again. One of his eyes is partially closed and his forehead wrinkled.

"What did you say?" I ask.

"If you still want to go to a council meeting, get dressed."

"That's what I thought." A long moment follows. He's really going to let me do this. Do I really want to? I don't think anything like it has ever been done. My pulse accelerates. "Why did you change your mind about letting me come?"

The line of his mouth tightens on one side. "Women in Envado are part of parliament. Did you know we have a queen?"

"What's a queen?"

"She's sort of like the equivalent of the Grand Chancellor."

"How can that be? A woman not only in government, but ruling? It's not possible." I try to imagine what it would be like to have a woman on the council with Father. I can't picture it.

He looks away from me. "The use of magic isn't a requirement for parliament."

"What a different place you come from."

In a voice so quiet, I almost can't hear him. "You have no idea."

It's even more different than I think? I can't imagine what else would surprise me more than a woman leading their government, but right now I need to focus on the council meeting. "I suppose I'll get dressed then?"

"It's up to you, but if you're going to come to one, you'll want to make it to this one."

What does that mean? I'm not sure if I dare ask and have more of my curiosity make him change his mind again. I can't believe he's asking in the first place.

"There's a condition."

Holding the door steady, I brace myself against it. "What is it?"

"You'll practice using your gun more and carry it with you at all times."

Which do I want more, to go to the meeting or to avoid the gun? I lick my lips. "I'll be ready."

A black cloak appears from behind him. "Wear this over your clothes. You'll stand out less." He starts down the stairs and calls over his shoulder, "Remember, forty minutes. If you're not there, I'm not waiting."

Without bothering to close the door, I ring for Waverly. I rush to my wardrobe wondering what to wear. None of my new things will suffice. Something more conservative. I grab the dress Father most approved of, though it doesn't have a slot for a gun like the others. I suppose I could still strap it to my leg, though I doubt there'll be time to grab it if needed.

Waverly enters with her usual tea tray.

"That was faster than expected," I say.

She sets the tray down. "Zade said you might need me early this morning."

I take off my robe and nightdress. "Yes, would you help me into this, please?"

She grabs the black dress. I step into it, already dreading it. As she works on tightening the back, I feel confined. I miss the freedom.

When I'm cinched, she puts things away while I eat breakfast. Nothing looks appetizing this morning. I grab a biscuit.

"What's the excitement about? Are you doing something for the ball? I haven't heard of anything."

I sip some juice. "No. Zade decided to let me go to a council meeting."

She drops the brush. "A council meeting?"

I put the barely touched biscuit back on the tray. "Yes."

After retrieving the brush, she says, "I'd better give you one of those boring buns then."

The tugging on my hair is familiar, though uncomfortable. I hadn't realized how much I've enjoyed her new way of styling my hair over the tight pulling. "Thank you, Waverly."

"No problem. If it's what Zade wants, I'll do what I can to help."

If she knew it was my idea and he's reluctant to let me, would she still be willing?

"There," she says. "All set."

The clock says there's still twenty minutes left.

"Would you mind giving me some face paint as well?"

"But you never paint your face."

"Today, I do." Though I'll hate every minute of the cakey mixture. "I want to make a favorable impression for Zade."

Without another word, she deftly applies a hefty amount of face paint. More than I've ever worn before, though not more than mother. Its chalky, fatty smell makes me sneeze. How have women worn this for years?

"It'll smear, so let it dry."

With pink cheeks and lips, eyes lined with black, I don't look like myself. But neither do I look like countless other woman who have painted their faces. There are angles to it, subtle, but there. Slashed at the corners of my eyes and across my cheekbones. I'm owned by a Chancellor, but on closer inspection, I'm different.

I close my eyes and take a breath. "Thank you."

She places a hand on my arm. "Courage."

I open my eyes and force a smile. After pulling on the cloak Zade gave me, I head for the door. I can do this. I will do this. The carriage leaves in ten minutes. I will not miss it.

\* \* \*

ZADE HOLDS out a hand and helps me from the carriage. Despite his spell aiding my carriage sickness, my stomach still feels off. Once I'm steady, I realize we're at Councilman Daniel's and Annabelle's house. This makes some of the tension leave, but not enough to really do any good.

A footman opens the door for us. He pauses when he sees me. Zade stares at him until, without saying a thing, he leads us to a long room. I hesitate at the door. The footman scurries back the way we came. Conversation drifts to us.

Zade's mammoth arms cross and a scowl mars his face. "Come along, woman."

Feeling shamed, though I'm sure it's only for show, I follow him alongside the table. It's almost as long as the room, with twelve chairs around it. A few warlocks are already seated. They fall silent as Zade passes. Or rather, when I trail after him. I hasten my pace.

A servant is behind every chair. They each wear a cloak like mine. That explains why Zade wanted me to wear it. At least I'll blend in a little more. At the end of the long table is another one, smaller and placed across the end to create the shape of a T. Three softer looking chairs spread across it. Two windows, behind the smaller table, let in light. When Zade reaches the chair furthest to the left on the smaller table, a servant moves toward it. He holds out a hand to stop the servant.

"My chair, wench."

The command is foreign coming from his lips, but I've lived in a world with commands longer than without them. I automatically do his bidding. When he's seated, I step behind him and slightly to the left since the servant is on the right.

The light from the window warms my back, but I don't move the cloak. I clasp my hands together beneath it. My body is rigid. Though I don't look up, I feel eyes on me. Watching me. Wondering about me. Waiting to hear a reason for my presence. Or to shun my presence.

Others enter, but I don't look at them either. I focus on the swirling pattern in the rug.

Someone asks, "What's she doing here?"

It takes me a moment to realize why I've stopped breathing. Father. He can't hurt me. I'm not his. I take a deep breath. No reply comes. I chance a peek at Zade through my lashes. He's scribbling away, pointedly ignoring Father. The floor returns to being my main focus. This is pointless. I'm not going to learn anything, but rather be reminded of how life is. How it still should be.

I draw the cloak tighter around me. Despite the warmth of the room, I'm more grateful than ever for the shield it offers. Several more minutes pass of men entering. Silence continues. Is it always silent or is it just me? Warlocks always seem full of talk and boasting, but I don't know if it's the same at a meeting.

Finally, someone says, "The Grand Chancellor."

I start to look up, but Zade's hand is behind his chair pointing to the floor. I duck my head back down. The only sound is the Grand Chancellor striding closer. His chair creaks as it's pulled back. He passes right by me, his cloak brushing against the tips of

246

my shoes. I force myself not to take a step back. It's easier since the window is close behind. I've nowhere to go.

He takes his chair. "Proceed."

There's a shuffle of movement. I chance another peek, though Zade is still pointing down. A tarnished is being led into the room. By the curves beneath her robe and delicate nose, I'd guess a woman. What's she doing here? I thought no woman had been before.

Her eyes are glazed, but her face is pure and clean save for the black tendrils of ink curling over her face. A servant helps her onto the table. My breathing quickens. What is going on? She lays with her head at the Grand Chancellor's place. The tournament flashes through my mind.

The Grand Chancellor casts a golden spell. After the gold recedes, silver gleams in his hands. At first I think it's part of the spell, but then realize the object holds its shape. The sharp blade of a dagger. It darts toward her.

My vision sways. Sacrifice. They're going to sacrifice her. My small breakfast threatens to come back. I focus on breathing. Once I've more control, I force my gaze away from the scene and clench my fists. No matter what happens, I can't do anything. No screaming, no fainting, no intervening. What would yelling do? The fact that I'm here is going to endanger Zade more. Calling out would only make his fate and my own worse, not save the girl.

There's not a sound. I count to twenty. Maybe it's not what I thought it was. I chance another glance, hoping I misunderstood.

The girl's eyes have gone from dazed to lifeless. Her face is white, making the ink more vivid against her skin. The tip of the dagger drips crimson on the table next to her.

A hole is above her collarbone. From it runs a thin, red line staining the side of her neck. No other blood taints the scene, but she's clearly dead. I bite my lower lip. Hard.

# CHAPTER 32

IT'S difficult to tell under the light of the sun, but the Grand Chancellor appears to be glowing again, just like after the sacrifice at the tournament. He claps three times. Four servants come in and take hold of the woman's remains. Pinpricks of light fill my vision. I hold my head down and take slow, deep breaths. Despite my efforts, I almost faint. I think of my sisters. Let them fill my thoughts. Finally, the world comes back into view. Though still dizzy, I resume standing straight.

The scraping of chairs and chatter of voices fills the room. I knot my hands together. The servant next to me moves to the Grand Chancellor. I sneak a glimpse. The council is relaxing, servants filling their glasses, one is getting his shoulders massaged. Once the glasses are filled, the servants return to their posts.

"Before we get to the agenda," the Grand Chancellor says, "I'd like to be informed why a female is in our meeting."

"Hear, hear," Father says. "If she were mine, I wouldn't permit it."

Zade straightens in his chair. "I believe that's no longer your decision. I've a right to do whatever I wish with my possessions."

"You can't break the law no matter your ownership. One of my own possessions has been informing me of what's going on in your household." Father's words cut into me. Bethany. What information has he gotten from the spell on her? Coming was a bad idea.

"What information is that?" The Grand Chancellor asks.

I hold my breath as Father says, "They've been visiting the tarnished area of town. Getting dresses that are two pieces and not just one. Dresses they can get in and out of by themselves."

Silence. Are they going to tarnish me now and kill Zade for not keeping control of me? I stare at Zade though I can't see his face. I didn't mean to bring this on him.

"I don't think there's a law that dictates how women dress," Councilman Daniel says. "There's only the guidelines in the Woman's Canon."

My chin quivers. I work to hold it still. Will his words be enough to save us?

"Unfortunately," Chancellor Ryan says, "he's correct. Maybe we should look into changing that."

"Put it on the agenda for a different day," the Grand Chancellor says. "Today is full and we have yet to address the issue of why a woman is present."

Will they really let us wear what we want? Not punish Zade or me for it? For now at least, it appears that way. But it also sounds like they are going to make plans to correct the oversight. I don't know whether to be relieved, angry, or sombered by the thought.

"But—" Father starts, but the Grand Chancellor ignores him.

"She may be your possession, Chancellor Zade, but I see you're still not used to our customs. No woman except the sacrifice has ever been allowed to our meeting. Are you offering her as one?"

My airway constricts. I picture myself laying on the table. I grip my hands tighter. Is the altar about to become my final resting place? I won't allow myself to be taken without a fight.

"I'm sure you'd love the power of her blood, but that's not why she's here."

Power of my blood? What does that mean? Is that why the Grand Chancellor was glowing? The magic in her blood combines with their own?

"Then, please do tell us why she's here so we can move on to more important matters."

"I felt it would be a good lesson, having her here submitting to my will. In fact," he turns toward the servant next to me, "give her the jug, she can keep my glass full."

The servant next to me thrusts the jug at me. Wine splashes on my cloak. I grab hold of it and try to mimic how the others are holding it. It's heavy.

A murmur fills the room.

"He's brilliant," Councilman Daniel says above the noise. "Jonathan, fetch my wife."

The servant behind him scurries from the room. The chatter grows louder. I almost don't dare hope Annabelle will arrive. Through my lashes, I watch the Grand Chancellor's body grow taut. Next to him, Zade lounges back in his chair, content to study the paperwork before him instead of the growing fray around him.

The voices speak too fast for me to keep track of.

"Can they really do this?"

"There's no law against it."

"We should make one."

"Wait, let's not be too hasty. Maybe it's a good idea."

"It is a good idea. Did you see how pale she was? I thought she was going to faint."

"She's still pale. I'm still expecting her to fall on the floor."

I grip the pitcher tighter and keep my gaze lowered.

"Women don't need to hear warlock's work."

"Not like it'll make a difference to them. Except maybe to teach them to be more respectful."

Their comments increase my desire to hold myself together. The debate continues. More are for it than I supposed would be. Not for the reasons I'd like, but it's better than nothing.

Finally, the door opens. Risking a peek, I see Annabelle wandering toward her husband looking confused. Relief fills me. She's halfway across the room from me and I can't say a word, but I'm no longer alone. Councilman Daniel motions for her to get behind him and promptly ignores her. She's given a jug like me, which she cradles to her body. She risks a peek at me, her face free of emotion, then lowers her head.

The Grand Chancellor taps a finger on the table. The arguing quiets, attention shifting to him. "First order of business?"

"Isn't it that there are women present?" Father asks.

"Clearly not, Councilman Stephen."

Father's face is a livid red.

Someone clears his throat. "Last time we didn't finish discussing the latest changes to the tarnished law."

Though I was already listening, I fix my full attention on the discussion and push the discomfort of the situation to the back of my mind.

"We've been arguing over this for months. Let's just pass it and get on with it," a warlock says.

"Or not pass it and get on with other things," another argues.

"I've given this a lot of thought over the break," a third, whiny voice says. "What if we compromise? Instead of forcing the tarnished to get marked and tracked monthly, they're rewarded for it. And before you brush this aside, I want you to really think about it. If we give them a reduced tax rate, it would be a good incentive and we'd get a good turn out."

I suppose this option is better than the original. Yet they'd still make them check in, taking more freedom, making them more bound to the warlocks. That would really affect Katherine. Would she be allowed to come to my house if they're tracking her? Or anywhere else she wants to go? What would it be like having someone always know where you are?

"How much of a tax break are you thinking?"

"We can discuss that, of course," says the man with the idea. "I think my biggest point is that we'd be getting what we want accomplished, but with less work for us and other warlocks."

"Why didn't you bring this up sooner?" Father asks.

Good question. Is this why Zade thought I'd want to be here today? And how did he know it would come up now?

"Didn't cross my mind earlier."

A previously silent Councilman says, "They'd still have to abide by our rules."

"And check-in regular like."

"You're forgetting one thing. How are we supposed to find funds to pay for this?"

"Raise taxes."

"Always raising taxes. You think we've problems now, we keep raising taxes and they'll get worse."

"Things aren't free, people have to learn that."

"We could make another tax on those who don't get monitored monthly."

"Added incentive," Chancellor Ryan says. "It'd be a good addition."

"You've been quiet, Chancellor Zade." The Grand Chancellor faces him. "What is your opinion?"

"Sounds like they've finally learned to compromise."

Does that mean Zade agrees? He's always so nice to Katherine, I thought he'd be different.

The Grand Chancellor turns back to the other side. "And you, Chancellor Ryan, you're for it?"

"I'd like the law to be stronger, but it'll do. As long as I don't have to do any of the tracking or ink spells myself."

"Let's vote then." The Grand Chancellor addresses the group.

"Those for the tarnished opting in to be tracked and marked in exchange for a tax break and raising taxes for those who don't?"

I hold my breath. Zade's shoulders are stiff.

The room fills with "Ayes."

"And those against?" The room stays silent.

Why isn't Zade saying anything? He knows Katherine. He pays the tarnished in the household. Why isn't he sticking up for them?

"I agree with the majority. Law passed. Chancellor Ryan, see to its implementation and recruit those you need to help."

"Yes, Grand Chancellor."

"Next item of business?"

Someone answers but my heart thuds so loudly, I can't pay attention. Just like that, my friend has lost even more freedom. And there's nothing I can do about it.

Thoughts of Katherine and what this might mean to her distract me. I wouldn't want a spell permanently cast on me, tracking me where ever I go. Most hexes are bad enough, but I would hate for them to be able to find me whenever they wanted. Hiding is one of my few escapes. Changing color monthly wouldn't be as invasive, but still too much. And having to be monitored so often. I can't fathom what it would be like.

The rest of the morning goes by in a blur of activity. I understand little of what they speak of. Things that have to do with which warlock can host what party and how much a woman should be punished for disobedience. The multi-wives law is mentioned briefly, but mostly they talk of things that seem to have little importance.

At some point, servants enter with food. They bring dishes of boar and venison, duck and fish. Cakes and pastries. The savory smells mix with the sweet in a sickening way. They lay it on the same table where the woman was sacrificed.

I'm offered nothing and accept it gratefully. I can't bear to watch the warlocks eat. The very idea is repulsive. I try to catch

Annabelle's eye, but she doesn't turn my way. My arms ache under the strain of the jug. I hope it's not too much for her.

The meeting progresses throughout the meal. Though it seems more like a boasting party as they top stories of one another's spells, occasionally speaking of how it relates to a law. Empty dishes are taken away, replaced with heaping ones. The men talk and grunt and laugh. Wine flows freely. The longer it goes on, the more food and drink splotches their clothes. Those with beards fall victim to the debris more often.

From behind, I can't get a good look at Zade, but he doesn't seem to be over indulging. The few times I've had occasion to see him after a council meeting, he's never been as soiled as his fellows. As they are now, it's more like the feast after my engagement ceremony than a meeting.

Looking closer, I realize there are a few others that aren't as piggish, one being Councilman Daniel. They're not all slothful then. The Grand Chancellor also abstains from almost everything. His servant never refills his cup, and he consumes only a little food on his plate.

"That was the last item," the Grand Chancellor says. "We'll reconvene in two weeks with reports as assigned. Dismissed."

Finally, I'll be able to set the wine down. One downside to Zade not drinking more, the jug never lightened. But the warlocks don't seem eager to go. They slump in their chairs, cradling their glasses and picking at the last of their food. No wonder most of them are so fat. Some of them, including Father, pull out a pipe. The room fills with an acrid, bitter cloud of smoke.

The Grand Chancellor is the first to depart. Everyone else continues talking, smoking, and eating. The air is choking with the pungent odor. Zade pushes his cup aside and reads over more papers. After a while, they start to leave. One-by-one. With so many hours of food and drink, it's a wonder they can move at all.

Chancellor Ryan stands, but instead of leaving, he leans over Zade's shoulder. I strain to hear what he's saying.

"Think you got away with bringing a woman here? You haven't. You've only succeeded in making the *visits* you've been getting more serious."

Zade's back stiffens, but none of the others seem to notice. Chancellor Ryan straightens and catches me looking at him. I know I should break the eye contact, but I can't. Each breath is a struggle. I want to collapse on the floor. If I heard right, it means Zade is going to die because of my constant insistence of having things my own way.

# CHAPTER 33

THE THOUGHT of me causing Zade's death seems to freeze time for several minutes. Yet it's probably only a moment before Chancellor Ryan sneers and slams his fist into my stomach. I groan and press my hands against the pain. Zade jumps to his feet. The room goes silent.

"Sorry," Chancellor Ryan says with a grin. "I tripped."

Zade's frame quivers. I bite my lip hoping he won't let his temper make the situation worse. They stare at each other. Every passing moment, Zade's shaking increases, the muscles in his face growing more and more taut, and Chancellor Ryan growing more and more relaxed.

Finally, he slaps Zade on the shoulder. "Won't happen again."

The pain is already receding from where he hit me, but the damage has been done. Chancellor Ryan strides from the room. The remaining council members begin to chatter again, though quieter than before and with gazes drifting to Zade. After a moment, Zade slams himself back into the chair without looking at me. I never should have asked to come.

The rest of the members don't linger. As the last one, save for us and Councilman Daniel, stands to go, he smirks at Annabelle and me. "Maybe it's a good idea to have the wenches around. Both are properly subdued."

Of course we are, who wouldn't be? Someone was killed, the tarnished are going to lose what little freedom they have, and my owner's life is under more threats. He may think it was a good idea for us to come when really, I made another mistake.

Zade doesn't look up from his papers, but Councilman Daniel grins. "We'll see you at the next meeting."

Once he leaves, my muscles loosen. The servants clear the remnants of the meal.

"You can put the jugs down, wenches," Councilman Daniel says.

I place the jug on the table and rub my hands and arms. My body aches, especially my legs, back, and arms. My feet are sore. Everything hurts. It's been a while since I've had to stand like that. It's a fitting punishment for asking to come, but not harsh enough for endangering Zade even more.

Zade breaks the silence, his voice sounds surprisingly normal. "Good showing, Daniel. The food is excellent."

"Glad you enjoyed it. I've something else you might like. A new hunting rifle."

"Great. Perhaps your wife could keep mine company while I take a gander."

Councilman Daniel snaps his fingers. "Annabelle, take her and keep out of sight."

I open my mouth to say something, but she squeezes my arm and shakes her head. Together, we scurry from the room. "What power the Council has. I knew they were impressive, but that was unlike anything I've imagined."

The table laden with a dead woman followed by an overabundance of food flashes in my mind. "It certainly was."

"I'd best be on good behavior," Annabelle says. "Can you

imagine if he makes me go to another one? I don't think I'd manage it without fainting." She steers me down a hall. "Let's stop at the water closet before strolling through the gardens. I'll have one of the servants bring us a bite to eat.

My stomach roils at the thought of food. "I'm not sure I could eat anything."

"It's been a long day, we'll at least try."

How can I even try when a helpless girl was murdered in front of me?

* * *

ONCE WE'RE SETTLED on a bench in the garden, Annabelle collapses against me. I lean into her and we support each other.

"That was a horribly long time," she says. "I thought I'd drop the jug. Guess I know why cook is frantic when it's our turn to host the meeting. Hope someone comes with food soon. I'm famished. Are you truly not hungry?"

"Not at all."

"Why not? It's been a full day."

I close my eyes. Even if it weren't for the Chancellor's threat, there's the sacrifice. Should I tell her about it? The dead woman on the same table as the food? A woman who will never get a chance at anything. It seemed normal for a council meeting. If it happens every time, how many more have been killed? How many more will be killed? The forgotten shadows are dying without anyone to care.

When I open my eyes, Annabelle's face is filled with concern. How much does she know?

I ask, "Has Councilman Daniel told you about the meetings before?"

"No, nothing. I only know he hates them, but goes so he can try to do good. When Jonathan told me I was wanted, I couldn't believe it. What were you doing there?"

"Same thing as you." But I shouldn't have pulled any of us into this situation. "You seemed concerned about what we said earlier, why?"

"You're good at avoiding my questions." She sighs. "Daniel always warned me that meetings are spelled. He said I should never go around them and if I had to, be careful of what I said. This place is protected, we can speak freely. You can tell me what's bothering you."

That makes sense with having to avoid meetings at Father's or Zade's. I drag my weary body up and move to touch the drying leaves of a bush. "Something happened before you came. Something that I think was normal to everyone else, but..."

"What is it? You can tell me."

I take a deep breath. "They sacrificed a woman."

A bird chirps in the distance, it's happy sound no comfort.

"But we don't have an altar. There's never been any signs of one. I've never seen a body. Are you sure?"

I feel myself growing more numb. "They used the table."

When she says nothing, the words tremble from my mouth. "The Grand Chancellor did it a few feet from me. He cast a spell and a dagger was in his hand. I couldn't watch, but he did something to her. When I looked again, she was dead." The sight of her won't leave me. "I thought I was going to be sick and afterward the warlocks laughed about it. Laughed and mocked and jeered. None of them even mentioned the fact that a person was just killed."

She flutters to me and throws her arms around me. I'm too numb to have it shock me, but the gesture lightens some of my load.

"I can't believe you had to go through that. No wonder Daniel always hates the meetings. I can't even—" She bursts into tears on my shoulder.

The only time I've comforted someone who's crying was one

of my younger sisters. I'm not sure how to help. Mostly, I feel like crying with her. Instead, I give her shoulder a pat.

From behind the foliage next to us, a male voice says, "Gertrude said you wanted—"

Before the thought is finished, Councilman Daniel and Zade come into view. Daniel drops the basket he's carrying and rushes to us. Annabelle latches onto him.

"What's the matter darling? Was it too much for you? I'm sorry. It's all my fault. The opportunity presented itself and I thought you'd want to take advantage of it. You won't ever have to do it again."

"It's not that," she says, voice muffled by his shoulder. "Serena told me what they did before I came."

Councilman Daniel meets my eyes, his brows drawn. Blast. I shouldn't have told her.

"Sorry, Daniel," Zade says. My chest tightens. He has yet to look at me. "I didn't think this would affect anyone but Serena."

"Don't worry about it. I've been meaning to tell her, but never knew how. If anything, I'm grateful she's knows."

I step back from them. Never have I seen a man and woman act as such. Something about it pulls at me. I feel as if I broke Annabelle. Broke her sunny disposition. Broke the way things are done. Broke everything.

Whether Councilman Daniel would have told her or not, Annabelle wouldn't be in tears right now if it weren't for me. I'm surprised he hasn't punished her yet. Then I realize, she always calls him by just his first name, not his title. And they're entwined in such a sweet way. Her fingers clasped behind his neck. His arms wrapped around her. He's whispering things in her ear. Perhaps there are others more like Zade than I thought.

Watching them feels like I'm spying on something I shouldn't. He rubs her back and says things too quiet for me to hear. She clings to him, tears trickling to a stop.

Zade moves closer, no longer ignoring me. "Are you all right? He hit you pretty hard."

My stomach's fine, but is the rest of me? No. Never will I be again. Especially if something happens to him. "Fine."

"No you're not." His hands are fisted at his side, jaw clenched. "Do you want to talk about it?"

Which part? I bring up the least bothersome of my problems, though it still seems like too much. "The new tarnished law, when will it start?"

"I meant talk about the sacrifice, how you're feeling." Not a word about the threat. Maybe he doesn't know I heard. "I didn't tell you because I wanted to see your genuine reaction. I'm sorry. It was wrong. I should've said something."

Would knowing about it beforehand change how hard it was to go through?

He puts a hand on his hip. "The law will happen when the Grand Chancellor decides. No other really knows."

I stay silent, contemplating.

"I didn't mean to stop your question, it just surprised me. Is there anything else you want to know?"

Lots of things. Coming here raised more questions than expected. Mostly I want to know how serious Chancellor Ryan was, but I stick to the easier topic. "Are the tarnished who are causing the problems really going to participate?"

"Many will have to participate because they have no way to earn money and pay taxes. But those causing the problems, it's doubtful they will."

"Then why bother with the compromise? It doesn't make sense."

"It's just a way to sneak the law in. They've been fighting the tougher law for so long, that the weaker law now looks good. The Grand Chancellor can act on it without anyone trying to usurp him."

"Is someone trying to take over?"

"He's aware some are unhappy with the way things are," he says. "And by doing it here, it makes Daniel appear in support of the law. The Grand Chancellor knows what he's doing. It'll probably grow harsher after people get used to it."

"So, things will keep getting harder for the tarnished."

"Do you think that's a good thing or a bad?"

Before my name was entered in the marriage pool, it would have meant nothing. Now I know how much it means. "Why didn't you vote against it?"

Immediately his expression becomes guarded. "I couldn't."

"Did you want to?"

After checking to see where the others are, he bends toward me. "Yes."

This makes sense with the way he's acted, but why wouldn't he say so in front of the council? Warlocks always say whatever they want, at least, I thought they did. Why is he different?

"The green in your eyes. I've never seen anything quite like it."

It's suddenly hard to breathe. "My eyes are brown."

He leans down, closer. "Yes, but there's a ring of green in the middle of them."

I've never noticed. No one's ever noticed. At least not that they've told me.

"Guess none of us are hungry," Daniel says.

I jump away from Zade desperately trying to get some air.

Zade is just like he always is, not affected by whatever it is that struck me. "No. We best be on our way. Thank you for taking care of Serena."

"It's not a problem. Thank you for bringing her," Daniel says.

"Yes, thank you." Annabelle smiles. "I'll see you soon, Serena."

Though her eyes are still red, her cheerfulness is returning. Wish I hadn't broken it in the first place. "You're staying at our house for the ball?"

"We are."

"We'll see you soon then."

On the ride home, I can't help but think of the tarnished woman, the glazed look in her eyes becoming lifeless. It's easier than thinking of Chancellor Ryan's threat, and what it could mean to Zade and me. I'm not ready to contemplate it, but the sacrifice... It could have been Katherine on that table. She has to know what they're doing.

# CHAPTER 34

KATHERINE SITS across from me in my room, looking at me with her big, dark eyes. Suddenly, I don't want to tell her. I want her free from the burden life has forced on her. It's a false hope. I have to say something.

"Two days ago I went to a council meeting." And had four shooting lessons since that time. It's been a busy week. Not the type of business I prefer. The metal piece is strapped to my leg. But even with the lessons, I doubt it will help Zade, or Katherine.

Her eyes widen. "How did you manage that?"

"I asked Chancellor Zade to take me a while back and he finally consented." I choke down the regret I feel for doing so.

"He consented? I didn't think a woman would ever go to a meeting and live to tell about it."

I cock my head. "What do you mean?"

"You were there, did you see what happened to the tarnished?"

"I tried not to." She already knows? "But how do you know it was a woman? How do you know about it at all?"

"Tarnished get taken whenever it's time for a meeting. When that happens, you get good at knowing about it and making sure you're not around," she says. "And it's always a woman. Always."

"Why a woman?"

"I'm guessing it has to do with magic. Some tarnished women have magic in their blood, no tarnished men do."

Magic in our blood. We can't use it, but the warlocks can. I remember the strange glow to the Grand Chancellor's skin after the sacrifices and Zade taking my blood during the ceremony. Didn't he say something about being more powerful after that? No wonder they want wives with lots of magic flowing through their veins. Or tarnish them and later use them as a sacrifice. How much more powerful will they become after draining our full life's blood?

Katherine says, "What was the rest of the meeting like?"

It takes me a moment to think of anything other than women being used for a power they can't access. "Horrid. Rather like my engagement ceremony, but not centered on me. Annabelle joined the meeting a little way into it. It was good to have the support of someone else, though we weren't next to each other."

"Two of you were there? That changes things even more."

"Probably not. I don't think we'll go again." How could I risk Zade's life more? And I don't want to keep being around sacrifices. But I do want to stop it. There's just no way that I can. "They did discuss something that will affect you and I wanted to make sure you knew."

Her face pales. "A law?"

"Yes. Revised from what they originally wanted, but it's passed."

Her hands tighten around the arms of her chair. "How bad is it?"

I explain the law as best I can. "It's not mandatory yet."

She puts the back of her hand to her mouth. "Might as well be."

"Chancellor Zade thinks it'll be the beginning of stricter laws. Are you—"

Before I finish, Katherine rushes to the washing bowl and

retches. For a moment, I'm stunned into immobilization. Once I'm over the shock, I pour a glass of water and take it to her.

"I should have broken the news more gently. I'm sorry."

She takes a sip. "It's not the news. Perhaps in part, I've been expecting it. It's just—" she drops into the closest chair. "I'm not a tarnished."

I stare at her.

She's not a tarnished?

It can't be. Can it?

"How's that even possible?"

She gives a half-hearted smile. "You'd better sit, you look worse than I feel."

My legs carry me to a chair. "Your marks are fake?"

"It hurt enough getting them to be real, but yes, by tarnished standards, they're fake."

"And your hair?"

"Shaved clean every morning."

"How can you not be a tarnished? You look just like one. You work and live in their section of town. Why would you do that if you're not one of them?"

"It's a long story."

"You can't say you're not tarnished without explaining. Please, tell me."

She sighs. "Father chose an old warlock to marry me. A really old warlock. Lots of money and power. He lived in another town. It was unlikely I'd see mother again. Plus, he smelled something fierce. Like rotting vegetables. So I ran away."

"You ran?" I slap my hand onto my chest. "Running never crossed my mind. How did you consider it an option?"

"One of the servants ran off when I was a little girl. It never left my memory. They caught her and hung her, but I always wished she had gotten away. When the chance came, I took it. Had I known what waited on the streets, I would have married the smelly old man." She shudders. "Now, I'm glad for the choice. Despite the hard work, I'm free as any woman can be in this country." Her voice cracks. "And after everything, it's going to end."

I switch to the chair next to hers and squeeze her hand. "We'll figure something out. Is this why you were upset when we came to visit?"

She nods.

It must have been hard dealing with this and no one to talk to. "You spoke of helping me escape once, could we make that work for you?"

"Perhaps. But it's not easy or likely with my inked face. Plus, I like my life and there are others I have to consider."

"What others?"

She breaks eye contact. "Friends I've made."

Is she hiding more from me? If she is, I can't imagine what else it could be.

Her gaze comes back to mine. "I like you. I'd hate not having you around anymore."

"But if they discover you, they won't tarnish you." The truth hits me like a pack of daughters. "They'll kill you for it, wouldn't they?"

Her lips form a thin line. She nods.

I sag in my chair and think. Is there any way to help her? Anything we can do besides sending her away? I don't want to see her go away either, but if it means she'll be safe, it would be worth it. "I have one other idea, but it'll be risky."

"Riskier than what I've already been doing?"

"Perhaps." Would asking Zade to help work? Especially with the trouble I've already brought him. Is there a way to find out without endangering Katherine even more? However I word it, he knows Katherine is the tarnished I talk with most. "I could speak with Chancellor Zade. He's different than the others. It's possible he might be willing to help."

Her silence says a lot.

"Forget I mentioned it."

"No, it's fine. You just surprised me." She lowers her voice further. "Do you really think he would be willing to help, or would he turn me in?"

It would be easier if I knew. "I can't say for sure."

She lifts her head. "When will it be implemented?"

"I don't know. Soon."

After a minute of silence she says, "He sought me out to pay me more than he should have for the dresses. I've seen how he treats you and your sisters. And Waverly. I think it may be worth it." A look of determination fills her. "Let's try. There are others who will need help too if it works and I want to know he's trustworthy before putting them in danger."

"Others pretending to be tarnished like you?"

"I'm the only one pretending. That I know of, anyway. I probably shouldn't have said anything, but if you're willing to help—" She shakes her head. "I know tarnished who would like to avoid the law."

I nod, curious, but not wanting to push her. "Let's see if we can find him."

Her face loses some of its color, but she stands and follows me out. It doesn't take long to find him. A servant directs us to his study. Why is it always the study?

My hands shake, but I don't hesitate to knock. I've already asked much of him. But this is the only way I can think of to help. I hope my instinct is right and he doesn't turn Katherine in and punish me. The thought makes my stomach churn. I want to take back my offer, but the door opens before I can do anything.

Zade looks us over, then opens the door wider. "Please come in."

Once we're seated, Zade at his desk shuffling through papers, he asks, "What can I do for you? Do you need more money for the dresses?"

"No, you've already given too much," Katherine says.

"It's something else entirely." I swallow, build my courage, and say, "Remember the new rules on the tarnished?"

He puts down the papers and stares at me. "Of course."

His gaze almost makes me lose the last bit of courage I have, but I push on. "Katherine was wondering— Or rather, I was wondering and Katherine agreed that we should ask if you could help. With the law."

"You want me to explain it?"

"I've done that." I tug at my gloves. How much do I give away? "We were wondering if you'd help her circumvent the law."

He pushes to his feet and paces to the window. "You know I'm already being threatened. If anyone knew of this, there would be nothing to stop them."

Which is exactly what I don't want, but I can't leave Katherine to be killed by them either. "I know."

"But I didn't." Katherine moves to the door. "Forget we ever asked."

"Wait." Zade turns toward us. "Forgive me, I didn't mean to burden you with my issues. I'll help."

Katherine pauses, gaze moving between the two of us.

I say, "Let him. Please."

"You're really willing to help me," Katherine says, "even though I'm nothing but a tarnished and you could die because of it?"

He lets out a huff and rubs the back of his neck. "They will probably be angry at me for risking it, but yes, I will help."

Who are they? It doesn't sound like he's speaking of the council, but who else would it cause problems for?

Katherine rushes over to him, throws herself at him in the form of a hug, and bursts into tears. "Thank you. So much. No one's ever willing to help a tarnished except other tarnished. But now I have Serena and you."

"Of course you do, we'll help however we can," he says.

The door bursts open. I leap to my feet. Phyllis. She stands there, a tray in her hands and a smirk on her face. "Your lunch *Master* Zade."

Fear rips through me. What did she see and hear?

# CHAPTER 35

AFTER SEVERAL DAYS I'm still haunted by Phyllis interrupting our conversation. There's been no word of any trouble because of it. Yet it gnaws at me constantly. Both Katherine and Zade have been acting as if nothing has happened, except to talk once of what they will do when the law is enacted. That time, Zade cast his salmon, no eavesdropping spell. Even I didn't hear that conversation.

Katherine sits calmly. She points to the bundles she left on the bed earlier before she met with Zade. "There are a few new dresses for you."

"You didn't have to do that. How did you find the time?" Especially with everything else going on.

"I've been able to hire four more workers." She waves her hand dismissively. "You've been good enough to wear the dresses to deliver the invites and it's brought business. I wanted you to have some new things to wear."

"You're too kind."

"If it brings as many requests for new dresses as my others have, you'll be the one doing me a favor."

I laugh. "Then by all means, you can make more whenever you like. Any other orders?"

"A few friends of Annabelle and Councilman Daniel came in. Each wanted at least three outfits. All of them wanted me to do their gowns for the ball. One is still skeptical. But Annabelle's more excited than you. She even took a pair of breeches."

"She did!" I try to picture the well-mannered woman in men's wear. The image refuses to come to mind.

"Don't worry. She looks great in them." A mischievous grin slides onto her face. "Your sisters should be trying on their dresses, should we go see?"

"I'd love to."

She stands. "Don't expect to see anything for the ball with your new things. You won't see your gown until that afternoon."

We head for my sisters' rooms. "I've never been so curious about a dress before."

"Glad to be of service."

We arrive at Cynthia's room and knock.

A muffled, "A moment please" is called through the door.

While waiting, Katherine gives a sly smile. "There's something else in there you may want to peek at when you're ready."

If it's not the ball gown, what could it possibly be? "What is it?"

She shrugs with her smile growing more sly. The door bursts open.

"Come in," Cynthia says.

Katherine enters, but I hesitate. "I need to check something. I won't be a moment."

"Don't worry about it. Bethany won't be ready for a while and I haven't even started."

I hurry up the stairs to my room. Several packages await me on my bed. Which one could she be talking about? I sort through them, feeling their weight. I grab the lightest. None of the others have been like this. Curiosity tugs at me. Bethany isn't ready yet. There's time. I run my fingers over the package. Opening it shouldn't take long. I undo the string. A nervous flutter dances inside me.

Despite my sudden misgivings, I push the wrappings aside. Black cloth sits before me. That's not so bad. No need to fear. But why is it so small? I pick it up and give it a good shake. Two separate pieces unwind, one on each side connected together at the top.

I yelp and drop them. They flutter to the ground. "Breeches?"

What was Katherine thinking giving them to me? I stare at them, and then move toward the door. Before I can open it, I sigh. I can't leave them sitting there for anyone to see. Waverly will be back before I am. And what if my sisters want to see my new dresses when they've finished with theirs?

Those tiny black things call to me. I inch to them and lift them, pinching the soft material with a thumb and finger. I move toward the bed. Under it should be good enough for now. When I get there, I can't bring myself to throw them under. This is ridiculous. I have no use for them. But, I can't bring myself to hide them. Finally, I've crossed the line. I've gone completely mad.

Yet, here they are, waiting for me. It would only take a moment to change into them.

"Ugh." I reach for the laces of my skirt. Soon I'm wearing only my blouse while holding the breeches. This was a silly idea. With a deep breath, I struggle into them and tie the laces at the waist. The bulk of the gun strapped to my thigh is visible. That won't work at all. I don't want to wear them around anyway, just curious.

They feel… tight. Though they aren't too tight, I suppose. I bend my legs. The material stretches with my movements. They aren't too snug, but more constricting than they should be. Will they damage my circulation?

I tread across the room. It's almost like walking around in my underthings. How can men stand wearing so little? It is easier to move though. Less material to get caught in things. Despite thinking they were constricting at first, I may be able to do more in them.

I stroll across the room again. And again, but faster. What else can I do? I run. Jump. Leap onto my bed. Just as I'm leaping off, the door opens. Phyllis's face flash across my view.

I slam onto the floor with a groan.

Before Phyllis has a chance to do anything, I stagger to my feet, ignoring my aching body. "What are you doing here?"

Instead of answering, she steps inside and closes the door. Zade's life is the one in danger, not mine, so I shouldn't be worried. But I am. My gun is useless, trapped under the breeches. I inch to the cord that will ring in the servants hall.

"Wait," Phyllis says. "I'm here to warn you, not harm you."

Once I'm within reach of the cord, I ask, "What do you mean?"

She eyes my breeches. "Why are you wearing those?"

"Not your concern." My hands bunch.

"You're right." Her voice loses the haughty tone its always had. "I've been reporting to your Father."

I raise my brows, but don't respond. It's hard to stay unaffected when her words set my heart racing.

"My family is deeply in his debt. We have no hopes of paying it off before we die. Which will be soon for my Father. He's old. If the debt isn't paid off before he dies, my sisters, mother, and I will be tarnished."

That could be me and my family if we were in debt. Even though I know the tarnished are so much like us, they're restricted in many ways. It makes my anger soften, but I don't budge. "And?"

"Your Father said the more information I told him, the more debt he'd forgive. When I made you drink the tea, he got rid of half the debt. Half!" Her eyes are wide and begging. "I've told him lots of little bits about the dresses and your seamstress, but he said it wasn't enough. He needed more and if I could find something big, he'd forgive the rest of the debt."

I stride toward her, fear and rage pulsing through me. "What did you do?"

"I told him about the conversation I overheard with Chancellor Zade, the one where he promised to help your tarnished seamstress."

My fist wants to fly into her. Hard.

Her voice is faint. "He's planning something, I know it. But he won't forgive the debt. Says I'm too valuable here and is going to keep me waiting. You helped the tarnished, can't you help me?"

"Help you?" My fist shakes from unreleased tension. "Help you? You've ruined us. Get out."

She doesn't move. I let out a half growl, half scream. She scrambles for the door. Now I know for certain, my insisting on helping Katherine will bring trouble. I can't have freedom for myself and trying to get it for her is going to cost all those I love. What will Father do?

# CHAPTER 36

"Come in," I call out.

A lower class servant I don't recognize enters. "I was asked to bring you this with utmost haste."

A chill flurries through me as she hands me a note. I barely notice her departure. Ever since I told Zade what Phyllis said and he told me not to worry, I've done nothing but. I've never had a note from someone outside the household before. Who would send me one? Does it have to do with what she said? The chill grows colder as I open it.

*Serena,*

*I feel I must warn you. Councilman Daniel and I have heard a growing number of rumors concerning you and the Chancellor. I'm afraid they aren't good.*

*I hate to be blunt, but feel I must. There is a hefty price on his life. Please be cautious.*

*Your friend,*
*Annabelle*

. . .

THE COLDNESS SEEPS clear to my heart with icy sharpness.

I don't know how long I sit staring, unseeing at the note. Finally, I grip it to my chest and run to find Zade. He's not in the study, nor the library, nor the sitting room. Am I already too late?

Where are all the servants? There has to be someone I can ask. Yet no one is in sight. I rush to the kitchen. There's always someone there. When I clang into the room, it is full of activity, Phyllis in the midst of it all. I want to scream at her again, but it won't do any good.

"Does anyone know where Chancellor Zade is?" I ask.

"I do," Phyllis says.

I round on her, the words flaming from my mouth like hexes. "Don't speak. You've already done enough damage."

Everyone stops working and stares. My stomach twists with regret at sounding so harsh, but the words are too true to take back.

A servant I don't recognize says, "I believe he's shooting."

Of course. We've spent so much time there I should have guessed. As I run out of the room I yell, "Thank you."

Finding him seems to go quicker now that I know where he is. If something had already happened, the servants would know, wouldn't they? When he comes into sight, I slow. Relief replacing some of my worry, but not enough of it.

He's practicing like he always does, casting a spell that looks like some sort of bird and then shooting it. His movements are sure and smooth. Every time he hits the spell it dissolves. I feel as if I could watch him all day. But as I come closer, his face doesn't match his confident moves. He's frowning, brows creasing together. When he spots me, he schools his features so well, I almost believe I never saw him uncertain.

"You know," he says.

"Why didn't you say something?"

"How did you find out?"

"Annabelle." I wave the note at him. "You didn't answer my question."

"May I?" He holds out his hand.

I give him the note, my fear replaced by confusion at his calm manner. He reads it over before throwing it in the air. An orange and red spell crackles from him, turning the note to ashes.

"It's true then," I say.

"It is." He sighs. "Does it do any good for you to know?"

None. "How soon?"

"No idea. Most likely before the wedding."

Before the wedding? That's only two days away. My stomach churns. "Maybe we can do something to stop it."

"We can't." He slams his gun down on a tree stump. "You've grown up with this life, you should know it better than me. Soon I'll be dead and you'll be back with your Father."

"They didn't succeed before, maybe they won't succeed now."

"Don't be stupid. They've set the price so high on my head, even those who already have a good sum of money will be after me."

His brutal response makes me stumble back.

"I'm sorry. I didn't mean it. I'm just so—" He picks his gun back up and shoots another spelled bird. Before dissolving like the others, it looks exactly like a dove except for the red light surrounding it. "There's nothing to be done about it."

"There has to be something." While trying to think of a solution, another thought comes to me. "If Father knows you're breaking the law, why isn't he taking it to the council?"

"He gets all my money and possessions if I'm dead. If he goes through legal channels, he'll only get some. And he cares a lot about his reputation. I've sullied it enough by being your owner, doubt he wants to add traitor to my bad qualities list."

He releases another bird, this one even redder than before. The shot echoes through the air followed by silence.

"You don't have to worry about Katherine. She'll be taken care of."

But what about him? Someone has to take care of him, too. I want to go to him and wrap my arms around him, but that's not the answer. Touching him won't save his life.

I remember Katherine once offering to help me escape. "We could run away."

"They're watching too closely for that to work. It'll only bring my death sooner and yours along with it."

He storms off in the direction of the house.

I grip my arms around myself. I've killed him and put myself back under Father's ownership. I should have quietly accepted the life I was given instead of striving for more. Because of my inability to be a good Chardonian woman, I've lost more than I ever thought I could.

# CHAPTER 37

GUESTS HAVE BEEN ARRIVING all morning. The ball is in a few hours, our wedding tomorrow, and Zade's still alive. Not a single attempt has been made on his life. At least none that I know of. It's left me more on edge than if someone had tried. Without an attempt yet made, they must have a sure plan. One that can only end with their success and Zade's death.

I'm exhausted from greeting everyone and wishing life was back to the way it was before there were threats on Zade's life. Once those staying overnight arrive, they'll have time to get acquainted with their rooms, and ready. Everyone else will arrive later, in time for the ball.

Zade sends the latest guests off with a servant. The way he acts, it's impossible to tell he knows death is coming. My heart aches watching him. I want to do something more, but there's nothing I can do.

The front door opens yet again. The Grand Chancellor and his son are followed by two women, both with heavy face paint.

The footman announces them. "The Grand Chancellor with his wife and his son Nathaniel with his fiancée."

The Grand Chancellor sweeps to a stop. "Thank you for the invitation. I'm sure it will prove an interesting occasion."

The fiancée watches the interaction, cowering away from them. The wife grabs her arm and yanks her forward. The Grand Chancellor scowls and zaps a fuchsia spell at the girl. She bites her lips, but doesn't call out. I want to kick all but the fiancée out of the house. The way she's being treated makes me want to protect her. Of course that won't happen.

"We do hope you'll be pleased with everything we have planned."

"We shall see," the Grand Chancellor says.

Zade motions to the next servant. "We have a set of rooms for you on the bottom floor. I hope you'll find them to your liking."

The Grand Chancellor raises his brows, but doesn't say a word as the servant leads them away. Once they are out of sight, it feels as if I can breathe again. My tension eases until Cynthia and Bethany join us.

"I thought we wouldn't be seeing you girls until it was time to dress." Mostly, I want them away from the danger as much as possible.

"I saw Father and the carriage arrive," Cynthia says. "We were hoping we could join you in greeting them."

"Certainly," Zade says.

Cynthia eagerly stands to the side. More sedately, Bethany also joins.

"Are you well?" I ask her.

"Fine. I'm anxious to see mother and hear how the little ones are doing."

But not Father. How will it be back under his ownership? I suppose I won't stay long. He's sure to have someone like Thomas already waiting for me. I suppress a shiver and focus on Bethany. "You can stay by me. I'm sure mother will be happy to see you."

She nods, but doesn't say anything. The door opens and the footman announces, "Presenting Councilman Stephen."

Zade puts his arm around me. The warmth of him envelops me. I'm grateful he's not as angry with me as he was yesterday, though perhaps he should be. Still, I take what comfort I can. I lean closer as Father enters, mother close behind.

When they reach us, Zade says, "Councilman, glad you could make it. I trust the journey was good."

"Fine ride out in the countryside." Father eyes Zade's arm around me. "Making the most of your goods I see. Nothing too untoward I hope."

Zade's arm tightens around me. "Only what you see." With his free hand, he motions to my sisters.

Mother takes a step closer and gives a small grin. She's pregnant again. Not that she's showing yet, but the darkness and lines under her eyes give it away. Another sister for sure. At least she looks happy.

"Thank you for allowing the services of your daughters," Zade says. "They've been very helpful."

"Of course." Father gives a sneering smile. "We wanted to make sure you had the proper help. I'd hate for your first public event to be disappointing."

"Little chance of that. They're fine girls."

"Good enough for a little entertainment planning, anyhow. It's sure to be a night to remember. When I—" he stops, his face growing red. "Cynthia, what are you wearing?"

I scan Cynthia's dress. It's a two piece Katherine designed, one more bold than I've seen. The colors are similar, but different enough that it's easier to tell it's not a simple dress. And those colors. Shades of jade hovering on being too bright. What's she doing wearing it now? Why couldn't I have realized before and saved us from the coming turmoil?

She straightens her back. "A new dress. Do you like it?"

"Is that a two piece?" His voice lowers to a growl. "Are you wearing tarnished clothes?"

Cynthia's lower lip trembles. "I—It…"

Leaving the safety of Zade's arm, I step forward. "It's something I told her to wear for greeting guests before the ball, Father."

Zade joins me as Father says, "You told your sister to wear tarnished clothes?"

Not today. Not ever, really. Why did she have to be so anxious to show it off? "It's just a trifle, Father."

His fist flies. Before I realize what's happened, Zade extends his own arm, blocking the punishment. Father waves his hand. If he can't hit me, he'll hex me. I reach in my pocket and take hold of the gun, but I can't shoot him just for hexing me.

Zade steps in front of me with a turquoise spell, effectively shielding me and part of Cynthia. Bethany huddles closer to us. I keep a firm hold of the gun, just in case. I don't know what I'll do with it, but it makes me feel better.

"May I remind you, Councilman, that Serena is no longer yours to punish."

Though I can't see him, Father's response sends chills through me. "That will soon change."

Will Father be the one to kill him? Right here? My hand aches from grasping the gun hidden within my pocket.

"You don't have as much power as you think," Father says.

"Perhaps," Zade replies. "But I may have more than you think."

The hall is quiet. I grip the gun tighter. Can I really use it if need be? Against Father?

"I hope you find your rooms adequate."

"Doubtful." Father smirks. "Cynthia, gather your things. You'll be staying with your mother."

Her head lowers and she moves toward the stairs.

Father adds, "Next time I see you Cynthia, it had better be in something suitable for a Councilman's daughter."

Father mutters after a servant. Mother spares us a glance, her lips pinched together, and follows him. Once they're out of ear shot, I face Zade.

"Why didn't you do something?"

"What can I do? I'm in enough trouble as it is and she belongs to your Father."

"She shouldn't belong to anyone." Tears prick my eyes. I let out an angry huff.

Zade watches me, his face drawn.

"Don't worry," Cynthia says. "It's my own fault. Thank you for trying to help, but I should have known better. I've been here so long, I'd almost forgotten how things are."

She heads up the stairs. Bethany calls after her, "I'll help."

"I can help, as well," I say, climbing the stairs after her.

"Wait, Serena." Zade pulls me to a stop. "We need to talk."

I look at Cynthia and Bethany. There's nothing more I can do for her that Bethany can't do better. Maybe Zade has a thought on how to help. Or maybe it's something to do with his death. "If you think we need to. I'll see you two later."

They nod and hurry up the stairs. I doubt they'll take long packing. If they do, they'll probably send a servant for the rest. You can't keep Father waiting.

The tears burn my eyes until a few trickle out. I brush them away and follow Zade to his study. The closer we get, the more my stomach knots. If any more guests arrive, they'll have to do without a personal welcome. We enter. He shuts the door and casts his spell that prevents eavesdropping.

"Why don't you have a seat? Or stand if you like. Whatever you want."

He paces over to his desk and shuffles through a few papers. After picking the chair closest to the desk, I perch on it. The maroon one still holds too many bad memories.

He pinches the bridge of his nose. "We've got to do this."

What can that mean? I grip my hands together.

Grabbing a nearby chair, he hauls it next to me and sits down. He clasps my hands in both of his. My breathing quickens. What's this about?

"Serena. I think I've found a way for you to not be owned by your Father again."

A puff of air escapes me. I don't want to think on his death. I lean back in the chair, our fingers trailing away from each other. "What do you mean?"

"Just what I said."

"You're giving me to someone else?"

"No." His face grows stern. "Never."

He's tarnishing me. I'm surprised he hasn't done so before now. But if it's my choice, what do I want? If his plan doesn't work, I want to be with him as long as I can, to the end. If my becoming tarnished works, I'll be like Katherine. Her life is hard and she has things easy for a tarnished. But if it will save his life, it would be worth it. And better than being back with Father.

"You can think on it. It's your choice. Stay with me or not," he says. "If possible, I'd like your answer before the ball."

I nod. "I'll think on it." My voice feels tiny. "If this is what was going to happen, why did you accept me in the first place? Why not leave me with Father?"

"I wasn't going to accept you. It goes against what I wanted."

His mention of being previously engaged comes to me. That was what he wanted. It must be what he still wants. To spare his life for an Envadi girl, perfect for him. Is his previous choice still waiting back at home or will he have to find a new one?

"When I saw how your Father was treating you..." Several moments pass before he can unclench his jaw to speak. "Still, I didn't want to force you into being stuck with me. I only brought the lawman to help me keep the Chancellor title and everything that came with it. Except for you. But I'd talked to others before I came to the meeting to try and decide how to handle it."

"Wait, why did you want the title? And what other people did you talk to about it?" Most warlocks would want it just for the power and money, but Zade's different. Why haven't I thought of it before? His work on the council, the way he keeps secrets, things he's said. Oh. He's— "You're an Envadi spy."

The muscles in his face tighten, but he says nothing.

"It's true, isn't it? I can see it in your face."

"You can't tell anyone."

"Who would I tell?" Though I can't be the only one that knows. Others must have guessed.

"Your sisters. Katherine."

Perhaps I do tell them a lot, but not this. "I know how to keep a secret. Aren't you a bit young to be a spy?"

"This is my first assignment. It wasn't even supposed to be. I was going to watch my Dad at the tournament. Help him get as far as he could and gather information. But then he got sick on the way here and I had to take his place. He and my mother aren't here because he's still sick."

"Is he going to be okay?"

His shoulder's slump. "I don't know. I hope so."

"You weren't supposed to be in the tournament?"

"No."

"Then how did you do so well?"

His cheeks turn the familiar shade of pink. "I've been trained since I was little. Best in my class."

"Probably best in more than just your class judging from how well you did at the tournament. I mean, you won against Thomas."

He squeezes his eyes shut. "I didn't mean to. I wasn't trying to kill him, it just happened. One minute everything is fine, the next I attacked instead of blocking and he was dead. Just dead. It was only supposed to knock him out, instead I killed a man."

I cup his cheek with my hand. His scruff scratches against my palm. My heart aches for him. "You didn't do it on purpose. I can't imagine what it must feel like, but I'm grateful you did. You've been kinder to me than he ever was."

With a deep breath, he opens his eyes. "I'm glad for that, at least. When you finally came out to meet me, you were clearly terrified of him, though you tried to hide it. Now I know that terror was justified. But then—" he shakes his head, "you looked just as terrified of me."

"You would have been as well if your future owner was so much bigger than you, and belonged to a country everyone says is barbaric."

"I can't do anything about my size, but I hope my barbaric ways haven't bothered you."

Warmth grows within me. I smile at him. "Not in the least."

His gaze pulls me, draws me in. I move toward him. Breathing becomes more difficult. We're only inches apart. I tilt my mouth toward him. He slants his head closer. Is he going to kiss me again? I want him to. Oh, how I want him to.

The door opens. Zade's salmon-colored spell zaps gone as he leans away from me. I sigh, disappointment creeping through me. Of course he wasn't going to kiss me.

"Are you ready to dress, sir?" Chadwick, his manservant, says.

Reality washes back over me. The ball, dresses, my sisters, and the one I want to avoid, but can't: his death. Those are the only things going on, not another kiss. I should be focusing on how to help, not kissing. I sit back in my chair and shake myself. What's wrong with me?

"I'll be up in a moment."

"Very good sir." He leaves, closing the door behind him.

Before Zade can utter a word, I leap to my feet. "I should get ready as well."

"Will you think on my offer? I don't want you trapped."

There's really no other choice. If it shows the council, and everyone else, that he can take control of women by tarnishing me and saves his life, it's what I want him to do. I just need a little time to process my new fate. "I'll think on it."

"Very well."

As I hurry to my room, I can't help but feel confused and uncomfortable. A spy. It makes sense. I should have guessed before. It makes sense he would want to get rid of me whether or not he was to be killed.

Being a tarnished wouldn't be so bad. Katherine said the hardest part was getting to where she is. I could do it. I can do it. I just have to leave him behind in the process. Leave him, to save him. Losing more freedom will be worth it.

# CHAPTER 38

I TWIST my hands together and wait for the door to open. It's been hours since I left Zade, and the strain of our conversation keeps pressing harder on me. My room seems extra empty. Cynthia isn't here and won't be coming. The dress made just for her won't be used. I've always been with her. How can I do this without her? She must be taking the brunt of Father's anger. Perhaps I should break her out. Easier than the other path I'm faced with.

The door opens. Waverly steps in. Not my ball gown then. Which won't fix my problems anyway, but would at least give me something to do.

"Zade wants to know when you'll be ready to talk with him."

It hits me. How she always says his name. How they're both from Envado. How they knew each other from before. How familiar he is with her. My stomach clenches. I grab onto the bedpost and cling to it. His offer wasn't just about saving his life or getting me away from Father. It's about his previous fiancée. She's the one he wants.

"Tell him…" that he doesn't have to worry about me. I'll do what I can to save his life and I'll figure something out with my own. "After I'm dressed I can talk. Katherine should be here with my gown soon."

"I saw her coming. I'll let him know, then I'll be back to help."

The last thing I want is to spend more time with her. She's been wonderful, but I can't handle being around Zade's love right now. "Why don't you get yourself ready? It's a big night for you, as well." I wonder if she knows how big yet.

"I want to help you though, it's my job." She stares at me a moment. "What if I brought my stuff back here? Then we could all get ready together."

I force a smile. "Sounds nice."

Before she leaves, Bethany enters the room. Her navy dress glitters with silver sparks of magic, hair twisted up between Chardonian strictness and Envadi freedom. A single tendril escapes behind her right ear. She must have already seen Zade because silver sparks also adorn her hair. Matching silver earrings and necklace glow faintly. Zade must have spelled those, as well. Her face paint is modest and becoming. A little red on her lips and cheeks. But the true beauty is the natural glow she exudes.

"She's ready, Katherine," she says into the hall.

Finally, it's here. I'll get to see it. I wait for Katherine to enter with my dress. I don't know why I'm so nervous all of the sudden. Easier to be nervous over a dress than saving Zade and losing the freedom I've gained being with him.

Katherine appears in the doorway. She holds a gown of burgundy. It shimmers in the light. She brings it to me, a grin gracing her face. Without a word, I run my hand across it. It's as soft as flower petals. So many emotions course through me. I wish Cynthia was here. And mother.

I want to wear this. I want to be beautiful. Tonight at least. Zade may love another, but we're still connected from the engagement ceremony. I'll make that connection worth having one last time.

"Put it on," Bethany calls.

Before I can move, the gown changes. It's a lovely green. The laces are on the sides and the arms go halfway down the dress. Simple, but gorgeous.

I suck in a breath. "What happened?"

Waverly beams. "Katherine made more than one gown and Zade spelled them together into one. It'll change every ten to fifteen minutes."

The causal reference to Zade twists in my chest. I try to ignore it and center my attention back to Katherine. "You made two gowns?"

She blushes. "Three actually. I was timing it so the best would be last."

The twisting in my chest turns to tightening. I swallow. "You shouldn't have done so much. It's more than I hoped for. Just these two are stunning." I stop before I begin to cry. "Thank you."

"Let's get you into the gown before it changes again."

"Yes, put it on," Waverly says. "I'll be right back to see it." She scurries out the door.

With Katherine and Bethany's help I change from my robe to the gown. It's not easy to get into like my new dresses, but I suppose for an occasion like this it's fine. If I waited until the first gown spelled back, I could manage on my own. It looked easy enough. This version still has a pocket with a slot to reach my gun. Knowing Katherine, they all do.

As they finish helping, I can't help but ask, "Is there a ring of green in my eyes?"

"Yes," Katherine says. "I planned some of your gowns to help bring it out."

"Really?" Bethany twirls me around to check. "Subtle, but there. Why the sudden interest?"

The room warms. "No reason."

Katherine's making a few adjustments when Waverly returns. "He said he'll be here soon."

I look away from her grin. It's not that I don't want her to be happy, I do. It just hurts. I try to shove the feelings away.

"Hurry," Katherine says. "Get in front of the mirror, it's already been thirteen minutes, it could change at anytime."

Once in front of the mirror, I can't believe my reflection. The dress is perfect. And then it changes.

One moment I'm wearing a green dress, the next I'm in a dress the color of pearls. Definitely not dark enough, but I've never seen a color so suited to me. Tiny, clear jewels are sewn on the full skirt and snug bodice, making it glitter in the light. The cap sleeves flow into the square neckline. The only problem is my visible engagement mark. Despite that, I'm stunning.

"You can wear just this one for your wedding tomorrow if you want," Katherine says. My wedding was supposed to be tomorrow. With planning the ball, I almost forgot. Just as well. "I know women typically wear black, but the Envadi wear white so you'll have an excuse. When I asked Zade, he said it would be a simple spell to unwind the dresses into three separate ones again."

I pinch my lips together. I would have made the most spectacular bride Chardonia has ever seen. But it's just as well. I don't want to get married. Zade deserves to live, even if it means I have to give up everything.

"You're an artist, Katherine." I embrace her, taking what comfort I can.

"Don't get tears on it." She pulls back and holds out a handkerchief.

Accepting the proffered cloth, I laugh. It comes out sharper than I meant. I dab my face dry.

"You look wonderful," Bethany says. "Katherine, you're talented. It suits her. Sit down Serena, and we'll finish getting ready."

I comply, letting them fuss over my hair and face paint. The paint is as light as I like it, if I have wear it. None of the white paint, but a shine to my lips and kohl to my eyes. My hair is twisted and coiled and puffed in a style like none I've ever seen. I can't hate a woman who can do this to my hair. Though at this moment I wouldn't mind if she was back in Envado.

I sigh. "Thank you, everyone. You're the best of friends." I turn to Katherine. "I wish you could come with us."

"All I want is to see how everyone likes the gowns I created. Zade showed me a nook on the second floor where I can watch the party without being seen."

"I'll have to be the jealous one then. This ball will be a better experience than last time I'm sure, but I wouldn't mind watching instead." I try to hold back my creeping emotions. "I'll make sure to bring you something to snack on."

Katherine says, "I admit, I've been wanting to try some of the Envadi treats ever since Waverly talked of them."

"I'll be sure cook sends some," Waverly says. "You'll be wanting to dine in Envado every night after this."

A knock sounds. I jump from my chair. As Waverly moves to open the door, Bethany gives me a half smile.

"Is it time?" I ask.

Katherine fluffs my skirt out. "Back to the white. Perfect timing. He's already seen it, but it will be better with you wearing it." She nods to Waverly who opens the door.

Zade stands at the entrance in a suit of black and a pearl colored cravat and folded handkerchief in his left pocket, same color as my dress. I realize he's been observing me while I've been perusing him. Heat floods my cheeks. I glance at Waverly.

"Everyone out," she says.

Anxious to have the man she loves free of me.

Katherine gives my arm a squeeze. "You'll do great."

"And don't forget to add sparkles to her hair," Waverly tells Zade.

Really, something so simple seems unimportant at the moment, but he agrees.

"Don't forget to have them announce you," Bethany says. "We'll make sure everyone is there and things are going smoothly." How smoothly will they go with the events that are to come? "Smile Serena. And don't scare everyone with it this time. Oh, and plan your entrance to have your dress change to this one shortly after you arrive."

"It will," Zade says.

"Thank you," she replies and they leave.

The room is back to being hollow, except this time Zade is here. I scrutinize my gloves, pearly to match my dress. Watching the sparkles in them is easier than looking at him. There's a warm glow to the fabric I didn't notice before. A sort of happiness not matched by my feelings.

I clear my throat. "Would you like to sit?"

"Would you?"

"Don't want to crease Katherine's dress before anyone has seen it."

He steps closer to me. I resist the urge to step back. "Are you ready?"

No. "I'll manage."

For a moment, he says nothing. He shifts like he's going to come closer, but then moves to stand by a chair, resting a hand on the back of it. "Have you thought about what I asked?"

"I have."

"And?"

And don't ask this of me. I want freedom and you. Not to be tarnished while you marry Waverly. At least you'll be alive and free to leave the threats on your life, which is what I owe you after costing your life in the first place. I close my eyes to keep the tears from coming. "I'll take your offer."

He nods.

A knock sounds.

"Come in," I call.

Waverly slides in. Of course she does. I clamp my hands together.

"Everyone's here. Seems they're anxious to begin. Bethany wanted me to let you know. I think she's anxious, too."

"Thank you," Zade says.

"Is everything all right?" she asks. "You haven't fixed her hair yet."

He walks to her. "Everything will be perfect. We'll be down in a moment."

It hurts to see them together, but I don't want them to see how I feel.

"Soon then." Waverly closes the door behind her.

Soon. They'll be together soon. Unless Zade's plan doesn't work, then he'll be dead and I'll be with Father. Even if it does, I'll be tarnished. Becoming tarnished isn't so bad, I remind myself. I keep reminding myself.

He moves closer to me. "May I spell your hair?"

"Yes." Despite becoming more accustomed to magic, the thought of allowing someone to spell me still makes me uneasy. I remind myself it's Zade and it's easier to turn around so he can reach the back better. "How long will these last?"

"About eight hours." There's a flash out of the corner of my eye. "All done."

When I face him again, my breath catches. It's so hard not to lean closer to him.

"Shall we?" Zade holds out an arm for me.

What is he doing?

"You put your hand here." He points at his elbow.

"Why?"

"It's the first step."

The first step to what? I lick my lips. Being at his side instead of behind him is appealing. I place my hand on his elbow. He grabs it with his own gloved hand and pulls it through the space between him and his arm, and rests my fingers on his arm.

"Like that."

He's so, so close.

"I see." I look through the open door thinking of what's to come instead of how good it feels to be next to him. "And there's to be a sacrifice, yes?"

Instead of answering, he guides me through the door, maneuvers us down the stairs, and slips my hand back on his arm as we walk down the hall.

"There will be a sacrifice."

The pounding of my heart intensifies. I've gone through it before. Another time will be no different. Except this is my home. My gathering. My only claim on the gathered warlocks of Chardonia. My last claim on anything. My ball will not stoop to their level.

"What if we skipped that part?"

Mid-stride, he stops. "The sacrifice?"

I wiggle my toes. "Yes."

With a small smile, he resumes our stroll to the ballroom. "First Katherine, now this. You're not the girl I won at the tournament."

Is that a good thing or a bad thing? A response never forms before we arrive. The oak doors wait. Waiting for Zade to sacrifice someone and make his name as Chancellor. Then to leave me as a tarnished.

"It will be fine." He pats my hand and nods to the footman.

As the footman opens the door, I can't help but feel as if I should run the other way. I don't want this. I don't want to be in any way a part of sacrificing another human. If I'm to be tarnished anyway, there's nothing preventing me from trying. What can I do to stop it?

# CHAPTER 39

ZADE WALKS INTO THE ROOM. When I don't come, he tugs me forward. My green dress flows around me, shimmering. The gathered crowd goes silent. All eyes are on us. There are so many of them. Despite helping with the guest list, there's more here than I thought there would be. Here to see how our ball turns out? To see us fail? To watch Zade die? Or simply curious? Whatever they want, they aren't going to get.

Remembering Bethany's words, I keep a smile plastered to my face. Is there anything I can do to stop the sacrifice? Perhaps there is. I could jump in front of her. There's no altar or girl in view though.

The stairs lead down to our left, leaving us at the top of a curving balcony. Although it's the largest room in the house, it's full. The only way we'll have space for dancing is by moving guests to other rooms we've prepared for sitting and eating, as well as the garden. The sight of so many makes my legs shake.

"Thank you for joining us." Zade's voice booms to the crowd below. "We hope you delight in the many surprises we have in store for you this evening."

Our clothes change in that instant, surely aided by Zade. The crowd gasps. A tingle of excitement zips through me. I'm ready for this. I hope.

"As you know, balls held by a Chancellor or Grand Chancellor are always proceeded by a sacrifice. Tonight will be no different."

The crowd watches us intently, eager for more. Suddenly, Zade shoves me forward. I reach out and grab the railing. The faces below me become blurs. I'm the sacrifice.

He's not tarnishing me, but sacrificing me? That's what he meant? Not to be his or my Father's? I won't belong to anyone if I'm dead. I grip the railing harder. Why is he doing this? I spin toward him.

"Zade," I whisper.

"It's fine," he whispers back. But it's not. He moves toward me, but then takes four steps down the stairs. For the first time, I'm looking down on him.

"My sacrifice." He waves his hand toward me.

This can't be happening. He's not saving both of us, just himself from death. I can't believe he'd do this to me. This isn't who I thought he was. This can't be happening. I want to do something, but I'm frozen to the floor. "Zade."

Again, he looks directly at me and whispers, "You're fine, Serena."

Does that mean it will be a painless death? None of the sacrifices ever called out. They didn't seem as alert as I am either. I was willing to try and stop a sacrifice, but how can I stop my own? Is it worth it if it saves Zade?

No. I'm willing to become a tarnished for him, but I'm not going to become a sacrifice so he can stay Chancellor. I tighten my legs. Maybe I can rush into him. It may not stop it, but it could prolong it.

He faces the crowd, hand still extended toward me. The perfect time. My muscles tense as I get ready to pounce. But his words stop me.

"My sacrifice. Serena, daughter of Councilman Stephen, I will her to accept my sacrifice of ownership of her. She's as free as any warlock."

Golden light bursts from his hand, surrounding me with its warm glow. I stare at him, unable to believe what he just said. My breathing becomes shallow. How could I ever have doubted him? I'm not bound by any one man. My body grows light as burdens I didn't know I carried lift. I'm free as Katherine, but without the constraints. Free. Truly free.

But how can he do that? He can't. The lightness shifts back into the burden I carry. The burden of being owned. Only now, it's worse. Knowing what I could have had, but can't.

The murmur of voices below me must agree. Their noise grows by the moment, confusion building to anger.

A warlock yells, "You can't do that. Women aren't able to be free. They need to be owned."

"He's right. You can't free her," another calls out.

Zade silences them by holding up his hand, the glow around me fading, but still present. "I can. Before you protest, I offer proof."

He holds something up. A book of some sort. Thick with pages I was required to learn. The Woman's Canon. How can that help?

"I've found," he opens the book to a page somewhere in the middle, "a woman must always submit to her Master's wishes."

It does say that, but it can't really free me. Can it?

The book slaps closed. Zade motions to a servant behind him.

The servant brings him a hefty book. Using two hands, Zade holds the book open. "While not typical, the law was used one hundred and eighty years ago. A man's wife never provided an heir. Despite wanting a new wife, he didn't feel his old one deserved to be tarnished. He used this law to free her, ultimately giving her the status of a man. The council upheld it."

Did they? My heart pumps again, but I refuse to let the load lift. The current council hasn't approved it.

"You're bending things to your own way, Envadi," a hairy man says.

"Come," Zade says. "Come look for yourself. Councilmen and warlocks, come. Then let your wives and daughters and sisters and mothers see."

The Grand Chancellor appears at the bottom of the stairs, those closest inching away from him. The murmurs from the crowd quiet. He says nothing, but climbs the stairs. Slowly, but deliberately. Once he gets to Zade, he takes the book.

For several minutes, he does nothing but study it. His eyes move back and forth as he takes in the words. I intertwine my fingers and place them over my mouth. What is he thinking? His expression is one of concentration and gives nothing away. Will he stop us from using the law in my favor?

Finally, he snaps the book shut and shoves it at Zade. His gaze bores into me, black with anger. The air grows cold. He hates me and I'm going to die because of that hate. I'm sure he'll kill Zade as well for trying this. There will be no need for a vigilante group. His nose flares, then the expression wipes from him and he faces the crowd.

"It is as he says. She's free."

He saunters down the stairs. Zade looks at me, a huge grin on his face. I'm free. Free as a man. Free!

The crowd's murmuring returns.

Zade quiets them with his words. "This is only the beginning of the delights we have planned for you this night. Please enjoy them."

He raises his hands above him and strikes them together. Black light surges from them, shooting across the room, plunging us into darkness.

A woman screams, but I'm not frightened. I wait anxiously for the next step. My whole body feels light and free. No Master. No punishments.

In the darkness, a single spark flickers. Then another. And

another. White at first, then the sparks growing in colors and brightness. They multiply quickly at my eye level, but above the guests. Soon there are enough to fill the room. It's as bright as a summer day. Bright as I feel inside.

Flowers appear in vases scattered through the room in full bloom. A scent comes to me. I know others are smelling whatever brings them the most happiness. Another spell I'm finding I enjoy. To me, the faint citrus scent smells suspiciously of Zade, but I don't let the thought dampen my spirits.

Music fills the air, slow at first, but steadily building into a familiar dance. The sound comes from all around.

Zade walks up a few stairs and says loud enough others can hear, but quiet enough I feel he's talking directly to me.

"You're a free woman now. Would you give me the honor of being the first to dance with you?"

I don't know what freedom will bring, but spending a dance in his arms sounds like a good start. "Of course."

He takes my hand and wraps it around his elbow like before. We make our way down the stairs. People part around us. A few couples head for the doors, but most are unable to look away from us.

Once we're in the middle of the room, I place my hand on his shoulder while he puts his on the bottom of my shoulder blade. Our free hands clasp together. We step with the beat. People have yet to mingle in other rooms, leaving very little room to dance. My awareness of them fades.

The music floods through me. Zade leads me through the steps. We work together. Moving and flowing. Light as cotton floating through air.

The only time I take my eyes from his is when required by the dance. I spin and twirl, his hands catching my waist. It feels good. Right and sure. My dress and his cravat flash to a new color. My joy bubbles up. I smile at him and move with the music.

As the song comes to an end, instead of standing and waiting for my curtsy, he does something new. He holds my hand and supports my waist then dips me backward. I slowly stretch up, wanting to keep moving toward him until our lips meet.

A new song begins. I shake my head to clear it.

"Another?" he asks.

Everyone is still staring at us. I'd rather dance again than deal with them and the ramifications of what he's done. What I now am. "Please."

He twirls me and beckons me back to him. This time, I try not to lose myself, but to watch the crowd around me. I can't let myself get caught up in him. Even more important now that I'm free. And he's free for Waverly. Some of my lightness slinks away.

A couple begins dancing. They spin past. Councilman Daniel and Annabelle. Another joins. And another. Soon, the floor is full of dancing couples and not staring people.

When the song ends, he brings my gloved hand to his lips and gives it a kiss. Warmth tickles the back of my hand. "Hosting duties call."

I sigh and follow him to the side of the room where those not dancing wait. We spend the next hour mingling. Or rather, he mingles. Lots of warlocks and even more women want to talk to him, but none want to even stand by me. Is this change going to help save his life or make them more intent on killing him? I thought they'd want to kill him more for it, but as eager as everyone is to talk to him, I'm not sure.

Either way, he's safe enough with so many enthused admirers. I drift away from him, moving in and out of rooms and the garden. The flowers are in full bloom and the temperature is cool, but not crisp, despite being fall. Bethany, Cynthia, and Waverly's ideas really mesh well together. Though people don't want to even look at me, they appear to be having a good time, smiling, dancing, eating, talking.

A warlock next to me laughs as his companion's hair changes color. This time they both drink from their glasses making both their hair change colors. Then they too make their way over to Zade. Someone squeals as one of the floating lights plummets toward them, but the sound quickly turns to glee as the spark transforms into a gold piece.

Nothing is like the only other ball I attended. The more time passes, and the more spells and surprises come, the happier everyone seems to be. I can barely see Zade with the crowd surrounding him. What would they think if they knew it was put together by a servant and two other women? At least the innovative ideas seem to help Zade.

At one point I see Bethany and mother. Bethany's hair no longer has the sparkles. Father must have unspelled them. At least she's still wearing her dress Katherine spent so much time on. I start toward them. Before I've taken a couple steps, Father spots me and rushes them to the other side of the room. Will I ever be allowed to see my sisters again? Will Father punish them in some way over my freedom? The thought makes me ill. Cynthia doesn't even know what happened. Will she think I abandoned her? Suddenly, being free doesn't seem as great.

I pass by Annabelle and Waverly at different times. They seem to be having more luck, chatting with lots of people. No doubt their spelled ball gowns are the attraction. Hopefully, the dresses will gain interest in Katherine designing more instead of casting a negative light on it like I'm doing. I hope she doesn't regret making it for me.

Others are wearing dresses Katherine clearly had a hand in making. A few are even spelled in some small way. Wonder how they talked their husbands into that. They also seem to gain much attention. It may be enough to offset the damage I've done.

A servant passes by with a tray of glasses, more drinks to change hair color or a potion that leaves you with a high pitched voice for several minutes? Maybe something else entirely. There are more potions and spells than I could have ever guessed. I wonder if Katherine has had a chance to try them. Plus, she may not know that I'm free. And even if she does, it'd be nice to know what she thinks of it. I might as well take her some treats.

I stop by the refreshment room. The food is so unfamiliar, I don't know what it is. I recognize some fish and a bowl of strawberries, but mostly I'm left to guess. Nothing looks appetizing in my current mood, but I grab things for Katherine. Hopefully a few of them are spelled in a way that she'll enjoy.

Despite the spell to keep the perfect temperature, I'm hot and thirsty. Maybe the spell isn't working or I'm nervous. Either way, I grab a drink for myself and an extra for Katherine. It sparkles on my tongue, somehow feeling like the sparkles on my dress. I make a mental note to ask Zade how he did that later. If he's still alive. I glance at him. He's laughing with a group of warlocks. He'll be fine.

Where will I live? I don't know. Not here. And I can't be a burden to Katherine. How will I make money and support myself? I don't know, but I can't stay. Maybe I should pack when I finish with Katherine, or sneak into mother and Cynthia's room. I really want to talk to Cynthia about what's happened. Father probably set a spell to stop her from leaving and people from coming.

With two glasses squished in my palm and the plate of food in the other, I set off to find Katherine. I traverse the stairs I stood on earlier. A woman coming down smiles at me, and I think there's hope of conversation, until her husband rushes her off toward the dance floor, which has just begun to glow a faint blue. I sigh and continue upward.

When I get to the top, I go to the doors, but a clang stops me. As I turn toward the gathering, the room falls eerily silent save for the music.

Warlocks, cloaked and hooded in black, form a wide circle around Zade. I was wrong. It doesn't matter what others think of him, of course Father wouldn't take the price off his head. My stomach cramps.

Smoky light moves from one cloaked figure to the next. Zade

is encircled by the warlocks. Trapped. A few people are caught with him.

"Our quarrel is with the Envadi," a raspy voice says. "The rest may leave our circle unharmed."

The trapped people hesitate a moment, their shadows enhanced by the glowing floor. Zade says something I can't hear. A man steps forward, hesitates in front of the light a moment, and crosses the spell. When nothing happens to him, the others scurry.

Zade stands alone.

"You've broken too many of our ways and have no right to free a woman," the voice says. "For that, you will die."

# CHAPTER 40

THE PLATE and drinks I forgot I was holding crash to the floor, soaking my feet.

For a moment, Zade looks at me. In that brief second, my heart feels as if it's been ripped from me. I've failed to help save him.

"I haven't broken any laws," he says.

"You break the spirit of the law. Too many people have complained. Now those gathered will see you pay the price."

They step closer to him, light fanning out from their circle toward him.

"No," I whisper. I can't watch this happen.

The crowd is knotted together, especially thick at the bottom of the stairs, preventing my running to him. Watching, but not anxious to be close to the action. They were so eager to talk to him before, was it all for show? Why doesn't anyone help him?

Waverly spurts from the crowd. Maybe she'll be able to distract them until I can get there and help. Though I don't know how I can. She dashes toward the circle. One of the robed men's hands darts out and knocks her to the ground. He zips a dark spell at her. She tries to curl away from it, but it slams into her back. Her body goes limp. She doesn't move. Is she dead?

"Don't hurt anyone else." Zade throws his suit coat on the luminescent floor, his gaze avoiding Waverly's motionless form. "I'm the one showing women they have a chance at freedom."

One of the cloaked figures growls. The spell creeping toward Zade intensifies. Suddenly it bursts, springing for him. An azure light zips from Zade's hands, surrounding him, shielding him in a dome from the attacking spells.

The steel light smashes against it, sparking. The warlocks raise their arms. The spell crashes and pounds against Zade's shield. A loud creak sounds. A fissure appears in the dome. The gray light pounces on the crack.

He's not going to make it. I can't just watch. I've caused it. I'll stop it or die trying. The knot of people is still too much to get through. They're tightly packed, standing as far from the fray as they can while not leaving the room.

Blast.

I kick my shoes off, pick up my green skirt, and dash for the railing. Without stopping to think, I thrust myself onto the railing and propel myself as far forward as I can. Toward Zade. I don't have to reach him, I just have to get close enough to cause a distraction. Maybe more if I don't die.

Air rushes past, my dress flapping. The engagement ceremony flashes through my mind, but I shove it away. A few faces of the crowd turn toward me as I hurtle down. Then a few more. And more. I'm almost to the ground. Tucking my legs and arms in, I brace for impact.

An amber light shoots from somewhere in the crowd. I plead it's not for Zade. My plea is answered. Instead, it sails toward me. Just before I collide with the floor, the spell reaches me, cushioning me. It lowers me several feet until I'm lying on solid ground.

I don't have time to stop and think. Something digs into my

leg. I roll over, jump to my feet, and rub the new bruise, wondering what to do next. The bruise is covered by a bulge on my leg. My gun.

My legs shake as I pull myself to a standing position. I reach my hand in my pocket.

"What are you doing?" someone asks.

The owner of the voice is behind me a bit, to the right. The Grand Chancellor's son, Nathaniel and his intended. Why is he so close? Another anxious to see Zade die? Ignoring him, I pull out my gun.

The crack in the dome surrounding Zade is widening, right above his face. If I was next to it, I could slide my hand through and touch him. He's sweating under the blue light. Someone from the crowd behind me shoots a burgundy spell. The crack widens. Suddenly, the room plunges into darkness, save for the lights of the dueling spells.

It can't wait any longer, a hex is going to get through. My hands shake as I lift the gun. They're shaking too much. I'm going to miss.

I point the gun at the hooded figure closest to me. I take a breath and hold it. I squeeze the trigger. The gun recoils in my hand. A crack sounds through the room. I missed.

Except the gun is still spelled to show where the bullet went. The tan light nicks the warlock's arm. He drops his hands, weakening the light attacking Zade. His hand darts out of his robe and touches his arm, it comes away darkened with liquid. He whirls toward me, bloody fingers stretched out toward me.

I haven't saved Zade, only caused us both to die.

The other robed figures hesitate. Maybe it will be enough to give Zade a chance, even if I'm losing mine. I wish I could see their faces. Know who's trying to destroy us. I aim at all of them one-by-one, starting with the figure facing me, quickly firing until I've used my other five bullets.

None of them hit an attacker, but it distracts them. Their spell weakens as they look for the commotion. The crack in Zade's shield shrinks, though he looks weaker than before. A bright green hex goes flying toward him and slips through the crack, slamming into his leg. My chest tightens as Zade lets out a growling yell.

Out of nowhere, a yellow spell zips from beside me, toward the attackers. Nathaniel stands next to me, hand extended, his fiancé by his side. They're going to help? A cry comes from the crowd. I look up just in time to see a black-tinged, crimson spell flung at me. I flinch.

A whimper from the side. Nathaniel's fiancé is on the floor. He crouches over her. One of the attackers moves toward us. Without a thought, I yell and leap for him.

He stops, but I don't. I force all my momentum into slamming my gun on his head. It hammers into him. We fall to the floor, his hood opening in the process. Father. I just hit Father.

For a moment, I can't move. He's unconscious. How many times has he done something similar to me? Deal with him later. I roll onto my back. He stays motionless.

Out of the corner of my eye, I see another attacker racing toward me. I turn to hit him or trip him or throw my gun at him. Anything, though it'll be too late. Before I can decide which to do, an aqua spell blasts into him from behind.

He searches for his foe. Zade's free, already casting another spell toward him, the other hooded figures are gone. The last one runs for the door, casting a tan wall behind him.

Zade saved me. Green spells fly from him, but hit the fleeing warlock's wall without doing a thing. Others from the crowd move to help, but it's too late. The attackers are gone.

Zade follows, but he's limping so badly there's no chance he'll catch up to them. He needs to come back here where it's safe and someone could look at his leg. Before I can go after him, Chadwick does. His servant should be able to bring him back. I search for Waverly, but don't see her on the floor where they left her. Did someone move her? Is she still alive?

A crowd of people have gathered around the fallen girl. Father is still beside me, several warlocks guarding him. I'd rather help the girl than deal with him. I heave myself off the ground and move toward her.

The crowd parts, not wanting to be by the girl with the gun, I suppose. Nathaniel is on the floor next to her. I kneel by him.

"How is she?"

He shakes his head.

I reach for her. Her skin is cold. Her chest isn't moving. Dead. She died because I stood up for Zade.

Why did they have to do this? I glance behind me, where I left Father. He's stirring, but Councilman Daniel, along with other warlocks, still stand guard. That will be sufficient, for now. I focus back on Nathaniel.

"I'm sorry I couldn't do more."

"Don't be. You're not the problem here. Someone else is."

"What is the meaning of this?" The Grand Chancellor shouts from above us, his white hair glowing under the lights, but his dark beard making the bottom half of his face seem too disappear. I swallow and stand.

He says, "I'm enjoying the gardens for a moment and someone kills my son's intended? Who has done this?"

The crowd parts away from me. Someone turns the electric lights on. The Grand Chancellor stares at me. Realizing I still hold the gun, I shove it back in my pocket and bite my lip. Can he tell she didn't die from being shot? Will he use it as an excuse to tarnish my newly freed state?

Then I realize he's not looking at me, but past me. I turn. The crowd didn't part to show me, they parted to show Father standing with his hood pulled back, a bruise forming on his head beneath strands of white hair. A bruise I caused.

"You're a part of this, Councilman Stephen?"

Father looks at me a moment. An expression crosses his face I don't recognize. He gives his attention to the Grand Chancellor. "I am."

"Why have you destroyed my son's possession?"

Possession? She was a person. Someone must have cared for her more than as a plaything.

Father puts his palms together in front of his chest. "I didn't mean to. We were only trying to get rid of the Envadi. Ever since coming here he's caused trouble. My reputation and daughter have suffered because of him."

The Grand Chancellor's voice is low. "This is because of Chancellor Zade?"

Councilman Daniel is close by. I catch his eye hoping he will defend Zade. My doing it would make things worse, but if he did it, it may help. Hope fills me as he steps forward.

"Grand Chancellor, if I may. There have been rumors that there's a price on Chancellor Zade's life. He's done nothing to break our laws. In fact, I think tonight has made it clear he's gone out of his way to follow our laws even if he wants things done a little differently."

Just then Zade limps forward, pale with dark circles under his eyes, Chadwick behind him. "We lost them."

Please don't take this out on him. I want to go to him, but my presence would only make this worse.

"Lost who?" The Grand Chancellor says.

"The rest of the warlocks that attacked me." Zade's voice is strained, as if just talking is an effort.

"How many were there?"

"Seven, counting Councilman Stephen."

The Grand Chancellor says, much too calmly, "Who are they, Stephen?"

Father clamps his mouth together.

"Did they kill my son's possession because they were here for a bounty on Chancellor Zade's life?"

Still, Father refuses to answer.

"If that's the way you want it. Anyone found even discussing the price on Chancellor Zade will meet the fate I'm about to deal you. None shall break our laws. Councilman Stephen, you are stripped of your title and holdings. Your things will go to Chancellor Zade since he is the closest living warlock."

My breath catches in my throat. If my family has to have an owner, none would be better than Zade. It can't be true.

"I believe, sir," Zade interrupts, "that the closest free family member is Serena."

The Grand Chancellor's mouth shrinks into a tight line. Did he just say what I think he did? Am I—? Could I—? Will I not only get to be with my sisters, but take care of them? Protect them? Or will the Grand Chancellor keep them from me?

Councilman Daniel steps forward. "If the law from earlier holds, then he's right. She has all the rights of a warlock. Everything would go to Serena."

Another man from somewhere in the crowd hollers, "It's true."

"Can they do that?" someone nearby says.

Everyone waits for the Grand Chancellor. My chest tightens. My sisters and mother. I might actually be in charge of them. My hand forms a ball and I put it to my mouth. Silently, I will him to uphold the earlier law.

He scans the crowd, pausing longer on those who gather around Zade. His lips turn down slightly. "It is as you say. The law stands. All of Councilman Stephen's holdings go to—" he waves his hand at me. He turns to his son and dead future daughter-in-law. "Someone clean this mess up."

He storms from the room. I'm stunned into disbelief.

Those gathered begin talking. Several men help Nathaniel with his dead bride. Zade motions more servants over to help and talks with him.

Suddenly, Waverly is at my side. "Too bad I got knocked out when the fighting was just getting started."

"Waverly, you're all right." I'm more relieved at her safety than I expect. I may want her far enough away that Zade can't be in love with her still, but apparently I don't want her harmed.

"Course I am." She rubs her temple. "Except for a headache."

"A little headache never got you down." Zade limps the rest of the way to us and gives her arm a squeeze. "Glad you're okay."

She gives him a smile. "You, too. I was afraid they had you."

"Not me."

"You're hurt though," I say. "Let me look at your leg."

"I'll be fine. Chadwick will help me with it in a minute."

Waverly purses her lips like she wants to say something but doesn't.

"Perhaps he should look it over right now." Because Zade truly doesn't look well.

"In a moment. I'm more drained than anything else." He takes my hand. "I'm glad you're not injured. When I saw you fly off the balcony, I thought you were going to die or be seriously hurt."

I glance at the floor. "I couldn't let them kill you without doing something."

"Those shooting lessons I gave you were worth it."

"I think it did more damage when I used it to knock out—" I'm not ready to think about him yet, "someone out. But when I jumped from the balcony, before I crashed to the floor something stopped me. A spell. Do you know who cast it? Was it Councilman Daniel?"

"Don't know. I didn't see."

"Is there a way to discover who it was?" I say. "I'd like to thank them."

"Just a moment, I'll see if I can find out." An almost invisible pale purple light comes from him.

"Thank you for helping him," Waverly says.

So she can marry her love, the spy. At least I'll be with my sisters now. And I won't have to worry over their punishments. "Of course."

"I can't tell exactly who it was," Zade says, not looking at me, "but there is one thing."

"What?"

"It came from that corner by the red flowers."

"Well, whoever it was, I'm grateful to them. I suppose we should help the guests get settled."

And once they're settled, I'll try to figure out what it means to be free, to have responsibility over my mother and sisters, and that Zade is still alive. The price on his head may not be completely gone, but hopefully close enough. I move to help, a bounce in my soaked feet.

# CHAPTER 41

CURLED up on the floor of the study, I stare out the picture window. Though it's been three months since the ball, it still feels like a dream. The sun is bright outside, warming the room. I keep waiting for someone to come in and punish me for something. But no one will. Not even my perpetually gloveless state is commented on.

With father locked away, no one is punished in this house. No one will ever punish my sisters again while they're under my protection. And I have what I wanted. My freedom. Except it still feels like something is missing. Something achingly big.

"Serena?" Cynthia stands at the door. "Waverly and Zade are here to see you."

Once I'm over my shock, I say, "Send them in. You can come, as well. Wait, why don't you get Bethany first. I'm sure she'd like to talk to them."

She smiles, bigger and brighter like she does now that father doesn't control our lives. Something is changing with her. "I will."

After she leaves, I can't help but let my nerves take over. I haven't seen them since we left the day after the ball fiasco. The day I was supposed to marry Zade. It's been so long I was sure we'd become nothing but a distant memory to them.

Without an introduction, Waverly and Zade enter. Zade is still limping, though not as noticeably. Chadwick insisted he get a healer for it, but the healer said was that it is an injury he will always carry. It hurts to watch him walk, to know his releasing me is partially to blame for the injury.

I can't bring myself to get off the floor even though it's not proper. To stand and show how easy it is for me, something he'll never have again. As long as mother doesn't see me entertaining this way, I doubt anyone in this house will care. Outside of the house, well, I don't want to venture too far yet and push the bounds of my freedom.

"Please sit," I say.

Waverly perches on the closest chair, but Zade surprises me sitting on the floor beside me. His nearness is both entrancing and disturbing.

"How have you been?" I ask.

"Fine," Zade says.

"Bored," Waverly groans. "And he is too, even if he won't admit it."

He shrugs. "I guess I got used to having you and your sisters around."

My heart clenches. "Things happen for a reason though. I'm sure you and Waverly have enjoyed the time to yourselves."

"We haven't," Waverly says. "I keep trying to tell Zade we needed to visit sooner, but he said you needed time to adjust. Glad I finally talked him into coming. We need something to do."

That's why it's been so long? They thought we needed time to adjust? And they probably wanted time to themselves. "I was planning on redoing this room." Though I don't know why they would want to help instead of being together. "It's the only reason I'm in here. Making plans to tear it apart and start over. Make it more my own. Do you have any ideas from Envado?"

"You know I do," Waverly says.

"I could help, too," Zade says. "You have anything specific in mind?"

"Not really. I just want a change."

"There's a lot that's changing."

It's so hard not to stare at him. I look at Waverly instead. It hurts as well, but not as much.

"I really don't mind helping, but I was also hoping I could have my old job back," she says.

"What?" Why would she want to go back to being my servant when she could marry Zade?

"I miss not helping. And not hanging out with you and your sisters. It's why I came here after all."

"Didn't you come for Zade?"

"Sort of. If it wasn't for him I wouldn't be here, but I really wanted to work. If money's an issue, I'll get Zade to continue paying my wages."

"No, it's not that." Ironically I have plenty of money. Money that Thomas paid father for me. I look back and forth at them. "I thought, well…"

"What?" she says.

"I thought you two would be getting ready to marry."

Waverly giggles. "Really? You thought—me and him?" She laughs harder.

Zade rubs the back of his neck, cheeks pinking.

Waverly edges farther out of her seat toward me. "Serena, he's my brother."

I jump to my feet. "He's your what?"

"My brother. And ew. We love each other, but not like that."

Shock roils through me, bouncing and jostling around until it finally bursts out by saying, "Why didn't you tell me?"

Zade says, "Because of my being a spy. It's dangerous for women here anyway, but if they found out she's my sister, it'd be even more dangerous. So please don't tell anyone. Not even your sisters."

"Of course not. I'll keep it a secret." And what does this secret mean for me? My mouth goes dry.

Waverly bounces to her feet. "If you don't mind, I think I'll show myself around."

"I can take you."

"No, no, it's all right." She heads for the door just as Cynthia and Bethany come. "Oh, look. You don't even need to worry about me. Your sisters will show me around, right?"

"We can," Cynthia says.

"I'd love to know how to make those crunchy little sweets that you suggested for the ball," Bethany says.

"Where's the kitchen? If you have the stuff, I'll make you some."

They leave, chatter fading as they go. Zade stands. I shift my weight from one foot to another. The silence makes me itchy to be moving. "I bought a horse."

"You did? Is he here?"

"She, and yes."

"I'd love to see her if you don't mind taking me."

"Are you all right with a long walk?"

He sighs. "I've gotten used to it. It's hard, but I don't mind. I'd like to go with you."

"Let's go then." I lead him through the house, my pulse doing strange things. "Sally named her Goldie."

"How are your sisters doing with the change?"

"Better. There's more laughter in the house now. I'm teaching them everything you taught me about shooting. Except mother, she thinks I'm crazy."

"It must be a hard transition for her," he says. "I'd be happy to help you teach them to shoot."

"Thank you. Teaching them to protect themselves would be good. After talking it over with the older girls, I've decided to wait on giving them their freedom like you gave me."

"Really?" We continue on to the barn. "Why's that?"

"I still don't know how things are with me. We've been staying here keeping the house running. A few women have visited me discreetly, very excited about the change. Katherine's orders are going through the roof."

"That sounds good."

"It is." Plus, she's safe. Zade has been spelling her tattoos, so she appears to be like any other tarnished following the law. "If you don't mind my asking, what's happened with Phyllis?" I've forgiven most of their debt, but couldn't bring myself to forgive it all yet. I will someday soon.

He rubs his forehead. "I couldn't kick her out. She'd be more likely to tell someone else what we're doing. I offered to let her stay if she'd let me spell her to remain silent. She was happy to take the offer. Though I prefer to keep her close, if she becomes more of a problem I can use some contacts to get her out of the country."

"Spy things?"

"Lots of them. Does that bother you?"

"Will it keep the threats against you away?"

He gives a wry grin. "Not really. I have the support of a few people, like my friend Chadwick. He's not really a servant, he's here helping along with others. But despite the help, with the way society is means there will always be threats to Envadi."

"I suppose we'll have to work on changing society's ideals then. Why are you spying on us? I heard that you want to steal our ideas and spells, but you don't seem to care about that."

"Envado is overrun with refugees from your country. I'm here to figure out how to help. Both for your people and mine. To make lives better. That's why I stayed instead of going back home after the tournament. There's more of us here working together than you'd think, but they need all the help they can get."

The thought is a startling one, but I hope it's true. I hope there are others that want to help Chardonian women gain what I have.

Then another thought hits me. "Does that mean being a spy is why you freed me?"

He laughs. "No, that came from you."

"What did I do?"

"You remember the journal you gave me?"

"Yes." I scowl at him. "You never returned it."

"I'll bring it next time I come."

My heart quickens at the thought of there being a next time. A next time with Waverly being his sister, not his love.

"In the journal, Julia wrote about her husband discovering the law."

"I don't remember anything about that."

He laughs. "You probably spent too much time on the gushy love parts."

My cheeks heat. I return to walking toward the barn, keeping a slow pace for him. "Chancellor Jacob was an uncommonly kind man."

"More than most people will ever know. He was trying to figure out the best way to use the law when she died. He was the Grand Chancellor's strongest opponent. I think after that he lost his will to do anything."

We enter the barn and stop in front of my new horse. He leans against the stall and we stare at each other. A fluttering fills me. I clear my throat. "This is Goldie."

"Serena." His voice is low, tantalizing.

Why am I suddenly so nervous? "I haven't ridden her yet, but I'm hoping to. I got a saddle."

"Serena."

"I'll learn one of these days."

He grabs my hand. I've never been so glad to be without my gloves. To feel another's skin on mine.

"Serena."

"Yes." My voice is whispery.

"May I kiss you?"

"What about your fiancé?"

His brows crease and then relaxes. "Technically that's you. I haven't known what the girl I was once engaged to is doing since before I beat Thomas. We were never really close, not like that. She was nice, but not the one I care about."

He doesn't care about her? Hope starts pounding through me. "But you freed me."

"We're still connected by the engagement ceremony." He reaches up and brushes his thumb across my neck, right where my brand is. "I don't know of a way to break the connection that I spelled to us, but I can try."

I lick my lips. "Does that connection take away any of my choices? Make me have to listen to you?"

"No. It just claims you as mine. Warlocks can cast a spell to read it and know that I have a claim on you. Like a contract, but there's no paper or signature. In my country a bride wears a ring that does the same thing."

Of course the country that was supposed to be barbaric finds a way to connect a couple without branding a woman. They're the least barbaric people I know.

His cheeks pink in the way that I've come to adore. "I don't want to own you."

I don't want to be owned either. I've barely gained freedom and no one can ever make me give it back. But I don't want him entirely gone either. When the idea comes to me, I don't hesitate to ask. "Is there a way for you to change it so it would say I'm protected, but not owned by you?"

He's silent a moment, his lips slowly turning upward. "I think I can do that. But before I do anything, you should know, I was sort of hoping to court you."

"You mean, get married?"

The pink of his cheeks darkens. "Not right away. More like us spending time together."

"Yes."

"Yes, what? You want to spend time with me?"

"Yes, I want to spend time with you. Yes, you can do the spell." I take several breaths, but it doesn't help. My heart still flutters wildly. "And yes, please kiss me."

I reach up, stepping on my tiptoes. He leans down. My pulse speeds as he moves closer, but time seems to slow. His lips hover over mine. Waiting. Soft puffs of air caress my lips. The fluttering in my chest becomes happy anticipation. He grabs my waist and pulls me the rest of the way to him. Our lips meet.

Gently and so sweet. I relish every second of him. Of being. Joy bubbles within me. My fingers twirl in his hair. I can feel his heart beating in time with mine. Too soon, our lips part.

Slowly, he puts me to the ground, his lips hovering over mine. He sneaks another soft peck. I reach up, about to go for another.

"Are you playing with Goldie?" Sally asks from the doorway.

I scoot away from Zade, my cheeks heating.

He grins. "Your sister was just introducing us."

"Did she tell you I named the horse?"

"She did. Did she tell you, she wanted me to teach her how to ride him?"

Sally's eyes grow wider. "She does?"

"Yup. I'm thinking she needs to go get some breeches on so I can teach her."

I laugh. "Sorry, trying them on once was enough for me. I found out women in Arllos use a side saddle. That's what I have."

"No breeches?"

"No breeches." I open Goldie's stall and grab the side saddle on the way out. "Think you can show me how this is supposed to go on her? I've been learning how to care for her, but we haven't covered anything about riding yet."

"I'd be happy to." He grabs the saddle from me and turns to Sally. "What about you little miss? You want to try breeches?"

"Can I, Serena?"

"You can do whatever you desire. You'll get no demands from me."

"Yay!" She races back toward the house.

As I watch her go, knowing my sisters are safe, I grab hold of Zade's arm. He brushes a kiss in my hair. This feels so right. Being here with the man I love. The man who loves me, but doesn't own me. Everything is mine.

# AFTERWORD

If you enjoyed reading this book, please consider helping the author by leaving a review where you purchased the book and/or on Goodreads.

You can sign up to receive notification when Janeal Falor releases a new book at http://eepurl.com/AL2s5 or www.janealfalor.com with a Release Notification link on the side bar, along with links to deleted scenes. Or talk to the author directly at janealfalor@gmail.com

Chapter One of MINE TO SPELL Follows

# OTHER BOOKS BY JANEAL FALOR

Mine to Tarnish (Mine Prequel Novella)

You Are Mine (Mine #1)

Mine to Spell (Mine #2)

Mine to Fear (Mine #3)

Sacrifice of Mine (Mine #4)

Ever Darkening (Darkening Light #1)

Savage Light (Darkening Light #2)

Death's Queen (Death's Queen #1)

Death's Betrayal (Death's Queen #2)

Death's Embrace (Death's Queen #3)

Death's Assassin (Death's Queen #4)

Bound by Birthright (Elven Princess #1)

Bound to Endure (Elven Princess #2)

Bound by Love (Elven Princess #3)

Goddess Ascending

A Genie's Heart

# CHAPTER 1

## *Cynthia*

SEVENTEEN TODAY. It should be a birthday like no seventeen-year-old Chardonian girl ever had before. Waverly made a cake I actually get to eat, and father isn't here to beat and hex his wrath on anyone. The dining room is crowded with my sisters, mother, and Waverly. The only warlock present is Zade, who's nothing like father. But the spell which just zipped in the window, and floats in bold over the table for all to see ruined the perfect day.

*Stephen's daughter, take control of your property or we will do so for you.*

PROPERTY MEANING ME. The words are glowing, bright and yellow with flecks of crimson, hovering above that perfect birthday cake. Waverly says that in Envado they have candles on cakes. Why they would do such a thing, I'm uncertain, but after this fiery display, it's not something worth even attempting. It's too much like the threat of a hex, burning hot, and ready to slam into me.

328

Zade zaps the spell with a flash of blue, but not quickly enough. Even the youngest girls know something is wrong. They hover together with their eyes wide. Even though they are only courting and not officially engaged still, Zade puts an arm around Serena as if it will protect her. A twist of longing aches in my chest for someone to care for me that much.

Though Serena may be feeling differently. Her chin is tilted up the way she does when she's determined. She's probably thinking on how to deal with this newest threat, but I'm doubtful it will solve the true problem. Me.

This birthday means I'm eligible to be sold to a warlock husband. Most girls don't get tested for magic on their birthday, but they at least have plans to even if it's a couple of years in the future. But the only plans here were cake and kindness. Obviously that didn't work out so well. Living in a society where only warlocks control everything and only they do magic was bound to ruin my day no matter how much I wanted it to be different.

"The property is protected," Zade says. "Nothing more than harmless threats can get in."

Probably true, but the way it cracked the joy from us only moments ago—it's not exactly harmless.

"Can we please return to enjoying the festivities?" Serena folds her arms like she's trying to keep herself together.

I'd do the same if I thought it'd help. Instead, I thread my fingers through my necklaces, keeping a neutral expression tightly in place.

"Certainly." Zade motions to Waverly. "Would you like to cut a slice for everyone?"

"I'd be happy to." She bounces over to the cake.

"Zade and I will be in the study," Serena says. "Please carry on and enjoy yourselves."

The girls giggle happily now that the spelled words are gone and cake is coming, easily covering Zade and Serena's exit. I wish

I could so easily forget, but instead, I go on pretending as usual. Despite being adept at it, I rather despise it.

"What an exciting day." The words are all too cheery spilling from my lips. "The only other time I've ever seen so many treats in one place was the tournament last year."

"Did they make a cake as pretty as Waverly's?" Sally asks.

I don't even recall if they had cake. "No one could make a cake as pretty as Waverly's."

"Only because I cheat." Waverly acts as if nothing has happened. She slides the first piece on a plate and passes it over to me. "Happy birthday!"

Her voice is a little too perky, but I chime back just as happily, "Thank you!"

Her smile becomes softer at the corners, less forced. At least my pretending appears to be good. Even if I'm faking my happiness, it's still satisfying to boost another's mood. The girls receive their treat, starting with the youngest.

Next, she serves mother, who's gained quite the sweet tooth with this pregnancy. The last thing father left us before the Grand Chancellor took him in to custody was another sister to be born sometime in the next several months. Mother seems to be taking this pregnancy like all the rest, but I can't help but wonder what will the baby's life be like never having his cruel influence in it?

My bracelets jangle as I force myself away from such thoughts to eat some of the white cake with pink frosting. Any other day, the rich sweetness would be fantastic, just not now. Instead, it sticks to my mouth like a giant gob of honey, and my throat wants to clamp shut, refusing admittance to its passage. That's just perfect.

I shovel in the bites regardless, not wanting to hurt Waverly's feelings, and take a big swig of milk after each one. At least that's easier to swallow. By the time I finish my slice of cake, my mouth and throat ache from forcing them. I never want to eat cake again. But it's done, and I've pretended long enough to make a getaway.

"Thank you again, Waverly." After pushing myself to my feet I say, "I'm going to wander around some."

"Check to make sure that Serena knows we're running low on sugar," mother says, clueless as to my real intent. Probably due to exhaustion. This pregnancy seems to be harder on her than I remember the others being.

But Bethany, the third eldest sister, and Waverly aren't as clueless.

"It will work out," Waverly whispers as I brush past her.

Bethany gives me a look that says she knows exactly what I'm doing. Not that it matters. As long as the little girls aren't worried, and mother's content, I can do as I wish. It's the first time my birthday has ever been celebrated, after all. Even if it's no longer much of a celebration.

"I'm going to make certain it does," I tell them.

I stride down the hall toward the front of the house, not bothering to knock when I reach the study. It's a simple thing to nudge the door open. It may be wrong, but catching Serena and Zade making lovey eyes at each other sends a giddy thrill through me. They'll both go red and start stammering, but won't lose the happy glow that they must get from each other. My sister is finally happy. Only when the door creaks open this time, neither of them has a glow to lose.

Zade is pacing one side of the study while Serena is on the other, rigid in her chair and staring out the picture window. The painful knot in my stomach tightens as I move into the room. It's worse than I feared.

I shut the door behind me and say, "I believe I should be included in this discussion."

"Who says we are discussing anything?" Serena retorts.

"You said we were going to do birthdays different now that father is gone, and I could have things the way I want. Well, I want to know what's going on. It's about the latest threat, isn't it?" Still neither says anything. "The threat was because of me. I deserve to know."

Serena jumps to her feet. "It wasn't because of you. It was because of me."

"Clearly, I'm the one whose blood should be tested to see what warlock wants to buy me, so of course it's because of me." Anger bites my words more than I meant to let out. I clench my teeth to trap it back inside.

"There's enough to fight out of this room, let's not bring it in here," Zade says before going to Serena. "She does have a right to know."

She bunches her fist. "My freedom was supposed to enable us to make choices for ourselves, not keep us locked up and scared."

"I know, but things take time. Hopefully, they'll get used to the way things are with you now," Zade says.

"But they aren't getting used to it fast enough," I say. "That's the seventh threat we've had this week, and by far the most foreboding. Most hinted about my coming of age and being sold, of which we've had no intention of following their expectations. The only other thing we could do is return to class, and that isn't an option. You remember what it was like. What they teach about women subjecting themselves to warlocks." And how I spent most of the time convincing everyone class was right where I wanted to be. At least it kept us safe, like we need to be now. Too much danger haunts my family.

Serena collapses back into her chair and rubs her temple. "I know."

The silence, thick with worries, doesn't last long before the door opens and Bethany slips inside, closing the door behind her. "Mother wasn't feeling well again and went upstairs to rest. Waverly's taking care of the girls. What's going on?"

"We're discussing the threats," Serena admits.

"Which are about me," I add.

Serena glares at me. No matter that it upsets her; it's all too true.

"What can we do?" Bethany asks. "It's not like we'll return to the ownership of a man."

Unless the council somehow forces us to. The way things are going, it seems rather likely.

Serena says, "We'll figure something out."

"How much time do we have left to figure something out before these threats become more than just threats?" I ask, trying to keep my emotions from flying.

By the tightening of her mouth, I know I've hit onto the real problem. What started as us staying around the house out of uncertainty has become us being caged out of fear. The servants, or Zade, bring everything we need, and even they are cautious. Yet regardless of this, there are a few who have ventured to us, like Councilman Daniel and his wife Annabelle who helped Serena at the ball, but mostly we are avoided.

"We can figure something out." But her repetitive words are as small as her voice.

"We can." I hesitate a moment but not long enough to really let the fact of what I've been considering since the threats started coming I'm going to do sink in. "I will enter the marriage pool."

Gasps sound from the girls, and Zade stares at me in shock.

Once she starts to breathe again, Serena says, "You can't!"

"Are you going to stop me?"

Her lips press into a thin line. The command not to place myself for sale is right there, waiting to tumble from her. I can see it in her eyes, but it goes against everything she's tried to do as owner master. As my master.

"No." Her words come out harsh, but firm. "I won't stop you as an owner. But as a sister, I'm pleading with you not to do this." I open my mouth to reply, but she plunges on. "Please, please don't do this. You know what they're like. How they'll treat you."

"I've always enjoyed the company of warlocks more than you

do." Her face crumples against my words. My true words. Just not true for the reasons she suspects.

"Perhaps, but being owned by one isn't what you want. I know it. You've reveled in the freedom more than any of the other girls. You've taken your own room with glee, enjoyed spending time alone and getting up in the middle of the night without repercussions. If you go back to being owned by a warlock, those are only a few of the things that will end. Much of your life will grow a great deal worse."

Exactly what I've been trying not to think on. With those big, begging eyes, it would be so easy to give into her pleading, so I switch my gaze to the person in the room most likely to side with the safety of my family. Zade. "If I enter the marriage pool, do you think it will ease some of their fears? Do you think it will help show them that Serena can... *handle* her property?"

His eyes stay perfectly trained on mine, and I have to wonder if he's struggling not to give into Serena's pleading as well. "I can't guarantee anything. You understand that, don't you?"

"I do."

He rubs the back of his neck. "It would probably go a long way toward helping. It would give those supporting us something to help prove that Serena isn't different from other warlocks. It would show people she's in control and willing to follow society's ways, which is something hard to dispute and fight against. Though there will still be those that are unhappy just with the fact that she's a woman."

He moves closer to me. Most of the time I forget that as an Envadi how much taller he is than me but at a moment like this, with my neck tilted back to look up at him, every inch of his height is a stern reminder of the seriousness of the situation. "You know if you enter the marriage pool there will be little we can do to prevent your ownership by a warlock. From when I checked before, we know the magic in your blood is more potent than Serena's, and there were many who tried for her hand. There will be many applicants, and she will have to choose one. I'm sure she will let you pick which one you'd like, but you'd still be giving your ownership back to a warlock."

Even though I already know all this, somehow his statement rages through me more than Serena's threats. But what will happen to my family if I don't show compliance to society's ways? It's not something I want to dwell on. My mouth is dry, making my reply harder to get out than it should. "I understand."

Serena moves next to Zade, somehow bearing down on me even more than he is, despite being my height. "Are you certain you do?"

I nod, even though the ever-growing desire to never have started this conversation builds. I almost wish I had never come to the study after them.

"They'll not only use you as a breeder to make powerful warlock babies, but they'll want the magic in your blood for themselves. It's too strong for them not to."

"I know."

"And you still wish to do this?"

I push past the choking in my throat, letting my words come out clear and strong. "It will help our family. I'll be happy to do my part."

Serena wrenches me into a hug. "We can find another way."

But we can't, and even if we could, would we discover it in time to help? Doubtful. I pull out the facade I spent years wearing, the one I hoped I would never need to use again. "Don't worry yourself over it. You know how I enjoy all the attention from warlocks." About as much as I enjoyed punishments from father, but I give her my winning smile, as if it will be the best thing that has ever happened.

She scrutinizes my expression, probably looking for some hint I'm faking this all. But she won't find it. Cracks don't happen.

"Are you certain? Absolutely certain? There'll be no changing your mind."

"Of course I am. I'll ready myself to go to the testing center."

Her eyes grow wider. "Right now?"

"You heard Zade. We can't let them doubt you any longer."

She gives a jerk of a nod and with a voice calmer than I expected, says, "I'll call the carriage."

"Thank you," I choke out, struggling to rein in the building frustration and loss so it doesn't come screaming out.

I turn to hurry from the room, but Bethany stops me. Her eyes are bright with unshed tears. She gives my hand a squeeze, a silent show of support and longing, and then moves to clear the way.

I saunter through the hall, past the kitchen, toward the stairs like I have some happy purpose, trying desperately not to let myself race to my room as I wish. The younger girls call after me, but I can't let myself do more than give them cheery hellos and hurry on. Vaguely, I hear Bethany saying something to them. She probably followed me out, anticipating such a thing. I step faster, up the previously forbidden stairs, down the empty hall, and into my room. My very own.

Serena was furious when she discovered there were enough rooms in father's house for each of us girls to have her own, and still have extra rooms left over. If father were around, instead of in a prison somewhere, I'm sure she would have knocked him out with her gun again. I felt the same. After cramming together in a couple small rooms our whole lives, realizing there was more than enough room to spare sent us both into a fit. But even if it wasn't a surprise, it was one more thing that we had no control over.

Apparently, there's still much we have no control over, even when I try to pretend otherwise.

But now we each have our own rooms, and she was kind enough to let me pick the one I wanted first. The choice has made it much easier to keep secrets.

I close my door, working extra hard to have it make the slightest click when it latches and not to slam it. After it's closed and locked, it doesn't take long to secure my room. It's almost without thought the motions come to me. Sally often likes to hide under my bed or in my closet which I double check for. Once I'm sure the room is clear of sisters, I draw the thick curtains, even though a tree thick with foliage is right outside my window, making it difficult to see in.

When I'm positive nothing that takes place in this room can be seen, I do one of the few good things I ever learned from father. I feel the power in me, the eager glow inside me flaring to life, yearning to respond to my will. I seize hold of it and launch it in a clear, save for a few crimson streaks, barely visible spell straight at my throat. It wraps around my voice just as I demand, blocking all sound. Then I scream.

# ACKNOWLEDGMENTS

There are many people who helped make this book what it is. Any remaining faults are only my own, and without all these amazing people know that the faults would have about a thousand times more. No lie. Hopefully I haven't forgotten anyone, but if it happens, please accept my apologies for my airheadedness is showing.

Serena may have fourteen good sisters, but I have a fantastic one that's better than fourteen combined. Karen C. Eddington, thanks for supporting, encouraging, helping, chatting, and being there. Best sister a girl could have.

Thanks Mom and Dad and the rest of my family, for asking about my books over the years and patiently listening to be babble on, asking about how my writing is going, and Mom for being willing to read. I'm the person I am today because of your love and support. I love and appreciated you guys so much!

RaeChell Garret – you know that one time that I asked you to review my novel. And then I asked again, and again and again. And every time you were like, of course! Your advice was always spot on rockin'. Plus the countless other details I'm always asking your advice on. Well, now the book is published so you can stop worrying I'll ask again...except for the tiny problem of the next book. Maybe I'll get under control sooner this time. Maybe. But truly, thank you for than many, many hours you've put into my book. Your insight is invaluable. You are next!

Thank you to Ashely Maker who Read, Reviewed, and Raved then help me Resolve a lot of issues I didn't even realize hadn't made it into the book. Apparently you win the thank you 'R' words award. It's a good one!

C.M. We found each other late in the critiquing game for this book, but your review helped me tweak some important things and gave me hope that I finally got this where it needed to be. Thank you! Looking forward to swapping more in the future. And Annalea Eastley with poetsinprose.com, thanks for pointing out all the little things I missed and helping making things less awkward.

Writing.com, namely the Novel Critique forum, has been very helpful especially during the early years of serious writing. My first 'real' manuscript was, well, quite sad when I look back on it. Your words and advice taught me much. And for this book I got some insight from the Young Adult Club. Thanks guys!

Michelle Pasket. When I finally worked up the courage to ask for your help, you were so happy and willing. Then when I got your feedback, I kept wondering why I didn't ask sooner. Your thoughts and catches really helped my words to shine. There's so many things you caught that would have never crossed my mind. I am so grateful you are willing to share your talents! Thank you, thank you!

Thank you Kathie Middlemiss with Kat's Eye Editing for helping polish my words. Not only did you catch some of my mistakes, but you were so patient answering my questions and helping me learn. I'm glad to have found you!

My dearest friend Loralie Hall. I already dedicated the whole book to you, but that's not nearly enough. And neither is this thanks. I'm getting all teary-eyed writing this (and more teary-eyed every time I edit it (seriously, like big, weepy tears that get weepier on each edit)) thinking of all you've done for me. Just know that the dedication says it all without saying enough.

My sweet, sweet children who put up with hours of mommy working and many more hours of mommy trying to get you to read and write your own books. Thank you. And a special thanks to my oldest who's getting to the point of being big enough to stay up 'late' reading and cuddling with me while I write. Those moments mean a lot to me.

The last, but biggest thanks to my husband. There's been innumerable hours devote to writing that could have been devoted to other things, like mopping the floor (when was the last time I did that?). Not once did you complain. In fact you only did the opposite. You encouraged me to follow my heart even when it meant no dinner on the table, a messy house, and countless other things left undone. Even offering to watch the kids when you have so many things to do yourself. But the biggest thing was the hours upon hours upon hours you patiently listened to me and bounced ideas back and forth. I love you forever and it doesn't seem long enough.

## ABOUT THE AUTHOR

Amazon best selling author Janeal Falor lives in Utah with her husband and three children. In her non-writing time she teaches her kids to make silly faces, cooks whatever strikes her fancy, and attempts to cultivate a garden even when half the things she plants die. When it's time for a break she can be found taking a scenic drive with her family, fencing, or drinking hot chocolate.

www.janealfalor.com
janealfalor@gmail.com

www.ingramcontent.com/pod-product-compliance
Lightning Source LLC
Chambersburg PA
CBHW050032030726
47506CB00001B/236